FAKING IT WITH THE FRENEMY

NADIA LEE

Faking It with the Frenemy

Copyright © 2020 by Hyun J Kyung

All rights reserved.

No part of this book may be reproduced in any form or by any electronic or mechanical means, including information storage and retrieval systems, without written permission from the author, except for the use of brief quotations in a book review.

AUTHOR'S NOTE

I always get asked how to pronounce Ceinlys. So I've decided to include it here for your reference: Cane-lis.

The inappropriately named treats from Japan in this book are real. They're seasonal/promotional items, so you might not find them if you visit Japan in the future, but they do exist. :)

I hope you enjoy *Faking It with the Frenemy*!

To The Boy, who never fails to make me laugh at least once a day.

1

Kim

You'd think having billions of dollars would fix all your problems, then give you what you didn't even know you wanted.

It doesn't.

I know, not because I have billions of dollars, but because I work for a man who does. And a statue he wanted last month is...well...not even close to being in his possession. Not because he can't afford it, but because the reclusive hermit artist won't return my damn calls.

Or texts.

Or emails.

So I follow up for the thirty millionth time, instead of doing actual productive work. Like coming up with something my boss wants before he even knows he wants it.

"Hi, François, this is Kim Sanford, calling—again—on behalf of Salazar Pryce. It's about your *Wife* statue. He would like to buy it from you. I know it's not a commissioned piece, and he's prepared to offer a very good price. Please call me back." I recite my number, then, because I'm desperate, I add, "I might send you a naked selfie if you return my call in the next twenty-four hours."

I hang up. Hopefully that will motivate him. He's been wanting me to model for him. He said it'd only be for four to ten weeks, depending on how his muse was feeling, and he'd put me up in his flat in Paris.

"Ma chère, just imagine! You will be immortalized!" Given where he was looking at the time, he probably meant my breasts would be immortalized. Actually, I think I exist *only* as breasts in his world. "But they are magnificent! Marvelously proportioned and shaped. A thousand years from now, people will admire your form!"

More like people will be jerking off to my bronzed tits. Not my idea of a flattering *artistic* situation. Besides, I'm not going to spend weeks sitting around nude in François's studio, not even for the sake of art that people might pay millions of dollars for...especially when the purpose of said art is to memorialize my mammaries.

Maybe I'm just plebian. I don't get fine art in general. I only buy what I buy because my boss wants it. And I'm pretty sure Salazar doesn't actually care that much for art. I overheard his financial advisor telling him it's a safe investment... Salazar just agreed with a small grunt.

But maybe François could use the naked selfies to inspire his next project—or so he'll likely claim—assuming I ever send him any, of course. I never promised.

Praying that the temperamental Frenchman deigns to listen to my message, I go back to my laptop to put the final touches on the special getaway itinerary my boss wants. He already rejected three earlier versions, saying they were too "plain." A hundred thousand bucks in two weeks is apparently just too basic.

I lean back in my seat in Salazar's elegant downtown office and purse my lips. His desk is empty; he's staying home today. I look out at the blue sky, interrupted by unevenly tall columns of buildings. I wonder what I can add to make the getaway even grander. Triple the budget and extend the length to a month? But what could he possibly do with his ex-wife for that long? And why in the world did they start dating again after they got divorced?

The cheery opening jingle from "Sleigh Ride" startles me. I

have an instant of total *WTF?*...then roll my eyes. *Jo.* She's the only one who would dare to change my ringtone, and she probably did it yesterday during happy hour.

I scowl at the annoyingly cheery music—spring is *way* too early for Christmas tunes—but suddenly realize *it might be François finally calling me back. Woohoo!*

"This is Kim Sanford," I answer, using the Bluetooth set lodged in my ear. Hope surges like a gathering tsunami. I need to hear his gravelly, accented greeting. I'd even welcome a few of his ridiculous innuendos. I know, I'll put us on video call so he can talk to my breasts like he prefers...

"Did you see those articles about your roommate? Why didn't you tell me she married Nate Sterling!" The familiar voice is breathless and fluttery, like an overly excited sparrow. But I didn't miss the small undertone of disappointment and censure because I'm not the one who married Nate Sterling, billionaire philanthropist and the last available bachelor from the filthy-rich Sterling family.

And who else but Mom would call to talk about tabloid articles?

Hope deflates like a balloon that hasn't been tied properly. "I was *busy*," I say, as flippantly as possible. Mom has this super radar when it comes to gossip involving rich men and their marital status. If she could tweak it so it was calibrated to detecting gossip about François's whereabouts, she could sell it to me for a nice chunk of change.

Or not. I'm certain she credits her radar for her success in life, if marrying five times can be considered "success."

"How can this be? She's only been in L.A. for...what? Ten months?" Confusion and outrage color my mom's voice. If she were here, she'd look like a puppy that was denied bacon that all its littermates got. "How can she already be set up for life when you're not? It's not fair!"

I say nothing and save the document on my computer. Mom needs to vent unimpeded. That way she won't call again about this topic for at least another week. The best course of action for now is just to let everything she says flow through one ear and out the other.

"You need a rich husband, Kim. Before it's too late."

"It's already too late." *How many times have we had this conversation?* "I can't do what you did. Five husbands is just... beyond my ability." Loveless marriages are sad, even if you're swimming in money. And it sucks even more for the kids. I know for a fact that I was an accident. Nothing ruins a woman's figure like pregnancy, and Mom's priority was to cling to youth and beauty for as long as possible in order to snag rich men. She only had me because it would have looked heartless to her fourth husband to have me aborted. And he only allowed it because it would make him look like a dick not to pretend he welcomed the new life he'd created with Mom.

I'm sure he regretted that when he realized he'd have to pay child support.

"Don't be silly," Mom says. "I had to struggle because I only had millionaires to choose from. You're surrounded by *billion*aires. One good marriage should do it."

"I'm not eighteen anymore, Mom," I say, suppressing a long, hard sigh. Only my mother would label being married to a millionaire a struggle. "No billionaire wants a trophy wife over the age of twenty."

"You're still pretty enough, but that won't last forever. Things are different now, so you can hang on to your youth for a little longer—at least facially—with Botox. But your breasts are another matter."

François disagrees, but I keep that to myself. No need to overexcite Mom. The elusive Frenchman is worth a few million bucks at least. But then again, he's *only* worth a few million bucks. Trophy wives seem to be setting their sights higher these days.

She continues, "Can't Botox your way to perkier boobs, dear. Gravity spares no one."

Only Mom would think about Botoxing your breasts. I look down at mine and shudder at the thought of injecting them with bubonic plague or whatever the latest anti-aging rage is. They're perky enough. And when they reach the point of needing injections or implants or whatever...

Well. I'll just have to find a man who appreciates my gravity-ravaged bosom.

"I simply don't understand why you aren't with a rich husband," she whines. "You've been in L.A. for *years*! You work for one of the richest men in the *world*!"

Eww. "Mom. Salazar is old enough to be my grandfather."

And even if he weren't, I'm not going to live my life like Mom. I'm going to be valued for something other than how young I look or my dress size. Like my brain and personality and professional capabilities.

Mom bulldozes my objection like it's a milk carton. "A woman's station in life in determined by the tax bracket of the man she marries. Billionaire, Kim. That's *nine zeros!*"

I can't even bring myself to sigh. "I'll have my station in life determined by my own hard work, thanks. That way, I hold my fate in my hands." I'll be damned if I let some man decide my future happiness and wellbeing, regardless of his tax bracket.

Besides, contrary to her worries, I'll be financially set within a month. By then, I'll have been working for Salazar for five years. I've never failed to deliver for him, and that means he's going to give me a five-hundred-thousand-dollar bonus, as per my employment contract. It isn't enough to set me up for life—not the way my mom's hoping—but as long as I'm careful and continue to work, I'll be fine.

Mom makes a sound that's somewhere between scandalized outrage and a patronizing "there, there." "You're so funny." Her tone says there's nothing funny about my attitude. "But really, dear. You're too old to hang on to such an unworkable idea."

I roll my eyes enough to get slightly dizzy. "It's *because* I'm older that I believe it." I've seen my share of gold diggers and parasites. They appear wherever Salazar is. The sad thing is, most don't end well. They're discarded like used Kleenex. I, on the other hand, am not only *kept*, but *valued*. And it's because I play a game called "Kim is so awesome at her job, she don't need no stinkin' sugar daddy."

"Maybe one of Salazar's sons will divorce." There's a desperate hope in her voice. "Billionaires often do. You should induce one of them to leave his wife. Someone's bound to be bored, stuck with the same woman for so long."

"Okay, *stop*. I'm not a home wrecker." She might as well call me a whore. "And even if I were so inclined, they're so devoted to their wives, it's unreal. Even if they were to become single again, no. There's a reason I didn't date them when they were still available." For one thing, it would have been way too awkward to continue working for Salazar if things hadn't worked out.

"Oh, fine." Her pout is palpable. "You're so picky. How about Milton or Byron Pearce? Or Edgar Blackwood?"

"Milton and Byron Pearce are not in my social circle." To be more precise, they aren't in the Pryces' circle, so there's no reason to run into them. "And Edgar Blackwood lives in Louisiana, of all places. I don't do long-distance relationships." Besides, I've never even met the guy.

"How about David Darling? He's seriously handsome. If I were forty years younger, I'd go for him. Bet he's great in bed."

Something sour floods my mouth. I so do not need to know Mom has a thing for a man young enough to be her son. "Didn't you hear what I said about long-distance relationships? He lives in Virginia."

"Not anymore, dear." Mom's voice is practically a purr. "Sweet Darlings opened a new office in Los Angeles."

And what does that have to do with me? But instead of asking that—because I'm sure Mom will come up with some inane logic twister—I reach for my coffee. Caffeine should perk me up, make me ready to continue working on Salazar's itinerary after this brain-cell-killing call.

"But if you're feeling too shy to throw yourself at him, how about Wyatt Westland?" Mom asks. "You two were close back in high school, weren't you?"

I almost spit my coffee, then check to make sure I didn't spill anything on my dress. Crap. That was close. "Wyatt? When did he become rich enough to suit you?"

Wyatt Westland is my nemesis. Maybe the full-blown Antichrist. He's the reason I couldn't have nice things back when I was growing up in Corn Meadows. The fact that I was dumb enough to like him and sleep with him still infuriates me. But his family has never been rich. His parents are ordinary middle-class folks, unless their bookkeeping service is really a front for some Mafia money-laundering scheme.

"This year," Mom crows. "He's loaded now! He sold some kind of technical thing to a company called Sweet Darlings and made over a billion dollars!" There is reverence in her voice, as though Wyatt ought to be canonized.

Well, that's some vomit-inducing news. "Isn't he married?" He dated and then got hitched to my former-best-friend-turned-tormentor, and I'll never forgive him for that. Not because he married her, but because he dumped me right after taking my virginity in order to be with her. There's got to be a special, unused corner of hell for that kind of asshole.

And that's not all. He also ganged up on me with his buddies after Geneva made me trip and fall in science class. I was carrying a beaker, which broke, and the edge sliced my jaw line, leaving me with a permanent and very visible scar. Mom wanted me to have plastic surgery—because men don't want scarred goods—but I refused, even though Wyatt & Friends started calling me Scarface. Because I knew, even back then, I'd leave the hellhole of Corn Meadows as soon as possible and never look back. I'd forge my own path and surround myself with people who wouldn't tie my worth to a scar or how perky my boobs were.

"No! He got divorced! He's eligible! Rich! And perfect!" Mom exclaims with breathless excitement.

"I'd rather lick a fire hydrant in a dog park."

"Do you want me to set up a date with him?" she asks.

Maybe the fire hydrant analogy wasn't clear enough. The ear-to-brain filter that lets her hear only what she wants to is not only highly efficient, it seems to be indestructible.

"You know what, Mom? The reception here in the office is horrible. Oh, gee, I'm losing the connection." I make some hissing static noises and hang up.

Unlike my mother, I actually have a career and a life, one that doesn't revolve around prowling for and pursuing rich bachelors. Me kicking ass at my job proves I'm not like Mom, and I never am going to be like her.

Ever.

And as soon as I get my bonus, I'm going to tell her I need a sugar daddy about as much as a Chihuahua needs a kale salad.

My phone beeps with a new text. Ugh. Mom should just get

the hint that I'm not interested. I pick it up, about to tell her I just dropped my phone and won't be able to talk or text with her for the next decade.

    –Salazar: Join me for lunch at noon. Éternité.

I stare at the message. Why does he want me to join him? If this were like even two years ago, I might've wondered if I was getting canned. Salazar has a certain...infamous MO. Step One: hire, as his assistant, a beautiful woman he wants to fuck, regardless of her ability or résumé. Brain definitely optional. Step Two: fire her for being incompetent. Step Three: screw her.

One of the reasons I have some respect and credibility is that he didn't fire me. That, according to everyone I know, means I'm too good at my job, which means I'm likely to be his first assistant to get the bonus.

But lunch? At a place as fancy as Éternité? It's the type of place you might take a date or maybe some business associates you want to impress, not your assistant. And it isn't like today is particularly special—not my birthday or work anniversary or anything.

On the other hand, maybe Salazar thinks I've done something to warrant a nice lunch. I shouldn't question the free meal. Éternité has the most amazing crème brûlée, worth at least an ovary or a kidney.

I check the time. Need to hurry if I want to be there five minutes before noon. I believe in being just slightly earlier than my boss.

2

WYATT

You'd think coming into a billion-plus dollars would make a person's problems go away.

Fact is, it doesn't.

People who I didn't know were my friends are contacting me, and people who I didn't know were my enemies are hating on me. My social media accounts are so flooded that I'm not even looking at them anymore.

But, most important, all my new money hasn't found me a suitable date for my ex-wife's wedding.

Normally I wouldn't bother, because I don't particularly wish her well. Not that I wish her ill. I just don't give a damn.

But my ten-year-old daughter needs closure. The counselor she was seeing back in Corn Meadows mentioned that attending the wedding might do her some good. I'm skeptical, myself...but what do I know about child psychology?

So here I am, my butt planted in a plush booth in a fancy Japanese-French fusion restaurant. Éternité has a waiting list that probably stretches halfway to Kansas, but we got a table immediately because Dane arranged everything. One of his brothers owns the place.

I tap the edge of the cream-colored leather-bound menu and take in my surroundings. The place is airy and bright, with lots of natural light. Translucent hangings with intricate embroidery from the ceiling create an illusion of elegant privacy. Even though it's not even noon, the place is already buzzing with conversation and the clink of silverware and glass. Probably corporate types with fat expense accounts and people with lots of money.

I don't like it. Not even a little.

Dane glances in my direction, his blue gaze sharp as a straight razor. "What's wrong?"

"Not to be ungrateful or anything, but some of this stuff looks a little...iffy." I gesture at the menu.

Nothing in his expression changes. But that's him—Mr. Poker Face. "What's wrong with it?" he asks, his voice cool.

"Just listen to this." I read off the menu to make sure I get it right. "Seared sashimi-grade otoro drizzled with wasabi-infused citrus sauce. Just what the hell is otoro, and...do people actually eat it?"

"It's a high-grade cut of tuna. Tasty."

"So is a bacon cheeseburger with fries." Probably better for you, too. At least you don't have to guess what you're eating, unlike this otoro thing. What's wrong with just saying "tuna," anyway?

"My wife likes it," Dane says, like that explains everything.

I'm happy he found a woman to be with, but there's a small part of me that feels slightly bad for my own situation. I thought marrying Geneva was the right thing to do, even though a nano-sized doubt was wriggling like a worm in my chest, as if my heart were an apple it was trying to eat its way out of.

That worm turned out be right. Marrying her was the biggest mistake of my life.

"Don't you think this place is too fancy for a meeting?" I say, looking at my chilled wine. *Maybe they have Budweiser here.*

"She's Salazar's assistant."

"So?"

"That means she's pretty enough to not embarrass you, smart enough to take directions and discerning enough to know when you go cheap on her."

Sounds like the ultimate in high maintenance. And I'm done with high maintenance. Been there and done that with Geneva, and look what I got—over a decade in a shitty marriage, and now a divorce.

What I need is a woman who doesn't mind bacon cheeseburgers and fries with extra ketchup and an ice-cold beer or two.

"It doesn't matter what she thinks," I say with a shrug. "David told me he's going to set me up with a date this week, depending on how our schedules line up. Someone named Bethany. She's apparently super smart. Speaks six languages."

Dane cocks an eyebrow. "Really?"

"French, German, Russian, Spanish and Italian." Or at least, that's what I remember from the text. "And English, I guess."

"French, Spanish and Italian are virtually the same language."

I'd bet a thousand bucks that Frenchmen, Spaniards and Italians would have something to say about that. Not that I'll interrupt Dane when he's riding the Sarcasm Express.

"And David's taste in women is deplorable," Dane states firmly. "He disagrees with that assessment, of course, but that's because he has more money than sense."

Despite Dane's less-than-charitable view, he's speaking without sneering. That means he likes David.

But of course Dane Pryce, David Darling and I are friends. We connected at a tech convention because Dane is in venture capital and David is with Sweet Darlings, which is a popular photo-storing and -sharing app. I happen to love tinkering with programming and own patents to a few security protocols that intrigued and eventually impressed both of them. That's how Sweet Darlings Inc. ended up paying me a billion and change.

"She's probably hot enough. David likes them hot." I don't even sound convincing to myself. Maybe I'm turning into a cynic like Dane, now that I'm divorced and all. He's always acerbic, and marriage hasn't made a bit of difference to him as far as I can tell.

"I thought the goal was to make your ex-wife eat her heart out," Dane says.

Ha. Never happen, because Geneva doesn't have a heart. "Something like that," I say, not willing to go into the whole situation with our daughter, Vi, again. Besides, I already have a course of action. I don't need to rehash it.

"Then hot isn't enough." Dane's tone is decisive and cool, his gaze calculating. Like a general planning a take-no-prisoners ambush. "You need to look happy. And show up with somebody who can pull that off."

Not quite believing what I'm hearing, I finish my wine and ask for a beer. It's that kind of day.

Our server manages a bland smile, but Dane wrinkles his nose. "Beer? Really? With Japanese-French fusion?"

"It's on the menu, isn't it? Or are you saying I should've ordered sake?"

His expression says I'm beyond help. "You need to spend some time with my brother Mark. He'll...educate you on this particular subject."

"I'm already educated. I'm divorced." Besides, I'm not spending my precious time with Dane's brother who, according to rumor, can name any wine's vintage after just a sip. I steer our conversation back to the more important point. "Anyway, you think your dad's assistant can make me happy? You know, for the wedding?"

He looks at me like I was dropped on my head early in life. "No. But she's good enough to fake it." He scrutinizes me over the rim of his wine glass. "Maybe you should take an acting class."

There must be something in the L.A. air that makes everyone want to take up acting or recommend it to others. "No time. I'm too busy at work, plus trying to move and help Vi settle in at her new school."

"You won't have to do much on the school front. It's a great place."

"I agree. And thanks for the recommendation. I wouldn't have known where to start without you." And it's true. Just because I'm a billionaire now—which sounds really weird—doesn't mean I know everything that goes along with being one.

He checks his watch. "She should be here soon."

I glance down at mine. Five till. "Isn't it a bit early?"

"She's always early. One of her many good qualities."

Right. But she still likes this kind of restaurant. Wonder if she

Faking It with the Frenemy

drinks mimosas and nibbles on smoked otoro slices piled on toasted bagels for breakfast. Or maybe not. She could be one of those gluten-free weirdos.

"Don't be negative," Dane says. "It's going to work out. I didn't make that idiotic bet with my father for nothing."

He keeps talking about that bet, but won't tell me exactly what it was. It could've been solving a multivariable calculus problem. To Dane, a lot of things are idiotic.

"Or get him drunk. The man's as immune to alcohol as I am." A hard, competitive gleam flashes in Dane's eyes. "Although he's gotten a bit less immune in his old age."

"Great job beating your ol' man."

Dane doesn't seem to notice the sarcasm. "He deserved it. And it's not like he needs his assistant. He's going on a trip soon."

In my peripheral vision, I note the hostess bringing a woman in a burgundy dress toward us. Dane shifts in his seat, his expression saying, *Finally!*

I paste on the pleasant, courteous and entirely meaningless smile I've perfected over the last decade with Geneva's parents. Even though I'm not too crazy about this setup or the super-fancy assistant of Dane's father who likes to be wined and dined at a restaurant that calls tuna otoro, I owe her some courtesy.

The hostess stops. "Here you are."

"Thanks." The assistant turns to us.

My brain stops for a moment as I take her in. She seems unbelievably familiar, but I can't quite place her. Her eyes are stunning, like warm, dark honey, her cheeks high and smooth. Her soft hair frames her gorgeous face perfectly and flows down her shoulders. The burgundy dress hugs all the dips and valleys of her body, the curves of her incredible breasts, the flare of her hips. Her arms and legs are long and shapely, as elegant as a ballet dancer's.

Hot lust clenches around my throat, even as my head warns me she isn't who I think she is. She is more than Salazar Pryce's assistant.

She smiles politely. "Hi, Dane...and..." Her smile fades away as hostility infuses her otherwise angelic face. I almost expect her to bare fangs at me. "*Wyatt?*"

The smart voice in my head crows, *Told you*. But where have I met her? At Sweet Darlings? At Vi's school? And why does she sound so mad? I don't recall offending a gorgeous, polished brunette recently. Or...anytime.

"You two know each other?" Dane's eyebrows are pinched together.

"Yes," she says.

"Uh," I say at the same time. "I don't think so..."

She looks down at me, full lips pursed. I have this insane urge to rub the pad of my thumb across them, make them pliable and relaxed.

Yeah, try that and she'll bite it off.

A derisive smirk twists her face. "Kimberly Sanford." She almost spits the name at me.

A physical slap wouldn't have stunned me more. "*Kim?*" Whoa. She was pretty in high school, but she didn't have this kind of smooth sophistication. No wonder I didn't recognize her. City life must be good for her.

And just like that, I know this is the beginning of a clusterfuck.

3

Kim

Everything inside me bristles at Wyatt's utter lack of recognition, and then surprise. It freakin' sucks to feel so insignificant that I don't even merit a couple of brain cells in his thick skull.

You're hurt.

Not me. My pride. But just because he was my first doesn't mean I was *his* first, despite what he claimed at the time. For all I know, he only said that because he knew he would be terrible in bed.

But he wasn't Terrible, that is.

Only because I didn't know any better. And I need to stop arguing with myself.

And I need to stop noticing how hot Wyatt is now.

So what if the James Dean, dark-haired devil look that made every girl in my high school swoon has matured into a delicious male package? And who cares that his eyelashes are long and thick, or that his eyes are stunningly blue? Not cold, but warm and arresting...like a sparkling summer ocean.

What I should do is punch and ruin that perfect blade of a

nose, which is sitting above a pair of full lips that can kiss like a dream. He deserves that, and more.

On the other hand, maybe not. I shouldn't let him know how much he still affects me.

Because I'm not affected. No way. Not in the slightest.

I'm just annoyed because he popped up after Mom did her best to waste away my morning, trying to convince me to marry into money. And not just any money, but Wyatt money. The fact that he got lucky enough to become a newly minted billionaire proves the world is an unfair place, that assholes finish first, and that we might as well send tributes...er...volunteers into a reality game to kill each other for shits and giggles.

"I'm here to meet Salazar," I say to Dane, keeping my tone as even as possible. "I didn't realize you'd commandeered his table." I start to leave. I'm not spending any more of my precious time in the company of Wyatt, of all people.

"Sit down." As usual, Dane's voice is cold enough to replace the restaurant's air conditioners. "We're waiting for him, too."

"You aren't on the agenda," I say, doing my best to match his frigid attitude. I refuse to look at Wyatt. I'd rather stare at a close-up of a cockroach's anus.

Wyatt clears his throat. "He made an exception for me."

That only stokes my irritation. My boss's schedule isn't something you alter on a whim. I'm the gatekeeper, the dragon guardian of his time and space. "And why would he do that?" I ask, doing my best to sound temperate, not because I give a damn about Wyatt, but because I don't want to make a public scene. "It isn't like you're his friend."

"As a favor to Dane. And we actually *are* friends."

Hardy har har. Salazar's eldest is so frosty that it's a miracle there aren't icicles sticking out from his body like hedgehog spines. Then there's the asshole factor. If Hallmark has Hallmark Moments, Dane has Dane Moments. He once called one of his brothers' wives a "charity case." And that isn't even the worst of it.

I wait for Dane to scoff, for Tyrannosaurus Rectum to emerge. Instead, he gives me a small nod.

"You have a friend?" I ask, stunned.

"Shocking, isn't it? He also has a wife and a child," comes Salazar's dry voice from behind me.

Oh, shit. My boss doesn't care for people badmouthing his children, especially when it's one of his employees. I manage to smooth my expression like nothing's wrong before turning to him. "Hello, Salazar."

He's old enough to be somebody's grandfather—in fact, he *is* a grandfather—but you'd never know from looking at him. His dark hair is expensively cut and styled, with just a hint of dignified silver at the temples. His glowing skin is almost wrinkle-free. It's also sag-free and age-spot-free. There's hardly any fat on his trim figure, and the man positively radiates mature, masculine perfection in an expensive tailor-made white dress shirt and dark slacks. There's a reason he was able to seduce so many twenty- and thirty-something women, and it wasn't all his money, although I'm sure that didn't hurt.

"Well! Now that we're all here, let's have lunch," he says jovially, gesturing for me to take a seat.

I hesitate, hating that it's a booth. Wyatt and Dane should share a bench, since they're such *good* friends. But no. I either have to sit next to Wyatt or Dane.

Chlamydia or gonorrhea. A rattlesnake or a water moccasin.

The world is full of crappy choices.

Salazar takes my option away by parking himself next to Wyatt. At the same time, Dane stands, takes a step back and gestures at me to sit down. My jaw slackens. When the hell did he become a gentleman? This has to be something his wife taught him.

Smoothing my face to hide my shock, I slide in, ensuring there's as much space as possible between us on the bench. I don't want to get frostbite.

It's actually not too terrible to be next to Dane, because at least I'm not next to Wyatt the Jerk. On the other hand, now I'm sitting directly across from him and am going to have to avert my eyes for the entire meal. Restaurant tables really should come with a partition. That way, you could raise it to block people you don't want to see or interact with, like with a business- or first-class seat on an airplane.

Since not even a place as fancy as Éternité has that kind of privacy option, I do the next best thing. I pull out my tablet and open a note-taking app, ready to get this farce over with as quickly and efficiently as possible. Not even Wyatt is going to stop me from being professional. "So."

"You can put that away. It's not that kind of lunch," Salazar says, his tone entirely too indulgent, and the Tingle of Terror shivers through my body. That particular tone of voice only emerges when he's about to ask me to do something he knows is unreasonable.

Shit.

Wyatt stares at me like I'm some kind of lab experiment gone wrong, then looks away, muttering to himself. It's probably something unflattering and mean, because that's how he rolls.

Dane lets out an impatient sigh. "You didn't tell her, did you?" he asks Salazar, his voice flatter than a freshly ironed sheet.

"I was busy," Salazar says.

"You're semi-retired. And you were supposed to tell her *two weeks ago.*"

"Tell me what?" I'm getting a very bad feeling about this. Just what the hell does Dane need from me that he needs to go through my boss? A kidney? No. Dane's too direct and arrogant to bother going through Salazar. He'd just take me to the hospital and tell me to my face.

Salazar shrugs, still looking at his son. "Told you, I was busy."

Yeah, busy rejecting my itinerary! But what does Dane have to do with this lunch, and why is Wyatt here too, rolling his eyes like this is all a huge waste of time?

Dane sighs again. "Tell her."

Wyatt shifts in his seat, full of the restless annoyance of a guy stuck in a pointless meeting. He picks up his wine glass and takes a healthy swallow, then taps the menu repeatedly, his mouth tight.

His crabby mood should make me happy, but it doesn't. It only makes me dread whatever it is that Salazar has done.

My boss isn't a normal man. He's the head of the Pryce family, one of the most influential and filthy-richest families in the world. He has no understanding of proper protocol or etiquette or even boundaries. Why would he? He's wealthy, powerful and damn good looking, the trifecta requirement of people who live *entitledly*, assuming that's a word.

"Tell me what?" I ask. "Salazar, what is it?"

"Nothing, really." My boss clears his throat. "It's just, well, see... Dane and I had a bet." He looks around. "I need a scotch."

The drink appears magically in front of him, two fingers, neat. He takes a swig, then tilts the glass this way and that, watching the ebb and flow of the liquor.

This does *not* bode well. It isn't like him to stall.

"What he's trying to say is, he lost the bet," Dane says, obviously losing patience. "And you're going to work for Wyatt for four weeks."

The words take a moment to sink in. I start to shake my head, feeling sick to my stomach. This has to be a nightmare. A terrible, horrifying nightmare. Maybe it is some kind of delayed, second-hand pot smoke trip, because it can't be real.

"Why on earth would I work for Wyatt if Salazar lost a bet to you?" It's the most logical question I can think of.

"Because he bet four weeks of your time, and I already have an assistant," Dane says as though he's stating the obvious.

"I'm not working for him!" I say, staring at Wyatt in horror. I fling a hand at him. "You have money. Hire an assistant yourself."

"I already do have one," Wyatt says tightly.

"Well then. Problem solved." I look at the three men. "He doesn't need me to work for him. Besides, it's against labor law to force somebody to work two full-time jobs." If not, I'm writing my congressional rep.

"I'm going to give you four weeks off," Salazar says, picking up a second scotch our waiter has thoughtfully provided. "With pay. That's only fair."

What's only fair is you not betting my time! But I'm not criticizing my boss in front of other people. I need to wait until we're in private to discuss the matter. "That won't be necessary."

"Yes, it will," Wyatt says finally, his tone as morose as a man about to choke down a steaming bowl of kale.

"Don't tell me you hired an assistant for her looks," I say, even though I'm convinced he did. Mom said he's divorced. What do single guys who come into lots of money do? Dumb shit. And what do divorced guys who come into lots of money do? Even dumber shit.

And hiring the first hot woman who applies to work for you without checking her résumé falls exactly under "Even Dumber Shit."

"I didn't hire her," Wyatt says. "My company did."

Boohoo. Like they'd hire somebody without consulting him first.

"She can't do what you can," Dane says.

From someone else, that would be an empty platitude to soothe my ego and manipulate me. From Dane, it's equivalent of a Nobel Prize.

Yeah, but it isn't Dane who you have to work for. It's Wyatt.

Wyatt, who's looking at me skeptically. Wyatt, who took my virginity to win a bet, then dumped me within a week to move on to Geneva.

Makes me wonder if this "bet" was also his idea.

Would it be justifiable homicide if I stabbed him with my fork? I could get lucky and hit a major artery. And I know a lot of good lawyers, having worked for Salazar for a few years.

"You'll basically only have one job," Wyatt says finally. "Find me a date for a wedding."

I raise my eyebrows. That's such a ridiculously easy task that nobody should take four freakin' weeks to get it done.

On the other hand, we *are* talking Wyatt. So maybe that's what's making this such a challenge.

Still, I'm not interested in working for him, even on something as silly and easy as finding him a date. "Get your assistant to go with you," I say, barely preventing myself from sneering. The hot co-ed he must've hired should be able to pull it off. It isn't like you actually have to appear smart or make interesting conversation at those things.

"Can't. She's married with two kids." Wyatt's expression indicates there's a lot more to it than that, but he won't be saying any of it out loud.

Still, it makes me blink. Because it isn't even a real date, and it shouldn't be that big of a deal for an assistant to make herself presentable for an afternoon on a weekend and some overtime pay. It isn't like anybody has to know she's married. How much of a dud did he get? He must've seriously pissed somebody in HR off. Not a surprise, given his personality. "So try Tinder. Get your assistant to screen the candidates."

"He needs someone hot enough to make a statement," Salazar says.

"This is L.A. It's full of hot women." He should know. He's probably fucked half of them.

"Ah, but are they hot enough to stick a knife in his ex-wife's heart and twist it around?" Salazar cocks his head at me. "For that, you need someone a step or two above just any old hot chick."

"Ex-wife? Is this *Geneva's* wedding?" I choke the words out, utterly disgusted. Spend a perfectly fine weekend pretending to congratulate that traitor? I'd rather sleep on a nest of wasps.

Wyatt looks dyspeptic, but I don't care. "Why would you do that? Are you trying to win her back? You'd be better off just swallowing a bunch of arsenic."

Dane gives me a reassessing look, like he's just realized I'm not a total moron. Just a regular moron, which is what he labels people with IQs over one hundred and five.

Meanwhile Wyatt is bristling. "*Why* is none of your business."

Huh. Well, I should've expected this kind of rudeness. He was a dick back in high school, and he's an even bigger dick now that he has money.

The fact that he's trying to crash Geneva's wedding makes me want to help just a tad. I can ask my super fashionista friend Jo to help me outshine the bride, and wouldn't that just piss Geneva off to no end? On the other hand, the idea that he's trying to win her back makes me *not* want to help...not even a little. I'm sure Geneva can make him miserable. That's her forte, making everyone around her miserable because she can—something I realized too late. But apparently he's even more miserable without her, so I'd rather he stay that way.

That's the least he deserves for the way he treated me back then.

I look over at Dane. "Excuse me."

"What?"

"Move. Get up. I need to go to the ladies' room," I lie, since I'm sure he's not budging otherwise.

Dane slides over and stands up. I do the same, then turn back to the table. "You know what? I don't have to honor the outcome of some dumb bet. I'm not"—I search for the right word—"*chattel* you can just trade around. If you have something to collect from Salazar, Dane, it's between you two, not me. Now, if you'll excuse me, I need to get back to the office. I've already wasted enough of my lunch break, and haven't had anything to eat yet."

"You're leaving?" Salazar asks. "But you haven't had the crème brûlée." He knows it's my favorite dessert, especially when it's from Éternité.

"Somehow, I've lost my appetite." I give Wyatt a pointed look, then smartly walk out.

4

Wyatt

"I knew it," I say. The second I realized who Salazar's assistant was, I knew the lunch was going to end in a total disaster.

"You should've told her earlier and prepped her," Dane says to his father, like it's all his fault, even though nothing would've made a difference. If I fell into a well, Kim would push large rocks down after me.

Salazar shrugs dismissively over his scotch. "Don't blame me. It's your fault for bringing it up so soon. She would've been more amenable after some crème brûlée. She loves that stuff."

"How are you going to make it right?" Dane demands.

"Me? You're the one who messed it up."

I raise my hand. "Stop. There's no point to arguing. She won't do it, no matter what."

"Why not?" Salazar asks.

"She and I have...a history." Which is putting it mildly. She said I sucked in bed and decided I gave her herpes and dumped me as soon as we slept together. The memory still makes me seethe. Not because I have feelings for her at this point—but because I really, really liked her at the time.

Although, to be honest, I still have some...thoughts about her. Her body, anyway. Her personality still sucks.

But that body...

My cock became chiseled stone every time I saw those tits. And it would love nothing more than to have my hands push them together, so I could drive into the tight, warm cleavage...

When the world ends in a zombie apocalypse and somebody eats my brain. That's when that'll happen.

Salazar shrugs. "Eh. I have a history with half the women in the city, and I get along with them."

Dane looks like he just chewed on some especially sharp glass. "That's inappropriate, not to mention irrelevant."

Salazar shrugs. "Just saying." He opens the menu. "I'm hungry."

"Me too. See you later." I stand and walk out. If I'm not impressing Salazar's assistant—and I'm not even going to try, since it's Kim—I'm not eating anything off a menu that weirdly relabels fish that have perfectly good English names.

Otoro, my ass.

I stop by a food truck on the way to the office and grab a hot dog. It's no cheeseburger, but at least it's honest. No pretensions. It's objectionable, as it tries to teach women how long and thick a man's cock ought to be—longer and thicker than the wiener stuck in the bun—and unhealthy, as the cheesy goo on it is probably as nutritious as toxic waste from a nuclear plant.

Easily tasty enough to scarf down before a meeting.

I arrive with ten minutes to spare. The Sweet Darlings office in Los Angeles is new, barely two years old. The company branched out after West Coast operations became too big for the space in San Mateo, and CEO Alexandra Darling decided to move some of the business functions out of the headquarters in Dulles.

The L.A. office occupies the entire twenty-sixth and twenty-seventh floors of a giant skyscraper. I never understood the point of having such tall buildings in L.A., even if land is at a premium. Earthquake evacuation would be a bitch from this high up. But people like to stand on high ground and look down on others, even if it's only from nine to five.

Faking It with the Frenemy

My temp assistant Melanie waves a well-manicured hand as I approach my corner office. She wears way too much perfume for the office. A thick glob of mascara weighs down her eyelashes, making her green eyes look smaller. Her desk has seven framed photos of her family, including her two boys, and four small potted plants that she dotes on at least once an hour. She likes to bring cookies every Monday, claiming everyone needs something sweet to make the beginning of a brand-new workweek more tolerable. She's always the first on our floor, if not the entire building, to dash out on Fridays. Her workspace is still littered with cookie crumbs from earlier, and I know they will stay until Friday, when the janitor finally gets fed up and sweeps them off her desk.

"Did you finalize the memo for the meeting?" I ask. It's a simple one-page document and only needed some corrections I made to an earlier draft entered into the soft copy and printed again.

She shakes her head. "Not yet. Did you get my text? The meeting got pushed back to two."

I pull out my phone. *Nothing.* "You sure you sent it?"

"Yeah." She checks, then frowns. "Oh, wait. Sorry. I sent it to David by mistake."

I don't know how that's possible, since D and W are on opposite ends of the alphabet. First names, last names...either way.

"Have the memo ready for me in the next ten minutes," I say, because I don't want her to forget or print it wrong or whatever. Then I step into my office and shut the frosted glass door.

After I sold my patents, part of the deal required that I work at Sweet Darlings Inc. for at least three years. The salary and bonuses I make are separate compensation from the billion bucks they paid me.

At least I enjoy the work, and it keeps me busy, so that's a huge plus. I text David.

–Me: Sorry my assistant bugged you.

–David: No prob. Melanie's not the most tech savvy. How'd your lunch go? Dane hook you up?

I feel my whole face purse like I just took a big bite out of a rotting apple.

–Me: No. I need to see that girl you mentioned earlier. Bethany, right?

–David: Yup. Tomorrow night good? She's gonna be free.

Might as well get it over with. There's no way Kim's going to Geneva's wedding. They get along about as well as two silverback gorillas sharing a four-by-four cage.

I check with Lori, the teenage babysitter I found via Sweet Darlings' HR. Everyone I spoke to recommended her. Gotta make sure Vi's properly supervised and fed.

–Lori: Sure, I can watch Vi tomorrow.

I text her my address, then add, *Thanks*.

–Lori: My pleasure.

I make a mental note to pay her extra for being so flexible. Besides, it's going for a good cause—her prom and college fund.

I let David know that it's a go with Bethany, put the phone on the desk and lean back with a sigh. If Kim were half as accommodating as most normal women out there...

A message drifts up from my nether regions. *She's really hot.*

Yeah, but that's about all there is to her. And I need more than a hot body. There has to be a personality, too. A kind heart. I'm not a single guy who can screw around and not worry about consequences. I can handle whatever fallout occurs, but Vi's been hurt before—*Thanks, Geneva*—and I don't want her suffering again because I've made a poor decision about the opposite sex.

Besides, so what if Kim's hot? I'm never going to see her again. She can be relegated nicely back into my past, where she belongs.

5

Kim

I grab an extra-spicy taco on the way to the office because it's that kind of day. Argh. As I gobble up the tongue-incinerating Mexican food, I stew over the fact that I got denied crème brûlée. And not just any crème brûlée, but crème brûlée that's good enough to cure menopause and erectile dysfunction. And it's all Wyatt's fault.

Annoyance still brimming, I suck down an icy lemonade and drive to the office to do my job. Even if my boss thinks I'm something he can just *wager*, I think what I do is worth more respect than that.

Dane probably led Salazar astray. Everyone knows he's the Lucifer of the family. But that doesn't mean I'm okay with my boss betting me. Like the way Wyatt fucked me to win a damned bet. And the salt on the wound? Dane deciding to hand me over to Wyatt. *What am I, anyway? An indentured servant?*

I shove every ostentatiously expensive location I can find into my boss's surprise getaway, lengthening it to a month and covering Europe and Asia and hitting all the major tourist attractions. That should do it. If not, he can just cry into his five-figure scotch, because if he complains about his vacation again, I might just strangle him.

Sometime later, Salazar walks up, holding a beautifully wrapped white box in his hand. He stops in front of my desk and smiles.

"I thought you were working from home today," I say stiffly.

"I thought maybe I should be here." He gives me another brilliant smile, the one he always flashes when he knows he's done something he shouldn't have, but feels pretty confident he'll be forgiven.

I shoot Salazar a thin smile in return. "That works out, because I was just about to text you about your good friend Churchill Phillips III's wedding."

Salazar considers for a second. Churchill is a dick who thinks being rich entitles him to grab a few unsuspecting asses. He almost tried it once with me, except he aborted the attempt when he noticed my boss was watching. However, Churchill's family was close to Salazar's late mother, and both families have some mutual business interests, so the ass groper's assistant sent an email about his fourth—or fifth?—wedding.

"Nah," my boss says. "Not going to bother attending. Just send him something suitably expensive and useless."

I raise an eyebrow, but make a note of it.

"Actually...never mind. I'll take care of it."

"You will?" Salazar doesn't know how to shop for anything himself, except possibly for cars, watches and jewelry.

"You look stressed. How 'bout some nice crème brûlée?" Salazar places the box on my desk. "You left before I could order one for you."

Oh, geez, I wonder why. And he's gotta do better than this. "It's fine. I can handle the gift," I say coolly, trying to stay strong.

"Don't bother. How hard can it be to send him a ten-thousand-dollar Amazon gift card?"

I almost choke. That is so ridiculous a gift, I can't even. On the other hand, that's more than that creep deserves, so maybe I should let Salazar do what he wants.

He continues, "Anyway, forget Churchill's wedding. Who cares about that ass fondler?" He gestures at the box. "I asked for two crème brûlées because they not only had the regular kind, but a *special chocolate one*. André came up with the recipe himself."

"Chocolate?" I simply can't stop myself. André is the executive chef at Éternité and a culinary genius. If he put it on the menu, it's going to be epic.

Salazar inclines his head, winks and oh so slowly pushes the box in my direction.

Damn it. I know I've lost because I can't stay mad and also have the damned chocolate crème brûlée. I open the box and see two elegant, almost dainty, desserts sitting in the box. André is French to the core; he thinks the American practice of stuffing ourselves with tarts, cake and custards the size of our heads is piggish and revolting. So items from Éternité tend to be smaller, as they are in France.

I pick up the included fork and take a bite of the chocolate one first. The rich, creamy flavor fills my mouth, and I close my eyes as a near-orgasmic pleasure shivers through every cell in my body. Who needs sex when you have this?

"Good, isn't it?" Salazar murmurs.

"Very." I lick my lips, then hit *send* on my email. "I just sent you the revised itinerary."

"Great." He hitches up one pant leg and puts half his butt on my desk. "So. Kim."

"Yes?" I say, knowing he's about to explain the situation. I'm not going to make it easy for him, even if he basically brought me an oral orgasm in a box.

"About that whole thing at lunch..."

"You mean that thing where you bet me like a piece of meat? Yes, I do believe I recall that."

He sighs. "He wasn't supposed to talk about it like that. Kids these days. No discretion."

"Right. It's totally Dane's fault that you bet me."

"Dane and I did have a little bet." He says it like he misplaced a dime somewhere. "I lost, and he's supposed to get a month of your assistant service."

"Didn't you think it was weird he asked for that? He has a team of assistants, and they're fantastic."

"He wanted you for his friend there, but said it was mainly

about the wedding date." Salazar shrugs. "I didn't think it was a big deal."

"Not a big deal?" My voice rises, so I take a bite of the divine dessert to help control my temper. Annoyingly enough, it helps. "You...you just *gave me away* like an old toy you don't want anymore. I've been with you for almost five years."

Salazar's eyes widen. "No, no, no, no, I'm just *lending* you. I'd never give you away! You're the best assistant I've ever had, plus you're super hot, which makes me look great in meetings."

I pinch the bridge of my nose. "Salazar. I'm about to get my five-year bonus, and I don't want this Dane bet thing to jeopardize it."

Salazar makes a spreading motion with his hands. "A separate matter altogether," he says with solemnity befitting a royal coronation.

I nod, accepting that he's serious. He might be a self-absorbed, over-the-top billionaire, he doesn't lie about things like this. "What was the bet about? There's no way Dane has something you want."

"Well. I was drunk and got...taken advantage of."

I give him a look. Salazar Pryce could drink double his body weight and still walk a tightrope. Everyone in his family can. And nobody takes advantage of him unless he wants it.

"Can't hold my liquor like I used to," he says. "Gettin' old here."

"Right." So now he can only drink one and a half times his body weight. Let me go grab a Kleenex.

"And we did rock paper scissors ten times."

"Rock paper scissors?" This is even dumber than his claiming he can't drink like he used to. I can hear my brain cells screaming as they die.

"He won three times, I won three and the rest we tied."

I can't decide if I should cry or bang my head against the wall. It wasn't even a real, dignified bet.

"Anyway, he wasn't supposed to say anything. It's embarrassing to talk details like that."

"What about me?" Doesn't he think it's embarrassingly ridiculous for me as well?

"Oh, no need to worry. I'm not a total asshole, so while you're working for Dane—well, his friend—I'm giving you a paid month off."

I stare, trying to decide if he's being intentionally obtuse or really is just this self-involved.

"*And* I made it clear you're not to work a second over forty hours a week." He spreads his hands with a magnanimous smile. "You deserve it," he adds, the very definition of an accommodating boss. But only because he's mildly embarrassed I found out about his dumb bet.

God. I want to wipe that smug "I know I'm forgiven already" look off his face. "Aren't you afraid I might leave you for Wyatt?" I ask.

"Nah."

"How come?"

"Because if you liked the idea of working for him, you wouldn't be all mad about the bet." Salazar can be self-involved, but he's not stupid. "And I guarantee he isn't as generous with rewards and bonuses as I am."

That part is true. Other than the five-year half-a-million-dollar bonus, Salazar has also given me semi-annual bonuses, worth about twenty percent of my salary, every year.

He continues, "Just grin and bear it for a month, okay? The guy's good looking enough. How hard could it be to go out with him once or twice?"

Typical male. "It'd probably be easier to get clean in a mud bath," I say. Salazar needs to stop because I think I feel hives breaking out. That's the only explanation for the shortness of breath I'm experiencing.

"But you're not dating anyone, right?"

"That *isn't the point*."

"If he makes any unwanted advances, let me know."

"Why? What are you going to do?"

"Remember my Aston Martin? The DB5?"

"Yeah…" It's the same model that Sean Connery's double-oh-seven drove. The license tag reads 2HOT4U. Salazar loves that car more than his own balls, and not even his children are allowed to touch it.

"I'll let you run him over with it."

My jaw drops. "You will?"

He taps the tip of his chin. "Actually..."

Ha! Should've known. He's feeling guilty, but not that guilty.

"I'll do it for you."

6

Kim

I spend the rest of the day pretending the lunch never happened, even though Salazar keeps shooting hopeful looks in my direction. I know he's big on keeping his promises, but if it matters that much, he should've bet himself, not me. There's no way I'm going to be Wyatt's date for anything. Not even for the chocolate crème brûlée. Four weeks' pay certainly isn't enough. I'd rather work in a salt mine.

For free.

And Salazar made the tactical error of telling me it won't affect my five year bonus, so I have even less reason to bother.

As soon as my laptop clock says it's five, I go to the barre studio to work out with Hilary and Jo. The three of us hit the studio two or three times a week, partly to exercise and stay healthy, partly to socialize and catch up. If we don't make an effort, we don't get to hang out with each other, especially with Hilary being married and her husband wanting her to spend time with him, too.

The workout helps me relax, but only a little. There's a teenager standing around, looking mulish, waiting for his mom to finish up. Wyatt was like that—all rebellious superiority—when he first saw me at a barre, although that was a ballet studio his sister and I went together. The memory puts me back into a crabby mood again.

Once the session's over, we head to a bar near the studio to unwind before heading home. It's our little ritual.

Hilary, Jo and I grab a table and order our usual drinks. While waiting, I suck down some lemon-infused ice water and look at the women I've known for years.

Salazar's daughter-in-law, Hilary, is a gorgeous, statuesque redhead. Her husband Mark has more than enough money to pamper her for life, but she continues to work as an assistant to one of the wealthiest fund managers in the country. I admire that about her—she hasn't changed just because she married somebody rich.

Of the three of us, Jo is easily the best dressed. Even after our workout, her long, dark brown hair is in place, her clothes absolutely pristine. But then, she's a fashion consultant and personal shopper. It's literally her job to look stylish.

"You seem a little grumpy," Jo says to me. "Anything wrong? You usually like barre."

"Trust me. My mood's gone up a lot since lunch."

"What happened?" Jo asks.

Our waitress brings out cocktails, giving me a moment before I have to answer Jo's question. And I need to answer; otherwise it'll turn into a persistent inquisition. She should've gotten a job with the CIA.

"Basically, I need a boyfriend."

Hilary stops in the middle of picking up her martini. "What?"

"Oh my God, is Salazar hitting on you?" Jo asks, thirty percent titillated and seventy percent scandalized.

"Don't be silly," Hilary says.

"Absolutely not," I say at the same time. "He's totally devoted to his ex-wife." Even as I say it, I want to shake my head at how ridiculous that sounds. If I saw it on a TV show, I'd throw popcorn at the screen. But it's true. The outrageous getaway I've been planning isn't for him and some side piece. It's for his *ex-wife*, whom he's decided is the true love of his life *after* their divorce.

"Fine, fine," Jo says, raising her hands. "So why do you need a boyfriend?"

Her confusion is understandable. I've turned down every single one of her attempts to set me up.

"It's just...ludicrous." I explain the basic situation of how Salazar wants me to date some dude I'd rather not, but I don't share the drunken rock-paper-scissors bet story because it isn't something I can talk about. No matter how annoyed I am with my boss, I can't just blurt out something he wants kept quiet.

"It can't be that hard," Hilary says when I'm finished. "I mean, it's only one...maybe two dates, max. And you get a month off."

"It *is* that hard. This isn't just any guy. This is my, like, archnemesis from high school, who screwed me and dumped me for my best friend in the same week. And that isn't even close to the whole story. Later he put a vibrator in my backpack and made sure it fell out in the cafeteria during lunch. I wanted to die on the spot."

"How the hell did he manage to do that?" Jo asks.

"Black magic. He's evil," I say. Even though Wyatt did his best to look innocent, I know he was responsible. The asshole was standing right behind me when it happened.

"Son of a bitch." Murder flashes in Hilary's eyes. "You know, I know a guy..."

"Don't bother," Jo says sourly. "Hit men aren't like in movies. They're incompetent."

"Sounds like you're speaking from experience," I say, eyeing her.

"Uh huh. I hired one for one of my exes."

"Oh my God. Remind me not to piss you off." Hilary and I exchange a glance.

Jo snorts. "Not to *kill* the guy, just scare the pants off him. That's the least he deserved for cheating on me."

"So did it work?" Hilary asks, leaning forward.

"Oh yeah. My ex got so scared, the fool tried to jump off his balcony to escape. He was living on the second floor, and there were plenty of bushes under the balcony. But he still broke both his legs."

I shake my head, trying not to laugh. "You're crazy." I wipe tears leaking from the corners of my eyes.

"Angry and determined was more like it. There were other options, but running someone over with a car is so passé. And I didn't want to dent my ride on his hard skull."

Hmm. Maybe I should mention that to Salazar. On the other hand, it's his Aston Martin that's going to get dented.

"So what are you going to do? You know Dane's not going to give up, right?" Hilary says, looking worried. She finishes her martini and signals for another.

"Who cares if Salazar owes his son a favor? And why should Kim have to pay up?"

I lean forward. Jo's devious mind is onto something. "What do you suggest?"

Jo snaps her impeccably manicured fingers. "Outsource the date. And don't get somebody nice. Sounds like Dane's friend deserves to be paired up with a warty-snatch ho."

I laugh. That is hilariously gross. On the other hand, Wyatt might not care. He married Geneva, after all. She might not have a warty snatch, but she definitely has a warty heart.

"I can ask around," Hilary adds. "I heard RentADate is pretty good if you want to use it."

"Better idea: GoldDiggers dot com," Jo says.

"For sure." I nod with a small, vicious smile. Maybe it's the alcohol or the company, but my friends are right. I don't have to attend the wedding myself, or even find someone nice for Wyatt. He just needs some pretty thing with a pulse. A rotten core will be a bonus.

And really, I don't even have to do the finding myself. He'll find a leech on his own just fine. He has the money, and is still young enough to be considered attractive, if the gold digger doesn't care about personality.

Feeling much better, I order another drink.

"But regardless of your situation with this...ape, you should still get a man of your own," Jo says.

I blink, then shake my head. "No time for that. My job keeps me busy, and I'm perfectly happy on my own, thank you very much."

"I know it keeps you busy, but if you had a boyfriend, nobody would expect you to date that man."

"True." Hilary nods. "Unfair, but true."

I wave away my friends' advice. "I can find him a lousy date. It's not that hard. If I have to, I'll get him an escort." And expense it to Salazar. If he wants, he can bill Dane for her services. It was their dumb bet anyway.

"Boyfriends have benefits," Jo says. "Keeping you warm, carrying heavy things, fending off intruders…"

"The sex can be nice, too." Hilary's gaze goes a bit dreamy. I bet Mark's great in bed. Maybe Jo's right about me being without a boyfriend for a long time. But I'm not going to lower my standards just to have a warm body beside me at night.

"And they kill bugs for you," Jo adds in case I'm not convinced yet.

I laugh. "Thankfully, my apartment is pest-free."

Jo gives me a long, assessing look over the rim of her drink. "Just think about it."

7
———

WYATT

THE TEMPORARY RESIDENCY SWEET DARLINGS ARRANGED for me and Vi is in a detached wing of a fancy hotel. It has everything—a full kitchen, two bedrooms and a living room. But you can't miss the fact that it's a *hotel* as you walk through the lobby with a huge front desk to enter and exit. It's just not a good environment for a child—all the guests coming and going make for a lack of the consistency she needs to feel secure—but we'll be moving to our real home tomorrow morning. It took a couple of weeks, but the new place is just the thing—the kind of normal home in a normal neighborhood that a normal family might live in. Providing Vi with the stability she hasn't had up to now is absolutely critical, and that means home-cooked meals, even though the leather-bound room-service menu on the living room table promises every culinary delight imaginable, including the bacon cheeseburger I didn't get for lunch.

I pull the two salmon filets from the griddle and sprinkle them with chopped dill. The steamed veggies are done—thanks to the microwave and instructions on the back of the bag.

They look pretty presentable, if I do say so myself. And it

only took me forty-seven minutes to make the dinner. Well, the concierge also sent me a recipe, just in case.

It's easier to just order something that looks healthy off the menu, but it feels a little too impersonal. Vi deserves home-cooked meals and good conversation a few times a week so we can connect and rebuild our relationship. I know I've neglected that, being busy with work and all, coming home late, traveling and working on my patents. I thought Geneva was taking care of Vi... but it turned out she wasn't. It pissed me off to learn that she fed our daughter nothing but takeout crap, then parked her in front of the TV after school. But what upsets me more is I didn't know until it was too late. It was my job to know. I'm Vi's dad.

Placing the plates on the table, I call out, "Dinner's ready!"

A moment later, one of the doors in the hall opens and Vi comes out. She's in a school uniform—a starched white shirt and pleated burgundy skirt. My little girl, so tall now, the center of my universe.

Right now, she's sporting a shocking shade of red on her lips... and *what the hell is that on her cheeks?* "What are you doing?" I ask.

"What?"

"That. Your face."

"Experimenting."

"Experimenting." When I was young, *experimenting* never meant anything good.

"Yeah."

"With makeup."

"Well, yeah. Duh."

"Isn't ten a little young for that?" What *is* a good age to start wearing makeup, anyway? "And where did you even get that stuff?"

She rolls her eyes. "I'm not a little kid anymore, Dad. Every drugstore has it. There's no age limit on buying makeup," she says like she's explaining the facts of life to an idiot. She comes over and sits at the table. "I was trying to *contour*."

My confusion must be obvious, because she sighs. *Dad, the clueless adult.* Then she wrinkles her nose. "I don't like salmon."

Finally a subject I can talk about with authority. "It's good for you. Growing kids need good fat, and fatty fish is full of it." I recite the information I read on a nutrition site.

Her mouth turns tight. "I'm not a kid."

"Actually, you are."

"I'm going to be in junior high soon."

"Not for another two years. And junior high kids are still kids."

"Elementary school is stupid anyway. I don't know why I have to go. Can't I just skip it?"

I do my best not to sigh. She's been struggling since the divorce became final late last year. Leaving Corn Meadows for L.A. two weeks ago didn't help, but it was necessary for the deal with Sweet Darlings. And Geneva getting remarried was a blow. Maybe Vi was harboring a secret hope that Geneva and I would reconcile, but that won't be possible. Ever.

I need to find her a new counselor she's comfortable talking to as soon as possible. I'm not qualified to deal with this on my own.

"You can't just skip everything," I say. "How are you going to learn what you need to know to be an adult? Besides, your school is one of the best in the city." Dane would never recommend anything less than the best, even if he does have questionable preferences in tuna names.

She sneers, and her attempt to appear older than she is wrenches my heart. Why does she want to grow up so fast? Can't she just stay my little girl for a while longer? I need to make up for the neglect she's suffered.

"Krystal does the best contouring. She said her mom taught her," Vi says, still refusing to touch her dinner.

"Maybe you can ask her to teach you, then." Still have no clue what contouring is. I make a mental note to Google it later.

"Forget it. It's stupid." She looks at the food with disgust. "And I can't eat this much, Dad. I'm going to get fat. Is that what you want?"

"What? No!" Why the hell is she worried about being fat? She's as skinny as a stick. Did Geneva give her crap about her weight? My ex-wife constantly whines about her diet, steps on the scale every morning and evening, and calipers her thighs and triceps on a regular basis.

"You gave me as much food as you."

I look down. Well…yeah. But only because that's how the salmon filets were cut! If she must, she should blame the grocery store. "If it's too much, you don't have to eat it all of it."

"Never mind. I'm going to go finish watching that tutorial." She slides off the chair and goes back to her room.

I stare at the door. I should probably go tell her to come out and eat. Or maybe threaten her. *If you don't eat now, you aren't getting anything later.* That's what my mother would've done.

But somehow I can't. Vi's attitude is… Well, it's messed up because of me. I should've known she wasn't getting the attention and love she needed from her mom because Geneva was too busy screwing around behind my back.

But even that isn't the biggest reason for my anger and frustration. It's that Geneva never wanted Vi…and I didn't realize until it was too late.

Princess hops up on the table. She looks at me long and hard, like she wants something. Instead of scolding her for being on the table, I scratch her head. Narrowing her eyes, she makes a weird half-growl sound in her throat. She's probably too unhappy about her circumstances to really purr. She was Geneva's cat, but was abandoned when my ex discovered her fiancé was allergic to felines. To Geneva, the only thing that matters is what she wants, nothing else.

You can always recover, I tell myself. Geneva might be gone, but I'm here. I'm going to take Vi to the damn wedding, give my daughter the closure she needs, and then I'm going to do my best to provide for Vi and give her a life of normalcy.

8

KIM

"YOU ARE AMAZING. INCREDIBLE."

Wyatt's voice is soft and mellow. And part of me melts away, as though I'm a piece of warm caramel and he's a source of heat...

Yeah. Like an incinerator.

Not like an *incinerator*. That's ridiculous. There has to be a better term...

A bet.

A dumb bet to see who pops your cherry first.

My heart races, but for a very different reason. Cold shivers through me, and I feel the old anger surging.

"I was drunk and taken advantage of."

Just another bet. And Wyatt wins again.

The fucker smirks as he picks up the scotch—the one my boss loves so much—and raises it in my direction. A toast!

Hilary hands me a phone. "It's a burner. A hit man. Discreet. Affordable."

Somebody falls off a balcony with a yell. I don't think it's Wyatt.

"You lost again." He laughs. "I always win, Kim. Always. Looooserrr..."

No! I'm not a loser. I'm not what I used to be. I'm more.
"Lo-ser! Lo-ser!"
"Scaaaaaaarfaaaaace!"
The taunts continue, and the laughter rings lou—

"Ack!" I jackknife up, blinking. I'm in bed. My bed. Alone. No idiot hit man or Wyatt or Salazar. Just me.

I slump and rub my temples. Just a dumb nightmare. Probably because I had to deal with *Wyatt*. No other reason to dream about the bet he made in high school, the one that humiliated me like nothing else. Didn't I suffer enough yesterday?

Inhaling deeply, I check the bedside clock, wondering how many more seconds of sleep I can squeeze in before I have to get up.

Six forty-two!
"Shit!"

I hop out of bed. The stupid alarm didn't go off! No time to figure out why; I need to get ready, pronto!

For once, I'm glad I had a horrible nightmare. Without it, I might've slept until it was too late.

I, Kimberly Katarina Sanford, am never, *ever* late for work.

I take the fastest shower in history, then wrap my hair in a turban so the towel can absorb the water. Not for the first time, I thank my stars that I won the genetic hair jackpot. It doesn't go poufy or frizzy. Just stays nice and sleek without needing to be blow-dried. Another huge towel wrapped around me, I trot to the kitchen to grab my vitamin C serum from the fridge. I put it on every morning and night. Looking my best is part of my new identity, and that means taking care of my skin, among other things.

Just as I finish patting the serum onto my face and put the bottle back in the fridge, the door to my apartment unlocks. Adrenaline spikes, making my heart race.

A burglar?

I dismiss the possibility as soon as it pops into my head. Who breaks into a place this early? It's barely seven in the morning. Criminals would be doing it at night or when people are at work. Not to mention the apartment complex has a locked entry that requires you to have a key or be buzzed in.

It's probably just Evie, my absentee roommate. She somehow

got finagled into a Vegas marriage, but plans to move back in as soon as she manages to divorce her crazy boss-cum-husband. Hopefully she isn't here for moral support, because I don't have time to lend a shoulder right now.

The door opens, and a man in a black T-shirt and jeans walks in. A baseball cap is pressed low on his head, covering most of his face.

Holy shit! It is a burglar!

Cold fear pounds through my heart. I freeze, clutching the towel in my fist as lurid crime headlines flash through my head.

Home Burglary Gone Wrong: Secretary Slaughtered.

Boyfriend Sexually Assaults His Ex.

Female Body Found, Assaulted.

Panic spikes. I have no weapon!

I take a fraction of a second to take stock of my situation. Can't run back to the bedroom—the kitchen's in a nook and the fridge is closer to the door. The fucker's going to get me—he has a straight path to grab me if I make a move back to the bedroom. What can I use as a weapon? A knife? I don't know how to throw it right, so that'd be like handing it over. Jut slash at him? What if he knocks it out of my hand and uses it against me? Besides, a kitchen isn't the best place to fight. I have a gas stove, and every action-flick kitchen fight ends with a gas explosion.

But there's a dirty wine glass in the sink. *Yes!* I grab it and hurl it at the invader with a scream.

"Shit!" he says, flinching and raising an arm in reflexive defense.

To my shock and irritation, the glass doesn't even hit him. It flies low and shatters on the wooden floor at his feet.

Damn it! It was my best chance at hurting the asshole, and I blew it! Should I just go for a knife anyway? I really wish I had a gun! Or a nice, large, intruder-fending-off boyfriend like Jo was saying yesterday.

"What the hell?" he demands.

Did he just say what the hell, like *he's* shocked and upset?

"Kim?"

Wait, what? "How the hell do you know..." Finally he looks up, and I see the still-gorgeous blue eyes and sexy mouth. The broad forehead and lean jaw line. Recognition hits me like a cast iron skillet in the face. "*Wyatt?* What are you doing here?" I demand, my terror turning into outrage.

"I live here."

"No, you don't! This is my apartment."

"But the—"

"No!" I cut him off before he can make any excuses or weird explanations. He'll probably say something asinine, like how he won this place on a bet, too.

My phone is charging on the small table by the couch. I'm calling the cops and getting this crazy bastard arrested. Getting a wedding date will be the least of his worries. Hopefully he'll resist, so the cops will have a reason to rough him up. I'm not asking for blood—just some good, solid punches. Maybe a broken jaw.

Gritting my teeth, I come around the kitchen counter fast. The bastard's eyes widen—ha! Bet he wasn't expecting that!—and he starts toward me.

Oh, crap! I leap for the phone, in my best *grand jeté* style, but he catches me with my toes still a few inches above the floor. His arms squeeze so tight that the air gets forced out of my lungs like ketchup from a squirt bottle.

Oh my God. He's going to crush me until I pop. "Let...me... go," I wheeze, squirming and kicking, refusing to die like this.

But the muscles I'm straining against feel like bunched piano wire, and I make about as much progress against Wyatt as I would against a piece of heavy construction equipment. This close, he smells like fresh pine soap and laundry detergent, plus a hint of mint toothpaste on his breath. I should've taken up karate instead of ballet. Then I could've broken his nose and legs by now, and been inhaling the scent of his blood instead.

"Jesus, will you stop?" he says. "You're about to cut your feet up." He moves, and there's a definite crunching noise from the floor.

The wine glass.

Wyatt carries me toward the sofa. "Damn it, Kim. The superintendent gave me the key to this place. I'm moving in today."

"Annie? Well, she messed up. It's the unit next door that's

empty," I say, even as part of my mind says something's off about this.

Then I remember I'm in nothing but a towel, and he still has his arms around me. *Shit.* I shove him away hard.

He lets me go and falls back. I clutch the towel like a shield—it's the only thing between us—and glare at him.

Wyatt's looking at me like *I'm* the loon here. That *I'm* hurting *his* feelings by treating him like he's a serial rapist.

"I'm going to ask you again. What the hell are you doing here?" I demand. Now that the shock is wearing off and my brain is working normally, I don't believe that bullcrap about Annie. She's always reliable and sharp. She wouldn't make a mistake like that.

"You're *welcome*. No extra charge for saving your feet from being cut to ribbons or anything."

"Yeah, well, there wouldn't be any broken glass in the first place if it weren't for your home invasion!"

Muttering, he takes the broom I left propped up against the kitchen pantry door and starts sweeping the floor. The gesture is unexpectedly nice, but I don't let myself weaken. He's Jekyll and Hyde. You think he's nice and let your guard down...and then *bam*, he slashes at you with a knife!

Well, figuratively, at least.

Since I'm resolved to remain strong, I cross my arms and ignore the way his forearms flex as he sweeps up. Unlike most guys, he isn't doing it wrong, either.

Super irritating.

So I say, "I wish this were Texas. Then I could've shot you."

"For getting the wrong key?"

"Oh, horseshit. What are really you doing here?" I demand for the third time, hoping he'll just confess that he's turned to a life of crime. Billionaires can be villains too. Just look at Lex Luthor. Comic books don't lie.

"I told you. *I live here.*"

"No, you do *not*. This is *my apartment.*"

He stops and looks at me, his head cocked to the side. Is he going to grab me and shove me face-first into the pile of broken glass he's gathered, so he can finish the job his ex-wife started back in high school? The scar on my jaw seems to throb at the memory.

"No, I mean this building." He gestures at our general surroundings when I don't move. One scar is plenty. "Anyway, don't sue the super. She was actually crying when I talked to her."

Yeah, right. Annie is a rock. She never cries, is never flustered and applies the rules fairly to everyone. That's why she's my favorite building manager-slash-owner.

On the other hand, she had to deal with Wyatt first thing in the morning, which would make anyone cry. He probably gave her a roach, like he did to me in high school. "You seem to have that effect on women," I mutter.

He shoots me a probing look—the one that used to make me want to babble, explain and then, when I was out of things to say, just kiss him so I wouldn't have to keep talking. The fact that I feel the same urge again makes me super pissed. I'm much too mature for that sort of reaction now.

"I'm not going to sue her," I say. *But that doesn't mean I won't sue you.* "And you need to go. I have things to do this morning, and they don't include chatting with old high school...memories." I fling the last word like ice cream topped with a panicked frog. Which is fitting, since he once actually did drop one on me, and it ended up in my ice cream sundae.

Fed up and now ultra-conscious of the time, I maneuver around glass on the floor, shove Wyatt out of the apartment and slam the door in his face.

9

KIM

DAMN WYATT. COMING INTO MY HOME IN THE MORNING like he had every right. I don't care if Annie gave him the key. He probably did some dark magic on her. And I hate it—hate, hate, *hate* it—that he *caught* me like that in the living room.

And I'm furious that I'm still thinking about how he smelled. I resent the hell out of the fact that he didn't have some medieval body odor like a sweaty *Game of Thrones* character.

Everyone should smell like the way they are deep inside, in which case Wyatt would smell like a sewer. And not just any sewer, but a rotting, rat-infested sewer.

It's his fault I'm in an Uber, rather than my own car, so I can apply cosmetics. I don't do makeup and drive at the same time. If texting is too distracting, making up one's face is suicidal. But I always report to work in full, flawless makeup. Maintaining the right image is part of the job description.

I march to my desk outside Salazar's downtown office. He isn't in yet, which is a relief.

First order of business is reviewing the day's mail and agenda. There's no correspondence that requires an urgent reply. No meetings for the rest of the day. I send Salazar a quick note letting him know, then think about how to get this *Wife* statue and have it delivered as soon as possible.

François is reclusive. He's also a dick with an ego so big it has its own field of gravity. And he seems to be highly disorganized, because he almost never answers his emails, calls or texts. Apparently my offer—sort of—of naked selfies isn't inducing him to call me back. Or maybe he hasn't even gotten the message.

But getting that statue is basically the final task I need to complete to claim my five-year bonus. I've worked too long and too hard to not get it over a lousy hunk of bronze.

There's gotta be a way—other than hiring a team of pilots to write out my message in the Parisian sky. But how? I can't send him an express mail, signature required, because he won't sign for it.

I inhale sharply as a light-bulb moment hits. *Catherine Davis!* Why didn't I think of her before? François is incredibly fond of her because she discovered him when he was a nobody and supported him. She's currently working as an art curator for Barron Sterling, who is Salazar's in-law, and undoubtedly has bought even more of François's works. I'm pretty sure François doesn't ignore *her* calls, with or without naked selfies.

And Catherine will reach out on my behalf without requiring any incriminating photos. I'll owe her a favor down the line, of course, but that's how this stuff works.

Happy with my solution, I pick up my phone.

"Hello?" she says, her voice soft and sweet.

"Hey, Catherine. Am I interrupting anything?"

"Not at all. What can I do for you?" she says, knowing this is no social call. It's one of the things I like about her.

"Listen, I'm trying to buy François's *Wife* sculpture, but I can't seem to get a hold of him at all. Do you think you could help arrange it? I'll owe you one."

"I'd love to, Kim, but it's already sold."

"What?" I straighten in my seat. "To whom?" *Please, God, let it be someone I can cajole into selling.* But fat chance. The people who buy from François are usually collectors.

"Don't you know? Dane."

"Dane Pryce?"

"Yup. He bought it last week. Which is sort of interesting, because I didn't think it was his thing."

I have a sinking feeling. "Did he get it for Sophia?" If so, there won't be any way to pry it out of him...unless I can prove that the bronze is radioactive and is going to cause cancer. The way he coddles and hovers over his wife... You'd think she was some kind of ancient Chinese vase.

"I really have no idea. Maybe...?"

Ugh. I place my forehead in my palm. Damn it, damn it, *damn it.* "Okay. Thanks, Catherine."

"My pleasure. Look, if you want something along the same lines as *Wife*, I can make a few recommendations."

I'm sure. She's plugged in to the art scene. But Salazar wants *Wife*, not some other similar sculpture. "Thank you," I say. "I might take you up on that, but let me contact Dane first."

"Good luck." Her voice is full of pity and sympathy, as though she knows I'm about to embark on a hopeless task.

And she's right. I might as well try to pry a seal out of a starving polar bear's clutches. But I'm not giving up. Girding my loins, I call the iciclehog...er...Dane. As Salazar's assistant, I'm one of the few people with his personal cell phone number.

"So. You're going to honor the bet?" Dane asks.

Hi, Kim, how are you? Why, I'm doing great, Dane, how about you? "Hello, Dane. And no, that's between you and Salazar. Nobody consulted me."

"He's your boss." Dane's voice is cool and flat, like he's stating something as obvious and mundane as the fact that air is invisible. "He doesn't need your permission."

"I'm not some carcass to be tossed around between two snarling animals," I grumble under my breath, but not too loudly, since I need something from him.

"Didn't catch that."

I'm not going to debate my agency with a man who thinks everyone should kiss his ass. "I'm calling about a sculpture you bought called *Wife*."

"What about it?"

Can he sound any meaner? What does Sophia see in him?

Surely money can't possibly make up for his gross deficiency in human decency. "Can I buy it from you?"

"No."

The answer is immediate and cold. Although I expected it, it still annoys me. "Why not? Did you buy it for Sophia? I can recommend something better." I'm sure Catherine knows some good stuff.

"I'm planning to give it to Wyatt," Dane says.

Huh? Did he just say what I think he said? "You're giving *Wife* to Wyatt?"

"Yes."

"But...why?" That's a pretty messed-up thing for a hetero guy —with a wife!—to give another man... Isn't it?

"A housewarming gift."

I pull my phone away and stare at it. If I didn't know any better, I might've thought Dane had a crush on Wyatt, but no way. Dane loves his wife enough to drive a pink car. "A housewarming gift," I repeat.

"Yes."

He doesn't explain. Figures.

"Thanks," I say, more out of habit than politeness, then hang up.

This isn't exactly what I expected, but the end result is the same. The statue is not available. When Dane makes up his mind about something, nothing can dissuade him. Well, Sophia might, but I don't know her well enough to ask. Besides, if he thought I was bugging his wife, he might hire a hit man. Not the incompetent kind Jo hired, but a really good one, like a former CIA agent or something.

But whatever Dane feels about his wife or Wyatt isn't my main problem. My main issue, contrary and weird as it is, is realizing that Wyatt fucking lied about moving in to the empty unit next to mine.

Fancy, artsy-fartsy statues like those created by François do not go into regular apartments. They belong in ostentatious mansions and penthouses, the kind that you see featured in glossy magazines for the rich and the famous. Or maybe some slick architectural digest on the latest trends in multimillion-dollar homes.

Obviously Wyatt was just screwing with me, just like he did in high school. There's a reason he's divorced. Not even a barracuda like Geneva could put up with him anymore. And I'm not at all bothered that he's still a dick. Not even a little.

Maybe I can tell Salazar there's something much, much better than *Wife* that's available. If I can convince him of that, I won't have to bother with François, and I'll still get the bonus.

And speak of the devil...

He walks in, whistling as he's texting on his phone, his eyes crinkled with affection. That's his "I'm in love" face, so it must be his ex-wife on the other side.

So. Weird.

I follow him into his office and shut the door. He sits down and looks at me. "Morning. Gorgeous day, eh?"

"Yes, it is." Sunny and clear, just like every other day in L.A.

"Well, everything's set. Ceinlys and I start our trip on Monday. Your itinerary's perfect. Exactly what we wanted."

"Excellent." I smile, happy he's pleased. Maybe it's going to make what I'm about to say go over better. "Um, I need to talk to you about something."

"Yeah?" His tone says he's not that interested.

"It's about the statue you wanted."

Now I have his attention. "You got it already?" Without waiting for an answer, he smiles. "I *knew* it. Thanks, Kim. You're honest to God the best. Gavin says his assistant is worth her weight in gold, but *I* say *you're* worth *your* weight in diamond-studded platinum." He winks. "You can tell her that."

"Tell her yourself," I say automatically, because Gavin's assistant is Hilary, who also happens to be Salazar's daughter-in-law.

"Probably be better coming from you." He laughs. "So. When is it being delivered?"

"Uh, that's the thing. I don't actually have it yet."

"You don't?" He frowns.

"I need to figure some things out." Like how I'm going to get Wyatt to hand over the statue once he gets it from Dane.

"Oh." He purses his mouth. "Well, that's not good."

I manage a properly chagrined expression. "Yeah. It's not. But like I said, I'm looking into getting it, but in case that doesn't work out…you'll need to pick something else."

Salazar shakes his head. "No. It has to be that statue or nothing. I mean it."

I clench my jaw, wondering how this man-child has managed to get through life to this point. *How old are you, again?*

"Look, Kim, don't fail me now. This is really important. You know that, right? I don't want to disappoint Ceinlys."

"Who cares about her disappointment? She *divorced* you" is on the tip of my tongue, but I swallow it. The last time somebody pointed out that Ceinlys was Salazar's *ex*-wife, things didn't work out so well for the guy. Salazar might consider me a great assistant, but that doesn't mean he would forgive me for reminding him of his current marital status. "No disappointing her. Got it. Let me see what I can do."

"That's my girl. Let me know when you have it."

10

WYATT

I arrive in the office for an afternoon meeting. The movers are done, except for Vi's room, but she said she didn't want anybody touching her things.

Melanie smiles. "Hey, Wyatt! How did the move go?"

"Pretty good, thanks."

"Here. A housewarming gift." She hands me a golden box of gourmet chocolate.

"Oh. Well, thanks. 'Preciate it." I force a small grin and accept the gift, even though gold-wrapped chocolate brings up some bittersweet memories. The first box of chocolate I bought for a girl was like this one, and it dented my wallet pretty good. But when Kim smiled in return, I felt like I had everything I wanted in life.

When things ended with Kim, I bought another box—the exact same kind—for Geneva. I thought Geneva's smile would make me feel the same way Kim's did. But it didn't. Wasn't even close.

Still, none of that is Melanie's fault. I put the box on the desk and head in to the meeting.

But gradually, through the long discussion, the crummy mood

Faking It with the Frenemy

from the morning returns and clings to me, like a film of paint you can't get rid of no matter how many times you scrub yourself. I'm pissed off that Kim thought I went into her unit on purpose. I'm doubly pissed the way my cock responded to seeing her in nothing but a towel.

She may look fuckable, but she isn't. Her reaction yesterday made it clear. I don't understand how she could get so offended just by seeing me, as though I was the one who did something wrong. I'm not the one who got used and discarded. And if she got herpes back then, it wasn't from me. But she was looking at me like I was some kind of human-sized genital wart.

Damn it, forget her. You've got bigger things to worry about.

Like this meeting. And the date with Bethany later. And figuring out how to connect with Vi, who these days speaks a language that sounds like English but never seems to mean what I'm expecting.

And this last agenda item here on the screen, because Sweet Darlings is paying me to work, not brood about a girl I thought was the one. Besides, wasn't I too young to know about that sort of thing anyway? Teenage hormones... Well, not just *teenage* hormones. They lasted into my twenties and made me do stupid shit, like marrying a harpy like Geneva.

After the meeting, I leave. I wish Melanie took decent notes, but that'd be like asking Geneva to have a conscience. I'm going to have to talk to David's assistant. Erin takes great notes.

"So. Big night, eh?" David grins. Like most of the Darling brood, he's your prototypical tall, dark and handsome. Popular among women, and he's been taking advantage of that by man-whoring around after breaking up with his last girlfriend. He's excellent at his job as head of marketing. Otherwise Alexandra would've kicked him out, family or not.

"Yeah." I force an enthusiasm I don't feel because I don't want to look ungrateful. "Something like that."

"Don't be nervous. I know you've been out of the meat market for a while, but it isn't that hard to jump back in."

"Uh-huh." He forgets I have a child and can't just hop from girl to girl the way he does. Not that I want to. The idea of sleeping my way through a bunch of available females seems about as appetizing as gorging at one of those hotdog-eating contests.

"Hey, you'll be fine." He slaps my shoulder. "You're exactly her type."

Somehow that doesn't reassure me, even though I'm not sure why.

11

KIM

ALL THROUGH THE DAY I THINK ABOUT THE DAMNED STATUE and how I'm going to pry it out of Dane's clutches before he hands it over to Wyatt.

Money won't work. He's too rich to be tempted.

Maybe a favor...? No. He already thinks he owns me because of that dumb bet with Salazar.

What, then?

Do I have to honor the bet? But even if I do, it still won't mean that he has to give me the statue. I want to tell Salazar to give up, but he's so, so determined to give the damn thing to Ceinlys.

Should I ask Ceinlys to tell Salazar she wants something more, mmm, *romantic* than *Wife*? But what if she asked for the damned statue? What if it was her idea?

Argh. I hate this!

On my way home, I buy a bottle of Merlot and some Kung Pao chicken. I deserve both after the kind of day I've had. Actually, the kind of week I'm having.

The bonus is the nice lady at the Chinese takeout place I love so much gave me a big bag so I could put everything in it. People like her remind me that the world isn't full of crazy rich people like my boss or subhumans like Wyatt and Dane.

I march toward my unit, happy to be home at reasonable hour and looking forward to enjoying dinner with my favorite wine. You've got to find little pieces of joy in your life somehow, or you'll end up being so miserable no therapy will—

Something on the hall floor catches my foot, and I stumble forward. Agh! Not the wine!

I manage to catch myself before I hit the floor. No food or drink is spilled. Relieved, I straighten up, about to kick away whatever it was that—

"Meow!"

I look down and see a small black cat. My annoyance immediately fades as I crouch and pick it up. It's gorgeous, its deep ebony fur soft and silky. The only place that isn't black is a crown-shaped patch of white on its head. I note it's a female and cradle her in my arms. "Hey, little kitty, are you lost? I've never seen you around before."

The cat licks her paw, ignoring me.

"Are you new? Are you Mrs. Lopez's?" She lives at the end of the hall, and she's been saying she wants a cat. I check for a collar, but although the cat has one, there's no tag. Maybe I shouldn't knock on Mrs. Lopez's door, in case this isn't hers. It might upset her because the reason she can't have one is her husband. Mr. Lopez has never made a secret of his dislike of cats, and Mrs. Lopez has said more than once he's an idiot she can't get rid of because she's a good Catholic.

I stand in the hall, unsure of what to do next. Maybe I should just take a picture of the cat and post it on the Facebook group for the building residents. Even if the owner isn't in the group, somebody might recognize her.

"I guess we'll just wait and see who comes to claim you. Do you have a name?" No response. "You know what? Since you have a crown on your head, I'll call you Queen. I think that's a fitting name, don't you?"

Queen looks up, her gorgeous green eyes startlingly wide, then paws me gently and purrs. She even seems to give me a feline smile.

Faking It with the Frenemy

"Guess I got it right, huh?" The cat rubs itself all over me, purring like the engine of one of the fancy European cars my boss loves so much.

Holding Queen in one hand, I unlock my door. As I turn the knob, loud, rapid steps come down the hall.

"Hey! You can't take my cat!"

I turn and face a small, skinny girl of maybe eight or nine. Her long, dark brown hair is straight, but messy and tangled as though she hasn't bothered to brush it—and nobody else has either. She puts her hands on her hips and looks up at me, her owlish blue eyes bright with fire and wariness.

She's in a starched white shirt and burgundy pleated skirt. A private school uniform, I decide. But I don't know anybody on my floor with a kid going to a private school. Maybe somebody upstairs?

But what's she doing this floor, then? And if her parents are well enough off to send her to a private school, shouldn't they be able to afford a hairbrush or two?

"This is your cat? Probably should keep a better eye on her, then," I say mildly, not wanting to alarm the girl. "I was just going to take her inside so she wouldn't get lost. Guess I don't have to do that, since you're here."

"Right." She nods.

I hand her the cat. "Okay, then. Here you go."

She takes Queen and thanks me politely. I stand, waiting for her to leave. I want to make sure she returns home, even though we're inside an apartment building. There are a few older kids I don't care for. They aren't in a gang or anything, but they have that "mean jerk" look all over them. I don't want her getting bullied.

Or maybe she already was. They could've done that to her hair.

But the girl doesn't move. "Aren't you going home?" I ask.

She shakes her head. "Nobody's home. I locked myself out looking for the cat. She's not supposed to be wandering around. She's an indoor cat."

I scowl. It's like... I check my watch. *Almost seven.* This girl shouldn't be alone. "How old are you?"

"Ten."

Geez. "Can you call your mom or dad?"

She shakes her head again. "I'm not supposed to bother them." Her shoulders droop for a moment.

"Oh." Sympathy stirs. It sucks when you're so low on your parents' priority list that you can't even call to let them know you're locked out. I know what that feels like.

I wonder if I should call 911 or something, but if I do, it's going to cause a *lot* of problems for her parents. And that probably won't help. At the same time, I can't just let her stay out in the hall.

"Want to come in?" I say. "I was about to have dinner. You can join me, if you'd like."

"Uh... I'm not really supposed to go anywhere with strangers."

At least she isn't totally naive. "Well, my name is Kim, and I live in this unit." I tilt my head at my door. "So you won't be going very far."

"I'm Vi."

"Nice to meet you, Vi. So..." Although I understand why she doesn't want to come in, a small part of me wishes she would just say *okay* so I can have my Kung Pao chicken while it's still hot. "About that dinner...?"

She gives it some thought. "Well...if you really live right here..."

I let her in and shut the door. She places the cat on the foyer and looks around.

I kick off my shoes and pad into the kitchen. "I got Chinese food. Have you ever had that before?"

"Yeah."

"You aren't allergic to anything, are you?"

"Just Max Iverson."

I try not to laugh. "Who's he?"

"This boy who sits next to me in class. He uses this soap that makes me sneeze."

"Well, he won't be eating with us, so you'll probably be okay." I spread the cartons and plastic containers out on the table. "Kung

Pao chicken, egg drop soup and some shrimp fried rice. Take whatever you like." I hand her utensils and a plate and a bowl. "I only have water," I say, giving her a glass, then serve myself a liberal dose of Merlot.

"Can I have some of that?" she asks.

"When you're twenty-one," I say. My mom was pretty liberal with alcohol at home and didn't care if I had it when I was underage—I'm certain she thought it'd make me grow up to be more worldly and more trophy-wifey—but I'm not giving it to somebody's kid.

She shrugs. "Thank you," she says, surprisingly polite, then portions a bit of everything onto her plate. "Is it okay if I give some to Princess?"

"Who?"

She points at the cat, which has approached and is hissing at her.

Weird. Shouldn't she be purring at the idea of food? "Oh. Her name is Princess? I thought it should be Queen because of the crown mark."

"Mom thought Princess was a cuter name. Besides, *Mom's* the queen, not some cat." Vi is speaking in that "I'm a cool teen" voice, but she's only ten. She can't quite disguise the unhappiness and wistfulness in her tone.

"Makes sense. So where's your mom? Working?"

"No, she's getting married. So she's really busy."

"Oh." That's...awkward. It reminds me entirely too much of how my own mother used to get married all the time. Well, not all the time. Just five freakin' times, each successive husband becoming older and richer. Thankfully I only had to witness the fifth one, but she told me all about the others in great, excruciating detail, with twenty photo albums. She even took pictures of her individual toes on the day of those weddings. "That's..." I search for a suitable word, but can't think of any. "That's...um... good for her, I guess...?" I say, hoping her mom isn't marrying for money, but for true love or at least some kind of course correction.

Vi scowls. "I guess."

I squirm. This is really uncomfortable. "Are you going to be in the wedding? Maybe a flower girl or train bearer or something?" My mother wanted me to be a flower girl for her fifth wedding. She thought it was adorable and showed her true love for the groom. When I told her I didn't want to, she made me do it anyway.

Vi looks down at her plate. "No. She doesn't really want me there."

But I hear more. *She doesn't really want me.*

Oh, you poor thing. Even my mother lets me know she loves me, although her way of showing it is pretty messed up. Like telling me to marry the richest guy available.

"She doesn't even want Princess, because her fiancé doesn't like cats. She says he's allergic, but I think that's a lie. He's a creepy perv."

"I'm sure Princess is better off with you," I say softly, not wanting to get into all the other drama. That's her parents' issue to deal with, not mine.

"Yeah, maybe." Vi forces a smile. "The girls at school are nice and so much more mature than the ones at my old school." Then she sighs, the sound small but audible.

There's no way ten-year-olds are mature, but obviously she's decided to be like them and fit in. Then my gaze goes to her hair. If she's trying to fit in with the "mature" girls in her school, she should never go to school with hair like that. "So. What's the new style in your school?" I have no idea what's cool in school these days, and I don't want to be like my mom, who just assumed that what was awesome to her would be awesome to teenagers.

"Something like this." She points at her own hair. "I teased it this morning, although it doesn't hold the shape very well. I think I need a new spray. The girl in the tutorial looked really great."

I bite the inside of my cheek. What she needs is better technique. Her hair looks like a raptor's nest. Besides, do little girls even tease their hair? Is that a thing, or is she just doing it because she saw it on some social media site?

I'm curious, but hold my tongue. It's none of my business. So instead, I say, "That should help, but you can also try something else. I used to tease mine too, and learned a few tricks. Want me to show you?"

Her eyes sparkle. "Really?" Then she stares at my non-teased mane. "But how come you don't wear it like that anymore?"

"It isn't really right for where I work. But I can show you."

She considers, then nods. "Okay. Thank you."

12
———

WYATT

DIPPING MY FINGERS IN WATER AND STICKING THEM INTO AN electrical socket would be less painful than this.

The woman—Bethany—across the table radiates a polished sexual energy. Her red hair glints, her brown eyes glint and her red nails glint. Every time she throws her head back and laughs, her teeth glint.

All that glinting reminds me of metal robotic claws...long, shiny ones, reaching for my bank account. The worst thing is that I'm certain she'd wrap them around my dick too if she thought that was what she needed to do get to my recent wealth.

I can feel it shrink in horror. *You better not! She isn't even that hot.*

Technically she *is* sort of pretty, in a luscious, overtly sexual way. I can see why David thought she'd be a good rebound date to take to Geneva's wedding. She might've been, too, if I were single and looking for a meaningless roll in the hay to pass the time.

Elbows propped on the table, Bethany is leaning forward intently. Her breasts look like they're about to explode out of her dress, and I wonder if she plans to continue leaning until her nipples pop over the low neckline.

Oddly, it reminds me of Kim. And the way her breasts felt against me yesterday morning—soft and firm at the same time. Why was that so arousing, especially since she acted like I was covered in raw sewage?

"So tell me everything," Bethany says breathlessly. "I've always been interested in those big tech deals."

Except she isn't really interested in the deal. What she's interested in is exactly how much I made off Sweet Darlings Inc.

I'm going to kill David for setting this up. "It was mostly just selling a few patents."

"But the articles said you made *billions*." Her teeth flash.

Billions... She can't even read right. The articles covering the deal have never said billions. Would she leave in crushed disappointment if I told her it was really just a little over one billion, plus a position at Sweet Darlings?

In my head, Kim's cool expression and immediate departure from Éternité play in a weird overlapping montage with this woman's excitement. I wonder what Kim would say if I explained my success to her. Would she be as admiring as Bethany? Or would she still turn away?

Whichever, at least it would be an honest reaction.

Yeah, just like how she called our time together a "mistake."

The reminder stings, even after all these years.

It's already after eight. I'm finished with my entrée—mainly because I gobbled it down in a hurry to get the hell out of the restaurant. Bethany's slower, but she only eats half, and in small, nibbling bites, like she's some kind of dieting rodent. She gestures for the dessert menu.

Oh hell no. Not doing this.

Dad raised me to be nice to women, but I know if I make him proud, I'm going to end up stuck here for hours because Bethany won't end it with just dessert. She'll want coffee...and cheese... and cognac...

Time to end this charade. Which means I need to start acting like the most direct and straightforward of my friends.

"I'm full," I say baldly, channeling Dane. "I need to get going."

"So soon?" Bethany says, fluttering her eyelashes. The fake

lashes' movement reminds me of centipede legs. I suppress a shudder.

Our waiter comes over as though he's sensed I need him. I hand him my credit card. The man's going to be tipped well.

"Maybe coffee? At my place?" Bethany asks, her voice so breathless that I'm afraid she's about to hyperventilate. If she does, I'll ask the waiter to call 911, but I'm not going with her to the ER.

"I have a kid waiting for me at home," I say, hoping she gets the hint.

"Can your sitter stay longer?"

Guess she's the self-centered, oblivious type. Been there, done that, got divorced for the effort. Not wasting any more time with another Geneva. "She has another gig tonight," I lie.

The waiter returns with the bill. I sign it, leaving him an extra thirty percent.

The barest hint of a frown is marring Bethany's forehead. "How about this weekend? I'd love to get together. You could bring your child along, if you like."

I resist an urge to rub my forehead. Bring Vi on a date? She wouldn't talk to me for a year. She might even run away from home. "Actually, I'm busy. Work." I give my watch an unmistakable look. "And I gotta get going if I want to be home in time. Nice meeting you."

Then I stand up and hurry out of the restaurant, without waiting for Bethany. The woman's a leech, and my politeness has a limit.

Sorry, Dad. But if you were here, you'd probably tie her to the chair so I could make my escape.

The valet brings my Audi around and I drive home. I'm going to have to come up with some other way to find a date to Geneva's wedding, since neither Dane nor David seems able to help.

When I reach the complex, I park in the garage and head upstairs. I like this apartment, and the normalcy it represents, even if I am stuck next to Kim. But it isn't like we'll run into each other much. I'm busy and so is she. If half the stuff I've heard is true, her boss is difficult to please.

I eye Kim's door as I walk past and unlock my unit. The light's on in the living room, but no one seems to be around.

"Vi? I'm home!" I call out, hanging my keys on the rack near the door.

Not even a disdainful meow greets me. Fine. I don't care if Princess wants to ignore me. She is a cat, after all, and I'm pretty sure she's unhappy her real owner—Geneva—isn't living with us.

But where's Vi? And Lori?

Maybe they're in Vi's room, arranging things to her taste. She's been...pretty particular recently. It upsets her when people touch her stuff or move something around.

I knock on her door. "Vi?" When she doesn't answer, I shake my head. Probably has that Bose headset on and music blaring into her ears.

But what about Lori?

Sudden panic squeezes my chest. I open the door and step into the room.

Empty.

Did something happen to Vi? I check my phone for texts, but there's nothing. What the hell is going on? Did Lori take Vi out to grab something? I frown as a thought strikes me. I hope she isn't buying her makeup.

I call Lori.

"Hi, Mr. Westland," she says, her voice perky and yet bored at the same time—a magic only teenagers can perform.

"Where are you?" I demand.

"Uh... Home?"

The frustration and annoyance of the evening roll through me, swelling and rushing like an ugly tsunami. "What the hell are you doing home? You're supposed to be watching Vi today!"

"Umm... Didn't Vi's mom call you? She texted me that she picked her up from school..."

"What?" That makes no sense. Geneva can't stand dealing with Vi. As a matter of fact, she hates it that she got pregnant in the first place, and said she considered Vi an unfortunate accident when we were in the middle of going through our divorce. The only value our daughter has is how good she can make her mom look, and Vi just doesn't measure up to Geneva's ideal.

"You might want to call her and see." Lori sounds mildly peeved. "Or, you know, maybe check your texts."

"I already checked. No messages from Geneva."

"Oh." She sounds vaguely more understanding now. "Oh. Well. Okay."

I inhale deeply. Whatever happened, it doesn't seem like it was Lori's fault. "Sorry I yelled at you."

"It's okay, Mr. Westland. But yeah, it was your ex-wife, so you should, you know...talk to her."

"Thanks. I'll do that." I hang up, then immediately call Geneva.

What the hell is she plotting? She's still irritated that part of the divorce settlement stipulated no further claims on each other's assets, ever. Her idea, because she was afraid I'd come after her and her rich fiancé. But I know it infuriates her that she can't claim a penny of the money from my Sweet Darlings deal.

If she's trying to use Vi...

Geneva finally answers. "What do you want?"

"Where's Vi? Is she with you?"

"Vi? Why are you asking me?" I can almost hear the wrinkling of her nose. "Did she say she was going to come see me? Ugh. You keep her at home. You know how Churchie doesn't like kids, and I don't have time right now. I have a wedding to plan."

She isn't lying. In my panicked anger, I forgot how self-centered she can be. Not wanting to hear her prattle on and on about her asshole fiancé and the wedding, I hang up, then finally remember I got Vi her own cell phone when we moved to L.A.

"Hey," she answers.

Relief flows through me. Followed almost immediately by a fury hot enough to singe my scalp. *"Where are you?"*

"Eating ice cream and watching TV."

"I didn't say what, I said where!"

"Dad," she says, all Miss Maturity. "Take a breath."

"Take a—?" She's lucky she isn't standing in front of me, because I might just throttle her. "You're grounded until you're sixty!" I yell, even though a small voice in the back of my head says maybe I shouldn't threaten that until she's home first.

"What*ever*. The most you can ground me is until I'm eighteen."

My blood boils. I inhale, whether to calm myself or to gather more angry words to fling at her, I'm not sure yet. There's some murmuring in the background, then a new voice comes over the phone.

"Hi. I just want to let you know there's no reason to worry, because your daughter's with me. I ran into her after work, and decided to keep her with me. Apparently, she got locked out of your apartment."

A woman. I relax a little. I know it's stupid—women can be just as vicious as men—but at least the probability that Vi is with a perv isn't as high. Her voice is familiar...probably one of the neighbors I ran into when I was looking at the unit. The people in the building seem like a friendly enough bunch...other than Kim.

"Hey, 'preciate it. Do you mind telling me where you are? I'll come get my kid out of your hair," I say, reaching for my keys.

"Sure. Apartment 1104."

I put the keys back on the rack, and go out into the hall. I'm in 1106. And 1104 is...

My head slowly swivels. That's...

Fuck.

13

KIM

I give the phone back to Vi. "You shouldn't give your dad static that way," I say. "He's just worried about you."

She rolls her eyes.

Oh boy. Why me? I'm not capable of guiding a young kid. "If he's that bad, do you want me to call the cops?" I ask, almost certain that she'll back off and realize she's having an unreasonable temper tantrum. "I can have him arrested for child neglect and endangerment. You'll never see him again, and you'll get a whole new dad."

Her small jaw drops. "You can really do that?" Something I can't quite read sparks in her eyes.

Does she actually want me to have her dad arrested? What the hell kind of dick is he? "Yeeeees," I say, suddenly unsure.

She gives me a considering look. "Would he be in jail for long?"

"I don't know. Probably not that long." Back in Corn Meadows, Mr. Felder went in and out of jail for being a drunken lout and a wife beater, but he never spent that much time inside his cell. His lawyer always got him off.

I reach for my wine and take a sip. Maybe I should've bought something stronger.

Vi shakes her head. "I don't want to do that. I heard jail sucks. All they do is toss each other's salad all the time." She makes a face.

I choke and sputter, but I'm too stunned to care about wine stains. "Where did you learn that? You're only ten!"

"So?" She looks at me like I'm the dumb one. "I'm old enough to know about jail. But seriously, who wants to eat salad all the time? Talk about a punishment."

Oh my God. Torn between laughter, horror and relief, I cover my face. Thankfully, there are three knocks on the door.

I turn to her. "I think that's your dad."

Her shoulders droop. "I know."

"Cheer up." I squeeze her hand and go answer the door with a smile...

Only to see Wyatt on the other side. "You! What are you doing here?" Did he come over to demand I honor that dumb bet?

He doesn't look any happier than I feel. "I'm here for Vi."

"Vi?" I gape at him. "*You're* her dad?"

He nods curtly. "She's here, right?"

"Yeah." I step aside automatically so he can come in, even as my brain's having trouble processing this bizarre turn of events.

Hands on hips, Wyatt walks over and stops in front of Vi, vibrating with annoyance. "Young lady, you're in so much trouble!"

"Why? I already did my homework." She flips her hair over a shoulder. Her hair's now neatly brushed and just slightly teased to give it some volume.

"You know why! Did you make Lori think you were with your mother?"

Guilt flashes through her gaze, but she shrugs. "Why would I do that? Mom wanted to come see me, but couldn't because something went wrong with the wedding plan. She said she tried to call you, but you didn't answer...as usual."

I almost shake my head. The girl is a terrible liar. She should at least look him in the eye when she lies. That way it seems more believable.

Wyatt is livid. "You're so grounded!"

Vi's stubborn expression says, *What else is new?*

"Wyatt." When he looks at me, I incline my head toward the door. "You can have your family argument once you're home."

Wyatt glares like I'm the cause of the situation between him and his daughter. I stare back levelly. It's not like I did anything wrong.

Eventually he relaxes slightly and inhales. "Thank you for taking care of Vi."

It couldn't sound more begrudging, but whatever. "No problem."

"Vi, let's go," he says.

She grabs the cat. "Thanks for dinner, Kim."

His lips thin even more, like it's a crime to feed his kid. *Hey, buddy, I didn't spit in her food or anything gross like that. Disgusting food toppings are your specialty, not mine.*

Wyatt nods once at me, then leaves with Vi.

I look out in the hall, just to make sure he actually leaves. He says something to Vi quietly enough that I can't make it out, then opens his apartment door and they vanish inside.

I pull my head back in and shut my own door. Then, as I'm cleaning up the dirty plates...it hits me. *Wyatt really did move in next door!* He really *is* my neighbor. But why? Doesn't he want a mansion to show off his billion bucks? And why is Dane giving him a statue that's going to end up looking ridiculous in that apartment? It's going to stand out like a Porsche in a pigsty.

I cross my arms and think. Wyatt can't possibly want a thing that costs, like, a million dollars in his apartment. And it's going to take up too much space. And unlike Dane the Iciclehog, Wyatt will probably be slightly more amenable to a trade, especially since he really needs a date. If his assistant were any good, she would've taken care of it by now.

I narrow my eyes and strategize. Because no matter what happens, I'm getting that damned statue.

14

WYATT

Vi hasn't said a word to me since yesterday evening when I dragged her out of Kim's apartment. Which is fine, because talking might just end up making things worse. According to a lot of parenting books, angry words are not the way to go with ten-year-olds who are trying to cope with multiple upheavals. My divorce, Geneva's new marriage, the move, the new school... It's a lot to take, and on top of everything else, I've been busy with the Sweet Darlings deal.

The silence continues as she leaves to go to school. I let out a sigh. Maybe I should take Daddy-Daughter Communication 101. Because this sucks.

Just as I'm on my way to work, I get a call from Dad. Smiling a little, I pick it up. "Hey, Dad."

"Hey, Wyatt! How's your new place?" he booms.

"Wish we were there to help you move," Mom says. He must have finally figured out the speakerphone function.

"The apartment is great."

"Are your new neighbors nice? Big-city people can be a little brusque. You remember how it was in New York," Mom says. She hates the Big Apple. Says it's a misnomer because apples are wholesome.

So I give her the only reassurance I can. "L.A. is nothing like New York."

"Oh, that's good. I don't want Vi to have trouble adjusting." Mom's voice is full of grandmotherly sympathy. My parents adore Vi, although they don't feel the same way about her mom.

"Vi's fine." But she isn't fine. She's going through a difficult patch. I really hope going to the damned wedding and getting some closure helps her get over...whatever she's having issues with, because I'm tearing my hair out. Probably going to need a toupee before the year's over.

"The witch is in town," Dad says. He only calls Geneva a witch when Mom's listening. When it's just me and him, the B-word comes out, among other more colorful ones, depending on his mood and if he had any alcohol. "And she hired a baker who looks like she should have been in that *Warrior Princess* series."

Warrior Princess? "You mean Xena?"

"Yeah, that's the one. Barely dressed and fighting with swords."

"I don't understand why Geneva wants to marry here in Corn Meadows when her grandpa groom lives L.A." Mom sounds positively peeved.

"Exactly. And what kind of man marries a woman a third his age?" Dad asks.

The rich, old kind?

"Better yet, what kind of woman leaves Wyatt to marry a man four times her age!" Mom adds, bristling with outrage.

I almost laugh. They're still mad on my behalf, and their math is charmingly creative. I swear, every time I talk to them, Geneva's fiancé gets older. The only thing I know for sure is there's a big age gap, he doesn't like children, is allergic to cats and this is something like his sixth marriage. I wish he'd met Geneva earlier, though, so I wouldn't have wasted so much time with her.

"That woman is probably a werefox," Dad says.

"A what?" I say, wondering when Geneva went from being a witch—or a bitch, depending who's around—to some kind of mythological fox.

"A werefox. I've been trying to expand my horizons a little, so we were watching some TV shows from other countries. And they say werefoxes are shape-changers. *Female* shape-changers. They lure you in with their beauty and the promise of sex...and then they eat your liver."

"Which kills you," Mom adds helpfully.

"But this happens after the men get laid," Dad says. "Nobody gives away his liver for free."

I really don't need to discuss the sex habits of mythical creatures from another culture with my parents. "I don't think Geneva wants my liver." More like money and being the center of somebody's universe to satisfy her narcissistic, sociopathic ego.

"Your heart!" Dad says, and I hear a loud clap. "Bet she rips out hearts, too."

"Eats," Mom corrects him. "Supposedly werefoxes eat the organs out of living victims. Now listen. You need to get a date prettier than Geneva, somebody who can outshine her. I really want her to look terrible at her own wedding, especially in front of Vi. Why, it would make my summer. I'm certain it would make Vi happy, too."

Mom can be super nice, but when she decides she hates you... "You said that Vi staying with you over the break was going to make your summer."

"Well, of course. I'm looking forward to spoiling her rotten, which that darling child deserves, but I can always use another thing to make my summer even more satisfying."

"What woman could outshine a werefox witch, though?" Dad asks.

"I don't know." Mom sounds entirely too serious, like they're debating where to invest their retirement savings. "Did we finish watching that show...?"

"This is really fascinating, but I gotta get to work." If I don't end it now, they'll continue forever on this asinine topic. A werefox that eats livers indeed. "Love you both."

"Have a great day!" Mom and Dad say together.

I can almost hear them wave and smile. I hang up and go to work.

When I step out of the elevator at the office, David finds me.

He looks fresh and pleased with the world. And why the hell not? He doesn't have a kid who lies to her sitter and imposes herself on a next-door neighbor who thinks he's a herpes carrier.

"So how'd it go with Bethany?" he asks with an arch look, a mug of steaming coffee in his hand.

"Terrible." There's no other way to describe the date. I start heading toward the break room because I could use some coffee myself.

David walks with me, confusion etched in every line of his face. "Why?"

I pinch the bridge of my nose as the terrible memory from last night resurfaces. I grab a mug that says *All My Darlings* over a bunch of baby photos, then fill it with coffee, dump two sugars in and stir.

"She said she'd even put out when she talked with me," David says, annoyed.

A little song goes through my head. *Glinty, glinty, little claws...* I shudder. "Seriously, man? And you still thought Bethany was a good idea?"

"Of course! Shouldn't you be happy you have a buddy like me? I thought you could use a little rebound action," he says, lowering his voice. "Best thing for getting over an ex. Trust me."

He would know. After he broke up with his girlfriend, he fucked half the eligible female population—discreetly, of course. His mom would murder him otherwise. She's big on propriety and family values.

"I have a kid. I need to set a good example."

David looks at me, scandalized. "Don't tell me you share *every*thing with your kid. She doesn't have to know. Besides, Bethany's hot. Perfect if you want to rub somebody pretty in Geneva's face. She can even do makeup to make herself look ten years younger. I've seen it."

"Yeah, if I want to flaunt an underage-looking gold digger who glints," I mutter.

David squints. "What?"

"Nothing. I need to prep for a meeting." It's a lie. I don't have a meeting until one thirty.

Melanie waves when she sees me. "Oh, good, you already got

yourself some coffee. I was wondering if I should grab you a cup, but then I thought maybe it'd get cold before you got in."

"You're in early," I say, more surprised she's early than the fact that she considered bringing me coffee. She's *never* here before me. Usually she isn't even on time.

"Oh, my husband's car broke down yesterday, so we're carpooling today. He had to drop me off this morning before heading to work."

"I see." I give Melanie a couple things to do, step into my office and come to a complete halt.

I blink and take a big gulp of my coffee. A lack of caffeine is the only thing that can explain the presence of Kim standing before my desk, looking like a hot, haughty model in a fitted red dress and stiletto heels. She's wearing plum-colored lipstick and there's a small smile on her luscious lips that does something crazy to my chest and dick.

I take another sip of my coffee to hide my reaction. "What are you doing here?"

15

KIM

I TILT MY HEAD AND LOOK AT WYATT. HE'S SURPRISINGLY well put together. Neatly brushed hair, a crisply pressed shirt, no tie and slacks with sharp creases. His blue eyes are alert, and he looks slightly surprised, wary and displeased, as is to be expected. I don't have an appointment, and he shouldn't be discovering me in here in the first place. But his worthless assistant didn't even try to stop me. Actually, she not only smiled when I told her I wanted to talk to Wyatt, but let me wait for him inside his office without any kind of supervision. What if I were a corporate spy? Or someone here to sabotage his work? He has documents lying on his desk. What if they're some secret project plans for the company?

But I doubt any of that crossed her mind. She was too busy fussing with her coffee and plants. No wonder he can't get his assistant to solve the simple problem of finding him a date to Geneva's wedding. She can't even perform the position's most fundamental duties.

I shouldn't say anything. It isn't any of my business if his assistant sucks. Wyatt probably pissed off somebody in HR with his insufferable personality and got stuck with her. And her carelessness has worked in my favor, because if I had shown up like this at the office any other billionaire I know, I would've been politely but firmly turned away.

"Your assistant needs to be retrained." Words I wasn't planning on saying slip out anyway, like somehow I'm concerned for him and how poorly his assistant is, well...assisting.

"What?" He stares like I've lost my mind.

"Your assistant. She let me in."

"So?"

"Her first duty is to be your gatekeeper." I can't believe I have to point this out. Has he never had an assistant before?

His eyebrows pull together, three deep vertical lines forming between them. "Did you come here to criticize Melanie?" There's a rebuke in his tone, like somehow I'm in the wrong pointing out the obvious.

It raises my hackles. "If she weren't so bad at her job, I wouldn't have been wagered like a sip of water between desert moles." After having seen Wyatt's assistant, I'm certain Dane got Salazar drunk and took advantage of him in order to help Wyatt. There's no other reason for that cold-blooded lizard to go through the trouble.

But I'm not here to discuss his assistant's inability to do her job. I'm here about the statue. *Must. Not. Get. Sidetracked.* "Anyway, forget about that. You're her boss, not me. I'm here to discuss the uncomfortable position I've been put in because of your sweet, loving friend Dane."

Wyatt sips his coffee, giving me a long, leisurely gaze over the rim of his mug. I feel it like a tangible touch, and can't suppress the shivers that run through me. They're probably from disgust. Because he's Dane's friend, and jerks of a feather flock together.

Then how do you explain the little spark inside your belly?

I'm lusting after his coffee. It smells really good... Like clean male and laundry detergent...and—

What the hell am I thinking?

No, no. We are *not* going there.

He finally lowers the mug and says, "Look, I—"

I raise a hand. "I'll act as your assistant for four weeks."

"—am not... What?"

"I can help you get the date you need. That's what you want, right?"

He looks at me warily, then nods once, slowly, like he's dealing with a snake.

And that annoys me, because I'm not the reptile in this room. "But I'd also like something in return, a small token of appreciation. I don't think that's asking for much." And I definitely don't feel that way after having seen his assistant.

"Okaaay," he says. "What do you want?"

I have two options and prepared accordingly. I can lie and twist and manipulate or I can just tell him straight. I haven't been able to decide, but I know now exactly how I need to approach it. Straight shooter. Why should I be a sly manipulator just because he's like that? "I know Dane's giving you a housewarming gift. Will you sell it to me? I'll give you the fair market value after a third-party appraisal." It's Salazar's money, and even though I'm not a huge fan of Wyatt's, I'm not enough of a bitch to take a multimillion-dollar statue from him without proper compensation.

Wyatt frowns. "A housewarming gift? But I told him not to worry about it."

"You should know by now that Dane does what he wants." I maintain a cool façade because I don't want to screw up and look overeager. That's not how you win a negotiation.

"But why his present?" he asks.

"Why not his present?"

He rakes his hair, messing it up. He looks gorgeous with his mane neat, but scorching when it's slightly messy, as though he's just rolled out of bed.

Don't think about bed.

"Look, Wyatt, it's a fair deal. After all, the wager between Dane and Salazar is…well, a deal involving the two of them, and I don't have to do anything to honor it. And in case you aren't aware, I'm a damn good assistant."

He thinks for a moment, then nods. "Okay. Fine. But I don't want you setting me up with some weird people off dating apps. And no gold diggers."

"Don't worry." I smile, satisfied that the deal is done, at least orally. "I'll have a contract drawn up and sent to you for signing."

"You don't trust me?"

Is that a hint of hurt I'm sensing? Couldn't be; in order to be hurt, you have to have a heart. I increase the wattage of my smile. "Things are just clearer that way. No false expectations. Oh, and I don't do overtime."

16

WYATT

I roll my shoulders as we wrap up the day's final meeting. It wasn't too bad, just *long*, with a bunch of interdepartmental issues. The company's trying to prioritize app features and security protocols. Not everyone wants to share their pictures with the world on social media, especially when it comes to photos of their children.

It's a quarter till five, which means I have a few minutes to get the final items off the day's agenda before I head home. But as I reach my office, I realize Melanie's not at her desk.

Huh. All right, well... Guess I'll ask her to bring me up to speed on whatever requires my immediate attention when she's back from her break—because those seem to pop up regularly, and always right before I'm about to head home. I pick up my phone, which I forgot on my desk, and check for messages and texts.

–Unknown: Did you sign the contract yet?

What contract? I check the time stamp; the text came while I was in the meeting. But there doesn't seem to be anything new on my desk. Did Melanie miss it? It wouldn't surprise me. She seems to miss everything but Macy's sales.

Just as I'm about to put the phone back on the desk and open my laptop, there's another ping.

–Unknown: I'm not joking around. No contract, no date.

Okay, this must be Kim. *How did she get my number...?* Probably Dane or Salazar. Then I remember her criticism of Melanie —that she sucks at guarding my office. So maybe she didn't guard my phone number either.

–Me: Did you actually send the contract? Or are you just complaining?

–Kim: Sent it before lunch.

She attaches a picture of the signed receipt. Somebody in the mail room got it, and it should've made it to my desk long before now. Robert, who runs the mail room, is nothing if not efficient and quick.

–Kim: So. Did you sign the contract? I'm not going to start until you do.

Rolling my eyes, I start to tell her I never got it, but then realize maybe I should check with Melanie first in case she forgot to bring it over. I look out through the frosted glass wall. No shadows moving around on the other side.

How long is her break, anyway?

I check my desk again to see if she left Kim's document during my meeting, but the usual stack of stuff is undisturbed. Then I see a sticky note in front of my laptop.

Came in early so I'm leaving now. Have a fantastic weekend!

–M

I stare at the yellow paper. As the meaning registers, sheer irritation and disbelief pulse through me. *What the fuck?* She never stays late when she arrives late, which is almost every day. Fuming, I check my email. Nothing...which means she also didn't finish the memo I asked her to draft for Monday's meeting.

My irritation turns into rage. I stride over to her workstation and check for the damned contract Kim said she sent. Melanie's desk is a cluttered mess. Fuck! How do you find anything?

As I go through it, I discover four dog-eared glossy magazines on travel and fashion, a pile of clippings on Ryder Reed and other A-list Hollywood stars—all of them male—a stack of junk mail with the coupons ripped out, a Harlequin romance novel with a broken spine and a huge Walmart barcode sticker. There are also four random Reese's Peanut Butter Cup wrappers.

I finally dig out a manila envelope with Kim's name on it from under all the crap. Kim stamped the envelope CONFIDENTIAL and URGENT in bright red capital letters. I guess Melanie didn't see that. Or didn't care.

Kim's criticism of Melanie's work comes back to me, making me grind my teeth. My temper turns even fouler. Even though deep inside I knew Kim was right, I refused to agree with her. Now I feel like an idiot, a sensation I absolutely hate.

I turn around, march back to my office and call HR. I've had enough of this.

"This is Nancy Beringer," comes an eminently professional voice.

"Hi Nancy. Wyatt Westland. When is my permanent assistant starting?"

"We're still looking. We're hoping for next month."

Jesus. Next month? "I see," I say, trying to sound calm. It isn't Nancy's fault that Melanie sucks.

"Is there a problem?"

"Are there any other temps available?"

Nancy pauses. "To replace the one you have?"

"Yes."

"That would take"—a keyboard clacks a few times in the background—"at least a week."

But if I have a permanent assistant starting within a month...

"Okay. Never mind. Have a good weekend." I hang up, praying I can put up with Melanie without killing her for incompetence and negligence.

That done, I rip the envelope open and glance at the paper. Kim's contract is not even half a page long and straightforward, in plain English. It just says Kim is supposed to find me a date to Geneva's wedding, and I'm to sell the housewarming gift I get from Dane at fair market value within a week of the ceremony.

I scowl, my earlier confusion returning. What is Kim's obsession with Dane's gift? It isn't anything to be this...weird about. I can just get it for her off Amazon.

And why isn't she doing that herself, instead of going through all this hassle? I feel like there must be some kind of trap, so I read the contract again, slowly.

Still not seeing any gotchas. So despite being slightly dubious, I sign it, then snap a picture.

–Me: Here. Signed it.

–Kim: Excellent. I have a date for you tonight.

Geez. That's quick.

–Me: Can't. I can't get a sitter this late.

Lori's undoubtedly busy. She's very popular as a sitter.

–Kim: I already took care of that.

I know that this shouldn't bug me, that Kim is doing what she thinks best, but it bothers me anyway. Not because I think Kim is negligent or anything, but Vi's *my* kid. I'm trying to be as hands-on as possible to show her she's important. And passing off the screening and hiring of a sitter to Kim feels like I'm saying Vi isn't important enough to warrant that personal effort from me.

–Me: I prefer you don't do that.

–Kim: Don't do what?

I feel my mouth go tight as I exhale.

–Me: Hire a sitter I don't know.

–Kim: Do you think I'd hire just anybody?

I don't have to hear her voice to know she's insulted. The outrage is in every syllable.

–Me: Yes.

I hit send, and a millisecond later realize I'm being a dick. *Shit.* Can't recall it now.

–Kim: Rachel babysits for Justin, Dane and Shane. That's Justin Sterling, if you don't know.

If she could, she'd send a sniffing sound. I close my eyes briefly. I'm annoyed with Melanie, anxious and irritated about having to attend Geneva's wedding, and I'm taking it out on Kim. She doesn't know how I feel about the situation with Vi.
She texts me a time and location.

–Kim: London Bailey is a wealthy heiress. Very pretty and likable. Try not to insult her.

I start to type *I'm sorry*, then hit the back button until everything's erased. I should apologize in person, and it's not like she lives far away.
I wrap everything up for the day and leave. I'm not sure about the woman Kim set me up with. *London*...a city name, just like Geneva. But maybe she really will be pretty and likable, and a good date for the wedding.

17

KIM

"It's seriously annoying how ungrateful he is." I swallow my martini in three big gulps. I swear, every barre studio should serve martinis for hydration. Or at least as an adjunct to stress relief and endorphin production. A workout just isn't enough to do it right now.

It's been a little over a week since the contract got signed, and I've done everything in my power to help Wyatt look good at the wedding next weekend. And how does he react? With anything but gratitude! He should be kissing my feet—not that I'd allow it, because I'm not going to think about his lips on my skin. Ever. It's a bad direction. But my point stands. He should be thankful!

"Who are you talking about?" Jo says, then takes an elegant sip. She's glowing after our session, hair and makeup still perfect. The barre studio should use her as a model to promote itself.

"The Antichrist," I say.

Hilary nibbles on the green olive that came with her drink. "Is this the guy you're supposed to help? Dane's friend?"

"Yes."

"How can he not be grateful? You're the assistant everyone wants to have but can't."

"Oh, *I'm* that assistant." Despite everything, I have to laugh.

Jo turns to Hilary. "Except nobody's even trying to hire you because... Well, you work for Gavin Freakin' Lloyd."

Hilary shrugs, but doesn't hide the little smile breaking over her face. She really is amazing at her job, and she mentored me when I was starting out. Without her, I wouldn't have lasted as Salazar's assistant or qualified for the five-year bonus. When I told her that and asked me what she wanted me to get her, she just said, "Pay it forward." Which is why I not only became roommates with Evie, but helped her out when she began working as an assistant to her now-husband.

"Did he say something to indicate he's unhappy?" Hilary asks.

"Look at this!" I show my friends some of the texts I got from Wyatt. "I've been trying to hook him up because that's what he wants, but..." I let out a small growl.

Hilary takes my phone and reads, deepening her voice a bit to sound more male. "'Are you serious? This woman is dumber than the concrete used to build the bridge in the real London.'"

Jo snorts, then laughs so hard that she almost falls off her chair. "Oh my God. You set him up with *London?*"

"Why not? She's rich, so she doesn't care about his money, and she's pretty. She looks especially good with that blond hair and those golden contacts, don't you think?"

"Well, yeah. But she is *actively* stupid." Jo uses her tiny martini sword to mime cutting something in two. "It's like her brain cells are half-sized."

"There's more," Hilary says, still reading. "'What's wrong with this woman? She's sticking so close, I can't piss without her trying to tag along into the men's bathroom!'" She looks up. "Who's this one?"

"Abby Stein. And she isn't *that* bad." I signal for another drink. "Besides, she's hot. If I were a lesbian, I'd totally do her."

"Do you know her ex got a restraining order against her when she showed up in his office, wearing only a trench coat and holding two dildos and a bottle of lube?" Jo asks, her eyes twinkling.

"I might possibly have heard something about that." I shrug, as mildly vindictive enjoyment tugs at me.

Hilary continues reading off my phone. "'She's thirty minutes late. I'm done.'"

"Ooh, ooh, I know this one!" Jo raises a hand. "Remington Brass! She's *always* half an hour late. Even if I tell her a fake time to get her to show up when she's supposed to, she's *still* half an hour late! It's like some kind of dark magic."

"You're pretty good at this, Jo," I say. "Maybe we should do a drinking game."

"'This woman only talks about shoes and purses.'" Hilary gives me a mock frown, although her eyes are bright with amusement. "'Can't she expand her repertoire?'"

"Maria Gomez, right?" Jo shakes her head. "She's awful. It was the worst when she hired me. She doesn't understand she also needs to get a dress, not just the peripherals."

"But she's *rich* and *pretty*. What more does he need for a wedding date?" But yeah, I do feel a teeny bit of guilt.

Okay, so maybe I'm picking women based on looks and net worth alone, which isn't what I'd do if I actually liked Wyatt. I'd consider the woman's personality and long-term potential. Or maybe just volunteer myself, since it's only a single afternoon.

At the same time, I don't think my choices are totally unreasonable. It isn't like he's looking for the love of his life. It's one lousy date to an ex-wife's wedding. And he's the one who stipulated nobody off dating apps and no gold diggers. My choices fit his criteria. If he wanted to narrow it down more, he should've put that in the contract.

"He's being picky," Jo declares. "Just get him an escort."

"I'm considering that," I say, although I'm really not. Vi might be going to the ceremony, too. And it's way outside my comfort zone to put Vi in close proximity to an escort. What if Wyatt suddenly decides he wants his money's worth?

The thought bugs me. A lot. Like sweaty hair sticking to my neck. Making me itchy.

Think about something else.

My phone beeps. Hilary hands it over, and I check the text.

It's from my superintendent.

—Annie: The exterminator came by again. I don't understand how you can still have bugs. But if you want, stop by after work. I'll be in the office late today.

"What's wrong?" Jo asks.

"It's my super. I have a bug problem." I glare at the phone. "She says she already sent somebody to spray, but I doubt that. Or maybe they half-assed it because I found another huge dead spider in front of my door this morning."

"Eww." Hilary and Jo both scrunch their faces.

"I thought your place was pest-free," Jo says.

"It was. But lately..."

"You could use a live-in man right about now, huh?" Jo asks, gloating slightly.

"Almost. Just so he could take care of the creepy-crawlies," I say, half serious. Nothing else gets a day started on the wrong foot like seeing a dead bug in front of my home. It isn't even always spiders. Sometimes it's crickets or a small mouse. The thing is, no one else on my floor is having the problem. I already asked my neighbors, all except Wyatt, because he's not a neighbor, but a pest himself.

And speaking of pests...

"What?" Jo asks, leaning forward. "You've got that light-bulb-moment look on your face."

"I didn't start getting dead bugs in front of my door until Wyatt became my neighbor." Is there a connection?

"Ooh." Jo blinks. "You think he's the one behind it?"

"Wouldn't surprise me. He once dropped a frog on an ice cream sundae I was eating."

Okay, so we were like twelve at the time. But he did it. That's what counts. Besides, he's dropped other creatures—and sneakily, too. I would've never found out if it weren't for Louis cluing me in after Wyatt dumped me. He's Geneva's twin brother, but unlike her, he's actually not a total psycho. A bit awkward, slightly overeager at times, but otherwise innocuous.

Anyway, thanks to Louis, I found out that even back then, Wyatt was the one pestering me. Louis called them "harmless pranks." I might've agreed if Let's Torment Kim hadn't gone viral after Wyatt and I broke up. His new girlfriend led the effort, and I'm certain he was egging her on. I just wish I'd known that about Wyatt sooner, so I wouldn't have made him my first.

"I should get going," I say, shaking off the old, unpleasant memories. "Annie said she'd be working late, and I want to catch her, let her know there's something weird going on."

We exchange goodbyes and hugs, and I head back home as quickly as I can. The super's office is on the ground floor, and thankfully the lights are still on.

I step inside, jingling the bell hanging from the top of the door. The office is neat and clean with two desks. Annie's at the one farther away from the door. She's in her late forties and dyes her short, curly hair auburn. A pair of red plastic-rimmed glasses sits on her pug-like nose, and her lips are thin and left uncolored. Actually, her entire face is bare, which is weird. She loves makeup. She and I sometimes chat about the best colors, sales at Sephora and so on.

Maybe she's having some kind of eye issue. They're swollen and slightly red. I know she has a pollen allergy, but she's never let that stop her from wearing makeup before. The hay fever must be pretty bad this year.

Something rustles behind her chair, and a dog stands up and ambles over. This is a surprise. It's the size of a golden retriever and looks like it should be one, but it's got a weird mane, and the shape of the nose reminds me of a…Pomeranian?

But that can't be right. Can those two even crossbreed?

Annie clears her throat. "Hi, Kim." Her voice is hoarse, like she's been coughing a lot. "Don't mind him. That's just Champ."

I hold out a hand so he can sniff me, then absent-mindedly scratch his head. "I didn't know you had a dog." I've never heard her talk about one. Ever.

"Not really mine." Her voice cracks a little. She plucks a Kleenex and blows her nose.

"He's adorable."

He twists around so he can lick my fingers. Maybe he likes the smell of martini lingering there, even though my hands are alcohol-free. When he seems to lose interest after a few licks, I start to scratch the soft spot under his jaw. His eyes narrow in bliss.

"So. You're here about the pest problem?" she says, her voice brisk but off. There's a teary quality to it, like she's about to cry.

Which is weird, because she isn't the type to break down. Maybe she's just having a really overwhelming day and isn't feeling well. I mean, there must be a reason she's still hanging out here in the office.

And that's starting to make me feel bad. I like Annie, and I don't want to pile on her crappy day if that's the case. But at the same time, dead bugs and mouse corpses are a real issue for me. "Well...yeah."

"Nobody else on your floor has mentioned anything, but I can send someone to spray the whole floor and your unit again tomorrow."

"That'd be great." I smile, trying to make her feel better. "I really appreciate everything you do."

"Thank you." Her voice cracks.

Oh shit. Is she going to cry? Her chin is trembling a bit, and her eyes are glistening in a dangerous way. What did I say...or do?

Sure enough, tears start to spill.

"Oh, no." Maybe I really *should* just get a boyfriend, one who can take care of dead bugs. It isn't like there are a lot of them. Just one or two in the morning, and they're outside my apartment, not inside. Besides, I haven't dated in a long time. Like, over a year. And a boyfriend is a great idea anyway. Make my life more interesting. And prevent me from making requests that bring my super to tears. "I'm really sorry," I say. "And don't worry about anything."

"No, no, *I'm* sorry." Annie starts dabbing at her eyes. The tears are falling faster and harder. "It's just my mom passed away over the weekend."

I stare, stunned. "Annie... What are you doing here? Shouldn't you be home?" Maybe trying to cope with her mom's death?

Champ whines, and I pet him, running my fingers through his soft fur.

"I thought work would distract me. My brother's handling the estate, while I'm taking care of the dog and the building." She and her mom owned the apartment complex together.

"Oh." I'm not sure what else to say, but at the same time, I feel like I should say something.

Champ looks at me with a huge doggy smile, like I'm doing everything right. It helps...a little.

"This probably makes me a terrible person, but I don't even know what I'm going to do about Champ." Her face crumples.

I look down at the dog. Is he somehow a problem? He looks healthy enough, and he's super friendly and adorable. Maybe Annie's allergic to dogs, and she can't bear to give him to some stranger...?

"I just can't look at him," Annie adds. "Every time I do, he reminds me of Mom, you know? But it isn't like I can give him to a shelter or something. He deserves better. Mom loved him."

"Yeah." I pluck a Kleenex from a box and hand it to her, wondering what I can do to help. I'm a problem solver, after all. If I can take care of Salazar's needs, surely I can help with Annie's.

"Thanks." She dabs at her eyes, then blows her nose again.

"Okay, look. Don't worry about my problem," I say. "What you're going through matters more."

"No, no. It's my job to make sure your place is, you know…"

"Yeah, but…" I wish I could just evaporate like a dab of rubbing alcohol. If I'd known, I would've never bothered Annie.

Champ looks over at Annie, and Annie starts crying harder. Obviously, the idea of sending Champ away to some random stranger is bugging her, even though she can't cope with him herself.

I make a decision. "You know what? I can take Champ for as long as you need, until you figure out what you really want to do with him."

Annie looks at me, her eyes redder and even more swollen. "No, it's okay," she says weakly. "I'll figure some—"

"It'll be my pleasure." I smile. It's the least I can do to make up for the fact that I made her cry, even indirectly. Besides, I like dogs, and Mom's fifth husband owned a golden retriever, so I have some experience. It isn't a big deal.

And it solves my boyfriend problem. A dog is probably more

reliable than a man anyway. Definitely more loyal. I don't know a single dog that would dump you for another girl right after you'd fed it.

"Well...okay. Thank you, Kim. And I'll give you a break on the rent to make up for the cost of feeding him and everything else."

"Don't worry about it. I'm good."

"I insist. Most people wouldn't have offered." Annie sniffs. "Thank you."

I nod, happy to be able to put her mind at ease a little. Annie runs her hands down Champ's head and neck, then whispers something in a low, soothing voice. The dog stares and wags his tail. She hands me a leash and a bag full of treats and kibbles.

She puts a couple of bowls in another bag for me. "These are his, too."

Champ watches the exchange, his eyes tracking the food bag, and comes back over to me when I take it. I rub his head. "You can just let me know if you want to see him. It's no problem."

She nods. "Okay. He's really well behaved and everything. Hardly ever barks. He just needs to be walked."

"Got it. I'll be a good mom, and if I have any questions about him, I'll text you. As a matter of fact, why don't I walk him a bit now, and then take him home?"

"Thanks, Kim. You're a lifesaver."

18

WYATT

When Kim offered to find me a date to Geneva's wedding, I thought she might be the lifesaver I needed, especially since Melanie has been proving to be more and more worthless every day. Dane said Kim was efficient, and Salazar sure acted like she could do no wrong.

But they're totally wrong. She's not a lifesaver. She's the devil. Evil incarnate.

Tonight's date sucks. Like, *I want to murder the woman* sucks. Every other sentence out of her mouth is a criticism or disparagement of someone.

"Look at that waitress. I'm surprised she can even get between the tables with a butt that wide."

"How can she walk around without covering her face when she has a zit that large? I'd just kill myself."

"Nobody gets food stamps because they need them. Have you seen those people? They're huge! They could use some serious dieting."

Does Kim really think a woman like this is an acceptable date? What the hell happened to her? Maybe she's gotten out of touch with the real world after hanging out with billionaires so much. She might not be one, but that doesn't mean she isn't part of their whole—

"So. I want to know if you want to have sex with me," Svetlana asks, her tone annoyingly coy.

I almost drop my fork. "Have what with you?"

She looks me directly in the eye. "Have sex with me. That's what rich men deserve. *Grrreat* sex." She gives me a smile I'm sure she believes is playfully erotic. It reminds me of a vampire. She flutters her eyelashes, then licks the cherry from her cocktail with some acrobatic tongue-work.

"No," I say flatly. "I'd rather get fucked by a horny mountain goat."

As soon as the words leave my lips, I realize I mean every syllable. I toss my napkin on the table and stand up. I'm not wasting any more of my life like this.

Thankfully, Svetlana seems too shocked to react. Maybe this is the first time anyone's turned down her offer of "great sex."

I pay for my portion of the dinner. Svetlana, being so superior to everyone, can pay for her own damned food. During the drive home, my rage builds. I park and stomp toward my apartment.

Kim has to be fucking with me to purposely set me up with one shitty woman after another. I should've known she still holds a grudge against me and wouldn't play fair. Otherwise she would've volunteered herself for the date. Because, like she said, it's just one lousy date, not a lifetime commitment. And she knows I'm not interested in commitment, long term or otherwise, with a woman who thinks I gave her herpes in high school. It doesn't matter that she's stunning, or that part of me just dies in sheer desire and longing when I see her. I don't want her.

I need to be more like Dane. Or at least David. He's pretty good at managing his feelings about women. He said breaking up and rebounding gave him a better perspective on life.

As I'm about to unlock the door to my apartment, I spot Kim walking toward her unit with a dog trotting behind her. She's smiling like she's been having a great fucking time. But then, why the hell wouldn't she? She got to spend time with a dog, not Svetlana of the Somersaulting Tongue.

I shove the keys back in my pocket and walk toward Kim,

anger and resentment twisting inside me. Since she's been ignoring my texts about the women she's selected, I'm going to do this in person. And now is the perfect time.

"Kim."

"Wyatt." She gives me a small nod.

When I don't get out of her way, she arches her eyebrows. And even now, she looks like some goddess. And I hate it that I'm noticing how pretty her eyes are.

What the hell is wrong with me? Or maybe there's nothing wrong with me. She's just too evil to be ugly. Like the snake that tempted Eve. How beautiful and mesmerizing must that reptile have been to get a woman to do what it wanted? Women usually run screaming when they see a snake.

I stay in the same place, wanting to erase the smile on her face, although I'm not sure exactly how yet.

"You're blocking the way," she says, slowly, like I'm stupid.

There must be something clever I can say. It's just at the edge of my mind, but I get a whiff of her scent—a hint of clean sweat and something sweet and soft. My blood surges south, which is the wrong direction. Now the clever thing that I almost had is gone. "You are seriously fucking evil," I say, the filter between my brain and mouth not working anymore.

"Me?" She blinks a few times. "Evil? I've been trying to help you."

"Your idea of help is matching me up with unacceptable women."

"Unacceptable? In what way?"

"Shallow, clingy, stupid, bitchy..."

"It isn't my fault that single women who aren't off dating apps and rich enough to not want your money are like that." Suddenly Kim gives a theatrical gasp and puts a hand over her mouth. "Or... wait a minute... Maybe it's *you* bringing the bitchiness out."

I should hate her for that, but instead I still find her hot. Damn it.

"You set me up. You never intended to take this seriously."

She stiffens. "You have no idea how seriously I take my job."

"Your job. All you want is the housewarming gift Dane is going to send me."

"Yes!" she says like she means it.

"That's the dumbest excuse ever. It's just like when you made me think you recipro—" *Okay, hold on.* High emotions and hormones don't make for the best confrontations, because you end up saying and doing things you shouldn't. Like telling her I assumed she felt the same way about me all those years ago... The fact that I'm still thinking about it shows she still matters in some way, and I'd rather skydive with a ripped parachute.

"Reciprocated what?" she demands, hands on her hips, a flawless picture of outrage.

She must've taken a lot of acting classes. She's been in L.A. for a while, after all. It pisses me off that she went this far to fuck with me.

Dad is wrong. Geneva isn't the evil werefox—*Kim* is. And she's after both my liver and my sanity. But I'm not going down without a fight. Revenge can be a two-way street.

"Well? I'm waiting," she says, tapping her fingers against her hips. "Hurry up, because I don't have all night, and apparently I've got to arrange *yet another* date for you."

You mean yet another disaster. She keeps on talking. God! The need to shut her up before I shake her teeth loose surges through me. I grab her and push my mouth against hers, bracing myself to hate it. After all, this isn't the girl I fell for in Corn Meadows. She's like a lizard's belly now. This kiss is going to put her in a box labeled "exes I never want to think about again." And most importantly, it'll mess her up, make her wonder why. Why I'm kissing her, why I'm holding her and why I'm not throttling her like a rational human being would.

But she doesn't feel especially reptilian. Her lips are warm and soft, and her taste reminds me of a cherry-flavored gelato I had once. Lush, sweet...addictive.

My blood roars in my ears, saying *more*.

She doesn't push me away, but goes absolutely still. Not even her breath tickles my skin, and I realize she's in shock...and at a point where she hasn't yet decided if she's going to kick my ass or participate. Her mouth stays sealed, and I flick my tongue over it, tasting more of her. Every cell in my body trembles for her. We're on a precipice, the danger and more in the connection of our lips, like we've both been waiting for this moment.

Suddenly her mouth turns soft and opens, her hand resting on my arm. The reaction hits me like a jolt of electricity—something that's been missing since forever. A quick intake of breath—hers—heats my blood until it's racing like lightning.

I slip my tongue between her teeth, and hers strokes it, tentative and hot at the same time. There's a hint of gin and vermouth that laces with her cherry flavor, and I feel like I'm drowning in a vat of liquor. My skin feels so tight, the need swelling so large inside me, that I feel like it's going to split. And her scent isn't helping. She smells unbelievably enticing.

I pull her closer, my blood like molten lava. My mind is no longer capable of thinking logically, just feeling and acting on instinct. She makes a small noise in the back of her throat. I'm already hard, pressed against her. She presses even closer, the feel of her breasts against my chest intoxicating. My cock throbs. I can feel my control slipping.

Suddenly, a warm body squeezes itself between our legs. She takes a step back, just as I move to see what's interrupting us. It's the dog she brought with her. It looks up at us, thumping its tail.

Shit.

I shake my head to clear it. Hormones fog my brain like I'm a teenager again. *What the hell?* I got way too involved there. Not part of the plan.

Kim stares at me, her caramel eyes dark and unblinking. Slowly, she brushes her lips with just the tips of her fingers. I see the muscles in her neck flex, and she breathes out hard.

"Wow. That was..."

Hot. Lush. Sweet. Not enough.

"...inappropriate," she says finally. She inhales, then finger-combs her hair. "Look, I have you set up with another heiress tomorrow night," she says, her words measured. "So turn around and go get some sleep."

Then she shuts the door behind her, taking the dog with her.

That kiss was supposed to mess with Kim's mind...but it doesn't feel like that's what happened.

19

KIM

WHY DIDN'T I STOP WYATT?

I should've slapped him when he laid his mouth on mine. Or at least shoved him away.

But instead I stood there like an idiot, unable to think as his lips softened on mine, like a butterfly alighting on a new blossom.

My lips tingle at the memory. Worse, my *breasts* are tingling, because I'm thinking about how strong and solid his chest felt against mine. I'm not going to even think about how what's between my legs is tingling because of how long and thick he was against my belly.

Ack! It's shameful I'm reacting this way. *Shameful!*

Humiliating, too. It's been over twelve hours, and *I shouldn't be feeling anything.*

And Champ isn't helping. Every time I see him I think of how he came between us, which reminds me of the kiss, which…

Argh! It's sad that a dog can indirectly make me horny.

On the other hand, maybe Champ isn't thinking about the kiss. His face is buried in his food bowl.

I change, put him on a leash for his walk, and open the door. There are two dead crickets right there in the hallway. Gross, but

Faking It with the Frenemy

not as bad as the roach that was there yesterday. I start to go back into the apartment to grab a paper towel to dispose of the bodies.

But Champ lunges forward and gulps down the brown bugs, saving me the trouble. Then he looks up, wagging his tail. If he could talk, he'd probably say, "Did you see that? Wasn't I awesome?"

"Yes, you are," I say. Crickets are just protein, nothing poisonous. "You're an awesome boy!" I scratch behind his ears, then grab a small treat for him. Good behavior always deserves positive reinforcement.

The walk is delightful, especially since I don't have anything urgent to do today. Salazar's promised paid month off has already started, so I'm going to take advantage of that and binge-watch some shows. I wish I could hang out with Evie, but she's busy getting ready for a "welcome to the family" party, hosted by her brother-in-law.

Champ pulls us along, ensuring the walk is brisk, but not taxing. I love how he's such a happy dog. I thought maybe he'd be depressed after losing his previous owner, but perhaps he realizes she would want him to embrace life. A bit deep for a dog, but some dogs are smarter and more intuitive than a lot of people.

After we come home, I shower and spend the rest of the day in my pajamas watching whatever Netflix serves up. Technology is marvelous. I don't even have to leave home to grab movies, and Netflix knows what I like—utterly mindless action flicks. *Terminator 3* isn't my absolute favorite from the franchise, but it isn't bad. I'm pretty sure Netflix is really Skynet with a super AI to make me park my ass on my couch and not join Team Human Resistance. Champ watches with me, snuggled against my hip and thigh.

I share a huge bowl of butter-free popcorn with him, making sure he doesn't get any kernels. My favorite is buttery caramel popcorn, but if I gorge on that I'll need to be at the barre studio until next year to undo the damage. And what I have isn't too terrible, considering. Champ isn't complaining about the plain flavor either.

My phone rings, and I answer automatically, assuming it's

about the date I have set up for Wyatt. See? He should be grateful! Look how hard I'm working for him!

And I'm not even his assistant, just a rental.

"This is Kim."

"Oh my God, darling! Tell me you're free next weekend." Mom sounds breathless in that familiar "I'm too excited to contain myself" way.

Which under-sixty billionaire just got divorced?

"Uh... I guess? Let me check my calendar," I say, not wanting to automatically confirm. This could be about anything. Maybe she needs somebody to hold her hand while she gets her breasts Botoxed. If anybody could find a doctor who was willing to experiment, it'd be my mom.

"Byron Pearce is attending an art gallery opening in San Francisco next Saturday! You should go! I have a ticket! I'm willing to give it to you!"

Oh my God. "Mom. Byron really isn't my type." If I tell her I found him to be pleasant enough, she'll never let me have any peace. She doesn't understand that finding a guy pleasant doesn't mean I'm ready to plunk down serious cash on a wedding gown.

"How come? He's worth over a billion, and still very much young enough that he can rise to the occasion without Viagra. I'm certain his stamina is excellent as well."

Ugh. I should've just gone for the buttery caramel popcorn, because I'm going to puke after this phone call. "That's so not the point."

"You have to give him a *chance*, Kim. He's *hot*."

She says that about every man with money. The more he has, the hotter he is. But at the same time... I have to admit that, objectively speaking, Byron Pearce *is* quite handsome. And unlike some rich guys, his reputation when it comes to women is pristine. He doesn't screw around, and he doesn't play games. It's like he's only interested in working and making even more money.

"I saw a recent picture of him," Mom continues. "It looks like he's been working out. And those eyes! Those lips! I'd love to be your age again so I could kiss him."

I so do not need that mental picture. On the other hand, the mention of lips and kisses makes me stop and think. Maybe the problem I had yesterday out in the hall was that I haven't had a boyfriend in a while. It's like food: if you get hungry enough, you'll risk eating an unknown mushroom or two. It could be that Wyatt emits some kind if toxin that confuses my brain and undermines my good intentions. And isn't it true that some poisons can make you tingle...?

"I'm just saying that you should consider the possibilities. Everyone has to marry. And if you're going to marry, you might as well marry somebody rich," Mom says, like she's trying to cajole me to eat my greens.

"Money doesn't buy happiness." I toss it out there, knowing she won't get it...again.

"Well, being poor certainly doesn't buy it."

"You know I'm about to get my five-year bonus, don't you?" I have to get the statue, but I'm confident that will happen. Wyatt signed the contract, and I'm sure that eventually one heiress or another will work out. If I have to, I'll put him on a two-dates-a-day rotation so we can find somebody faster. The wedding is next weekend.

"You mean that pathetic five hundred thousand dollars?" She tsks. "After taxes and so on, it won't be that much."

Just like Mom to dismiss my accomplishments when they don't align with how she wants me to live my life. "I also have savings."

"Not a billion dollars' worth, I'm sure."

I hiss out a breath. She needs to try a different strategy if she thinks this is going to make me want to consider dating Byron Pearce.

"I've already mailed you the ticket. Just go. You don't know what's going to happen. And if Byron bores you, just think of his net worth. If that fails, look around. There will be other men."

Totally not helping.

"I have faith in you. You're still very pretty," she says. "I gave you good genes. You look younger than most women your age."

My age. I'm only twenty-eight! "So you're saying I look like jailbait?" And after telling me last time not even Botox could help my breasts?

"Doesn't hurt. Quite a few men go for that..."

Oh my God. I'm not going to bother with the gallery opening, but I make a noise in the back of my throat, loud enough for Mom to hear. She'll interpret it however she wants, which is fine by me. "I gotta go. I have to work." *I need to watch more Netflix and forget you talked about Viagra and kissing men not even half your age.*

"Fine, fine," she says. "I'll check in with you later."

Please, don't. Once we hang up, I turn off *Terminator 3* because it has too much plot for me to handle right now. I start a mindlessly violent action flick to erase the last few minutes with Mom. Within the first three minutes, four bombs go off, at least seven cars explode and tons of extras are dramatically blasted into the sides of buildings. Bullets fly and more extras go down clutching their stomachs or with geysers of blood bursting from their heads. Other than screams, there's zero dialogue.

Perfect.

There are knocks on my door. I decide to ignore them. It's barely two o'clock, and I haven't placed a single Amazon order in the last four days. And I'm not going to find the One True Path because some random stranger at my door just happens to know something the rest of humanity has missed.

But Champ has other ideas. He goes over and wags his tail, standing expectantly at the door.

Something bad slithers down my spine. Is Wyatt on the other side? If so, why? Shouldn't he be working, making Sweet Darlings even richer?

I sit up, wishing I'd at least powdered my face. Then irritation surges. Why should I care how I look to Wyatt? It's not like I'm trying to impress him.

But maybe it's Annie. I push myself off the couch and walk over to look through the peephole. It's Vi.

I open the door. Champ tries to rush out and sniff her, but I grab his collar.

"Shouldn't you be in school right now?" I ask.

"We got out early." She glances at Champ with a small smile. "Oh my God! I didn't know you had a dog! He's so cute!"

Champ wags his tail as though he understands and agrees with her.

"What's his name?" she says, trying to walk into my apartment.

I shift my body subtly to block her. I haven't forgotten her elaborate babysitter lie. And she's not going to skip school to play with my pet. "His name is Champ, and we're not talking about my dog. I haven't heard anything about school letting out early today."

Her sitter isn't scheduled to come until four. I know because I set the appointment up. It's part of the package deal of working for Wyatt, mainly because I don't think Melanie would remember to take care of that kind of detail, and it's the kind of minor thing I'd deal with if I were doing it for Salazar. But neither Wyatt nor Melanie told me about this so I could have Rachel come early.

"If you snuck out of school, I'm taking you back."

"It's a short day. You can check if you want."

I don't think she's fibbing, but then, what do I know about kids and their school schedules? Hell, I fibbed when I didn't feel like going. I ask Vi for the school's name, and she gives it to me. Still blocking the door, I go to the homepage and log in using Vi's last name and zip code. Sure enough, her class got out at one thirty because of some emergency plumbing check. The notice is dated yesterday.

I curse under my breath. "Did you tell your dad?" I ask, just to be sure that *I'm* not the one who screwed up with the sitter scheduling. My professional pride is shivering with horror at the possibility.

She shrugs. "Yeah, but he probably forgot. He's busy."

I thought Wyatt cared about his daughter. He seemed pretty upset when he found Vi at my place without her sitter, but maybe I was mistaken. My estimation of him drops. The validation that he's just as bad a human as I remembered should give me some satisfaction, but it's just disappointing. Vi doesn't need to suffer because of him.

"Come on in," I say, since I can't have her hanging out in the hall on her own. *Again.* But I will have a very stern conversation with Wyatt about this.

"Thanks."

She steps into the apartment. Champ starts licking her

fingers, and she pats him. He looks at her with absolute adoration. Based on his expression, you'd think Vi had a halo around her head and her hands were made of crispy bacon.

At least her hair doesn't look like a bird's nest today. "So. No more teasing your hair?"

"Yeah," she says, going to the couch and sitting down.

Oh, crap. I realize I paused the movie at a part where bullets are flying and bodies are getting shredded. I turn off the TV, hoping Vi didn't catch any of it.

Champ lies at Vi's feet, giving me a "you're a negligent adult" look.

Yeah, yeah, stop being so judgmental. I wasn't expecting a ten-year-old to show up at my door.

"Nobody at my school does anyway," Vi says suddenly.

It takes me a moment to catch up to the conversation. *Oh, teasing hair.* I park myself next to her. "So why were you doing it?"

"Mom used to do it all the time. I was just curious." She looks down at her hands, running her thumbs over the tips of her neatly trimmed fingernails. "Just trying to be more like her, you know?"

I nod, since I can't voice what I really think. The last person Vi should ever want to emulate is Geneva, who's not just your garden-variety crazy, but an honest-to-God sociopath. Not the kind of truth you can tell a child, though. Every child should be allowed to believe their parents are wonderful and loving...until they're old enough to figure out the truth for themselves and cope.

"But I really want to learn how to contour. It's so annoying because it looks so easy on YouTube," Vi says.

She's way too young for makeup. Shouldn't Wyatt be on top of this? On the other hand, if I *tell* her she's too young, it'll only make her want to do it more. I need a different tactic. "You know," I say slowly, like I'm giving it some serious thought, "I think your skin's too good to cover up with makeup."

"Really?" She can't hide the sparkle in her eyes, even though she's trying her best to look cool and unaffected. "But you have perfect skin and you use makeup."

"Perfect? Ha." I lower my face and pull my hair back so she can see some unmade skin. "See the dark spots here and here?" I point at my cheeks and neck. "And this little blemish on the tip of my chin?"

Vi squints, then nods. "Yeah. But they don't look that bad. I mean, I didn't even know you had them when you had stuff on your face." Her eyes narrow. "Hey, you've got a scar."

"Yeah, but it's not a big deal." I smile to put her at ease. I know it bothers some people. It still bothers me at times, but mostly because it reminds me of how poorly I selected my friends when I was younger. In retrospect, it's obvious Geneva only liked me because I helped her with her homework and I had a couple of rich dads who gave me lots of stuff. "But anyway, the flaws in my skin are what I'm trying to cover up when I use foundation. Now look at your skin, Vi." I reach into my purse and pull out a compact. There's a small mirror inside the case. "It's flawless. And everyone who uses makeup, you know what they're doing? They're trying to have *your* complexion."

Her mouth forms a small O.

"And your eyelashes are long, curly and thick." She has Wyatt's lashes, luckily. Geneva's have been always a bit thin and short. God must've realized she didn't deserve any better. "Again, what I'm trying to have with mascara. If you really want, you can try some light eye shadow, but the only thing you really need is a good sunscreen, which should help you keep your skin nice and healthy for a long time. I wish I'd started using it earlier. I didn't start until four years ago."

"Oh." She stares at my face, deliberately keeping her gaze above my jaw.

It makes me squirm a bit. I don't like it when people stare up close. "Tell you what. If you want, I'll take you shopping." Whoa, what the hell made me say *that*? It isn't like I like shopping with kids. It's just... Well. Vi seems like she could use some older female help, other than what's on YouTube or based on her experience with Geneva.

"Really? Now?"

"No. Not right now. Maybe later, if your dad doesn't mind." I don't feel comfortable taking her shopping without her dad's permission. Wyatt might have plans...to take her himself or something. "And you need to do your homework first."

She makes a face. "Do I have to? Nobody needs to learn math. We have computers for that."

"Yeah, but what if Skynet takes over the world, and you can't use computers?"

She thinks for a moment. "What does a cable company have to do with using computers?" she asks, confusion still lingering in her eyes.

I almost laugh. "Skynet isn't a cable company, although it sounds like maybe it could be. It's a super-evil worldwide computer network that controls killer robots and causes an apocalypse."

The confusion's gone, replaced by the mild cynicism and arrogance of a child trying hard to look more grown-up that she really is. "So it isn't real."

"No. But it could be, at the rate AI is improving."

"Yeah, but we can control it. Otherwise we wouldn't be making it."

Oh, my sweet child. If people only made things they could control, they wouldn't be making babies. Just ask my mom.

"Anyway, you *do*, absolutely, positively, *have* to know math." Since Wyatt is being a substandard daddy, who forgets when his kid's getting out of school, it looks like I need to step up and do what's right.

She sighs, a monumental heave like the world is ending. "Fine."

She drags her backpack over to the dining table to start her homework. While she's busy, I check my email, but there's nothing urgent. I browse Amazon to see if they have stuff I didn't even realize I wanted.

Then I suddenly stop. Vi is a growing child. She probably wants a snack.

I get up and go to the kitchen. "Are you hungry?"

"Yeah." She looks up from her homework. "What do you have?"

I check the fridge. "Yogurt. Some fruit chunks. And spinach salad, but you probably don't want that, huh?"

She wrinkles her nose adorably. "Eww, no. I'll have the yogurt, please, as long as it isn't plain."

"Okay." Relieved I have something the kid will eat, I take out a strawberry-and-banana-flavored tub and give it her with a spoon.

She starts eating. "Hey, Kim?"

"Yeah?"

"Do you think people are proud of their children if they get straight As?"

"Well... Yeah, of course," I say, unsure where this is going. But people are proud of their academically gifted children, right? My dad was when I brought home As. And my stepdad used to give me fifty bucks every time I got an A because he believed in "proper incentives and compensation."

"So. If I *don't* get straight As, are they ashamed?"

"Oh no. That's not it at all." I feel like I've fallen into a trap. I should've told her parents don't care about grades at all. And honestly, this is the kind of thing Wyatt should be telling her. Or maybe not. He could be pressuring her to get good grades, and some kids just aren't that into academics.

"But you said—"

"There's a difference between pride and love," I say hurriedly, trying to claw myself out of the hole. "Parents love their children no matter what."

Vi looks skeptical...naturally, because her mom is a narcissistic psychopath and her dad can't even remember when she's getting out early. I suppress a sigh. The need to explain until Vi realizes I'm right is overwhelming, but I keep my mouth shut. This isn't something she's going to get from someone's words. It's something she has to feel for herself because her parents put her first, as I know from personal experience. My mom told me repeatedly I was her number one, but it wasn't true; I was never the rich man she'd set her sights on. And my dad said he cared about me, but what he really meant was he cared about hiring a lot of people to take me off his hands because he had better things to do with his life.

"I wish I could meet Mom's fiancé," Vi says. "But I can't until the wedding. She says he doesn't like children." There's a pause. "Even if they get straight As."

I squirm in my seat. This is waaay over my pay grade. I might as well try to navigate a minefield in nothing but Jo's favorite Jimmy Choos.

Vi continues in a small voice, "He's making my mom give me up. Dad and Princess, too. She must really love him to do that."

Oh, Vi. My heart breaks as she looks down at the handout, her shoulders so narrow and fragile. I can't believe Geneva managed to have a child this sweet and vulnerable. And I hate my former best friend for hurting her kid this way.

And Wyatt isn't much better. Unless I misunderstood the wistfulness in Vi's tone, he didn't really want to end it with Geneva. So needing a hot date is probably his way of rubbing it in Geneva's face. Which makes him a petty, shallow bastard, even if she does deserve it.

I give Vi some OJ because there isn't any other way for me to comfort her. As for me...

I really need a drink.

20

Wyatt

Unlike my previous dates, Miri is cultured, well mannered, and fun to talk to. Not offensive in the slightest.

There's only one problem...

"To be honest, I'm really not into men," she says from across the table at an elegant Italian restaurant.

"You're not into...? Oh."

She sighs. "My grandfather is ultra-conservative, and he has a bad heart. So I'm kind of faking it until he, you know"—she shrugs delicately—"passes away."

I feel bad for her. "Why are you telling me this? Aren't you afraid I'm going to out you or something?"

She shakes her head. "You seem like a decent guy, and I don't want to string you along. At the same time, I don't want to date you, either, not even to trick my granddad. I already met somebody I love, even though it's sort of a secret at the moment." Her expression softens, going a little dreamy.

"Well... Appreciate your honesty," I say. "I hope we can be friends, though."

"Of course." She smiles.

She insists on paying for her own meal, and I let her because I can sense it's important to her.

The date ends up lasting longer than my previous ones, since Miri and I actually enjoy each other's company. It's nice to chat with somebody decent who has no expectations or ulterior motives. But I still make it home by nine, when it's time for Rachel to leave.

She's a pretty, twenty-something brunette. She used to nanny for a wealthy Hong Kong family, but they went back to Asia. Right now, she's doing work for a bunch of different parents. She isn't cheap, but she's very nice and capable. Most importantly, Vi likes her.

"Vi's already done her homework and is texting with her friends right now," Rachel says with a smile, gathering her phone and purse. "She came home early and stayed with Kim until I got here."

What? "She did? Her school schedule says she doesn't get home until ten after four."

"They apparently had a special short day."

Except I haven't heard anything about that. I asked Melanie to sync Vi's school calendar with mine, but obviously that hasn't been done yet. Still, wouldn't Vi have said something? *Maybe she did and I forgot,* I think as a sliver of guilt slides into my gut. "Thank you."

She hands me a printout. "This was in her backpack. I think she forgot to give it to you yesterday."

It's a notice about an emergency plumbing check today. The note said the school is sending this as well to ensure every parent is informed, in case the email alert didn't reach us.

Shit. I didn't see the alert, but then, I have more new emails than I can ever read in my inbox.

I pay Rachel and lock the door behind her.

Then I head to Vi's room. "Hey, sweetheart."

"Hey," she says distractedly, her back resting against the headboard of her brand-new bed and her legs stretched out on the sheet. Her gaze is glued to her phone.

"How was your day?"

She still isn't looking at me. "Eh."

I sigh. Talking to Vi can be harder than pulling a shark's

teeth. "Rachel told me you got out early today."

"Uh-huh."

Frustration starts to bubble up. I'm not certain she even heard what I said.

"I saw that you didn't give me the paper from the school yesterday."

"Uh-huh."

"It's important you give those to me, Vi," I say, while vowing to check the academy's website every day, just to be sure.

"Sorry. But it's not a big deal. Kim was home."

I guess she is listening. "Yeah, but if Kim hadn't been home, you wouldn't have had a place to go. I wouldn't want you hanging out in the hall until I get home." Maybe I should get her a key, but I don't like the idea of her being home without adult supervision.

"Okay, yeah. Fine."

I rein in my impatience and try to see the week from her point of view. I haven't been around much because of the dates Kim arranged. So maybe Vi's feeling neglected and is acting out like this. Didn't I promise myself to be a good and attentive father, to undo the damage Geneva's done? And I really should've synced her school calendar with mine myself, since Melanie isn't going to do it. I'm the adult here—her dad. "Tell you what. Why don't we go shopping tomorrow? I know you want to buy a new dress for your mom's wedding."

That gets her to look at me. *Finally!*

"Really?" she asks.

"Yeah."

"Don't you have a date or something?" It's almost like she's blaming me for needing a plus-one for the wedding.

That makes me feel guilty and slightly defensive, because I'm doing the best that I can. But I don't try to make excuses. After all, this isn't about me, but about her dealing with the crappy situation. "My only date tomorrow is you and the mall."

Vi smiles. It's a small one, but still precious. Warmth pools in my chest, and I give her a hug. "Sorry I've been busy. I'll make tomorrow extra special."

"With ice cream? A double scoop?"

"Don't push your luck." But I'm smiling as I say it.

21

KIM

"You think I need to get laid?" I ask casually as I look over the dresses on the clearance rack. It's Saturday, and I'm on my retail therapy at a department store in the mall. It keeps me from thinking about the damned kiss again.

And I refuse to think about that damned kiss. Nope. No way. I haven't even confronted Wyatt about the situation with Vi yet because I'm too afraid that facing him might remind me. Or worse, make me want to do it again. It's bad enough I thought about it last night in bed, even knowing that he's a shallow asshole. Then I exacerbated the situation by wondering if he kissed Miri, because she's actually a normal, decent human being. She's too good for him, though.

Jo glances over. "What?"

"Do you think I need to get laid? Like, have sex," I add, in case she isn't clear on the concept. I feel like not having been laid in a long time is the only reason I'm obsessing about the kiss. I should be repulsed, especially after what Vi told me yesterday.

"Yeah, uh, pretty sure I know what the phrase means. But what's this about?" She's standing hipshot, and posed like that, looks like a model in her fitted blue top and skinny jeans. She says she has to look like she's just stepped off the cover of *Vogue* because her clients expect her to be stylish.

I, on the other hand, am dressed in a white Hollywood T-shirt, cute cropped denim pants and flip-flops, hair pulled into a ponytail. Still looking good in a weekend-casual way, even if I'm not up to Jo's standards.

"It's just... I feel like I've been depriving myself. I haven't dated in, like, a year," I say.

"Your last time was...who? Marco?"

"Yeah." I can feel my face twist. *Marco the cheater.*

The most outrageous part? He said it "wasn't his fault" that his dick fell into another woman's vagina because "accidents happen." Oh, and it's a biological imperative for men to spread their seed as far and wide as possible. The survival of the human species depends on it. So really, what he did was a noble service to humanity.

If I'd been holding a knife, I might've stabbed him.

Jo shakes her head in sisterly commiseration. "He's the kind of guy who could induce any penis-loving woman to become a lesbian. Or a nun."

"True that." After him, I went on a dating fast.

"Look, if you really just need to have sex with a warm body, my cousin might be able to help," Jo says somewhat seriously. "Hugo loves women, and some of his exes told me he's, um, the best lay they'd ever had." She makes a TMI face.

I scrunch my nose. "Isn't he, like...twenty-one?" Jo told me about changing his diapers when she was younger.

"No! Twenty-six. Old enough to know the score, but still young enough to go Energizer Bunny on you."

I shudder, shaking my head. "No. I can't take a guy whose diapers you changed seriously."

"What are you talking about? I never did that. It was my other cousin because she wanted money for a new prom dress. Anyway, I thought I'd offer him because he needs a favor from you."

"He does?" He and I have never met. I didn't even know he knew me.

"He's applying for a job and wants to see if you could review his résumé. Apparently this is a position he absolutely *has* to get or his life is going to be over."

That's dramatic, but then, Jo's family has always been pretty over the top. "Well, he certainly doesn't have to sleep with me to get me to look it over. He can just email it to me. Or drop it off, whichever is easier."

"Cool," Jo says. "You're the best. I'll tell him to get in touch with you. I offered to look it over, but he basically told me I didn't know anything about being gainfully employed or having a boss. But apparently you know all about it, so I'm supposed to get you to help him out." She rolls her eyes.

I laugh. "Did you tell him that dealing with fickle clients can be harder than dealing with a fickle boss?"

"Yeah, but he doesn't get it. He doesn't respect what I do." She waves a hand. "Anyway, if you don't want to jump Hugo's bones, how about you just listen to your mom?"

The Tingle of Terror prickles at the back of my neck. "Oh, no. Did she call you again?"

"Uh-huh. Asked me to help you pick out the perfect dress for the art gallery opening. Said you wouldn't know what to do without my help. I told her you aren't that bad, but..." Jo shrugs.

"Oh my God, I'm so sorry. She needs to quit calling you. Did you tell her that using you as leverage wasn't going to work?"

"Yeah, but I don't think she understood. Or maybe she decided I was speaking Spanish because it wasn't what she wanted to hear." Jo shakes her head.

I sigh. *Why, Mom, why?*

"You might disagree with her on other stuff, but you gotta admit, Byron Pearce is hot. And single. And not dating anybody, from what I can tell."

Jo's right, but that doesn't mean I'm going to agree with her. It would feel like I was letting my mom win her battle to get me to date rich guys.

"And he's probably great in bed, so he could totally scratch your itch. If you don't like him afterward, I'll take him for a spin."

I start to say no, then stop and wonder if kissing Byron would feel as nice as kissing Wyatt. Hard to tell. I've never really fantasized about the man. On the other hand, he *is* really good-looking. There might be some chemistry.

And I've never heard any stories about how Byron mistreats children.

"Ooh, look at this." Jo pulls a red dress out of the rack. "Off the shoulder. Chiffon. That slit on the side is brilliant. It'll make you look like a flame to be devoured."

"It's the *flame* that devours," I correct her dryly. "Or burns."

"Ha. Not if you're doing flaming shots! Anyway, you know what I mean. I can lend you my Jimmy Choos. I haven't worn them yet, and they'll match the dress perfectly. I can just imagine it." She closes her eyes briefly. "Byron sees you in red across the gallery floor. He gets struck dumb with desire. He romances and seduces you. And you invite me to your billionaire wedding!" She claps as though she's the one getting married in her fantasy. "It's going to be so exciting!"

The mental picture she paints has all the right elements. But somehow it's about as exciting as overcooked pasta.

22

WYATT

The mall is a collection of horrors, but I made a promise to Vi, so here I am at a department store, trying to help her buy a dress for Geneva's wedding. Except...what do I know about clothes for little girls? Just because I'm wearing an Avengers T-shirt doesn't mean I'm a superhero when it comes to girly fashion.

As a matter of fact, we aren't even in the right section. The dresses are way too big—adult-sized, actually.

Still, Vi lingers, admiring them. "I want to be taller."

"Why?"

"So I can wear this," she says, running a hand over a black number with a plunging neckline.

My jaw tightens. *Over my dead body.* She could be ten feet tall, but she's still not wearing anything with a neckline like that for at least the next thirty years.

Then I hear a familiar voice...

Kim?

I turn my head, and hot lust seizes me. A stylish brunette in designer clothes and shoes is with her. But Kim looks better.

Sweeter. More touchable. Her lips are bright red, tempting me like a bullfighter's cape.

Shit. Stop thinking like that.

Too late. My mind is already conjuring up how she felt in my arms when I kissed her in the hall. Sweet. Delectable. Hot as hell. The memory heats my blood, which is flowing in the wrong direction—again! Damn it. I do *not* need this kind of physical reaction when I'm out shopping with my child.

Then the brunette starts talking about some guy named Byron Pearce. The name is vaguely familiar—somebody David mentioned once as someone I should meet.

But the more the brunette and Kim talk, the more irritated and annoyed I become. If Kim needs somebody to "scratch her itch," she doesn't need this Byron guy. And she certainly does not need that sexy red dress the brunette is holding, or any Jimmy Choos. And she definitely does not need to go to this art gallery thing and try to catch the man's attention.

I haven't even met the guy, and I already hate him.

Not because I'm jealous. It's not that kind of thing. It's just that… Kim needs to focus on finding me a date to Geneva's wedding.

Without thinking, I move toward them, cross my arms and shoot the brunette my most disapproving look. It's the look I've been reserving for Vi's first boyfriend. "Red isn't Kim's best color."

Kim turns around, her face going tight. "What are you doing here?"

Despite the hostility bristling through her, she's cute. And she smells amazing. Like ripe peach and flora body wash. I shift a bit to ease the pressure down below.

"Buying a dress for Vi," I say, praying that talking about my daughter will cool me off a bit. And it does, as long as I hold my breath so I don't smell Kim or look at her mouth or tits. So I keep my gaze squarely on hers. "But I have no idea where the girls' dresses are." I look over my shoulder and see Vi talking with a clerk. Hopefully she isn't asking how much the plunge-to-the-navel neckline dress costs. "Maybe she's finding out."

"Why does she look like she's here to buy a hazmat suit?" the brunette asks.

"What?"

"She looks...grim. Way too serious."

Kim nods. "Most girls are happy to shop." Her narrowed brown eyes say she blames me for Vi's lack of shopping joy.

I glance at Vi again, who does look a little concerned. Wonder why. Has she sensed my discomfiture at being in the mall? I haven't set a budget or vetoed anything...yet.

But I gotta admit, I'm feeling lost. I thought once we got here, the dress Vi needs would just, I don't know, materialize on a rack in front of us. But I don't even know exactly what she should wear to Geneva's wedding. All I'm sure of is that Vi wants something more than just a dress. She wants to make an *impression*, although it better not be of the Hollywood sex symbol variety.

"We're struggling," I say. There's no way to hide it. And there's no shame in admitting that you haven't mastered something yet. "Actually, *I'm* struggling. I'm not exactly sure what she should be wearing."

Kim purses her mouth for a moment. "If you want, I can help."

"Really?" I didn't expect her to do anything more than the absolute minimum to fulfill our contract. Then I look at how she's dressed, and think about how she's always so perfectly outfitted, and relief loosens the knot in my chest. "Well, yeah, that'd be great. Thank you."

"My friend Josephine here"—Kim gestures at the brunette—"is a personal shopper extraordinaire. Her service is *very* exclusive, so you'll have to be prepared to pay big."

Josephine blinks, then leans over and whispers something furiously into Kim's ear. Kim whispers back, and they go back and forth like that.

What is this, some secret clubhouse code? Or maybe Kim is explaining to Josephine what Vi needs.

Vi comes over. "*Kim!* I didn't know you were here!"

I haven't seen such an openly joyful expression on Vi's face for so long that it's hard to take a breath. And it's Kim who put it there. An odd mix of tangled emotions pulses through me.

Kim looks back at her with a wide grin. "Just doing a little shopping with my friend." She gestures at Josephine. "This is Josephine Martinez. Josephine, meet Vi."

Vi stares up at Josephine with her mouth open. "Wow. You look amazing," she whispers.

Josephine is dressed to the nines, if you want to look like you're ready to go to a fancy restaurant, but I like the way Kim's dressed better. Like someone you could share cheeseburgers and fries and a couple of cold beers with.

Josephine beams. "I know. I'll make you look as good as me." She winks and takes Vi away to a different section.

Vi seems to instinctively trust Josephine on this matter, so okay. I just pray Josephine doesn't pull a Kim on me by selecting one crappy dress after another for Vi.

23

KIM

As I watch Jo take Vi under her wing, satisfaction and guilt twine inside me. Satisfaction because Jo will do a good job. Guilt because it's Jo's day off.

To make matters worse—and likely to ensure I don't forget today's her day off—she hissed into my ear, "I don't work for clients I don't know."

"His name is Wyatt," I whispered. "Now you know."

"Wait, is this the guy who you've been trying to set up with London and Maria and all...?"

"Yes."

"You never said he was *hot*."

Of course Jo had to focus on the least important point. Or so I decided forcibly, pointedly ignoring how great his arms looked in his shirt. "Oh, just shut up and do this for me. I'll buy you whatever drink you want." I gave her my best pleading face. "I'm doing this for the kid, not *him*." I don't want Vi to feel awkward because her dress isn't quite right. And I don't trust Wyatt to know what to buy. "He thinks red isn't my color. You know he's totally wrong about that."

Jo's conflicted expression said she agreed with me, even

though she really didn't want to. "Girlfriend, you owe me more than a drink. You owe me a blow-by-blow when you hook up with him," she said.

"That's not happening."

Jo's eyes narrowed. "We'll see."

You can narrow your eyes all you want, but it's still never happening. "Sure." I smiled thinly.

Jo better not complain when she never gets the story she thinks she's going to get.

Wyatt and I follow Vi and Jo until they reach the appropriate section of the store. He leans against a wall, watching them, and I stand next to him. As I do, I realize I've made a tactical error. I should've helped Vi myself. Or at least assisted Jo. Now it's too late to join them without looking weird, so I'm stuck with Wyatt.

Crap.

We aren't standing too close together, but close enough that people will probably assume we're friends. His body radiates so much heat. Although it's hot today and I should be gravitating toward the cool AC, his warmth pulls me closer, making me want to lean just a few degrees in.

It's not just a thermal attraction, I decide. It's also his scent. Not aftershave, but the laundry detergent. Something custom ordered from Satan, no doubt. I don't know of any laundry soap on any Walmart shelf that smells this amazing.

My eyes dart in his direction. He's looking at me, like he wants to say something. Or do something. Is he going to kiss me again? Maybe he's wondering about it...like me. Or maybe he's just trying to mess with my mind like he did before. And I'm letting him win by being weak.

Must. Stop. This. *Now!*

"You should've been more aware of Vi's schedule," I blurt out, bitchier than I want.

He frowns. "Yeah, sorry about that."

"She said she mentioned it to you." I exaggerate a bit because she never quite put it that way. But she sort of implied it, so close enough. "But you probably didn't hear." *Because you have other, more important priorities.*

The creases between his eyebrows deepen. "She did?"

I nod, relieved to be distracted from thinking about how hot he looks and smells. *Focus on all the reasons he's a terrible human being.* That should dampen my misguided attraction.

He sighs. "I could swear she didn't, but I've been busy and distracted this week with all the dates."

"Hey, don't you go putting that on me. I'm doing my best to help you out."

"I know." Brackets form at the corners of his mouth. "I'm just thinking maybe I shouldn't bother."

My gut tightens. "Why?" I'm not going to lose out on my bonus because Wyatt can't do his part in finding a date. I need that statue! And knowing him, he won't sell it if I don't deliver.

"Because the date doesn't really matter," he says, sounding slightly resigned.

"It doesn't?" That doesn't jibe with what I've been hearing. "But you obviously want one. You even had Dane ambush Salazar to get me to help you."

"I could care less about the wedding, but the thing is, Vi hasn't really been coping. I think she needs some closure. To really understand that her mom isn't coming back."

"But you want a hot date," I say, totally confused. "You want to make Geneva sorry."

Wyatt shrugs. "If I do, great, but if not, it doesn't matter. I just want Vi to stop trying to please Geneva and start thinking more about herself. What's best for her."

I'm starting to get a bad feeling about this. I look at him for any hint of deception, certain his motives can't be this pure. He could be messing with me again. But he's looking straight at me, and his mouth is set in a firm line.

And I feel lower than slug slime. I totally misconstrued his intentions, assuming he'd want to get back at Geneva. If he's really going to the wedding to help Vi get emotional closure, the women I've been picking out for him are totally inappropriate.

Before I can tell him I'm sorry, Vi and Jo approach with a dreamy pink dress that is not only modestly cut but also sophisticated. I knew my best friend could pull it off.

"This one," Vi says, her eyes shining. "It's so *perfect!*"

Wyatt flashes a grateful smile at Jo. "That looks fantastic. Thank you."

Jo waves a hand. "Ah, she's a great kid. Easy to shop with."

Vi grins up at her.

"You're awesome," I tell Jo, thankful she didn't try to be like me and give Vi a horrible dress only somebody like Svetlana the Snob would find acceptable.

Jo picks out shoes and accessories for Vi, to ensure everything is coordinated for maximum effect. Afterward, Wyatt and Vi go off on their own to "rustle up some ice cream." Jo and I find a nice navy cocktail dress I can wear to parties...or to the office, if I put a jacket over it. Jo doesn't look for anything for herself, since she wears only the latest fashions, and she won't find those hanging on a clearance rack.

"She's a really nice kid," Jo says. "And that Wyatt is seriously hot."

"You think everyone's hot," I say, doing my best to sound careless. I'm not admitting to Jo that I think he's hot.

"Not *every*one. Just the hotties. I'm stingy with praise."

"Uh-huh."

"It's weird he's taking his kid to his ex-wife's wedding, though."

"It's for a good cause," I say vaguely, not wanting to share his reasons when he hasn't told me I can. And it isn't just about him, but Vi, too. When I was growing up, I hated it that people knew about my mom marrying over and over again for money. It was just too humiliating, and I was too young to know how to handle the situation. I don't know exactly how Vi feels about her mom and the wedding, but I suspect it isn't on the warm and fuzzy side.

I purchase the navy dress and the red one Jo picked out earlier. The latter costs a little more than I'd like, but I don't give a damn. The color is so me.

Afterward, Jo and I hit a few more stores before we call it quits. Despite the balm of retail therapy, I'm distracted. I keep thinking about what Vi said yesterday about how she feels like she isn't loved unless she does something her mom is proud of and how she's no match for that fiancé in her mother's affections. And also what Wyatt told me at the department store. I think about it more on the drive home.

Pairing him with an heiress rich in assets but poor in personality is out of the question now. But I honestly can't think of anybody I can set him up with who would be suitable. Most decent heiresses I know are either married or engaged or in a relationship. Miri is an exception, but that obviously didn't work out. Predictably, because Miri likes her men slim, mild-mannered and unassuming...and Wyatt is none of those things. His arms alone are so thick and muscled, sometimes I'm tempted to bite into a bicep to see if it's as hard and strong as it appears.

Maybe I should just go to the damned thing. It's like Salazar said—just one lousy date. And yes, it's the hateful Geneva's wedding, but I can probably grin and bear it for Vi's sake. I don't know why I care so much, because it isn't like she's my child or I've known her for long. Maybe it's because I sometimes catch glimpses of myself in her. It would have been nice, back when I was a kid, if there'd been someone around to let me know I was okay the way I was.

I finally decide to tell Wyatt not to worry about a date because I'll do it. And it'll free up his evenings to spend more time with Vi. I hadn't even thought about that in my petty desire for revenge, but if she's as emotionally lost as she seems to be, she's going to need her daddy around for moral support.

Feeling pretty good about the decision, I park and go up to my apartment to drop off my stuff before talking to Wyatt. Princess is in the hall, her black fur glossy and beautiful. Wonder how she got out. Did Wyatt forget? It isn't the first time I've seen her wandering around. Or maybe she's finding ways to escape to explore the area. One of the trophy wives Mom hung out with had a cat that used to run away a lot, but he always came home.

Just like Princess right now.

She seems to have something in her mouth. I look more closely, but can't quite make it out. Maybe an old kibble?

She purrs softly and wraps herself around my ankle. Her warm body vibrates against my bare skin, making me smile. "Hey, beautiful. Haven't seen you in a while." Not since the day I first met Vi.

The cat looks at me adoringly, then places something on my left foot. It's a dark brown, bullet-shaped corpse with six disgusting legs folded like death traps. "*Aaagh!*"

I jump, my heart pumping a million beats a second. If I were a cat like Princess, I would've gone through the hallway ceiling.

I kick hard, trying to dislodge the roach on my toes. It gets flung away, along with my flip-flop, creating twin arcs through the still hall air. I stare down at my toes to make sure there aren't any roach flakes, revulsion shuddering through me. I have to disinfect them now, but only because I can't cut them off and regrow them.

I look down at the hall, wondering what disgusting detritus lurks on the floor. You never know. There might be finely ground roach powder all over.

Princess is mewling, sounding particularly displeased. But it isn't the poor feline's fault. She's just being a cat, and probably doesn't even know that she's being set up by Wyatt.

Yeah, it's far-fetched, but there's no other rational explanation. Why else would *his* cat bring *me* bugs? Cats give bugs to their owners, not their neighbors!

I hop on my right foot toward my door, which is really hard in a flip-flop. When I manage to get inside my apartment, I slam the door shut in Princess's face in case she's going to cough up a hairball full of dead tarantulas or something.

Champ rushes over and buries his nose in my crotch. I move him out of the way, take off my other shoe and hop toward the bathroom. He follows, tail wagging and completely clueless as to how traumatized I am and how much I need a drink right now.

But first things first.

Under the sink, I find a first-aid kit and a brand-new bottle of rubbing alcohol. I dump it all over my contaminated toes, then wait for the roach germs to die a horrible death. I can almost hear the screams.

One. Two. Three...

When I hit one hundred, I run warm water over my foot, then wash it with extra care with antibacterial soap.

Three times.

Just to be sure.

Afterward, I dry my foot and stare at the towel. Maybe I

should throw it away. Not because it's contaminated, but because it feels gross. On the other hand, it's a damn good towel. Argh, the inner conflict! Maybe I can wash it with extra bleach. It's white, after all.

I finally go back out to the living room, walking gingerly, and plop down on my couch. A long, hard sigh escapes my parted lips, and Champ tries to lick my freshly washed toes.

"Don't!" I say. "They touched a cockroach, like, two seconds ago."

He looks at me, then gives me a doggy smile and hops up on the couch, sidling next to me. I hug him, burying my face in his fur.

Damn ambush. I totally didn't that coming.

There's only one explanation for this. *Wyatt.* He must've trained Princess. He's dropped roaches and frogs on me before. He might feel like he's too old to do it himself now, but *his cat*... It isn't easy to get a cat to what you want, but if you're determined, it's possible. Maybe even *easy*, if you're as evilly super-powered as Wyatt. He made me tingle and think about that damned kiss for days. He can totally control a pussy...

A cat. *A cat, dammit!*

Ugh. And here I've been thinking he's a changed man. More mature. Sexier. And nicer.

But Princess has set me straight. My mouth tightens. I wish I could change my mind about being his date to Geneva's wedding. Under any other circumstances I would, but Vi shouldn't have to suffer because she drew a short straw in the parent lottery.

Twice.

Okay, no more overthinking, no more assigning desirable qualities to Wyatt. I'm going to put on my big-girl pants, go to the wedding, fake my congratulations to Geneva and whatever poor sucker she's marrying—because God knows nobody deserves Geneva as a wife—get the damned statue, collect my five-hundred-thousand-dollar bonus and live happily ever after.

The end.

24

KIM

SINCE I DON'T HAVE TO WORK, ON MONDAY I START MY DAY lazily. After sleeping in for half an hour, I select jeans, then, after some deliberation, pull out a red T-shirt from my closet. Wyatt doesn't think red is my color, but that just shows he's color-blind.

I grab Champ's leash and we head out the door. Nose to the ground, he finds another bug present in the hall and immediately consumes it. Hopefully it wasn't another roach or, God forbid, a tarantula. I rub his head, grateful he's keeping me safe. "You're such a smart, brave, wonderful boy."

I walk him while sipping coffee from my travel mug. It's nice to have an easy pace for once. Then I remember Evie had that party with her husband/boss's family. I text her to see if we can have lunch together to see how she's coping. She seems so panicked about her marriage.

The walk is refreshing and clears my mind after the hours of TV shows and movies I had to watch last night to clear the trauma delivered by Princess. Champ matches my pace and explores the area, sniffing any and everything. By the time we're done, I'm finished with my morning brew. Caffeine courses pleasantly through my veins, making my brain feel lubricated and turbocharged.

When the elevator doors open on my floor, I spot Wyatt right outside his unit. He's in a T-shirt and worn jeans.

Shouldn't he be at work? Or maybe he's deathly ill. Or maybe he got fired.

Or maybe he's leaving me another bug.

I take a glance at my door. *Nothing.*

"Why are you still here?" I ask, suspicious. He could always pull a toad out of his pocket and throw it my way.

"Working from home today. I just drove Vi to school."

Champ wags his tail at Wyatt. That poor dog is a terrible judge of character. He has no clue Wyatt is really evil inside.

"Do you do that a lot?" I ask. "Work from home, I mean."

"Couple times a month, depending."

Hmm. That's a couple of times too often. It gives him more opportunity to train Princess to send disgusting critters my way. I wonder what fresh horrors he's got in mind, although it will be hard to top roach-bombing my toes.

"Listen, thanks again for helping out with the dress. Without you and Josephine, Vi might not have picked such a good one. And it's really important to her."

I stare at him, confused and annoyed. When Wyatt's like this, I can almost believe he's a good guy who means well, who's doing his best. It's crazy because *I should know better.* It's probably those blue eyes. They're so gorgeous and earnest. When they focus on me like this, I feel like I'm not only getting his undivided attention, but absolute, soul-baring honesty.

Stop getting sucked into this. He has a plan, and it's not good for you. Remember the roach assault by proxy.

Right. Mustn't forget that. Ever.

"I did it for Vi," I say. "And I bought that red dress because, despite what you think, red looks fantastic on me." I point at my shirt for emphasis.

He looks chagrined. "I didn't mean it like that. It's a great color for you."

"But you said it anyway."

He opens his mouth.

I wag a finger. "Nuh-uh. Don't need an explanation. I know why you did it."

"You do?"

"To mess with me because that's how you get off."

He gives me the strangest look, like I'm the loony tunes here. Bastard.

Since I can't kick his ass, I add, "And I know what you've been doing with your cat."

"Huh?"

"Yeah, yeah. Keep playing dumb." I'm not fooled. He must've mastered some way to make his cat do what he wants. It can't be harder than making a billion dollars. I crane my neck to look at his backside. "By the way, blue jeans make your ass look flat."

"What?"

"I know you can't handle the truth, but..." I shrug a shoulder.

Before Wyatt can respond, I go into my apartment, slam the door shut and toe off my shoes. That was a terrible lie. Jeans make his ass look fantastic. His ass has always been perfect. Captain America has nothing on this guy.

But let him wonder. It will give me great pleasure if he burns every single pair of jeans he owns. Or spends an hour or two in front of a mirror, twisting around to see how his ass really looks.

I go to the kitchen and grab myself some ice-cold water. As I chug it down, it hits me that I've been so focused on blitzing him with all those women that I forgot about the most important thing —him being my next-door neighbor. I thought he'd move out soon. After all, billionaires buy mansions and penthouses and beach homes. But who's been helping him find a suitable property? Certainly not that terrible assistant who can't even guard his office competently.

And he's too busy with Vi to buy a bunch of dumb stuff, like most normal guys who suddenly came into a billion dollars would.

Salazar said the main thing I need to do for Wyatt is finding him a date to Geneva's wedding. But he never said I couldn't do more with all the free time I have on my hands. So I'll take on a special project.

Find Wyatt A Home.

Or FWAH. It's like a sound a baby might make when it's happy. Fitting, since I'll definitely be happy when he's out of my hair.

Besides, Vi deserves a better home. Something with a pool and a butler. If Wyatt moves out in the next two weeks, I might even consider getting him the butler as well.

My mind made up, I call Rick the Realtor. He's sold a few properties to Salazar and his son Iain. Rick knows all about billionaire-appropriate homes.

"Hello, Kim. A pleasure to hear from you." He's mellow and cordial, as always. I wonder if it's how he always sounds, or if it's part of his professional persona.

"Hi, Rick. I'm looking for a property. For a single father and his daughter. The man's worth over a billion, so something fitting."

"Does he have any particular preferences? I have some properties with amazing gardens and pools. One has a water garden."

"Mmm, not a water garden." That's wasteful and silly in SoCal, what with all the droughts and water shortages. But what about the other places? I remember Wyatt's mom having a green thumb, but I doubt Wyatt's into pulling weeds or shoveling fertilizer. There's a reason he chose an apartment. He probably likes the convenience of somebody taking care of everything, and he likes the height. "Do you have a penthouse or something like that?"

"I have three. One of them is extremely new. The builder just got finished last month."

"That sounds perfect. If you're not too busy, I'd love to see them this morning, before lunch." Evie texted and said she could meet for lunch.

"Sure. Should I pick you up at your boss's office in, say...one hour?"

"Actually, pick me up at my place. I'm off today." I give him my address. "See you."

I hang up and change into a form-fitting magenta dress and heels. Then I put on makeup. Although I'm not working for Salazar this month, I still need to look perfect, especially around people who associate with him and his family. It's part of being somebody like Salazar's assistant.

Three penthouses. That's not bad. Hopefully one of them will work.

25

WYATT

Blue jeans make your ass look flat.

Do they? I'm twisted around, staring at my butt in the mirror. It doesn't *look* flat. I change into dress slacks and check again.

Nope. About the same.

Was she just saying that to mess with me?

My ass is one of my best features. I work it off in the gym, even though recently I've been too busy to go.

Dammit. I need to stop worrying about what Kim thinks. Working from home doesn't mean screwing around. I actually have things to do, and I need to focus.

Even if Kim's comment does keep popping into my head.

My phone rings, and as soon as I see the name, my mood plunges. Geneva never calls unless she wants something. I'm really tempted to drag my finger to the left, but then, what if this is the one-in-a-million occasion where she might actually need to discuss something concerning Vi?

"Hello, Geneva. What can I do for you?"

"I decided Vi can be here, *if* she'll be part of the ceremony and throw flower petals," Geneva says.

It makes me clench my jaw. Isn't it enough that she's making our daughter feel unwanted? Now she wants to use her?" "I already told you she wasn't going to do that. She just wants to be there to meet her new...*stepdad*." The word sticks in my throat like a half-wet, moldy biscuit.

"He's not really interested in children. He isn't marrying me to have babies." Her tone clearly says, *Unlike you.*

Except I never wanted to have children, not so young and not with somebody like her, who thinks nothing of abandoning her own flesh and blood over a man. She said he's a billionaire, as though the man's net worth justifies what she's done. The guy could be a trillionaire for all I care.

"Then just accept that Vi isn't interested in the farce, either," I say coldly.

"What do you mean?"

"Do you honestly think she wants unicorns flying over a rainbow for your wedding?"

"Why the hell not? She's my kid! She should be happy for me!"

The scary thing is that Geneva sounds utterly convinced. Not for the first time, I wonder what it takes to be this oblivious and self-centered. "She *was* happy for you, until you decided to dump her for a new husband."

"What?" There's a pause. "Kids are so weird these days."

"Yeah. God forbid one would actually want her mother to give her some priority."

She sighs. It's the same sigh she always lets out when she can't think of anything to say back. "Do you think you can manage to bring somebody fitting for the ceremony? I know you aren't coming alone. Just don't bring a hooker or anyone like that. It's a classy event."

A muscle under my eye starts twitching. Now I wish Vi weren't going so I could pick up the trashiest hooker available for this *classy event*.

"My baker's even going to put my cake on Instagram! I'm going to be part of it, too. She's got a huge following, and it'll probably go viral," Geneva continues. "So I don't want anything that looks wrong in the photos, you know? Oh, and can you also use your company to help publicize the photos? I know Sweet

Darlings' app is for privately sharing photos, but maybe you could have the ones of me pushed to their users?"

Geneva doesn't need a new husband. She needs a mental hospital. "You have to be kidding."

"Of course I'm not kidding. Why would I be kidding? If you—"

"I gotta go. I have a meeting," I say, and hang up. If I could, I'd block her number. But there are times we need to chat because of Vi. So like it or not, I'm stuck.

I go back to the project planning, and when my stomach growls, I leave for a late lunch. I want nachos with extra jalapeños to cleanse my palate. And there are a lot of great Mexican restaurants near the apartment.

When I get back, I see boxes outside Kim's door. A cute blonde I've never seen before is adding to the pile. Maybe Kim's getting a roommate?

Actually, never mind. It looks like the blonde is moving out.

"Hey. Need some help?" I ask.

The blonde turns around.

"Sorry, I should introduce myself." I gesture at my apartment door just as Kim appears. "I'm—"

"Just leaving," Kim cuts in with a thin smile. "And no, we don't need any help. Evie, let's go."

What's going on? I don't mind helping, even if she accused my ass of being flat. "Kim—"

"We're very busy. Oh, don't forget to take your cat."

I look down and see Princess at Kim's feet. What's she doing here? I thought I left her at home.

Then it reminds me of what Kim accused me of earlier—that she "knew what I'd been doing with Princess." Has the cat been bugging Kim somehow? Ugh.

I pick Princess up and go inside my apartment, since Kim's obviously annoyed with me. I shake a finger at Princess. "Don't bother Kim. She doesn't like cats." At least, she doesn't like them as much as dogs.

Princess blinks in response, doing her Sphinx act.

"Yeah, yeah. Look, I know you miss Geneva, but she isn't here, and Kim isn't Geneva. She's a lot nicer...even if she is crazy, with her weird mood swings." At least she's consistently nice to Vi.

Princess licks her paw, ignoring me.

I place her on the floor with a small sigh. Part of me wishes Kim weren't so difficult, and that we didn't have the kind of history we do. Then maybe we could get along better.

26

KIM

THE OTHER BEDROOM FEELS REALLY EMPTY WITHOUT EVIE'S things in it. Actually, the whole place feels empty, especially now that she's officially moving out. Oddly, I miss her even more.

Since she's married to Nathan Sterling, whose home is already furnished with super-expensive and nice furniture, she left her bed, but promised she'd send somebody to take it off my hands. I told her to take her time. It isn't like I'm dying to get a new roommate or anything. With the break Annie is giving me on the rent, I don't really need one anytime soon.

I nuke a frozen meal, the official Dinner of Executive Assistants Everywhere. While the microwave works its magic, I check up on Salazar.

–Me: Everything good, boss?

–Salazar: I thought I gave you time off.

–Me: What, a girl can't check up on her favorite boss?

A little sucking up never hurts. Especially with Salazar.

–Salazar: Everything's great. Having a marvelous time. And Ceinlys says to say thank you.

Ah-ha. If Ceinlys is happy, I just got an extra Brownie point or two. I pour myself a glass of chilled rosé and sip the slightly sweet wine.

–Me: My pleasure. ;-)

The microwave dings. I pull out the heated chicken breast and veggies, and take a bite of carrot. It's a little soft, and still tastes like boring old carrot. We have such advances in science and technology. Why can't someone make carrots taste like chocolate? Even caramel would be an improvement. Maybe you could wrap them in bacon or something...

My phone buzzes. Probably Salazar again, just remembering something he wants.

–Wyatt: What's going on with tonight's date? Do I have one? I can't find anything about it.

Oh crap. I forgot to tell him about my decision to go with him to the wedding. In my defense, I *was* busy trying to roach-block him.

I shove the rest of the carrot into my mouth. I need to work up to sharing my decision.

–Me: No date tonight. Enjoy dinner with your kiddo.

There. That should make him happy.

–Wyatt: But I don't have a date for the wedding yet.

–Me: Yeah, you do.

–Wyatt: Who?

I'll tell him later. I want to finish my dinner in peace while it's still hot, because that's what's making it palatable. I push the veggies around, then take a bite of the chicken. The sauce isn't too terrible—a little thick and floury—but the poultry has the texture of soft rubber.

Hey, at least it's soft rubber, my mind says, trying to find a positive in the situation. *You won't need to see your dentist about a broken tooth.*

Champ looks at the bit of chicken still pierced on the end of my fork, licking his chops. The longing in his gaze says he totally agrees with my mind and more.

There's an urgent pounding on my door. Wyatt. Has to be.

Sighing, I stand and go look through the peephole. Yup, Wyatt. His hair is sticking up and he looks rather concerned.

"You absolutely cannot pick one of my previous dates," he says firmly. Like a man in a middle of divorce proceedings telling his lawyer that his wife isn't getting a penny more than what the law requires.

"Okay," I say, mildly amused.

"Okay. So who? The wedding's this weekend."

"I know, but it's okay. Don't worry about it."

He narrows his eyes until they're brilliant blue slits in his gorgeous face. "You lied about wanting the housewarming gift from Dane, didn't you?"

The reminder of the statue makes my spine stiffen. "No, of course not. I want it more than anything." It's the only thing standing between me and my five-year bonus.

"Why? It doesn't make any sense."

"I don't have to make sense to you." I step aside. "Anyway, come on in. I was going to stop by to chat."

"You were?"

"Yeah. And where's Vi?"

"Watching TV."

I consider. The talk won't take that long, so I bring him in and shut the door. The entire floor doesn't need to hear my decision.

"I'm going to go to the wedding as your date." I feel slightly resigned that it came to this, but also slightly proud I'm going to fix this problem for him and get the statue and the bonus I deserve.

"You are?"

"Yeah."

"But you don't meet the criteria."

"Oh, really?" I put my hands on my hips. "Which part? The 'not wanting your money' part or the 'pretty enough' part?" If he says I'm a gold digger, I'm going to punch him. If he says I'm not pretty enough, I'm still going to punch him. If he says both, I'm going to punch him into a mushy pulp, then feed him to Champ.

"I thought you were going to get me an heiress."

My outrage dies a bit. "I never said that. The only reason I set you up with them is that a rich woman won't usually want your money. Anyway, most of the eligible heiresses around are taken. Kind of like all the decent men."

He frowns. Well, he can ponder all he likes. Doesn't change the truth. "Look, I'm doing this because I want you to spend more time with Vi," I say, giving him half the truth. "You've been busy with all the dates lately, and I feel bad about that. Also, freeing up your evenings means you can do a special father-daughter bonding activity I planned for you guys."

"You set up a father-daughter bonding activity for me and Vi?" he says slowly, like he just heard something horrific and unimaginable.

"Yes." I go to the couch and dig through my purse until I find the brochures and glossy papers Rick gave me. I hand the stack to Wyatt. "Your new home."

"What?" He barely glances at the colorful papers with a frown. "I don't want a new home. I just moved here."

"Yeah, because your assistant doesn't do her job. You're a billionaire now. Your daughter deserves a home with a pool." I point at the pictures of the pools. Every single penthouse I saw today had one.

"Kim, I picked this apartment because I wanted Vi to have normalcy. I need to give her what I had when I was growing up."

I sigh. It's so weird how a man as smart as he is can be so... dense. "Normalcy isn't just a *house*. It's how your home makes you feel. Do you feel safe? Cared for? Do you feel like you can let your guard down? That's what makes a good home for Vi, not an apartment your parents might've gotten in Corn Meadows." I gesture at the papers in Wyatt's hands. "And you know what? She's the daughter of a billionaire, whether you can wrap your mind around that or not. She's going to a school that's full of rich people's kids. And she's going to wonder why you won't spend the money on a better home. If she doesn't, her classmates certainly will."

Wyatt's eyes have widened slightly. After a pause, he says, "Never thought of it that way."

"I know," I say, pleased to be able to set him on the right path to complete FWAH.

"Okay. Thanks."

"Anyway, just go have a look at them. The realtor's info is on the top sheet. Rick's a fantastic guy. And he loves kids."

Wyatt nods.

Man, I'm good at my job. And if he does as I ask and moves out in the next two weeks, I'm definitely going to find him a butler.

Suddenly, a thought crosses my mind—that I'm going to miss him and Vi if they move. I slap it down *hard*. Vi, maybe...but I want *him* out of my hair. I'm trying to go back to a non-pest-littered life, so I can leave home without having to check the damn floors first.

But the thought refuses to stay down.

27

KIM

"His attitude is much better with houses," I say at the bar after our exercise session.

Jo and Hilary both look at me, then Hilary sticks her hand out. I give her my phone, and she scrolls down and finds texts from Wyatt.

"'This is a really nice home. But too big for just two people,'" Hilary reads, then sips her cosmopolitan.

"Yeah, that's the three-level place Rick loves so much."

"As opposed to what multimillion home?" Jo says. "He just loves the commission."

"Your cynicism is astounding, Jo. He works hard for his money."

"Kim's right. There's nothing he wouldn't do for his clients," Hilary says.

Jo snorts. "You mean for his clients' *money*. Don't get me wrong, the guy's good at his job. But he has a highly prehensile approach to cash."

Hilary chuckles and continues reading Wyatt's texts. "'Don't know about this one. Too sterile. Feels like a hospital.'" She tilts her head. "I have to agree. It's too white and...I don't know. Utilitarian?" She flips the phone around so Jo can see the picture.

"Yeah. But some people like that," Jo says.

Hilary's eyebrows rise. "Who?"

"People who are afraid to put their mark on a place, so they want it just sort of...plain. Or people who think the functional minimalist look is a thing to aspire to. Like God."

"I'm pretty sure God likes color," I say.

"And I'm grateful every day for that," Jo says. "I wouldn't have the job I love otherwise. And speaking of jobs, Hugo wants to know if he can stop by tonight."

"Sure. Any time, as long as it's before nine."

"Got it." Jo starts texting.

"By the way, are you going to that art gallery opening?" Hilary asks.

I look daggers in Jo's direction. "Did you tell her?"

"It just came up." Jo's smile is entirely too innocent as she puts away her phone.

"I couldn't even if I wanted to. I have another..." I think for a moment. Not a *date*. And *appointment* sounds weird. "Engagement," I say, using the word my boss likes so much.

"With who?" Jo asks eagerly.

"Somebody we know?"

I suppress a sigh. I hate it that I'm going to have to prove Jo right. Not to mention I owe her a blow-by-blow report of how he and I are going to get together. Crap. I should've promised her a bottle of Salazar's favorite scotch instead. "No one you know," I say to Hilary.

"But *I* knooow..." Jo singsongs. "You've got a date with Wyatt!"

I make a face. There's no hiding it. Not that I could anyway.

"You have to tell me *everything*." She cackles like a witch.

Hilary leans closer. "I thought you were setting him up with an heiress."

"It didn't work out," I say. "And he really needs to be paired up. We're low on time, and I decided to step up because I'm professional like that."

"It's the kid," Jo says to Hilary. "I knew it when I saw the girl.

Kim can never resist being nice to a child, especially when she comes from a broken home."

"It isn't like that," I say, not caring for the *broken home*. Being away from a parent who doesn't want you doesn't necessarily mean there's something wrong with your home life. "I like Vi a lot. It has nothing to do with her background."

"I need pictures of these people," Hilary says.

"There are none," I say.

At the same time, Jo says, "Kim can take some tonight. He's her neighbor, after all."

"Uh, *no*. That would be creepy. I'm not going to stalk him," I say, then finish my drink. "Anyway, I gotta go and walk Champ."

"Oh, I almost forgot!" Hilary hands me a thermos.

"What's this?"

"Mark's attempt at a pork chop. André told him not even a dog would eat it, and he wants me to give it to you for Champ. He wants to see if Champ will eat it or not. It's all cut up, too."

A porkchop in a thermos. "Why is he making pork chops?" I ask. If Hilary's husband wants pork chops, he can just drop by one of his fancy restaurants and ask one of his superbly trained chefs.

"Because he wants to impress me on my birthday."

Now Jo looks even more befuddled. "Your birthday was, like, five weeks ago."

Hilary's smile is resigned. "*Next* year. Apparently, Dane told him nothing shows a woman how much her husband loves her like a home-cooked meal. He already made pot roast for Sophia, which she said was very good. It was surreal how he kept bragging about it."

"Were you high? Or drunk? You could've imagined it," Jo says.

"One hundred percent sober." Hilary raises a hand, the other one over her heart. "Not a drop of alcohol."

I shake my head. I just can't picture that human icicle doing that. Ever. He'd melt near a stove. Besides, if all men believed Dane's theory, restaurants would be out of luck on Valentine's Day.

But I take the thermos and head home. At least Champ will

have something other than kibbles. Mark uses the best cut of everything, so the meat is going to be great. I just hope the taste doesn't kill the poor dog. Mark has many talents, but cooking isn't one of them.

Once I'm home, I walk Champ, then, with some trepidation, serve him the pork chop. He sniffs it first. God. Not even Champ trusts Mark's cooking. Then he takes a piece into his mouth and gobbles it down.

I watch anxiously to make sure he doesn't keel over. Maybe I should've sampled it first. I feel like serving Mark's food might qualify as animal abuse.

Champ, however, takes another bite. Hmm. Maybe it is okay.

The intercom buzzes, and I glance at the clock. *Almost eight.*

"Yes?" I say into the speaker.

"Hi. My name is Hugo Martinez. I'm Josephine's cousin?"

Oh, right. Totally spaced that. I buzz him in.

Champ's at the door before Hugo knocks. I open it and almost blink. Jo never said her cousin was this hot. Dark bedroom eyes, longish hair that brushes his collar, flashing, straight white teeth and a cute dimple on his smiling face. His body is just as gorgeous —long, lean lines and strong muscles underneath a T-shirt and jeans. Didn't she say he could go all night, a la the Energizer Bunny?

Damn. I wonder if he and I have any chemistry. That way, Wyatt won't distract me with his next-door-neighbor sex appeal.

Maybe I can ask Hugo to kiss me. Fair compensation for reviewing his résumé. Then again, it'd probably be weird. And he is Jo's cousin, so I might run into him again.

But it could be like a vaccine for the unwanted tingling I feel around Wyatt...

God. This situation is killing me!

"Come on in," I say with my best friendly smile.

"Thanks." As he walks in, Champ sniffs and then licks Hugo's fingers. Hugo scratches the dog's head.

"Don't mind him. He likes to have a taste of everyone who comes by." *Maybe I should have a taste.*

"No prob. Seems like a nice dog."

I lead him over to the dining table. "So. You want a job, huh?"

"Yeah." He gives me that flashing grin and takes a seat. "Jo said you're the person to talk to."

His smile is devastating, but for some reason, my body isn't responding. *Come on, hormones!* "She isn't exactly wrong, although it depends on what you're looking for. Something to drink?"

"I'm good, thanks," he says.

I take a chair opposite him. "So. What do you want to do?"

"I want to be an assistant. An executive assistant. Like you."

A little unusual, but there are a lot of great male executive assistants.

He pulls a résumé from a leather folio and pushes it toward me. "Here."

I skim it. He's graduated from… Columbia Law? What…? My head snaps up. "Why do you want to be an assistant when you have a law degree?"

"Well, I haven't passed the bar yet."

It doesn't seem like he failed, though. He seems a bit too uncaring and unashamed. "Did you take it?"

"No. Not sure if I want to bother, to be honest."

"Why not?" If I had a law degree from an Ivy League school, I'd definitely want to be a lawyer. Not just any lawyer, but the kind people cower around.

"It's my life." His expression remains friendly, but his tone is firm.

"That's…true," I say slowly. I know when I'm being politely told to butt out.

I read the résumé and mark a couple of places that could use some tweaks, especially if he wants to be an assistant. He makes notes, his expression serious, like he was Moses taking stenography from God.

"So. Is there someone in particular whose assistant you want to be, or are you just casting around?" I ask, unable to suppress my curiosity. There has to be a story behind his decision.

"I want to be Samantha Jones's assistant." He says her name like I should know her, and his eyes go all gooey.

So he has a crush on this woman. Except the only Samantha Jones I know is a cynical attorney in her forties. She handled the divorce between Salazar and Ceinlys. "What does she do?" I ask, wondering if there are other Samanthas. It isn't like Jones is a super unique name.

"She's a lawyer. Fantastic. Practices family law."

"Practices family law" is a nice way of saying she lives to make her clients' enemies bleed. If Hugo hadn't gone to Columbia Law, I might've thought he was confused about what "family law" entails.

"And...you don't want to join her law firm as a lawyer?"

"No. I'll never get to be around her if that's the case." He shoots me an extremely earnest look. My expression must be saying I don't understand, because he adds, "If I can't spend time with her, how am I going to convince her we're meant to be?"

Oh my God! *Is he serious?* "Aren't there bars where she hangs out, or...?"

"No. She doesn't drink much, period. Says alcohol makes her dull." His eyes shine with admiration.

I can't decide if I should shake my head or wish him luck. It's weird to imagine Samantha as the object of desire by a man as young, smart and hot as Hugo. Not that Samantha herself isn't attractive or smart. It's just that her views on love are...dim. Actually, they're pitch-black. I doubt Hugo's bright, youthful optimism would be a match for that.

"Anyway, I've taken enough of your time. Really appreciate the help," Hugo says, standing up.

I walk him to the door, debating if I should tell him to have a Plan B. His Plan A is unlikely to work out, to put it mildly. On the other hand, he's a big boy, so maybe he can handle the heartache. What doesn't kill him...

He turns around in the doorway. "Hey, listen. If there's anything I can do to repay the favor..."

He smiles. The dimple shows on his cheek again. He's gorgeous. Young. Smart.

I inhale, taking my time. He smells nice, too, with a hint of aftershave and laundry detergent. Just like Wyatt.

Maybe this is my chance to prove that whatever weird pull I've been feeling with Wyatt is a fluke, that it's all due to my not having dated for so long. On the other hand, I can't ask Hugo to date me when I know he has a thing for another woman. I wish I were clueless about his attraction for Samantha so I could just impulsively kiss him to test my theory.

Well. I'll just have to do the next best thing.

"Why don't you just give me a good, tight hug?" I ask.

If the pull between me and Wyatt is just a result of me being deprived, I'll feel a zing with Hugo, too. My breasts will be crushed against his chest, and his arms are going to be around me. It's a perfect test case.

"Hug a pretty girl?" Hugo's grin widens. "I can live with a repayment like that."

I wait for something to stir. His tone is sweet—all-American nice guy, not smarmy in the least. But...*nothing*.

Maybe I need physical contact. After all, Wyatt touched me.

But you felt something from his voice, too.

Yeah, but maybe I'm just immune to voices now. I might need more.

I step into the hall, and Hugo and hugs me. His arms are strong and tight, and he's warm and solid.

But there's no zing. No crackle. None of the jolt that makes my nipples hard or my body tingle in places that haven't tingled in a long time. I even bury my nose in his chest, trying my best to inhale his shirt. The mix of laundry soap and male scent fills my nose.

Still no frisson. Hashtag Experiment Fail.

Shit. How can this be? What's missing? Eau de pheromone de Satan?

Hugo lets go with a smile. "Thanks again."

Such a nice guy. And I feel nothing for him.

I manage a smile of my own. "My pleasure."

He goes off, disappearing into the elevator.

"Wow. Is he even legal?"

I turn around, and like the proverbial bad penny, there's Wyatt, watching me with narrowed eyes and arms folded across his chest. You could snap a photo right now and stick it into a dictionary for ESL students to teach them the meaning of "disapproving."

My hackles rise, and I cross my own arms over my chest. I

want to look tough. And also to hide the fact that my nipples are getting a bit...hard. *Shit.* "Oh, he's definitely legal. Just a bit younger."

He cocks an eyebrow. It's a gesture of sheer arrogance. And rudeness. But somehow it's hot. And now I'm tingling in places where Hugo's hug didn't induce tingling.

What the hell?

But I'll be damned if I let anybody know, much less admit it to myself. "And I *do* like a younger man." My voice is buttery sweet. "They're more accommodating and not as damaged. Smell nicer, too."

Liar! Hugo did not smell better than Wyatt.

A muscle in his neck twitches. "I guess you need them undamaged if you plan on giving them herpes."

It takes a second for the meaning to sink in. "Are you telling me I have herpes?" I demand as fury surges so hard inside me that I feel like my head is about to explode.

"I'm not telling you anything you haven't already said."

What does he have to be resentful about? He isn't the one who just got accused of being a herpes spreader! "I can't believe this. I agree to go to the stupid wedding, and you accuse me of having an STD?"

His jaw slackens. "Are you kidding? *You're* the one who said—"

I'm tired, and I've had enough of this bullshit. I raise my hand. "You know what? I have something more important to do at the moment. Like watch Champ puke up his dinner." I slam the door shut and, to make a point, turn the lock loudly, making sure the entire floor can hear it *click!*

Then I fan myself hard, as heat that has nothing to do with anger courses through me. Must be a delayed reaction from the hug. It's gotta be.

28

Wyatt

I shouldn't have mentioned the herpes. That wasn't just immature, it was plain stupid. Now she knows how the note she left is still bugging me.

Yeah, so what if it still bothers me? She's apparently moved on. She's even dating that kid. Well, not really a kid. He looked pretty full-grown. I was just being mean because I really didn't like the way he was hugging Kim. Nobody hugs a woman like that unless he likes her.

"You aren't even listening," David says around a mouthful of sandwich.

We have a small table to ourselves in the company cafeteria. The place has an amazing array of food, even if they don't serve burgers.

"I was thinking," I say.

"About what?"

So I tell him the gist of what happened two nights ago, annoyance resurfacing. He was hugging her too long. Probably a perv trying to feel her up on the sly. Except he can't fool me.

David nods. "He definitely wanted to sleep with Kim."

"Right?"

"Yeah. Unless the woman's underage or, like, sixty or something. A man who denies it is a liar. Basically the same as a woman who says she likes chocolate, but doesn't want to eat it."

I nod, feeling vindicated, even though I feel bad about bringing up the herpes thing. Not that I'm going to share that with David.

Maybe I should do something to make it up to her... "Hey, when you put your foot in your mouth, what's the best way to recover?"

"Depends. You want to sleep with her, right? Not just be friends?"

My mind opts for "friendly," but my nether regions are definitely voting for "wild monkey sex." I scowl at the terrible direction my dick's heading. David's exact words were "sleep with," but it doesn't seem to care. Probably has an internal translator that changes everything into something it wants to hear.

"Okay, so you want hot monkey sex."

I almost jump. Is David telepathically linked to my junk? "What makes you think that?"

"You hesitated."

"So? Could've been because I didn't want it."

"Oh, you want it."

Shit. David can be difficult to fool. He knows me too well.

"A box of Belgian chocolates should do. Even Dane agrees with me." He texts. Then he frowns when his phone pings.

"He called you on your bullshit, didn't he?" You can always count on Dane to douse a man's enthusiasm better than a thunderstorm over a campfire.

"No. He says, 'Eighty percent dark. Swiss.' That's probably his wife's favorite."

God damn it. I can't believe Dane failed me. He wasn't like this before...but then, he wasn't married before.

Although I'm skeptical about the suggestion, I still find myself in front of Kim's door after work, holding a box of Belgian chocolates from the fancy chocolatier David recommended. It isn't like I have a better idea. And I should probably apologize for what I said yesterday anyway, because the whole herpes thing is from a long time ago. For all I know, maybe she forgot about it, or maybe she wants to forget it ever happened in the first place.

Regardless, I'm not going to hold it against her. I can be the bigger person. I *am* the bigger person.

Still, I still feel awkward as I knock on her door. It takes a while before she sticks her head out. She looks great, but somehow her makeup seems like a shield to block me out than something that she did to make herself look better.

I'm probably just being oversensitive. She doesn't care enough to put up a defense like that.

I clear my throat. "Hey."

"Yes?" She stares up at me like I'm something she'd rather not see. Like a puke stain on her couch.

"Uh, yeah. I thought maybe I should talk to you about..." I gesture with my hand vaguely. "Mind if I come in?"

She purses her mouth, and some sort of calculation flashes in her eyes. Finally, she says, "Okay."

I walk inside. Her dog comes out with a soft whine and licks my hand. I pat him. *'Preciate the friendliness, buddy.* Suddenly the back of my neck tingles, and I lift my head. Kim is watching me with narrowed eyes, her arms crossed over her chest.

"Here." I thrust the box at her.

She stares at it. "What's that?"

"Chocolates."

No response.

"They're Belgian."

Instead of accepting it with a smile or thanks, she pulls back, her arms tightening around her. "What did you do?"

"What do you mean?"

"Did you sprinkle them with rat poison? Herpes virus, maybe?"

What the fuck? Back to herpes again? And here I am trying to mend things so we can at least be civilized at the wedding!

She arches an eyebrow, obviously having taken my silence as some sort of acquiescence. "Trying to make sure I am indeed the super herpes spreader, huh?"

Maybe she smacked her head against something hard sometime after she left Corn Meadows. She's the one who said she has herpes because *I* gave it to her way back when. On the other hand, she isn't acting like she has brain damage.

She's just crazy. Hot, but crazy.

And David's an idiot. Dane, too. I could've gotten her chocolates from the god of cocoa himself, and she'd still be saying this kind of shit. I almost wish I *had* given her herpes, so this bullshit accusation wouldn't sting so much.

"They're just plain old chocolates."

The eyebrow crawls up her forehead, making for her hairline.

I muster up a smile, all the while telling myself, *I'm the bigger person, I'm the bigger person, I'm the bigger person.* "Thought we should smooth things out, since we have to go to the wedding together with Vi and all."

Kim continues to give me the same "I don't trust you for shit" expression. I'd bet my entire bank balance she's looking for an ulterior motive. Just how hard is it for her to accept that not everyone has a secret agenda? Or maybe she can't. Maybe her head is so full of hidden schemes that she can't imagine anybody else being a straight shooter.

"Let me make something clear. I'm a professional," she says finally, her voice full of faux sweetness. "I can play my part at the wedding without a bribe."

Trying to get Melanie to draft a decent executive memo would be less frustrating than this. I put the box on the kitchen counter and walk out, since there's no point in even talking to Kim at this point. I shouldn't have bothered. I shouldn't have even felt bad. I don't know why I softened...or cared about her reaction or feelings. Maybe it was the damned kiss. That messed with my head more than the games she's been playing with all those idiot heiresses or asking me for Dane's housewarming gift.

When I step out into the hall, I almost run into a neatly groomed guy in a suit. Unlike the other one she was hugging, this one looks older and more—how can I put it?—mature...? Certainly more successful, from the air of wealth and command around him.

Is this some new man Kim's going to hug...and more, since I'm not going to be around to interrupt?

Somehow, the very idea pisses me off. Not because I give a

shit about this man's herpes status, but because I just don't like Kim being near him. He's probably a player. And a dick. And even if he isn't, she shouldn't be hugging and...doing things with strange men, especially in the hall. Actually, she shouldn't do them at all, period, even in her own home.

Before I can figure out why I find the idea so distasteful, I say, "She's not interested."

The other guy frowns, his gaze flicking over me with the slight wariness of a person dealing with a possibly rabid dog...or a time bomb. "Great. I'm not interested either."

Haha. Yeah, right. "Who are you?"

"Her potential roommate."

What the fuck? But before I can say anything else, he slips inside and closes the door in my face.

I do my best to rein in an urge to kick the damned thing down. *Potential roommate?* Why in the world is she getting a male roommate? There are millions of women in the city looking for roommates...aren't there?

Something sour and ugly unfurls in my gut. It feels an awful lot like jealousy...but that can't be right. Probably ate something bad at lunch with David. There's no way it can be anything other than indigestion. The outrage I'm feeling right now is...is... *It's about setting a good example for Vi.* Right! What will she think if she sees Kim living with some guy she isn't even married to?

Since when did you become so medieval in your attitude?

Since I had a daughter. And I'm not *medieval*. I'm just...

I put a hand over my belly. I just have an upset stomach.

I'm absolutely not jealous.

29

KIM

NATE'S SUDDEN VISIT IS SURPRISING, BUT I SHOULD'VE expected it. He and Evie are having some issues, and even though Nate and I aren't super close, we do know each other. Nate's family is related to Salazar's by marriage. And I'm the one who helped Evie get a job with Nate in the first place, so he probably thinks I owe him some advice.

But it's okay. Helping Nate fix things with Evie will keep me distracted for a while. And it's hilarious he let Wyatt think he might become my roommate. I'm not looking for anyone, but Wyatt doesn't know that. And I don't want Wyatt to even possibly suspect I felt anything for him after our kiss.

So I give Nate what advice I can. But I'm no love doctor and I can't guarantee what I told him will mend things between him and Evie. Once he's gone, I sigh and turn away from the door, only to notice the box of chocolates Wyatt left behind.

The brand is familiar. It's one that Salazar likes—because his ex-wife-slash-current-girlfriend loves it—and Salazar has me order myself a box on my birthday every year. Just because he deigns to remember my birthday doesn't mean he's actually going to go to the trouble of getting me a gift himself. But I don't care. They're seriously the most intensely orgasmic truffles I've ever had. It's almost as good as the crème brûlée from Éternité.

Still, I feel like the box Wyatt brought is a nuclear warhead, armed and ticking. Not because I think he actually put herpes virus or rat poison in it. I'm feeling slightly guilty about having reacted that pettily earlier. What he said yesterday was uncalled for, but I didn't have to stoop to the same level and be a total bitch when he was trying to apologize.

It's just…it's hard to not get annoyed when he keeps swinging between nice guy and asshole. It keeps me off balance, and it's the worse when he acts like he's totally justified in his douchebaggery because of something I supposedly did. The thing is that no matter how I rack my brain, I can't think of what I could have done to cause it. Okay, so I paired him with one brainless heiress after another, but it wasn't like he didn't get me back for that. I still think he's using some kind of secret animal training to get his cat to leave me dead bugs. There's no other explanation when I'm not even the damn cat's owner! As a matter of fact, I found a spider carcass not even half an hour before he came by with the chocolate.

Maybe it's animal hypnosis…

There's a knock on the door. *Wyatt again?*

I inhale, trying to calm my conflicting emotions. I'm going to be a nice, reasonable person here. I can be mature. I *am* mature.

I open the door, only to come face to face with a beautiful, slim Asian woman. Her taut, smooth skin is milky white with a hint of gold, and her makeup is absolutely professional. Long, straight auburn hair cascades down her back. Something about her seems really familiar, though. Where have I seen her before?

"Hi," she says with a wide grin.

"Hi."

Champ sticks his nose out and tries to lick her, but I block him. *You can't just lick everyone who comes by.* He's a fabulous dog, but a little too friendly at times.

My gaze falls to the two large suitcases next to her. Oh no. Maybe she looks familiar because she's one of those door-to-door salespeople I've been ignoring. So what if she's carrying Louis Vuitton luggage? They're probably knockoffs.

"I don't buy things from drop-by salespeople," I say coolly.

"Cool. Me either." She continues to smile, looking like she expects me to let her in.

Nope. She needs to move on. Like...to Wyatt's place next door.

Finally, something dawns in her eyes. She glances at her luggage. "Oh, don't worry. They're not for sale. And even if they were, I don't know if you could afford them."

Huh? I cross my arms, feeling mildly insulted. *Lady, whatever you're selling can't be that expensive.* She's in a cheap T-shirt, jeans and no-name brand shoes. Snobbish, but I can't help myself from judging.

"Who are you and why are you here?" I demand.

"Mind if we talk inside?"

"Yes."

She sighs and appears slightly put out. "Court told me you'd be nice."

"Court...?" Does Salazar have another illegitimate son I don't know about?

"Harcourt Blackwood? He said he heard from Nate that you don't have a roommate anymore because Evie moved out."

Okay, so she isn't making stuff up. I know who Court Blackwood is, even if we've never been introduced. And it's no secret he and Nate are close.

But when did he—or Nate—become my real estate agent? I haven't even hinted to anyone that I was in the market for a new roommate.

She sticks her hand out. "I'm Yuna Hae. I know the name probably doesn't mean anything, but I'm Ivy's soul sister. That sort of makes me Court's sister-in-law, by the way."

"I know who Ivy is." The story of her and her husband, Tony Blackwood, is pretty well known—infamous, even. But...*Yuna Hae... Yuna Hae...* Where have I heard that name before?

Something clicks, and I snap my fingers. "Wait. Are you *the* Yuna Hae from the Hae Min Group?"

She nods with a small smile.

Holy shit. "Why didn't you say so?" I say, hoping she isn't offended I mistook her for a door-to-door salesperson. "Come on in."

The Hae Min Group is one of the biggest family-held multinational conglomerates in Korea, and Salazar has done business with them before. If she's here, it must be something important. I'm just not sure why she didn't have her people send me a message. That's the normal protocol.

On the other hand, I'm not going to tell her she's doing things wrong. Her father and brother are two of the more important people on Salazar's contact list. And I know enough about them to know that she's not to be messed with. Not because she actually does much at the Hae Min Group, but her father, the chairman of the conglomerate, overindulges her. I've heard rumors that Byron Pearce lost a deal with the corporation because Yuna didn't like him.

Damn it. Did I screw up? In my defense, I've never met her, and it's pretty unexpected for her to show up at my place, unannounced.

I help her bring her suitcases in and shut the door behind her.

Champ sniffs her and then—since I'm too far away to stop him this time—licks her, wagging his tail. She rubs his head and says something in Korean. "Your dog is adorable."

"Thank you. So...is there a reason you came by?" It must be something really important for her to find out where I live, then show up like this in person.

Yuna looks around, taking in the dining room, kitchen and living room like she's examining a hotel suite while the front desk manager waits to see if everything's to her liking. Finally, she nods. "This is great."

"Thank you," I say again, feeling increasingly confused. Surely she didn't come all the way here to compliment my apartment.

"You didn't get a new roommate yet, right?"

"No..." *Can you just get to the point?*

She claps her hands together. "Perfect! Can I be your roommate, then?"

What? This doesn't make any sense. Doesn't she have a suite waiting at the Ritz or the Four Seasons? Or maybe her English isn't as good as I assumed, based on the fact that she's speaking without an accent.

"Could you, um, say that again?"

She sighs. "I want to be your roommate, if you're okay with it. Please?"

"Aren't you staying at a hotel or something?" Maybe her assistant forgot, in which case I feel sorry for the person. But even then, it isn't like every top hotel in L.A. is full. As far as I know, there aren't any major conventions or events happening right now... *Oh no. Did Court tell Yuna she could stay with me?*

"The hotel? Ugh." She waves a hand. "Don't even bring that up. It's more like jail."

First time I've heard a suite at a five-star hotel compared to prison. But I wait for her to elaborate.

She gestures at my couch. "Is it okay if I sit down? I'm a little tired."

"Yeah, of course," I say quickly, feeling terrible as I realize I've been a crappy host. "Want something to drink?"

"Do you have wine?"

Nothing like what you're used to. None of the bottles I have cost over twenty-five dollars...at the most. "If you don't mind a California rosé...?" I offer after a moment of debate. If she really wants alcohol, cheap wine is better than nothing.

"Anything is fine," she says.

I pour two glasses and hand her one. She sips it without a hint of distaste or condescension. After finishing about half the glass, she says, "Do you know how hard it is to shake off the evil agents?"

A frisson of fear and concern travels along my spine. "Evil agents?" Is she being targeted by kidnappers or something? Shit.

"My mother's spies."

"Spies?" Yuna's English must be worse than I thought. She has to be misusing words.

"Mom assigned some people to follow me around. Spies."

"You mean, like...bodyguards?" I say, trying to correct her gently. I don't want her to get upset and ruin whatever business relationship my boss and his family have with the Hae Min Group.

She shakes her head. "Not bodyguards. *Spies.*" She speaks slowly, like she's talking to a child with a poor understanding of the world. "They report everything I do to my mom. They probably tell her how many times I go to the bathroom." After a moment, she adds, "How long I stay there, too."

My lips twitch. It can't be *that* bad. Her mom's probably just worried about her. It's actually sweet and cute.

"I finally had to go to this place called... What's the name again...? Oh yeah, *Walmart*. I had to go to Walmart to get myself a decent disguise."

"What disguise?" She's wearing normal clothes. And that hair can't be a wig. For one, I doubt Walmart sells them, and two, her tresses look too silky and real.

"This." She sweeps her outfit with her free hand. "I had sunglasses on, too. Put my hair up under a cap. Neither of Mom's spies realized it was me." A smug smile curves her red lips.

"Really?" That kind of cloak and dagger sounds like something from a spy novel.

"They were looking for somebody in Versace. I've been a little obsessed recently, although I'm getting bored with it now. Dior's new collection is really nice this year, don't you think?"

I just nod because I have no idea what Dior's new collection looks like. Yuna should talk to Jo if she wants to discuss that sort of thing.

"Anyway, I know it's really sudden, and it's a huge imposition. But I'm a great roommate," Yuna says. "I'm neat, and I can give you free piano lessons. Or I can play. I'll buy you a piano if you want."

Ugh, no. Most people who claim they can play are so awful that their "music" feels more like screws being drilled into your ears. Maybe Yuna has an inflated sense of how good she is. She's undoubtedly surrounded by sycophants.

Yuna laughs. "I can see what you're thinking. But I'm actually really good. I went to Curtis. You've heard of it, right? They offer you a full scholarship if you're accepted. Only the best of the best go. And I love dogs, so I can help you take care of this big guy. If you like parties, it's even better, because I throw the best parties. And I'll lend you my clothes. But not my shoes. I think sharing shoes is gross, don't you? Feet just aren't very hygienic in general. So what do you say?" She looks at me, her eyes bright. "I'll pay half the rent and utilities, obviously."

"Um... Look, I don't know. This is really sudden." Should I say yes? What if I get tangled up in some crappy family drama and get screwed in the process? But I don't want to upset Yuna, either. I need to find a delicate way to turn her down.

"It's just... I just don't want to get more dossiers to review," Yuna says with a forlorn sigh, the corners of her mouth drooping.

"Dossiers?" This really *is* starting to sound like a spy novel. Or maybe she's just got the wrong word...

She opens an outer pocket on one of her suitcases and pulls out a thick manila envelope. "Have a look."

I take it and pull out the papers inside. The first page has a picture of an impeccably groomed Asian man. There's a chart, which I assume it has stuff like his name and so on. I flip to the next page and stare at an enormous, detailed stock portfolio—ticker symbols, share price when acquired, share price at the moment, the number of shares and so on. "Wow. This is...thorough." It really *is* a dossier.

Yuna takes the document and starts flipping through pages. "Medical history. Family tree. High school and college transcripts. And so on and so on, blah blah blah. It's in Korean, but trust me. It's *all* here."

"Who is this man?" I ask, wondering why she has such private information about anyone.

"One of the guys my mother wants me to consider marrying. He's the oldest son in a cosmetics empire in Korea. It'd be a great merger, because Hae Min always wanted to go into cosmetics, but it's highly competitive, you know?"

Merger. Oh, man. I start to feel terrible for her. I thought only somebody like *my* mother would tell their children to marry rich. I always assumed rich parents didn't bother their kids with stuff like that. Why should a rich woman have to marry for anything but love? But...apparently not.

Yuna's case actually seems worse because she doesn't need a man's money or position. And unlike my mother, her mom is sending *dossiers*—it really is the only word—to review.

If Yuna just needs a break from having to deal with her matchmaking mom, I guess there's no harm in that. And maybe it'll force her mom to lay off a bit, especially since Yuna is obviously not interested in marrying any of the dossier men.

"Okay," I say. "You can stay here for a while."

She brightens. "Really? Thank you! You won't regret it! I'll be the best roommate you've ever had!"

Her enthusiasm makes me smile. For somebody with enough power and wealth to make some of the heiresses I set Wyatt up with look homeless, she's awfully easy to please. And I'm not sensing any entitled brat attitude. I just hope I'm not making a mistake by taking her in.

30

WYATT

POTENTIAL ROOMMATE.

I keep thinking about that guy. He's the right age. Seemed confident. Well dressed. And as much as I hate to admit it, he isn't that bad looking. Okay, fine, he's pretty. I can see a woman going for that.

Is he Kim's type?

The moment the question pops into my head, I force it out. Who the hell cares? More importantly, why should *I* care?

He said *potential* roommate. He didn't say he *was* the roommate. Kim will probably say no. Most women don't want to share a space with some guy.

Unless they're involved...

My phone pings with a text.

–Kim: For the wedding, we're going to keep our story simple. You and I met when you moved in next door. We started chatting and got close. We decided to date. And that's why we're going to the wedding together. If anybody asks, I'm fond of Vi.

Not what I thought she'd say after our...unpleasant encounter this evening. Can she actually fake it?

Another text from her pops on my phone.

–Kim: I expect you to memorize the story and play your part accordingly.

–Me: What about you? Can you handle it?

–Kim: You don't have to worry about me. I'm a professional.

Her disdain is palpable. I'm skeptical. Most women I know are terrible at hiding their feelings, especially when they include hate and contempt.

I'd feel a lot better if she'd just taken the damned chocolate with a smile. Regardless of her claim that she's a pro, I bet she was fuming about herpes the entire time she was texting me.

If the *potential roommate* hadn't shown up when he did, I might've turned around and tried to fix things. Or maybe gone back after dinner to have a calm, rational conversation. Might've even taken her a slice of the pecan pie Vi and I had, so Kim couldn't claim it's contaminated with a virus. Even she would have to admit I wouldn't give a piece of contaminated pie to my child...

The sound of a door slamming pulls me away from my thoughts. Normally I'd tell Vi not to slam doors, but I decide not to at the moment. I need to stop obsessing about Kim, the wedding and the guy, and it's a good interruption.

"Job done!" Vi says loudly, then washes her hands at the kitchen sink. Toweling them off, she adds, "By the way, did you know Kim got a roommate?"

What the...? The guy moved in that fast? He only just saw the place a couple of hours ago! "No..."

"Well...she did. We met in front of the garbage chute."

"Did you guys talk?"

"Yeah. I mean, just to say hello." She shrugs. "Seems nice enough."

"Appearances can be deceiving," I mutter. He's probably dirty-minded. A pervert.

"What?"

"Nothing. Are you finished with your homework?"

"There *is* no homework." She rolls her eyes. "We're on summer vacation starting tomorrow, remember?"

I clear my throat. "Right. I remember." I just got distracted by that roommate. Another mark against the man.

Maybe I should force him to move out. It'd be doing the entire floor a service. The guy looked slick, and people who look that slick are bad news. Just ask Dane.

Right. Because who does Dane think is good news?

Shut up. I've already decided. Nobody likes noisy neighbors. I go grab my toolbox and pull out some nails and a hammer.

Vi looks at me. "What are you doing?"

"Gonna nail this wall." I size up the one between our unit and Kim's.

"Uh... Why?"

"Hang some pictures."

"We don't *have* any pictures. Not to hang."

"Yeah, but later we will. This is prep. Being prepared is half of success."

Shaking her head, she goes into her room.

I start banging with more noise than necessary. And I don't stop with one. Why should I, when I have a box full of nails?

After I bang twelve or so into the wall, Vi comes out. "Dad, can you knock it off? It's after ten."

"So?" It isn't like she needs to go to bed early tonight.

"I didn't get good sleep last night, so I want to go to bed a little early. Besides, we have to go to Corn Meadows tomorrow, remember?"

Damn it. Why did she have to have a bad sleep yesterday? More importantly, why did Kim have to get a roommate?

But there's nothing I can do about either one, so I put away the tools.

Vi goes back to her room. I glare at the wall for a long time, telling myself I'm doing this to get a pervert out of the building, not because I care about him living with Kim.

31

WYATT

THE NEXT MORNING, VI AND I DRAG TWO BIG SUITCASES OUT into the hall and I lock the door. Since she's spending the summer with her grandparents, she insisted on taking everything she might possibly need. But knowing my parents, she'll probably end up buying even more luggage because they'll take her shopping and treat her to whatever she wants. Hopefully not more contouring products. Or makeup. Or anything else that she can use to "experiment."

I wish Vi was spending the summer here in L.A., but I also understand she misses her grandparents and her old friends. I don't want to create some weird competition of affection between me and the people she left behind in Corn Meadows. That's the kind of manipulation Geneva pulls constantly to see if she's the number one priority in your life, and Vi deserves better from me.

Despite my resolve to play it cool and unaffected, my gaze slides over to Kim's unit. Did she and the roommate stay up late, chilling? Hanging out? Breaking the ice?

Or did Kim do the responsible thing and go to bed early so she'd be ready for the drive to the wedding?

Like she could've slept through the ruckus you were making last night.

Yeah, but I stopped when Vi asked me to. It wasn't that late...

What the hell am I doing? Kim said she could be professional, and so can I. Besides, I'm the bigger person.

Kim's door opens, and she comes out with a black purse. She's in a scarlet fitted dress that does something amazing to her breasts, pushing them up until they're like flaming beacons I almost can't tear my eyes from. It also clings to her hips and ass, and that ass is amazing enough to bring about world peace and tame dragons. Her heels are a hot scarlet as well, and they increase her sex appeal tenfold.

At the same time, it's probably another dig at my "red isn't her best color" comment. Even though I said I was sorry, I know she didn't accept the apology. I don't think she considers anything out of my mouth sincere unless it's something insulting.

So I'm not apologizing again. Even if I do, she'll probably accuse me of sprinkling her seat with herpes. Or rat poison. Although... Since Vi's around, maybe Kim won't say any of it out loud. Just text me all her wild accusations.

Kim's gaze flicks in my direction. Is it me or is she checking out my chest and ass too? I took care to dress in my best suit and tie for the wedding. Not because I give a fuck about Geneva, but because I don't want anything to embarrass Vi. My kid's suffered enough from that horrible marriage—one of the biggest mistakes of my life.

"Hey, Kim!" Vi says with a big grin. "It's so cool you're riding with us!"

"I know!" Kim says with the same happy smile as we make our way to my car.

It's all I can do not to shake my head. I knew Kim was a great liar, but this is just more proof. I should film it so she can't ever claim she's an honest soul.

When I texted her this morning, she sounded anything but happy about sharing a car. She actually wrote, *I need my own wheels. Independence. You know you can't go anywhere without a car in that town.*

Except I don't know why she feels that strongly about it.

Faking It with the Frenemy

We're going to be there for the few hours that it's going to take to watch the ceremony, and then most likely skip the reception unless Vi really wants to go. Only when I mentioned it was something Vi was looking forward to did Kim relent. Actually, my daughter didn't care how many cars we took. She just wanted to ride with Kim, and I didn't want to be excluded when she's already spending the entire summer with my parents. She's my kid, damn it. But somehow she seems to be bonding with Kim better than me.

Must be a girl thing, I decide, even though a voice in my head says Vi never bonded this tightly with Geneva. But Geneva has always treated Vi like an unwanted pest, not caring if it hurt her feelings.

But that still doesn't explain why she's not bonding well with me.

You've been busy for a long time, my guilty conscience reminds me.

I spent a lot of time working to satisfy Geneva's need for more —more money, more comfort, more...everything. I thought if I made more she'd be satisfied, turn her attention from *things* to our daughter. It was a terrible miscalculation on my part. Something I never plan on repeating.

Now all I can do is take one day at a time with Vi. Someday she'll realize—and accept—that I love her to pieces, but please, God, let that day come sooner than later.

"You look great," Kim says to Vi. "I love the dress."

"I know! Josephine is fantastic," Vi says, flushed and a little breathless. "This is exactly the kind of thing I wanted."

"Thanks again for introducing us," I say, popping the trunk of my Audi and placing Vi's suitcases inside. Regardless of our unresolved bad feelings, I can admit that Kim's been incredibly nice and helpful to Vi.

For a moment Kim looks uncomfortable, then she clears her throat. "Don't mention it."

She starts to take a seat in the back, but Vi shakes her head. "You should take shotgun," she says.

"Oh, that won't be necessary." Kim's tone is extra sweet, but I know she's turning it down to avoid sitting next to me.

And that annoys me for some weird reason. Makes me want to tell her herpes isn't an airborne disease. I might, if Vi wasn't around.

"It's kind of cramped in the back," Vi says. "You'll be more comfortable in the passenger seat. I'm okay 'cause I'm shorter."

Still, Kim hesitates.

Enough of this. "We need to get going if we want to be in Corn Meadows in time for the wedding."

Vi gets an anxious look. "I don't want to be late."

That does the trick. Kim shrugs, says, "Okay," and takes the passenger seat.

Once everyone's settled, I start driving. Vi chatters about all sorts of things, her voice bubbly. I can't remember when she's talked so much, or in such an excited tone. When I try to get her to say something, it's like trying to pull a rabbit away from a hungry jaguar.

But she isn't talking to *me*. She's talking to Kim. And never once does Kim act like she's annoyed or bothered. Her patience with my kid loosens something in my chest. I realize I've been worried that Kim would act uninterested in Vi...like Geneva. Kim isn't passively making noises, either, pretending to listen. She's actually participating, asking Vi questions, offering up opinions and thoughts. And every time Kim says something, Vi lights up like it's Christmas. Gratitude mixes with relief and happiness. I owe Kim big—not just because she's going to the wedding, but because she put that joyful look on Vi's face.

Yeah, and doesn't that make Kim a hundred times hotter, too?

I frown. Of course... I mean, I *appreciate* her. She's being nice. Her smile is bright and sweet, the light in her eyes brilliant and irresistible. Anybody would find a woman like that attractive.

But not every woman as nice as Kim has a chest like that. Or a mouth like that. Or tastes like she does...

Shut up, *shut up*. I'm not going to think about the kiss with my kid in the car. And I'm certainly not going to get turned on when Vi's sitting right behind us.

"I'm super excited about spending the summer with my grandparents. They're awesome," Vi says. "They have the *sickest* farm. I love their goats and dogs."

"They have a lot of goats now?" Kim asks, although she can't possibly care about my parents' animals.

"Yeah. Like, ten. Didn't they before?"

"I think they had maybe two when I was in Corn Meadows." Suddenly Kim yawns, then blinks a few times, something I noticed some women do when they want to rub their eyes, but don't want to ruin their makeup.

"What's wrong?" Vi asks.

The anxiety in my kid's voice makes me hold my breath. *She's worried that she's finally boring Kim.* Everything inside me chills as I wait and pray Kim doesn't do or say anything that will hurt Vi. She's too sensitive.

"Sorry," Kim says with a small smile. "I didn't sleep very well last night. Seems that *someone* was banging on the walls."

Damn it. Now I feel like a dick. "I stopped," I say, even knowing it's a pretty feeble attempt. My effort *better* make the roommate want to move out. I don't want it to be in vain.

"Yeah, but then I couldn't sleep afterward because I kept wondering if it was going to start again." Kim's voice is extra saccharine.

"I'm sorry," Vi says before I can respond. "Dad was getting ready to hang some pictures that we don't have yet."

Oh, fuck me. I rub a hand over my face and avoid looking at Kim.

"Really?" Just from the tone of Kim's voice I know her eyebrows are raised high in her forehead. "Why would he do that?"

"Because being prepared is important to success."

The skin around my neck heats, and not even the cold air blowing from the AC vent can cool me down. Now I wish we'd taken two cars. That way I wouldn't have to listen to this. I sound like a loon. And I can't even offer anything to redeem myself, because Vi isn't saying anything I didn't.

She continues, "And I had to tell—"

"So, Kim! How's your new roommate?" But the second the question's out there, I wince. I do *not* want to talk about that guy.

On the other hand, it's less embarrassing to talk about the guy than to talk about how you tried to run him off with your banging.

"Seems fine so far. How did you know I got one?" Kim asks.

Is she kidding? Doesn't she remember I saw her *potential roommate* yesterday?

"I told him," Vi says. "She's so pretty and funny. I saw her yesterday."

Wait a minute. *She?*

I recall the man I ran into yesterday. He's as tall as I am, broad-shouldered and looks like he works out. Definitely not "so pretty."

Vi sighs longingly. "I want to have her body when I grow up."

I shudder with horror. "You don't need eighteen-inch arms."

"What?" Kim says. Vi's scowl in the rearview mirror shows confusion.

Am I the only sane person in this car? "I don't know what magic you performed to make that man look so pretty, but—"

Kim starts laughing. "Oh my God."

"What's so funny?"

"You! You think *Nate's* my roommate?"

"That's that guy's name?"

"She said her name was Yuna," Vi says.

What? "Who's Yuna?"

"My new roommate," Kim says. "Nate didn't work out, so I ended up with Yuna." Her demeanor is prim, but her lips are twitching.

Vi sticks her head through the gap between Kim's and my seats. Or at least tries to, as much as the seatbelt will let her. "I can't believe you thought she was a man! She's really pretty, Dad."

Well, now I feel stupid. But how was I supposed to know it was a woman? Or that Kim had multiple roommate interviews set up last night? "I ran into a candidate, and it was a man."

"Was he hot?" Vi asks.

"Vi!" I say, shocked. My kid's too young to care about that kind of stuff!

"He's nice. And very much taken," Kim answers. "He's in love with my former roommate."

The knot in my belly dissipates. If the woman seated next to me weren't Kim, I might've thought I was jealous or something.

But of course I'm not. You don't care about a woman who accuses you of giving her an STD and treats you like cholera. It's one of the unwritten rules of dating.

"Aww." Vi sighs.

"It's very romantic," Kim says. "And really, every woman should marry a man who not only loves her but treats her like a queen."

"Yeah. But he has to be hot, too!" Vi says, making my teeth grind together. She needs to stop with this *hot* obsession!

"That's a factor, but a small one," Kim says with a smile.

"No way!"

"You'll see I'm right when you're older." Kim's lips twist, but she turns her head so Vi can't see it.

Somehow I feel like the look on Kim's face was directed at me. Which is weird. But whatever. I need to not overthink all this and just get through the wedding. The objective is to give Vi the emotional closure she needs, not to obsess about this...weird interaction between me and Kim.

32

Kim

It takes half an hour longer than expected to reach Corn Meadows, thanks to a small fender bender slowing down the freeway traffic. Not that I mind the delay. The closer we get, the more I have to consciously relax to relieve the tension gathering in my neck and shoulders.

I've never wanted to come back to this horrible little place, home to so very, very few decent memories. The only reason my mother, with all her divorce money, even settled here in the first place was because she wanted to be a "person of importance," as she put it. And that wasn't going to happen in a big city like New York or Los Angeles.

If it weren't for the fact that I need to attend the wedding and get Wyatt to sell the statue, I'd never set foot here again. I've trashed every letter and brochure from my old high school, including the invitation to the latest reunion. I've asked more than once not to have them sent, moved without giving them my new address...but somehow the school finds me again. It's like a faucet that drips every so often, just enough to drive you crazy, but not seriously enough to call a plumber.

But then, nothing is logical and sane when you're dealing

with Corn Meadows. Even the town's name is ridiculous. No one grows corn here. The soil apparently isn't right for it, but the founders thought they could, and named the town after the crop they wanted to raise. If they'd been pecan farmers, the place would've probably been called Nutdale.

Nothing much has changed. Still the same old streets with the same old stores, like all the multinational conglomerates somehow missed Corn Meadows during their quest to build big-box stores in every town in America. Or maybe they thought it was too small to bother with. Either way, it feels weird, like I've been thrown a couple of decades back.

Maybe people are different now. As in, learned to mind their own business.

Hopefully. Ideally. I pray for that, even though part of me doubts that particular aspect of Corn Meadows has changed. The place doesn't even have a McDonald's. People are going to need some form of entertainment, and nothing entertains like gossip. It's free and in endless supply.

My phone pings. A text from Mom.

–Mom: OMG! I saw a picture of you and Wyatt in a brand-new Audi! Are you in town right now? I can't believe I'm in NY and going to miss it!

Oh, thank *God* she's in New York. I purposely didn't tell her about this visit because I knew exactly what she'd do. The last thing I want is for her to embarrass me in front of Wyatt, going on and on about how I need to marry him before my boobs deflate, because he's rich. And Vi! The poor kid's already going through the pain of her own mother's gold digging. She doesn't need to wonder if I'm around for the same reason, especially since it isn't true. And I'll be damned if I let anybody, especially Wyatt, think I'm into moneyed men the way my mother is. It's a matter of pride.

My phone pings again. This time Mom forwards me the picture. From the background, it's obvious it was taken maybe ten minutes ago. Gossipmongers move at 4G speed. Shouldn't Corn Meadows get fast food before fast Internet?

–Mom: This is so exciting!

–Mom: Look how wonderful you look in that car! People will hardly recognize you! I had to tag you on the photo so they'd know! I'm so proud of you!

She's only proud because I look good. And I'm in a car with a billionaire who is currently unattached. She hasn't gotten to that yet, but she will if I give her enough time. I really hope she'll disappoint me on this point, but I have a feeling she won't.

–Mom: Did you take an Audi because there's a child in the back?

–Mom: Next time, come in a Ferrari! Or a Maserati or Lamborghini! Italian sports cars are the best!

–Mom: On the other hand, I've always thought Bentleys were very dignified and upscale. Does Wyatt have one?

–Mom: He's single. A billionaire! Grab him before it's too late. He even has a child. It's like getting a ready-made family without the stretch marks. You do realize that sort of thing devalues a woman, don't you?

–Mom: You aren't as young as used to be! This is your chance!

The more she texts, the more bitterness fills my mouth. I feel my face twist. Not a single word of concern or worry. She knows Wyatt and I broke up years ago. She knows I was hurt, even though I never told her the exact details. She could at least ask if Wyatt is a better person now, or if he ever apologized for dumping me like that for Geneva. And Vi is not some mail-order kid I'm going to pick up to suit her inane fantasy of having a child without loose belly skin. The whole idea is gross, and the fact that my mother ever even thought it makes me more embarrassed and resentful. How come she's the one who says shameless things, and I'm the one who has to suffer the humiliation?

My silence must be spiking her anxiety. My phone rings, seeming louder than normal. I hit the red button.

It rings again. *Maybe I should take out the battery.*

"Go ahead," Wyatt says. "Sounds like it's urgent."

"It isn't." I put the phone on silent mode and smile.

"I don't mind," Vi says. "I'll even put my hands over my ears if it's, like, a secret or something."

Her earnestness makes me laugh a little. I shake my head. "Trust me. It really *isn't* that important." I turn to Wyatt. "Are we going to be on time for the wedding?"

"Yeah. It's not that far." Then he adds, "John's Orangery."

Geneva's a terrible human being, but I have to give her credit for decent taste. John's Orangery is the best place in Corn Meadows for an outdoor wedding. Despite the name, it doesn't have that many orange trees or the enclosed space for them. What it does have is an amazing garden—surrounded by small, rustic one-story white buildings—and a huge kitchen suitable for catering. Also, dressing suites for brides and grooms. A lot of girls growing up in Corn Meadows dream of getting married there.

But not me. I'll be dammed if I get married in this town. I don't know where I want to get married, but it isn't Corn Meadows. Nice as it is, John's Orangery couldn't pay me enough.

"Weird for her to pick the same place again," I mutter. Knowing Geneva's propensity for showing off, I can't imagine her having her first wedding anywhere but John's Orangery.

Wyatt glances over. "We didn't get married there. Just had a small private ceremony." His tone is flat, his eyes narrowed as he goes back to focusing on the road. "No money or time. It was...sudden."

Ah. Mom told me Geneva was getting married because of a surprise pregnancy way back when. Guess she's trying to live out her fantasy with her new groom. "Have you met the guy? The groom, I mean."

"Once, when he came to give her some moral support."

Wyatt doesn't elaborate, but I can guess the man must've been on Geneva's side during the divorce.

"He's"—Wyatt's mouth tightens, until his lips almost turn white—"interesting."

His tone says the guy's a fucking bastard.

"I haven't," Vi says. "I'm sort of looking forward to it."

She's a bad liar. I turn around and give her a smile, wanting her to know I've got her back her no matter how things go today. Besides, even though she might not agree, she's better off without a mother like Geneva. I'm biased, but it's obvious she doesn't care about her child. And Vi has to know, even if she doesn't want to admit it to herself. Kids always do—I know, from my own experience.

We reach the venue. The place is packed with more vehicles than I thought possible for a town like Corn Meadows. Did Geneva invite everyone she knows in the country?

As I climb out of the Audi, I spot a few vaguely familiar faces from my high school years. Just seeing them takes me back to one of the worst phases of my life, and I can almost feel hives breaking out over my skin. Feeling like I've just stepped in a fresh pile of goat poop, I ignore the sensation and grab my purse from the car.

"Kim? Hey, long time no see. Whoa, you're smokin' in that dress!"

I look over a shoulder and spot a tall, skinny guy. Dirty blond hair, dark brown eyes and a pointed chin. The suit on him looks awkward and poorly color-coordinated—and fits about like a child trying on his dad's outfit. But there's no mistaking that overeager and slightly over-the-top grin.

"Louis...?" Of all people, Geneva's twin isn't who I thought would come over and say hello first.

It isn't like I have any terrible history with him. Considering what's between me and Geneva, Louis's and my relationship, such as it is, is pretty benign. He did his best to tell me all the "pranks" Wyatt pulled on me, including the vibrator in my backpack disaster. But there's something new that sits uneasily in my belly for some reason. It annoys me I can't put my finger on precisely what's bugging me.

He's disloyal.

I almost flinch. But the thought doesn't go away. He was a bit too eager when he told me what Wyatt had done, even though he was supposed to be Wyatt's friend, not mine.

Faking It with the Frenemy

If he's anything like Geneva... She was my friend too, until she wasn't.

Louis's eyes dart to Wyatt and Vi. But he doesn't say hello to either of them.

The mayor of the city hurries over to Wyatt before he can get around the car to join me and Vi. Did Geneva invite him, too? He's a freak who doesn't age—he's always looked like a zombie—and he's been mayor ever since I can remember. He greets Wyatt effusively, and Wyatt responds with a polite smile. Guess he can't just ignore the mayor. Even if he doesn't live here anymore, his parents do.

"I had no idea you were still close to him." Louis jerks his chin toward Wyatt, sounding mildly disapproving. I'm surprised to find that it grates on my nerves.

Since I'm supposed to be a nice, subdued date who doesn't do things like make scenes, I put on a bland smile. "We live in the same city." I don't elaborate. I don't feel like revealing any more than I have to.

Louis moves closer, placing a hand on my shoulder. It feels damp through my dress, like mud, and I cringe at the unwanted contact.

As I start to shrug his palm off, Vi says, "Hi, Uncle Louis."

He gives her the annoyed look of a man who just got interrupted in the middle of an important football game. Vi's smile slips a notch.

What a dick. I pull away from him and step closer to Vi, placing an arm around her in silent support. *Don't believe the overly friendly appearance he's putting on. I'm not that close to him, kiddo.*

"Yeah?" he says roughly, glaring at the girl like it's her fault his palm isn't on my shoulder anymore.

"We aren't late for the wedding, are we?" she asks, her voice small.

"Do you hear the wedding march? No? Exactly," he snaps.

"Hey." I glare at him, pissed off at his nastiness, especially when I see how Vi flinches. "What's your problem?"

He looks shocked that I'm defending Vi. Just what kind of an entitled asshole has he become to think people are going to let him talk to a child like that?

Finally he gives me an awkward smile. "It's been a very stressful day," he says, as though that excuses his terrible behavior.

Subhuman trash. This isn't even his damn wedding, so what does he have to stress about? But then I decide he isn't worth my time. It isn't like Vi will be dealing with him much while she's staying with Wyatt's parents. Given Louis's attitude, he probably won't bother spending any time with her, even if he still lives around here. I just want to get this farce over with so Vi can have the closure she wants and move on, instead of wasting her mental energy on people who don't deserve it.

"Did Mom already change into her wedding gown?" Vi asks.

"Kind of has to," Louis says, rolling his eyes. "To get married."

It's obvious Vi wants to see the gown and maybe say hello before the ceremony starts. "Where's her dressing room?" I ask, doing my best to keep my voice level. I'd stick a stiletto into his head, but my shoes deserve better.

He gives me a bright, smarmy smile. "I can take you there."

The hopeful light in his gaze reminds me of a greedy little bully eying an ice cream sundae that doesn't belong to him. I suppress a shudder.

"That won't be necessary. Just give me directions and I'll go with Wyatt." I glance over my shoulder. Wyatt's still speaking with the mayor. Is that vampire trying to get him to contribute to his political campaign? I can't imagine any other reason for him to be yammering on and on into Wyatt's ear. And it's about time he ends the pointless conversation and comes over.

Louis frowns. "You think that's a good idea? Geneva's very sensitive."

Sensitive like a T-rex. And I don't care if seeing Wyatt upsets her. If his presence is that objectionable, she shouldn't have invited him. "I think it's a *very* good idea." I smile thinly.

Louis shoots Vi an evil look, obviously blaming her that I'm not leaving with him. "Maybe after the wedding we can hang out...and, you know..."

Hell fucking no. "Yeah, maybe," I say, only because I don't want to tell him what I really think in front of Vi.

Faking It with the Frenemy

"Come on. I can give you a ride back home."

I'd rather eat a frog-topped ice cream sundae. "It's really far. I live in L.A.," I say, hoping he'll get the hint. It's a good three hours away, even without traffic.

"I don't mind." Louis winks a few times, which makes him look like he's trying to get rid of lint in his eye without using his hands. He leans in like he's going to give me some *sotto voce* gossip. "And why would you want to hang out with a guy who gave you herpes, am I right?"

Shock paralyzes me. I can't even speak. Finally, I manage to croak out, "What?" Did he somehow hear about the things Wyatt told me while we've been neighbors? But that doesn't make sense. Wyatt said I was going to give it to Hugo. He never said anything about giving *me* herpes.

Before I can probe, Vi says, "What's herpes?"

She overheard. "Nothing," I say, glaring at Louis.

He starts to back away. Maybe my death glare is working. Then I feel Wyatt's hand at my elbow. Louis is now at least two yards away.

"The ceremony's being held up a little," Wyatt says. "Apparently the groom needs some more time." Displeasure is evident in his narrowed eyes. I don't think he particularly cares about Geneva's happy ending, but more about giving Vi what she needs. "Oh, hey, Louis," Wyatt says. His words are friendly, but his tone is cold. Guess they aren't that close anymore. Even without the divorce, the way Louis talks to Vi would be hard to overlook.

"Hey, Wyatt. Looking good, man."

"You too." Wyatt's smile widens. "That tie is inspired."

I bite my lip, trying not to burst out laughing. Louis's tie is a sickly neon yellow, and it clashes horribly against the dark charcoal of his suit.

"It's from an ex. I'm still friendly with her," Louis says, looking from me to Wyatt. "Sign of a man's maturity, when he can get along with his exes."

Oh, please. His ex hates his guts if she gave him that tie. He probably needs good insurance to pay for anti-delusion meds.

I loop my arm around Wyatt's and lean closer to him, like

we're super tight. I know he's my enemy and we're just faking it. But Wyatt seems a thousand times safer than creepy Louis.

"Let's go," I say, reaching out to hold Vi's small hand.

We walk away from Louis. Wyatt pulls his arm from mine, and for a moment, it seems like he doesn't want me touching him at all or thinks I went too far. But then he puts it around my waist, pulling me closer. Although the sun's warm and pleasant on my skin, the heat from Wyatt's body is warmer and more pleasant. Actually, more than just pleasant. Body-tingling good. Making-my-breath-uneven good. It reminds me of the kiss...and how he felt when he took my mouth, pressed into me...

Stop thinking about that! He isn't doing this to seduce you. It's just for show, remember?

I need to think about something else. Anything but how my body's reacting to his nearness, his scent, his heat...

"I want to say hi to Mom," Vi says suddenly. "Can we go to her room?"

Wyatt nods. "Yeah. The dressing rooms are over there." At my questioning look, he adds, "I was here once for a friend's wedding."

He leads us to one of the squat white buildings. They have open hallways that exit directly out to the green field that forms the center of the orangery. We knock on the double door. It opens, revealing a bridesmaid. The pink fairy-princess dress is a dead giveaway. That and the fact that it's Abigail Madison, who replaced me as Geneva's best friend after Wyatt and I broke up.

Abby hasn't changed at all. Her slightly narrow-set green eyes are still mouse-beady, and her nose is still hawkish. The combination was jarring in high school, and it's even more jarring now because her makeup sharpens her features until they look almost feral.

"You." Her tone says she's just encountered something unpleasant. Should've expected that, since she was a card-carrying member of Torment Kim Club when we were in high school.

"Hello," I say with a smile that's faker than a spray tan.

"What are you doing here?" Abby demands.

Putting on the bored "I'm a billion times superior to you"

expression I've seen on Salazar's face too often to count, I tilt my head in Wyatt's direction. "I'm his plus-one."

She puts her hands on her hips. "So that photo was actually real."

For a moment I wonder what she's referring to, then I remember the one Mom texted me earlier.

Geneva pops up behind Abby, then comes forward, pushing her out of the way to take center stage. "So, you're an escort now?"

I'm torn between sighing with resignation and smacking her hard enough to knock the ridiculously large tiara from her coiffed and bleached platinum hair. In a blindingly white designer gown, she should look bridal, but there's an ugly sneer on her red lips... and an empty coldness in her eyes, which are currently dark blue, thanks to colored contacts. I doubt they went from hazel to that unnatural shade on their own.

"Geneva, be nice," Wyatt says.

She rolls her eyes. "'Be nice, be nice,' always so bossy and annoying. You know she's only here because of your money. Nobody cared about you. They still don't. They just like your bank account now."

"Sort of like why you're marrying an old man," Wyatt asks. "Or do you just love that pale, saggy skin?"

Oh my God. Go, Wyatt!

"It's totally different. Don't be jealous."

Like we're going to be jealous of her becoming somebody's trophy wife. But then, the whole point of the wedding and inviting everyone—even Wyatt, her ex-husband—is about making everyone envious. I know her too well to suspect any other motive.

She sneers at me. "Gold digger."

Oh, for God's sake. I inhale, ready to ream her. "You're—"

"Mom...?" Vi's voice is small, but it stops me better than a shout.

Shame is immediate and scalding. *What am I doing?* There's a child watching, and this isn't about me putting Geneva in her place. This is about Vi.

Geneva looks down. "Well! I thought you weren't coming."

"Of course I wanted to come. It's your wedding." Vi's smile is tentative as she looks up at Geneva.

"Your *father*"—Geneva's voice grows pointed—"told me you were too busy and important. I wanted you to be part of the ceremony."

My jaw tightens. It's the same kind of manipulation my mom would always use. Worked, too, until I got out on my own. An urge to defend Vi pushes at me, but I keep my mouth shut, since I have no idea what was said between Geneva and Wyatt.

"That *isn't* what I said," he protests. "I said—"

"I don't mind helping," Vi says. "I mean, if it's not too late."

Geneva's sneer grows nastier, and my heart starts to break for the kid. This isn't going well. As a matter of fact, nobody should've ever thought it would give her any kind of closure. Geneva has always been a selfish bitch, incapable of empathy. The only thing she cares about is what she wants.

"Well, it *is* too late. I don't need you now, so just...go take a seat. You can have some cake afterward." She crosses her arms and studies Vi with a vaguely dissatisfied look. "Or maybe not. Have you put on weight?"

My hands itch with a murderous desire to strangle her with her own veil. Except that wouldn't solve the problem. "Vi looks fantastic just the way she is," I say, gently squeezing the poor kid's trembling shoulder.

"That's a real compliment coming from you, Scarface," Geneva says.

"Not just me. Josephine Martinez thinks so, too. You've heard of her, right? The one who dresses all the important people in Los Angeles?"

Geneva expression rapidly goes from surprised—showing she has heard of Jo—to stricken. I guess she couldn't get on Jo's client list.

I give her a smile full of teeth. "You might be interested to know that Jo chose Vi's outfit *personally*. Said she's never had a client so delightful and lovely to shop for." Okay, she didn't really say that, but Geneva doesn't need to know. And besides, this little lie is for a good cause. Vi needs something to bolster her self-esteem at the moment.

Wyatt tightens his arm around me for a second, silently communicating his thanks. I appreciate his gratitude and support, but even without it, I'd still be defending the hell out of Vi.

"Anyway, we'll be going, since you're too busy to be nice to your guests," I say.

Just then, Abby's shrill voice comes from behind Geneva. "Oh my God, then just find him the old-fashioned way." I lean to my right and see her on the phone. "Well, search the damn buildings! We can't go ahead without the groom."

Geneva's face turns red, and she slams the door in our faces.

"Guess the groom's missing," I say.

Wyatt grunts, the sound eloquently communicating that he doesn't give a fuck.

"Maybe he just went to the bathroom," Vi says.

Sweetie, nobody stays in a bathroom this long...unless he's puking his guts out over the dawning horror that he's marrying a sociopath. "Could be. He might've eaten some bad shrimp or something."

"More like he's hiding somewhere, getting drunk," Wyatt mutters just loud enough for my ears.

"Maybe we should look for him," I say, even though I don't really want to. But the wedding can't start without the groom. And with every passing second, Geneva's going to feel more and more upset. Then she's going to lash out at everyone. Vi doesn't need more nasty attacks from her own mother today. She's suffered enough.

"Let's not." Wyatt's tone says he'd rather have the groom vanish forever and leave Geneva humiliated.

I don't blame him, especially after her nastiness. Usually people mellow out as they mature, but somehow that hasn't happened with Geneva. She's just gotten worse.

"Do you want to stay here any longer than we have to?" I whisper, hoping Wyatt says no. Maybe he wants to catch up with his old buddies in town. He must be an object of admiration—maybe even envy—after his billion-dollar deal with Sweet Darlings. And I just want to get out of here.

His face still says he'd rather leave the groom finding to someone else.

Fine. I suppress a sigh. Never let it be said I'm not accommodating. "Okay. Why don't you go get Vi settled somewhere? I need to use the bathroom, then I'll join you."

Wyatt nods. "We'll be over there." He tilts his chin toward the field, where the altar and chairs are set up.

I watch them walk off, then start toward one of the four smaller buildings in the orangery. I spot a huge pink and white truck with a logo that says *Bobbi's Sweet Things* in a bubbly font. Must be the baker. Is the cake big enough to fill the entire back of the vehicle? Might be, knowing Geneva's vanity.

I hope the cake is freakin' awesome, because I'm going to let Vi have as much as she wants. The hell with Geneva and her judgmental attitude. Vi deserves all the dessert she can eat.

I soon realize I should've asked for directions, because there doesn't seem to be a map or information about where anything is located. The two small buildings I've been to already actually don't have bathrooms.

"Crap," I mutter as I head to another building. I don't really have to go right now, but I'd rather not get up in the middle of the ceremony, especially since we don't know when it's going to start. How the hell do you lose your groom on the day of? You'd think Geneva would've superglued him to the altar.

During my search, I walk past several former high school classmates. They gawk like they can't believe their eyes, but I ignore them, preferring to wander without directions. Every one was a member of the Torment Kim Club, and would be more likely to send me into a booby-trapped minefield than a bathroom. And I have no illusions that they've changed for the better after having seen Abby and Geneva.

Nothing that looks like a bathroom in this building, either. This is stupid. Surely the orangery doesn't want people peeing in the bushes.

Annoyed, I start to stalk through the open hallway, then stop. *What was that?*

I listen for a moment. There's another moan, like somebody's in great pain, coming from one of the rooms to my left.

Worried, I move toward the noise. Another groan, trailing off into a kind of whine. The sound is somewhere between a pig

Faking It with the Frenemy

about to get butchered and a cow giving birth, farm noises I never want to hear again.

Is someone having a heart attack? Isn't Geneva's groom supposed to be old? He could be dying in there, without anybody knowing. He might need CPR or even an ambulance.

I turn the knob. The door opens easily enough. I stick my head inside. "Is everything oka—"

"What the *fuck*?" A loud, high-pitched shriek pierces my eardrums like a needle.

The scene practically slaps me in the face. Some old dude, black slacks down around his ankles, is screwing someone in a bridesmaid's dress. But not Abby. It's a blonde.

One thing is immediately clear. I really don't need to see his saggy ass.

He whips around. "You!" he says, eyes wide.

"Churchill?" What the hell is he doing here? Isn't he supposed to be getting married soon? Salazar is planning to send him a ten-thousand-dollar Amazon gift card for the wedding.

Shock rings in my head like a gong, and I stay frozen for a moment. And then it happens. *I see his post-sex dick.* It looks like a half-filled albino sausage.

I need to bleach my eyes. *Now.*

"Shut the door, you bitch!" the woman screams. "Someone's going to *see!*"

Right, and yelling like that is the best way *not* to attract attention, especially in a building that opens onto the central field. I can already hear footsteps coming up behind me.

Somebody pushes me away from the door. I stumble, then feel an arm wrapping around my waist, preventing a total fall. I look up to see Wyatt holding me.

Geneva blows past me in her wedding gown. Schadenfreude wars against sympathy within me. She doesn't deserve to be happy after the way she attacked Vi earlier, but this level of humiliation should probably get at least a wince all the same.

A crowd is gathering behind her.

"Where's Vi?" I ask Wyatt urgently. She doesn't need to see this.

"Hanging out with some of her friends." He gestures at the field behind him, where the chairs are set up for the ceremony.

I sag with relief. But that only lasts a few seconds. Geneva marches forward aggressively.

"Churchill! What is the meaning of this?" she demands, her arms flinging around like windmills. "This is supposed to be our *wedding day!*"

"Yes, I know." He straightens, pulling his pants up and zipping up the flies.

My jaw almost hits the floor at his ballsiness. The crowd holds its collective breath, titillation palpable. Many—actually, most—of them are holding up phones to film the drama.

"We're supposed to be faithful and true to each other!" Geneva screeches.

"And of course we will be, dear. But we haven't exchanged vows yet."

Face, meet palm. I've always known he's a dick, but this sinks him to a whole new level of assholehood.

"Nobody would've known if it weren't for her." He tilts his chin in my direction.

If he thinks he can deflect the blame on to me, he has another think coming. "If you hadn't cheated on your wedding day, there wouldn't be anything to know," I say coldly.

Suddenly, Geneva whirls around to face me. "It's all your fault, you bitch! You never, ever wanted me to have anything nice! You always pretended like you were so good, but we all know you're just a jealous cunt!"

Oh boy. I'm torn between incredulous laughter and the urge to smack her a few times. She must've been living in a fantasy, because I've never, ever been jealous of her, of all people. Unless she's confusing contempt and distaste with jealousy.

"Shut up, Geneva," Wyatt says.

Thanks for speaking up, but really the wrong tack to take here, I think, wondering how he could not know this. Now she's going to think she's being persecuted.

Geneva's face turns bright red. "*You* shut up! It's disgusting how you gang up against me! This is why I had to leave you. Because no matter what I do, you're always defending her!"

"When did I do that?" Wyatt says, utterly confused.

He probably said something that wasn't mean about me, and that made Geneva think he's against her.

Geneva rushes out. Churchill rolls his eyes and follows her, doing up his pants. Wyatt and I go as well. Well, I think Wyatt is chasing her to get the answer to his question, while I'm going because I really don't want to be stuck in a room where Churchill just had sex. The place is likely contaminated with who-knows-what and needs to be disinfected by the CDC. Twice.

Out in the field, Geneva maneuvers through the chairs. Guests who hadn't followed her to the room start to stand and gather, apparently sensing a scene about to unfold.

I scan the area and see Vi with a group of girls on the far side. When she makes eye contact, I wave. *Stay there, kiddo. Don't come any closer.*

"You asshole! I hope you fucking choke on this!" Geneva reaches for the giant ivory and pink five-tier cake.

Hopefully she isn't going to try to throw it at Churchill. The cake's way too big for her to pick up.

Suddenly a woman large enough to play an Amazon warrior in *Wonder Woman* steps between Geneva and the marvel of bakery art. "Stop!" she says. "I have to upload the pictures to Instagram."

Geneva tries to reach around her, but the woman handles her easily. "I don't care about Instagram!" Geneva stamps her feet.

"Hey, I'm posting the pics, no matter what. It's in the contract. You can't destroy the cake until after."

Even without any contractual stipulation, Geneva shouldn't waste the cake on Churchill, period. It's too beautiful. Looks tasty, too.

"I hate you! You've ruined *everything*!" she screams at me and Wyatt, her face mottled even through the makeup.

I watch her unravel, unable to decide if I'm pettily pleased or sad. If she actually loved Churchill, I might feel some sympathy, despite our ugly history. But knowing what I know about him, I doubt it was his personality that won her over. And since she can't spare a single kind word to anybody, even her own child, sympathy isn't exactly welling up within me

"You just can't let me be happy!" Geneva continues. "You spineless, dickless asshole! She said you gave her *herpes*! Don't you have any pride?"

I... *What*?

Wyatt stiffens. "How the hell do you know that?"

I swivel my head toward him. What is this? And how come *I* didn't know about it?

"Because *I* sent the fucking text!" She's yelling so hard that she's actually spitting. "You're so goddamn stupid you didn't even realize it wasn't from her!"

My gaze jumps back and forth between the two of them. Wyatt looks like he just got sucker-punched.

"What is going on?" I demand, furious. If there's anything I hate more than drama, it's drama that I didn't even know I was participating in. The sunlight hits all those raised phones, all those pairs of California sunglasses, and disgust wells up inside my chest. There's a Facebook group for this stupid town, and everything that happens here is undoubtedly going to be on it. For all I know, it's being broadcast live so everyone can gossip.

But you know what? I just don't have any fucks to give. It isn't like I did anything wrong, and my employment contract doesn't come with a morality clause.

"You wish you had that brat with her, don't you?" Geneva keeps on screeching at Wyatt, ignoring me.

I feel my face harden as I realize who she means by "brat." I can't see Vi right now, not with every adult standing up to watch the shit hitting the fan, but I hope she's too distracted with her friends to hear it. Better yet, she found the bathroom I couldn't and isn't around to witness this horror show.

Wyatt glares at her. "Shut up, Geneva."

"That useless thing *ruined* my figure. I'll never be able to un-stretch my belly. But I got the best man I could, and you still had to wreck *everything*! I can't go through with this now because everyone saw what happened in that room, and who's going to pay for all...this?" Tears in her eyes, she gestures at the venue— from the guests to the flowers to the cake.

For the briefest moment, I feel almost sorry for her, for sinking so low that she thought marrying a man who cheats on her on their wedding day would be okay as long as people didn't know about it.

Wyatt looks terrible...murderous. He might actually throttle her if it wasn't for all the witnesses. He takes a step toward her, but then stops and turns. I turn as well and see Vi. Her face is colorless, and tears are glistening in her wide eyes.

Now *I* want to murder Geneva.

Praying desperately she didn't hear what her mom said, I run to Vi and put my hands over her ears. I wish I could go back in time and take her away from the scene so she'd miss all the horrible things her mom said. And I'd ignore the noises Churchill was making so he and Geneva got what they deserved —each other.

Sighing softly, I hope that despite the wedding being cancelled, coming to Corn Meadows gives Vi some closure. But even with everything going on, I can't help coming back to what Geneva said about herpes and the text.

33

KIM

Wyatt and I take Vi away from the orangery. Our steps are hurried as more yelling and obscenities fly behind us. Vi doesn't resist, but stumbles along like a rag doll. And that makes my heart ache more than her screaming or throwing a tantrum ever could.

I sit next to her in the back of the car as Wyatt drives to his parents' home. We don't say anything. Vi's lips are pressed tight and she's blinking hard, as though that will hide the tears gathering in her eyes. I hold her cool, limp hand in mine, unsure what to tell her to make it hurt less. But there are no words to take away the pain she's feeling.

Wyatt's parents come out the moment we pull into their driveway. A plaid shirt and worn jeans stretch over his father's tall and now comfortably rounded body. He has less hair than I remember. His mother is in a long house dress that flows around her like a cloud as she moves hurriedly. Their expressions are tight. Guess they saw the videos. Geneva's wedding has to be the biggest event of the summer for this town, if not the year.

But as Vi climbs out of the car, they smooth their faces and paste on big smiles.

"You're here!" Mr. Westland says, picking Vi up.

Mrs. Westland pats Vi on her back, then hugs Wyatt. Finally, she turns to me. "How are you, Kim? We haven't seen you in ages."

That about sums it up. If I had it my way, we would've never seen each other again, since I wouldn't be back in Corn Meadows. But I'm grateful she seems to know what to do with Vi. And despite my and Wyatt's falling out, these folks were always nice to me. I give her a small smile. "Hello, Mrs. Westland. Mr. Westland."

"Jenna and Pat. You aren't in high school anymore," she says. "Come on in. I was just making some lemonade. Want some?" Even though she's supposedly speaking to me, her gaze is on Vi.

There's no reaction from Vi, and the light in Jenna's face dims. But smoothing things out is one of my numerous duties at my job—and I'm damn good at it. "I'd love that. Wouldn't you, Vi?"

She nods a little, even though she's still looking down. I should've shoved Geneva's face into the damned cake before leaving.

We all go into the house. Nothing much has changed. The sofa is worn but comfortable. The dining table is huge, the surface slightly scratched from years and years of use. The interior feels homey, and nothing about it indicates the sudden exponential jump in their son's wealth. I admire and slightly envy that. If it were my mom, she would've not only upgraded her home but would've made sure to let everyone know about her change in circumstances.

Wyatt and Pat take Vi's suitcases upstairs, while Vi and I follow Jenna to the kitchen. She pours us fresh lemonade, and Vi sips it quietly. There's none of her earlier bubbliness, and it upsets me that she's so miserable. I didn't think she'd be able to make up with Geneva, but I thought she'd maybe accept how things are with her mom, rather than pining over a mother-daughter relationship she doesn't have. I used to be like that too, and I wasn't happy until I accepted that people will never change for me, no matter how much I wish it were otherwise.

Soon Wyatt and Pat join us. Jenna tilts her head at me, and I nod and follow her out to the garden. I'm certain she wants to talk about the ceremony.

"I saw what happened," she says. "The wedding. It's all over our Facebook group."

"Yeah, a bunch of people had their phones out." The busybodies of Corn Meadows never rest.

"There's a thread where Geneva started to brag, and everyone posted videos in the comments..." Jenna shrugs.

Figures. That's totally Geneva. She obviously considered Churchill the ultimate matrimonial prize...until he stuck his stick shift into somebody else when he should've been parked at the altar.

"I don't suppose Geneva controlled herself very well." Jenna's tone says she wants me to contradict her, even though she's certain I won't.

"She really lashed out." I let out a sigh. It's infuriating there's nothing to be done about it...or her. "Vi's going to need some comfort and reassurance from you and Pat."

Jenna's mouth firms. "Well, we'll give her all the love she needs. I still find it unbelievable Geneva managed to create something as wonderful as Vi."

I nod. There's nothing redeemable about Geneva. "Was she better with Vi when she was younger?" I ask, unable to contain the curiosity. I just don't understand why Wyatt would marry her otherwise.

"No. Never."

Poor Vi.

"Wyatt would've never married that she-devil if she hadn't gotten pregnant. I wonder if it really was an accident," Jenna says.

Holy... That's a pretty serious thing to doubt...and explains so much about Jenna's unhappiness. Although she called Geneva a "she-devil," it's obvious that isn't quite the word she really wanted to use. "Why?"

"Because I'm pretty sure he was about to dump her. Who could put up with her for long anyway?"

Not many people. But I'm surprised she went that far to keep him. Was she in love with him?

Does it matter? Look how hateful she is to him and their child now.

The door behind us opens, and Pat comes out, letting out a long sigh. "I need a beer."

"What's wrong?" Jenna asks.

"She's upset, and Wyatt doesn't seem to know how to comfort her. Not that I blame him, because I don't either. Geneva's lucky I wasn't there at the wedding."

Guess it's about time Vi lets it all out. It'll probably good for her to do that, rather than letting it fester silently inside. But of course Wyatt's clueless about how to deal with this. He was raised by two normal and very loving parents. He's never going to quite understand what she's feeling right now.

"Why didn't *you* try to fix it?" Jenna asks.

Pat stares at his wife as though she just accused him of being an ax murderer. "You think I know how when her own daddy doesn't?"

"You're her grandfather…"

While they bicker, I slip into the house and follow the murmured conversation coming from the living room. Vi and Wyatt are seated on the sofa, and she's looking at the tips of her shoes. I want to reach out and hug her until there's a smile on her face again.

"Of course it isn't the same. Why would I?" Wyatt says, utterly bewildered.

"Because you lived together for so long. That means you like the same things." Vi kicks her left foot, then stops abruptly. "And don't like the same things."

"Honey, that's not always the case. And if you haven't noticed, we aren't together anymore," he says.

"Because she left you. Just like she left me." Her chin trembles a little. "For him," she adds in a voice as small as mosquito buzzing.

Oh no. Empathy swells, making it hard to breathe. My mom did the same. Although she never remarried after Husband Number Five left her for a younger and perkier trophy, it wasn't for lack of trying. Dating new, rich men always came before me, even if it didn't lead to the engagement she was hoping for.

And Geneva hasn't proven herself any better than my mom. Instead of providing Vi with some closure, the clusterfuck of a wedding has given her even more of a complex. Now she thinks she's worth less than that idiot Churchill.

"Vi," I say, walking toward her. "Your mother didn't leave you. She *lost* you. There's a big difference."

Vi jerks her head in my direction. "How?"

"Haven't you ever picked something...only to regret it later? Maybe ice cream or a dress or makeup?" I squat in front of her, so she can see my face without having to crane her neck. I want her to be able to look down at me, and hope that the position makes her feel more in control.

She nods.

"Okay. So your mom decided to pick Churchill over you...but look what happened today. He betrayed her. Right? You understand that?"

"Yeah."

"So now she doesn't have him. But she also can't go back to how things were with you and your dad. She already did too much...hurt you too much." I pause to let it all sink in. "Can you ever forget what she said to you?"

I wait for her to process, while holding her hand gently in mine. These are things I wish somebody had told me back then when I was hurting. Even though I never had anyone to hold my hand and make it better, I'm glad to be able to do it for her.

Vi hesitates, then finally shakes her head.

"You're worth more than you can ever know, Vi. Think how much your grandparents care about you and love you. Think about how your dad loves you."

She continues to look down, then finally asks in a slightly louder voice than before, "How about you?"

The vulnerable question hits me harder than a tight fist in the chest. I swallow a hot lump in my throat and smile. "Of course I care about you, Vi." I run the pad of my thumb over her knuckles. "You're one adorable young lady."

She nods slowly, then finally lifts her chin. A smile would make me feel better, but this is enough for now. It'll only make things worse if I push too hard.

She slowly leans forward and wraps her arms around me. "Thank you, Kim."

Something as warm and sweet as caramel spreads in my chest. I place a soft kiss on the crown of her head. "It's my pleasure, kiddo."

34

WYATT

IF THE FACEBOOK UPDATES ARE TO BE BELIEVED, GENEVA totally lost it after we left, and she ended up falling into the giant cake while yanking the hair of the woman Churchill screwed. But the baker did manage to put up a bunch of Instagram pictures she took before the destruction by Bridezilla. Fucking priorities.

I push the gas harder, wanting to get the hell out of Corn Meadows as soon as possible and leave the damned wedding behind. I'm pretty confident that Vi's going to be okay, especially after that talk with Kim. My parents will make sure.

My eyes slide over to the passenger side. Kim's been quiet, checking her phone. I don't know details of her job, but she probably has to check in once in a while to make sure her boss is having a good time in Europe. And that he's finding his way home properly. Dane mentioned his parents were coming home this weekend the last time we spoke. It's was earlier than scheduled, but apparently his mom misses her grandkids.

"Thank you," I say, once we're finally on the freeway back to L.A.

Kim lifts her head from the screen, then puts the phone in her purse. "For what?"

Faking It with the Frenemy

"Talking to Vi. I'm terrible at figuring out what to say to her."

"It was nothing. I just didn't want to see her hurt because of Geneva. She doesn't deserve that." Kim pauses for a moment. "By the way, can we talk about what Geneva said about herpes?"

"Sure," I say, even though the topic makes me squirm a little. But we need to get this resolved.

Judging from Kim's reaction earlier, she didn't know anything about the text. And it's pretty clear my harpy ex-wife not only engineered it, but hid it from everyone...including me. If it weren't for the wedding imploding in her face, she might've never lost her cool enough to admit it out loud.

"What did she mean by how I accused you of giving me herpes? When did that happen?" Despite her neutral tone, her gaze is intent on my face, and I swear my cheek's about to be laser-burned.

"After we, uh, slept together." Embarrassment heats the skin around my neck. But she deserves the full truth. "You remember you were gone from school for a couple of weeks right after? You sent me a text saying that you got herpes from me and had to get treated."

She jerks like she's been cattle-prodded. "*What?* I couldn't go to school because I got the flu! And I never texted you anything about herpes. I *think* I would remember something like that!"

My shoulders tighten. "Yeah, I kind of didn't believe you had the flu."

"Why on earth not?"

"Because I didn't get sick. I figured I should've gotten it too, since we'd had sex and all. And the text, well... It came from your phone."

"Well, I certainly didn't—" Kim suddenly goes quiet. "Oh...*shit*. Mom said Geneva came by to drop off some handouts. And I was asleep some of those times."

"So it's possible she used your phone to text me..."

"And then deleted the text afterward to hide the fact that she'd sent it."

Wow. Now I feel gullible. I should've confronted Kim back then. Instead I just—

"So that's why you dumped me and started dating Geneva?"

Dancing naked on national TV would be easier than this. "Yeah. She was there, and I just...didn't know what to say to you. I was too young to..." I rub my forehead. "You were my first, Kim. And I thought I was half in love with you at the time. When I got that text...it just wrecked me. I typed out a hundred responses, but deleted them all because I thought they made me look stupid."

Kim says nothing.

Every inch of my skin prickles. I shift in my seat, trying to get more comfortable, but it isn't working.

"I had no idea," she says. "Did anyone else know about the herpes thing?"

"No. Never told a soul." The words tumble out fast. I don't want her to believe I spread any rumors.

"I just wondered. Everyone was so mean to me after...you know."

Jesus, that makes me feel even worse. I knew Geneva and she had some kind of falling out, and wondered if it was because of me. But Geneva swore it had nothing to do with me. Just "Kim being a bitch." I didn't realize other people were nasty to her as well. Maybe Geneva was right when she told me at the beginning of our relationship that I could be a little oblivious.

"I thought you dumped me just because...well, because you wanted a more popular girl. Geneva was certainly the queen bee in our class." She sighs. "No matter how angry and hurt I was, I didn't know how to confront you about it and protect my ego at the same time. I didn't have anybody to talk to, either, since you were with Geneva, who I always thought was my best friend. I couldn't figure it out, so I just decided not to say anything. The only person who was sort of friendly was Louis. But I wonder..."

She trails off. After a few moments, I say, "What did he do?" I'm getting a bad feeling about all this. Louis is a dick.

"I wonder now if he was in on it with Geneva. He told me you were the one who put the vibrator in my backpack that time."

"What?" I remember that incident. I thought it sucked for her, even though I looked the other way because my youthful pride decided whatever happened to her wasn't my problem anymore. "It was *not* me," I say, wanting to make that extra clear.

"I don't doubt you, now that I think about it. He also told me it was you who put dead bugs in front of my lockers and on my desk."

What a fucking traitor! That weasel acted like he was my best friend until I caught him treating Vi like trash behind my back and almost knocked his teeth out for it. "That's why you thought I had Princess leave you bugs in front of your apartment."

She nods. "I figured you were just continuing the tradition."

"It wasn't me." I muster all the sincerity I can, praying she doesn't really think I'm that much of a dick. "Kim, I swear. I can't get that damn cat to sit on my lap."

She shifts until she's facing me fully. "I believe you."

A knot eases in my chest. What Kim thinks of me matters a lot, even though I don't want to probe the reason too closely at the moment. "No wonder you hated my guts. I'm sorry." Even if there was a misunderstanding between us, I should've been more mature about it. And I hurt Kim by not being honest with her from the beginning. If I'd just asked her about the text, all this could've been avoided. *So much time and energy wasted.*

"I'm sorry, too. I was...well, petty when you needed my help. I set you up with unsuitable women on purpose, just to make you suffer. And...um...I thought you deserved to be stuck with one of them."

I shrug. "Probably would've done the same if the situation was reversed. But you came through when it counted, and you were kind to Vi when you didn't have to be. You could've taken things out on her just because she's Geneva's child. Plenty of people might've done just that."

"I would *never*—"

"I know." I give her a small smile. "That's why—" I stop, swallowing the rest. Was I just about to say that's why I still...adore her? *Whoa.* That's... No. Way too fast, too early and too weird. We just cleared up a years-long misunderstanding. No way we're moving to the adore phase this quickly.

"That's why what?" she asks.

"That's why I think you're a great person."

The rest of the ride back passes quickly as we talk about old friends and high school events. When I shut the engine off in the parking lot, I discover that I don't want the evening to end. I don't want her to go when we just cleared up the ugly misunderstanding from our past. "Hey, you want to have a drink? I got a really nice bottle of scotch. Also have wine..."

She smiles. "I love scotch."

35

KIM

I PROBABLY SHOULDN'T HAVE SAID YES TO THE OFFER OF scotch. My new roommate and Champ are waiting for me at home, although that's a flimsy reason, since Yuna texted me earlier.

Just to let you know, we're doing fantastic. Champ is a perfect dog. And a black cat came by, and I fed her. Hope you don't mind, but she was purring and I couldn't resist. She's really cute. I wonder if her owner's going to get mad if paint her little crown pink. Pink is definitely prettier than white, if you ask me, and it goes well with black fur. Anyway, have fun. Take as much time as you need. Don't forget to bang the best man, assuming he's hot. I understand that's an American tradition.

Ah, Yuna. If you only knew.

To be honest, even without her text, I would've found some excuse to make a detour. I really want to see Wyatt's place. I'm curious what it looks like...what it might reveal about him. Although we talked about what happened before, and I realize he's not the jerk I thought he was, it's been a long time since we had any nonprofessional interaction. Who knows how he's changed in the last decade?

I'm pretty sure he wasn't planning on asking me into his apartment when we left this morning. And that means he considers it presentable enough, but nothing's staged to sway my opinion one way or the other.

The first thing I note is the tidiness. Everything is exactly where it should be and set just so. No clutter, no knickknacks except for a dog-earned young adult paranormal romance novel Vi must've left on a side table by the leather couch. No hint of the statue anywhere, either, but I doubt he'd keep that kind of thing at home with a young kid around. Besides, the apartment is too small for *Wife*, which is reportedly life-sized. And while our complex is nice, the building doesn't have good enough security for such a valuable item.

The organized part of him hasn't changed. He was neat in high school as well. I doubt he has somebody coming over to clean for him, because I would've noticed in the last few weeks I've been home.

The place doesn't feel sterile or cold. Splashes of burgundy and cream add to the décor, and a comfy-looking afghan is draped over the back of the couch. I run my hand over it, feeling the softness against my skin.

"This is nice," I say.

"My mom made that for Vi," Wyatt says as he heads to the kitchen. "She likes to wrap it around herself and curl up to read or watch TV."

The mental picture that creates is lovely. A longing for something I can't quite put my finger on pulses through me. My mom's gift ideas tend to run to self-improvement, with particular emphasis on enhancing physical assets. She used to worry about the scar along my jaw, but right now she's obsessed with the perkiness of my breasts. She sends me reviews or her own thoughts after having used plastic surgeons and spas, but has never offered to pay. When I point out they're far too expensive for someone on an assistant's salary, she says she didn't get enough alimony to afford to help out.

I take a seat on the couch. It faces a huge, top-of-the-line TV —something every man on earth seems to have. I gaze at the blank screen and let my mind wander.

I always thought Wyatt couldn't say sorry enough times to make up for what he'd done. I vowed I'd never forgive him. Or at least make him kneel and grovel before I accepted an apology. And I was certain that any apology would only be a pathetic balm over my old, painful memories.

But our conversation about what happened somehow soothed the decade-old wound. And when he said he was sorry, I actually felt better—calmer and happier. Like the words really did have the power to heal.

How weird. No other guy I ever dated was able to do that. Their *sorry*s always felt empty, like they were only saying it to get forgiveness for what they'd done.

But I shouldn't have compared Wyatt to them. He's one of a kind.

The realization is startling and uncomfortable, mainly because I'm not sure what to do about it. We really liked each other before Geneva engineered our breakup. Even so, a lot of time's passed and a lot of things have happened, including the kiss.

That makes me think maybe there's still something. But where do we go from here? I'm in unfamiliar territory, and that's weird. I'm all about pre-planning—careful and deliberate. Otherwise I wouldn't have lasted so long as Salazar's assistant.

Needing something to distract myself, I look around some more and see nails sticking out from the wall Wyatt and I share. What Vi said in the car pops into my head and I smother a laugh.

"So... That's where you're going to hang the pictures you don't have yet?"

"Yeah." Wyatt comes over and hands me the scotch, then parks himself next to me on the sofa. Our legs brush, and I suppress a shiver at the contact, even through the fabric of his slacks. And my fingertips tingle where we touched.

To hide my reaction, I murmur thanks and take a sip. Lots of smooth heat and a hint of oak. It's a really good scotch. Something my boss would love.

"So you thought you could just hammer Nate out of the building?" I tease.

Wyatt shrugs, although he looks vaguely guilty. "Something

like that. Most people don't like noisy neighbors. Figured you probably didn't disclose that fact."

"Because you weren't noisy until yesterday."

He clears his throat, then hides his face behind the crystal tumbler as he knocks his drink back.

"Thankfully, my real roommate is very understanding." Yuna said she'd put up with the noise for the greater cause of staying hidden from her mother's spies.

"I was..." He pauses for a moment, as though gathering himself. "I hated the idea of you living with another man. I thought maybe he was like that other guy."

"What other guy?"

"The one you hugged in the hall." His voice is tight, and his expression is tense enough to make me wonder if he's actually pissed off about that rather anemic embrace.

"Hugo?"

"Is that his name?"

"That's Jo's cousin. And he has a huge crush on another woman. I'm not desperate enough to go for a guy who isn't going to be into me."

"But you were acting like you wanted to kiss him," Wyatt points out.

"Oh. That." I take a drink, hiding my face. That was such a dumb, embarrassing attempt. I can see that clearly now. Maybe I should ask for more scotch. A finger isn't going to do a thing. My tolerance is too high.

Wyatt shrugs. "Since we're being so honest today... I was jealous."

His admission erases the awkwardness I'm feeling, filling me with something warm and sweet. "Were you now?" I prop my chin in my hand and gaze at him. The long lashes. The brilliant blue of his eyes. His full mouth.

He's gorgeous, but it's not just his handsomeness making my heart flutter. It's what the honesty represents—vulnerability. And it cracks the shell around my heart faster and more effectively than any expensive dinner or gift ever could.

I realize I really like this honest Wyatt, who tells me how he really feels. It's nice not to snipe at each other or brace for conflict, to be able to let my guard down.

"You shouldn't have been jealous," I say with a small smile, ready to return his candor. "I only tried to kiss him because I wanted to know if what I felt from *our* kiss was exclusive to you or not. I wanted to pretend it wasn't, but I needed another guy to test my theory. The thing is, I couldn't really kiss him because he has a crush on somebody else. So I just settled for a hug."

"And...?"

"And"—I shrug, wishing I could travel back in time and tell myself not to bother—"nothing. I mean, he's nice looking and he's a decent guy, but that's about as far as it went. Kind of anticlimactic."

"Not anticlimactic. Very satisfying." He grins. "I was thinking about the kiss too."

"Is that so?" I say slowly, pleased that it was on his mind, too.

"I was...upset when it happened. I thought you were just messing with me, and I wanted to mess with you back."

"You succeeded. It screwed up my headspace."

And the crazy thing is that I really liked it. The pounding of my heart. The feel of his lips on mine. The hot, tingling sensation that spread all over me.

I finish my drink, then place the empty tumbler on the table. Resting my elbow against the back of the couch and propping my head in my hand, I gaze at him. Inhale his scent. He always smells so delicious—clean male, with something woodsy in there, and now the tiniest hint of scotch. Yummy.

He leans in. "Fact is, it backfired on me. That kiss was pretty much all I could think about for a while, and I hated the fact that you wrote that herpes text because I thought... Well, I didn't know you didn't."

"And I was thinking it was unfair that I was attracted to a guy who dumped me so unceremoniously. So we're even." I smile. "Evenly foolish."

"Not foolish. We were just too proud and too young to talk about it."

That's true. We were too young. I don't know if I'd let him get away with it now. I'd probably bash his head with a wine glass... one that isn't broken from his earlier home invasion.

"Well, we're older now," I say.

"Yep. But not too old."

I can feel his breath against my cheek, feathery soft and slightly ticklish. Is he going to taste like Wyatt and scotch? The combination seems irresistible.

I start to narrow the distance between us, and he moves, taking my mouth.

He cradles the back of my neck, the touch hot and possessive, nothing like the awkward moves he made when we were in high school. But his lips touch mine with care, giving me a chance to pull back. I stay still, fusing our mouths. His kiss remains gentle and sweet, exploratory. My heart thuds in my chest, blood pumping through my veins.

The hell with it. Wrapping my hand around the base of his skull, I come up off the couch, pushing into him, onto him, flicking my tongue freely over his lips. A groan vibrates in his chest as he presses closer. The sound stokes me, pulling me happily into the web of bliss he's creating around me. His mouth opens, his tongue sliding along mine. I dip into his mouth, just as he does the same with me. He tastes delicious, instantly addictive, and I know I can never give this up. There's something about him that makes me feel drunk on life, on pleasure, and I want to have him *now*.

He caresses my shoulder, moving down my arm. Goosebumps rise, and I let out a shaky breath. There's a crackling electricity between us—a deep, endless thirst that's going to be impossible to satisfy.

I clutch at him, then fumble in trying to unbutton his shirt. I can't seem to stop, or even slow down. My whole body tingles, my skin tight, like there's a honeyed lust growing and expanding inside me. I need him. I want to reclaim the man who was my first. *Right now.*

"You have too many buttons," I say between kisses.

"I can take care of that."

Gently pushing my hands out of the way, he grips his shirt and rips it apart. The sound ignites fire in my blood. The heat travels all the way down past my belly and pools between my legs.

Oh God.

Whimpering and unable to wait, I straddle him on the couch, my skirt hiking up. He smooths his large hands down my thighs, leaving trails of fire. The naked desire in his eyes is driving me crazy. There's an almost uncontrollable urgency to his touch, and it's intoxicating to know that his need equals mine.

His erection presses against me through my underwear. My mouth fused to his, I grind against him. His breathing grows rougher and he moves against me, pushing away the straps of my dress and unzipping the back, releasing the red satin. My breasts hang free.

"You aren't wearing a bra," he whispers, his gaze on them.

"This dress doesn't look good with one," I say, glad that after half an hour of earlier debate, I decided *whatever* and zipped it up *sans* bra. The stark expression on his face is priceless—and sexy as hell.

"Good thing I didn't know. I don't think I would've been able to control myself."

I smile, feeling powerful and wicked at the way he's looking at me. "Well, they're all yours now."

Wyatt makes a sound that's halfway between a pant and a rumble. He lowers his head, pulling one of my nipples into his hot mouth. I whimper as electric pleasure winds through my core, digging my fingers into his surprisingly soft hair. He closes his free hand around the other breast, brushing against the tip with his thumb. I moan. It's crazy how amazing this is, how liberating. Maybe it's because we cleared the air between us, reached an understanding. But whatever it is, I feel safe with him.

He stands up, lifting me in his strong arms and moving down the hall. My heart flutters because I know exactly where we're going. He takes me to his bedroom and lays me down on his bed. The sheets are cool against my back, and I love how they smell just like him.

I watch him discard his clothes, enjoying every inch of hot, hard masculinity that's revealed. He's gorgeous, more powerful and muscled than he looks in clothes. It's turning me on to realize he's mine to touch and take. I quickly sit up and I start to toe off my shoes, but he shakes his head.

"Leave 'em on."

"You have a shoe fetish?" I tease, slightly breathless from anticipation.

"No. I have Kim fetish. And those shoes look amazing on you."

He kisses me again, slipping his hand between my legs, sliding his fingers along my clit and folds, while he drags my underwear down my legs with the other hand and flings it over his shoulder. Oh God, he's killing me, I think, as blissful delight pulses through me. I can't think of a time I was this into sex.

"You're so fucking wet," he says, his voice guttural. He presses his thumb against my clit and pushes his finger into my pussy. But it isn't enough. It's nowhere near enough, because it isn't what I want. I want both of us to feel really, really good.

"I want you. Inside me," I demand. "Right now."

He leaves me for a moment, reaching for a condom from a drawer on his nightstand. Once he's fully sheathed, he pushes into me. I gasp at the thick, rigid invasion. He goes still for a moment, his eyes on mine. I smile, letting him know I'm more than fine. Only then does he start moving in and out, and I sigh at the delicious friction. I pull my knees up, holding them in my hands.

He kisses me hard, his thrusts harder and harder, every one creating a new hot wave of bliss.

I arch into him, reveling in the way his control slips a notch, his breathing growing rough, the guttural vibration in his chest. And I don't try to hide my reaction, wanting him to know exactly how he's making me feel. Pleasure builds and builds, making it nearly impossible to breathe.

Suddenly, an orgasm breaks over me. My back arches, and my knees slip from my hands. Wyatt's fingers dig into my ass as he pushes into me one last, straining time. He groans against my neck as he climaxes. I hold him tightly, enjoying the moment when we're both utterly helpless.

We stay entwined for a bit, clinging to each other. My vision's a little blurry, and I can't seem to focus as blood roars in my head.

This is the best sex I've had since...well, ever. As much as the languid satisfaction turns my muscles to goo, I also sense a bit of vulnerability creeping over me. We both said a lot...did a lot. I wonder if this moment means as much to him as it does to me. Then I shake myself inwardly. What am I? A teenager? It's very natural for two healthy adults who are attracted to each other to give in to it.

You call that...what? Justification for sleeping with Wyatt and feeling things maybe you shouldn't?

Wyatt pulls me closer, wrapping his arms around me. I snuggle into him, ignoring the pesky voice in my head.

"Stay here tonight," he murmurs. "With me."

My heart stops for a second as a tiny hope stirs inside me that this could turn into more than just...physical fun. I place a hand on his warm, whisker-rough cheek. "Okay."

36

WYATT

I WAKE UP WHEN SOMETHING WARM SHIFTS NEXT TO ME. I tense up for a moment, wondering who it could be. Haven't shared my bed with anybody in a while, with Geneva and I refusing to use the same room long before the divorce became final. But almost immediately I realize it's Kim and relax. I prop my head on my knuckles and study her. She looks so peaceful asleep, sweet and... *What else am I feeling here?* I realize it's protectiveness. She looks so defenseless and trusting with nothing but the sheet wrapped around her. I want to do everything in my power to keep her safe.

She shifts again, and the sheets twist around some more. We were pretty insatiable last night. We didn't fall asleep until I'd had four orgasms. I think she came at least ten or twelve times. Or so my ego says.

My dick's already hard. *Ready for number five.*

Yeah. That sounds like a great idea, except Kim looks too tired. She said something about needing her sleep after her final climax. *Eight hours of sleep or I'm going to turn into a psycho pumpkin witch.*

Today's Sunday. No need to wake her up yet. It's just the two of us here, and we can afford to be lazy. Have brunch or something. Hang out. She used to like eating popcorn and watching movies. Wonder if she still does. I'd love to hold her on the couch, while she giggles at some joke or gasps at an over-the-top action scene.

I brush my lips over her shoulder, enjoying her softness...and the most amazing scent clinging to her skin. After breathing her in one more time, I get up, brush my teeth and shower. Then I note the bathroom countertop is pretty bare as I dry myself. Won't Kim need her things in the morning—like lotions and creams? Geneva used like a hundred different types twice a day.

On the other hand, we aren't in a relationship where we leave stuff like that at each other's places. Besides, I don't know if she wants to leave anything here even if we were. The woman lives next door.

Then again, if she were anything like Geneva, I'd say she would, because Geneva hates for people see her without full makeup. Kim isn't that shallow or obsessed about her looks. If she were, she would've done something to get rid of her scar.

But my perverse mind conjures up images of a bathroom full of Kim's favorite body wash, shampoo, conditioner and bottles and jars of skin lotion and creams anyway.

Whoa. Slow the hell down.

I don't even know what Kim's thinking about all this right now. She might just want something casual and simple. She's obviously devoted to her career, and might not want anything that would distract her from that. And it isn't like I can just jump into a serious relationship without considering the consequences. I have a kid to think about. Kim and Vi get along well, but that doesn't mean Vi's going to be okay with me and Kim dating. Vi's counselor once said kids can be irrationally contradictory. And she said that includes Vi feeling like I'm trying to replace her mother with another woman when she isn't ready to cope with that yet. Even though Vi thinks Kim's pretty damn awesome, she might not feel that way if she thinks Kim and I are dating.

Or...Vi could *think that you and Kim together is the best thing ever...*

Damn it. I try to pull my thoughts together, which isn't easy without coffee. But I manage. Vi's gone for the summer. Kim and I can explore what we have between us for the next few weeks, then figure things out. Not every decision has to be made right now.

I pull a new toothbrush out from the stash of extras and lay it on the counter. When I'm out of the bathroom with the towel around my waist, Kim sits up, her back hunched and her head in her hands. She rubs her eyes, yawning. God, she looks so cute, like a sleepy cat.

"Thought you were going to sleep in," I say.

She lifts her head and looks at me. "I've got to get up. Otherwise I'm going to pay the price tomorrow morning, and I have to go to work."

The raspy morning huskiness of her voice tugs at my dick. I go over and kiss her. *Rolling around in bed counts as getting up, right?* I mean, neither of us would actually be sleeping.

Before I can convince her of my brilliant logic, she pulls back, her expression somewhere between dreamy and grumpy. "I need coffee."

I laugh at how cute she is. "Coming right up. With breakfast." I can seduce her after I feed her. "Left you a new toothbrush on the bathroom counter."

She smiles. "Thanks."

I put on a shirt and shorts and go to the kitchen. Then I start the coffeemaker, lay some bacon strips in the frying pan and take inventory. *Not a lot around here that a woman would like for breakfast.* There's a box of cereal, some milk, one small yogurt—something Vi left behind—eggs and cheese. I haven't been to the store this week. Hopefully Kim's okay with eggs and bacon. I don't want to have a mini-argument about it, and having to choke down "calorie-dense" bacon is something Geneva would've lost her marbles over.

Kim's not Geneva.

Right. Gotta keep reminding myself of that.

Kim comes out of the bedroom in one of my dress shirts, sleeves rolled up. The hem stops several inches above her knees, exposing a lot of smooth, shapely leg.

I always thought wearing a man's shirt was an overly calculated seduction move, because women only do it hoping to look sexy the morning after so they can stick around. But it's not only hot, it's *intimate.* Having a woman put on your clothes in the morning, so she smells like your laundry soap... It's like she's living with you, sharing a space and a life.

"Hope you don't mind," she says. "I can't wear my dress again. It's wrinkled to death." She takes a stool at the island.

"Don't mind a bit." I gesture at the frying pan. "You like bacon?"

"I love bacon."

Great. I take the strips out of the pan and put them on paper towels, then crack a few eggs into the pan.

Kim says, "That smells *so* good. I'm starving. I didn't even get to eat the cake yesterday." She sounds even grumpier now. "And it looked really good. Probably the nicest thing at the wedding."

No kidding. And since I've just been reminded, I check my phone to make sure everything's okay with Vi. The latest text from my parents says all's well. There's also a screed of messages from Geneva, most sent after two in the morning.

–Geneva: It's all your fault.

–Geneva: You're going to pay!

–Geneva: You owe me money!

–Geneva: How am I going to marry Churchill now?

I exhale roughly, anger and pity tugging at me from opposite directions. She was probably drunk and needed to vent. And it's just like her to blame everyone but herself for her own bad choices.

"What's wrong?" Kim asks. "Is it Vi?"

I shake my head. "Geneva."

She arches an eyebrow, so I hand her the phone. "Oh, for fuck's sake. She's certifiable."

"Don't have to tell me." I pour a mug of coffee. "How do you like it?"

"With some sugar and cream. But I can manage black."

I put a dash of sugar and cream in it. I just add sugar to mine, then take both cups to the island.

Kim accepts hers with thanks and wraps her hands around the cup, then takes a sip. "Can I ask you something?"

"Sure."

"Why did you decide to marry her?" She clears her throat, then hurriedly adds, "I'm not judging, but I'm really curious. Mom told me things, but I want to hear from you in case what people are saying isn't, like, how it happened."

"It's sort of stupid." Talking about it is going to make me feel ridiculous, because the whole marriage was a bad idea. I was just too close to see things clearly.

"We've all done...dumb things."

Yeah, but there's dumb, and then there's plain, flat-out *dumb*.

I take half the bacon off the paper towels and place it on her plate, then load some eggs along with it. The rest goes on mine. I swing myself onto the other stool and bite into a strip.

If anyone but Kim was asking, I'd gloss over the whole issue or just refuse to talk about it. But she deserves to know what happened, especially in light of how low Geneva sank to break us up back then. I take a couple sips of coffee, hoping the caffeine will give me a clear head so I don't muck up the story of my personal failure.

"Okay. So at first I dated her because she said she wanted me. But I knew we weren't that well matched. It was a rebound thing."

Kim nods while chewing slowly, her expression carefully neutral.

"I was thinking about ending it because I knew we weren't giving each other what we needed. Even back then, she was unhappy, and I wasn't too thrilled with our situation either. Then she got pregnant."

"Wow." Kim's doing some math in her head, I can tell.

"It was way before I made any real money." I push the eggs around on my plate.

"Were you angry?" she asks quietly.

"I think I was shocked. If I'd already made that Sweet

Darlings deal, I might've suspected she did it on purpose, but back then... We were doing okay, but there wasn't a whole lot of extra cash floating around, if you understand what I'm saying."

Kim nods. "Yeah."

"Once the shock wore off, I needed to do the right thing. Single moms aren't a big deal these days, but let's just say I can be old-fashioned about some things."

She reaches over and squeezes my hand. "You just wanted to do what was right for Vi."

I look at our hands and sigh, feeling a bit of old guilt. "I'm not sure if that's what I was trying to do. I think back on it sometimes and ask myself if I felt that the pregnancy was messing up my plan to break up with Geneva. It wasn't until I heard Vi's heartbeat that she felt like a person to me, a new life I was responsible for, you know? I wonder if Vi knows that, deep inside. Maybe that's why she doesn't like me that much." And as I speak, I realize the sense of guilt has been weighing on my mind for a long time, maybe even before my divorce. And I feel sad, wondering if I'm being dumb and overcompensating somehow, by trying to give her a normal life and all that by insisting on living in a typical middle-class apartment, while sending her off to one of the most exclusive and expensive private schools. A lot of what I've done hasn't been that consistent, and Vi's smart enough to get that, even if she can't quite put it into words.

"I doubt Vi feels that way," Kim says. "She loves you. She just doesn't know how to express it yet."

"I hope so." I smile, wanting Kim to be right and wishing I knew exactly how to show Vi how much I love her in a way she can process. "Thanks."

"For what?"

"You know. Just being understanding and nice."

"Don't mention it. I don't want to see you and Vi hurt because of what Geneva did."

As she spoons her eggs, her head tilts a little, and I see the scar Geneva gave her. Geneva said it was an accident, but nobody believes she didn't mean to make Kim trip and fall.

I reach out and gently run my thumb over the jagged line,

chin almost to the ear, and she goes still. Then lean over and I kiss it, all the while thinking I don't want to see Kim hurt by anything.

And I realize the small voice in my head is right. What I feel for Kim goes beyond just a new toothbrush on my counter. I want to see how far we can go together this time.

37

KIM

I HELP WYATT CLEAN UP AFTER BREAKFAST, BUT I REALLY have to get going. I need a fresh set of clothes, not to mention a shower and makeup. But somehow I don't want to leave him, not even for a second. The sex was fantastic, but the morning after was even better, more intimate and open. I love seeing this new side of him, the vulnerability that makes me want to open up to him in return.

I finish my second cup of coffee and start to put the empty mug in the dishwasher. Then I hear it. A loud, weird noise—something between a whine and a bark.

"What's that?" I ask with a shudder. The sound is horrific. I might suspect Champ, but Yuna is with him. If something was wrong, she would call.

"I don't know," Wyatt answers, looking a little alarmed.

It happens again, and he turns toward the Wall of Unhung Nails. "I think it's coming from...there?"

Holy cow, Wyatt's right! Panicked, I grab my purse and dash barefoot to my apartment. I should've known better than to just assume Yuna would do a good job taking care of my dog! She probably can't comb her own hair without an assistant. Anyone born that rich can be helpless about the most basic things.

Wyatt follows and stands protectively as I fumble with my keys. Finally the door unlocks, and I step inside.

"Hello? Yuna?" Champ rushes me and Wyatt, tail wagging. He isn't giving us his usual doggy smile, but I don't see any sign of abuse or neglect. On the other hand, it's only been a day.

Wyatt reaches for the light switch and turns on the recessed lights in the living and dining rooms.

"Oh, thank God you're back," comes from a vibrating leather chair that doesn't belong in my apartment. It's Yuna, but she's facing away from us.

Champ makes the same creepy whine-bark sound again.

"Argh," she says. "Never mind. I thought he'd stop if you came home."

"Obviously not," I say, mildly annoyed. "What did you do? And where did you get that chair?"

"I didn't do anything except walk him earlier and feed him. I think he's just upset the cat disappeared."

Yuna must be talking about Princess. I'm not too worried about her, since even though she's a house cat, she seems to be able to take care of herself.

Yuna continues, "She left this morning—I'm not sure how she got out, since all the windows were closed. And I bought this, obviously. Do you like it?"

"I don't know," I say. "It's vibrating."

"To the untrained eye. But this is fourth-generation undulating relaxation tech."

Sounds like a euphemism for a high-tech sex toy. But I keep the comment to myself. Wyatt's watching, and I don't want to embarrass Yuna.

"I'm trying to finish this mask without getting damaged. UVA spares no one."

"Well, let's see the thing. You have curtains over every window." I start toward them, walking past the sex chair.

"No, don't open them!" she yells, obviously having sensed my movement. "UVA is an equal-opportunity ager."

I turn around and almost trip over my feet. Yuna's hair is in a tight topknot, and she's in a black tube top and shorts. Her face, neck, shoulders, chest, arms and hands are covered with a thick, dark goo. Two slices of cucumbers sit on her eyes. She pulls them off, holding them with her fingertips.

Champ immediately goes crazy, making the same goosebump-raising sound.

Wyatt's shocked as he places a comforting hand on Champ's head. "That's...your roommate?" What he's really saying is: *That's who my daughter wants to emulate?*

Who can blame him? Yuna looks terrifying. A monster that's risen from a mud hole. The creature from the black slime lagoon.

Regardless, I remember my manners. "Um, yes. This is Yuna Hae. Yuna, this is Wyatt Westland, our neighbor and my..." I pause, wondering what the right word to describe him is. *Lover* sounds weird. *Boyfriend*... Are we even dating? Ugh. I should've just ended with "neighbor" and been done with it.

"Boyfriend," Wyatt says decisively.

It's a little surprising to hear him use the word. On the other hand, it definitely does make me feel all warm and fuzzy, like a girl who just learned the boy she has a major crush on likes her back. If he wants to call himself my boyfriend, he isn't looking at us as a one-time thing. And to be honest, at this point I'm not either.

"Hi." Yuna waves. "I'd shake hands, but I'm sure you don't want my seaweed mask all over you."

"That's *seaweed*?" I ask. It looks like some kind of alien fertility gel.

"Yes. And I don't know why Champ is acting up so much. He knows it's me. I smell like me."

"It's your face," I say. "And the rest of you. And your seaweed glop smells briny."

"So are you saying he's going to act weird if I put on a new perfume? He shouldn't be so sensitive."

"How long do you have to leave that stuff on?" Wyatt asks.

Yuna checks the timer on her lap. "Ten more minutes."

"Champ may have an aneurism before then," I say.

"Let me keep Champ calm," Wyatt offers, then turns to me.

"Why don't you go shower and...do whatever is it you need to do?"

"Okay. Thanks." I flash him a grateful smile.

I rush through a shower, but Champ is quiet the entire time I'm in the bathroom. Wyatt must be doing a great job of keeping him under control. I wish I'd spent the time to talk about where Wyatt and I are going with this...thing between us in more depth, maybe even lay down some ground rules, since there's a kid involved, but I wanted to satisfy my curiosity about why he married Geneva. Regardless, we can figure out everything before Vi comes back. I hope she doesn't mind too badly. I looked at my mother's Husband Number Five with wariness since... Well, I didn't trust my mom to marry for anything but money. Being a good father to me was never on her list of requirements in a man. But I think Vi's going to know Wyatt and I aren't like that.

After applying mascara and lipstick, I pull on a sundress and walk out to the living room, my hair slightly damp. Yuna's gone, and Champ's thumping his tail, panting at Wyatt, who's sitting on my couch.

"All done?" Wyatt asks.

"Yeah. Where's Yuna?"

"Gone to wash that stuff off." Wyatt casts a glance at her room. "Is she always, you know...like this?"

"You mean, does the mask and stuff?" I sit next to him. "Maybe. I don't know her that well. I only said yes because she needs a place to stay and is friends with some people I know."

He nods. "Neighborly of you," he says, although his expression says he doubts Yuna is really lacking in alternative living quarters, given the super-tech chair she brought in. It looks expensive.

"She may move out soon. I'm pretty sure this isn't the type of place she's used to." I eye the fancy chair. Yeah, she's not going to last long in my very ordinary home if she can't survive even one weekend without something like that. Then I turn my attention back to Wyatt. "By the way... Wyatt?"

"Yeah?"

"We're, um, you know... Dating for real, right?" It feels important to ensure we're on the same page. I don't want any more misunderstandings or assumptions like before.

"Yup." He searches my face, then smiles. "Don't know how you can ask that after last night."

Pleasure and a small bit of embarrassment heat my face. "Sex doesn't always mean anything." That's been my experience, anyway...although maybe I need to revise that slightly. I thought Wyatt betrayed me because of what Geneva did. But if she hadn't interfered, it wouldn't have ended the way it did. It'd be small of me to hold what happened against him.

This is a new beginning. The proverbial clean slate. He shared things openly when he didn't have to, and he deserves for me to treat him the same way.

He holds my hand, then brings it slowly to his lips.

The warm, sweet touch of his mouth on my skin leaves me shivering.

"It does in this case."

38

WYATT

Kim and I spend the rest of Sunday grocery shopping, then eating in and watching old movies while cuddling. And having sex. Because you can't have a great day with your girl without sex. Well, you *could*, I guess. But why?

Princess hops on the bed and deposits a cricket on Kim while we're wrapped up in each other, breathing hard. Kim gives a high-pitched scream loud enough to pop my eardrum. I glare at the feline, but of course I have to get up and flush the cricket down the toilet and wash my hands. Nothing less will satisfy a woman when it comes to bug disposal.

Princess has the audacity to hiss at me as I come back into the bedroom. Since Geneva only left her with me because Churchill is allergic, I wonder if I can send this demon cat back.

Princess hisses harder, her hair rising.

"Fine, I won't send you back," I mutter.

"What?" Kim asks, sheet pulled up to her chin like a shield.

"I said I'm not sending the cat back to Geneva."

I wait for Kim's reaction. She might very well say we need to send her back.

Kim purses her lips. "Of course not. That would be animal

abuse." She sighs. "I don't know why she keeps bringing me things."

"Me either. She never brings *me* anything." Not that I want her to, but I'd rather have the cat dump bugs on me than Kim.

Monday starts out hectic. Kim has to go back to work, and that means she needs to rush back to her apartment as soon as her eyes open. No breakfast, no coffee together.

"I'll text you," she says, then kisses me and leaves.

The bedroom goes quiet. I sigh at the closed door, then heave myself up and get ready for work. Just because I have more money than I can spend doesn't mean I'm going to slack off on what I do at Sweet Darlings.

The first thing I check when I walk into my office is my email. And I see one from HR with the subject line: Your New Assistant.

Finally!

I open it immediately and skim the attached résumé. Loren Vincetti. Graduated from UCLA with a degree in sociology. She's only looking for a new position because her boss got relocated to London, and she didn't want to uproot everything and go with him. According to HR's note, the previous boss had nothing but praise for Loren.

I hit reply to the message.

When is she coming in for an interview?

Then I go back to clearing out my inbox, taking all the urgent items off my plate first. HR's response arrives when I'm almost finished.

That's why we're emailing you. We sent a note last week, but never received an answer.

My blood pressure hits the roof, and it takes a moment before my vision clears. *Melanie.*

The saddest thing is that if she were even the tiniest bit competent, I'd think she was just trying to extend her temp gig. But I know better. I look at her desk through the frosted glass. She's probably eating cookies and clipping coupons and pictures of hot Hollywood stars. She doesn't seem to understand that Sweet Darlings isn't paying her to sit around drooling over Chris Hemsworth's abs.

I pick up the desk phone and hit the extension for Nancy in HR.

"Nancy, this is Wyatt Westland. How quickly can you get Loren in for an interview?"

"How soon do you want it?"

"I wanted it last week." I check my calendar. "How about this morning? If not, any time after three is fine."

"I'll check."

"Call me on my cell or text me directly."

"Sure. By the way, I feel like I should let you know something, even though I'm certain what your answer's going to be."

"What?" I ask, wondering why she's giving me such a long preface.

"Melanie asked for a permanent position last week."

"As what?" Not as a stocker for the break room, hopefully. We'll be out of coffee in hours.

"As your assistant. She says you're an easy boss to work for."

Oh, for fuck's sake. "Of course I'm easy to work for. She doesn't do shi— Excuse my French. She hardly does anything."

Nancy sighs. "I thought as much. Anyway, I'll contact you directly."

I hang up, then glare at Melanie's back. Now I'm thinking that she purposely hid the message from HR to ensure I'd be stuck with her.

Not gonna happen.

I attend two meetings, with memos and docs I prepared *and* printed because Melanie forgot again. The second one with the marketing team goes pretty well, considering I'm missing one of the presentation slides, which David apparently sent to everyone's assistants last Friday.

As David and I are leaving the conference room, my phone pings with a text. I pull it out of my pocket faster than a gunslinger unholstering his iron.

–Kim: Lunch today?

I was expecting a response from HR, but still feel a smile coming on.

Faking It with the Frenemy

–Me: Sure. What are you in the mood for?

–Kim: Something simple. Burgers and fries?

A woman after my own heart. It's like she knew exactly what I wanted at that restaurant where you couldn't call tuna...well, tuna. My smile gets bigger.

–Me: Perfect.

David sidles up, trying to get a look at my screen. "You hook up with one of the bridesmaids? Sly."

I shake my head. Only he would think that. "You know the wedding didn't happen, right?"

"Of course. Saw the videos on Facebook because I just had to know about this particular ceremony. But that means there were some disappointed bridesmaids, am I right? I read the groom got caught humping one right before the ceremony." He clasps my shoulder like I just invented a vaccine for prostate cancer. "I'm proud of you, son. You're doing the right thing. Soon you'll forget why you ever married that crazy bitch." He pauses. "You did get digits for more than one maid, right?"

I roll my eyes. "I'm not going to plow through half the city like you did."

"No need for past tense. But *plow* is correct. Why do you think I volunteered to be relocated? Mom was getting too nosy about my personal life."

"Well, I'm not going to drown myself in women. I have a kid."

"Uh-huh. But that was an 'I got laid and I'm gonna get laid again' smile."

I shake my head. "More to life than just getting laid, partner."

"Only if the sex is bad."

"And I do believe I'm settled on one woman," I say, completely ignoring him.

"No way! You're finally single and you're going to limit yourself to one? *Already?*"

"I know what I like, and what I like isn't sampling every meat in the market."

Another ping interrupts us. *HR*. Finally!

–Nancy: Three today. She has another interview this morning.

Damn it.

–Me: Is she going to take the other job if they offer or at least wait until the interview with me?

–Nancy: She said she's going to look at all her offers first.

"Everything okay?" David asks.
"Yeah. A possible new assistant."
David frowns. "Melanie not working out?"
"If by 'working out' you mean 'making my job five times harder,' yeah, she's working out fine."
"That's too bad. She bakes great cookies. And she really wants to be here."
My jaw slackens because he's the second person to say this. I never thought she wanted to be at Sweet Darlings long-term, especially based on how little she cares about doing her job. "Did she tell you she wanted to be my permanent assistant, too?"
He nods. "Didn't you know? She's waiting for you to make her an offer."
It's like hearing that the Pentagon decided to test nukes on the moon. "Why in the world would she think that's going to happen?"
"Aren't you?"
"No. She's the worst assistant, ever."
David nods. "I guess your ex-wife isn't the only deluded woman around."
"Got that right. Some people can fool themselves into anything. But anyway, I gotta go."
"I thought we were having lunch with Dane today."
Were we? I forgot. But... "Sorry, bud. I got a better offer."

39

Kim

Wyatt picks me up from the office lobby. It's been only a few hours since I saw him, but a small hitch forms in my chest when I spot him in the lobby scrolling through his phone. He fills out the pale blue dress shirt and slacks perfectly, his shoulders broad and waist trim. His sleeves are rolled up, showing sinewy forearms. The sunlight pouring in from the huge glass behind him creates a halo effect. A group of women on their way to lunch check him out, but he's oblivious to them.

Then he lifts his head and an electric tingle shoots through me when our eyes connect. I smile to hide the intensity of my reaction and walk toward him on slightly unsteady legs. If we weren't in my office building, I might just hold his face in my hands and kiss him. Or drag him down on the floor.

Bad hormones, bad! Salazar's coming back today, and I need to be back before then. There's no time for lunch and a nooner, and no way I can skip a meal, unless fainting from low blood sugar has become the new standard of professionalism.

Wyatt offers his arm. I link mine with it, like it's the most natural thing in the world and I've done it a million times.

A few curious gazes bore into my back. I turn my head and

see the security guards watching, like they can't believe their eyes. I've never had a lunch date come pick me up like this before. But let 'em wonder. I'm enjoying being with Wyatt way too much. Besides, it isn't against my employment contract.

The burger joint Wyatt takes me to is a hole-in-the-wall, small and neat. But the place is surprisingly busy, with a long line, and as soon as we get within olfactory range, I understand why. There is a positively crack-tastic aroma coming from the kitchen and tables. If their food tastes half as good as it smells, it's going to be killer.

With a hand at the small of my back, Wyatt bypasses the line and goes straight to the bar. A man with silver hair and laugh lines fanning from the corners of his eyes walks around the counter and comes over, an apron loose around his comfortable girth. "Wyatt, good to see you! Your table's over there."

"Thanks, man."

"You take reservations?" I ask the man, surprised. This place doesn't seem like the type to do so because... Well. Just look at the line.

"No, but an exception can be made for a friend of Dane's." He winks.

I resist an urge to wiggle a finger in my ear. It's hard to imagine that Dane is this well liked in the city.

We sit down, and the man walks back to the bar, leaving us to his server. The waiter brings our water. I pick up a laminated sheet and look at Wyatt over the bright yellow and red on the menu.

"You have to tell me the story between that man and Dane," I say. "I can't believe Dane was nice enough to someone to get special treatment."

Wyatt laughs. "There's no big story. The owner over there was having some financial issues, and Dane invested in the business."

"This is a pretty small business. Doesn't Dane usually operate in a larger financial space?"

Wyatt shrugs. "He just likes the burgers here a lot."

I look at the menu dubiously. *Dane likes them so much, huh...* "They aren't poisoned, are they?" I can see him feeding them to his enemies while sneering, *Eat 'em and die*. Dane himself, of course, would be immune.

Wyatt laughs. "Dane's not that bad."

"Yeah, the jury's still out on that. So what do you recommend?"

"Bacon cheeseburger and fries." Then he hesitates and adds, "But you can also get a salad, if you want. They have a couple."

My mom's texts from this morning pop into my head.

You're going to be in your thirties soon. Your metabolism's going to slow down and nothing will stop you from becoming too fat to be an acceptable wife.

My eyes start to narrow.

Not even those barre classes will save you. Do you know what being fat does to a woman's market value?

"Kim?" Wyatt asks.

I pull myself back to the present. I texted Wyatt so we could have a nice time together, not so I could dwell on her toxic messages and let them ruin our date.

"Are you kidding? Why would I want a salad?"

"Well... You know."

Oh geez. I rub my forehead as it becomes clear. I've seen countless women who say they want one thing—*Oh my God, I want the richest chocolate you can find!*—then complain when they get it because it'll make them fat. I had to deal with those asinine complaints for my boss more than once when he was still in his player phase. A couple even accused me of trying to sabotage their size-zero bodies so I could snag Salazar for myself. Obviously, Wyatt's had one too many encounters with those types. "I'm getting the burger *and* the fries," I say firmly.

Wyatt grins. "My kind of girl. You won't regret it."

When our waiter comes by, we place our order. Since we have to go back to work afterward, we get soft drinks. I need to be clearheaded to deal with my boss because there's no telling what he's going to throw at me after a month away.

I sigh longingly at their beer options. "I bet it'd be great with a cold Pacifico."

Wyatt places a hand on his chest. "Be still, my heart. Maybe next time."

We chat about nothing in particular. He lets me see some pictures from his mom, which show Vi having a lot of fun with her grandparents. I smile at her light, happy expression. Good for her. She deserves some fun after that clusterfuck of a wedding. Thinking about it spikes my blood pressure again. There's a special flaming hole in hell—no, *below* hell—with Geneva's name on it.

"By the way, you know anybody who's looking to become an assistant?" Wyatt asks.

"Not at the moment. Why?"

"I need one. I have an interview this afternoon, but I'm not sure if she'll work out. She had another interview this morning. If it weren't for Melanie, I would've already had a new one by now." He tells me how Melanie conveniently "forgot" to tell him about the potential candidate.

Wow. I knew his assistant sucked, but this is full-blown sabotage. "I'll ask around," I say, although I'm not too optimistic. All the best assistants I know are already working. Bosses who know what they're doing treat their assistants well, especially if they're good at their job. "But let me know how things go with your candidate this afternoon."

"Thanks." He smiles.

Just then, our order arrives. The bacon strips are perfectly browned, the cheese still melting over the sizzling patties. Since the food looks so amazing—and because I'm feeling a little catty—I pull out my phone, snap a picture and send it to Mom. She can look at my lunch and weep, while gnawing on raw radishes and celery to maintain her trophy-body thinness.

That done, I pick up the huge burger and take a bite. *Holy cow.* It's so, *so* good—hot, juicy and flavorful beef enhanced by salty cheese and crispy bacon. The sour hint of pickles adds to the overall effect. No wonder that asshole Dane invested with the owner.

"Like it?" Wyatt's eyes are twinkling.

I nod, chewing my food and swallowing. "Yes. It's amazing." I take another bite, then another. The fries are great too, especially dipped with their specialty ketchup, which has a perfect balance of tanginess and sweetness.

After a few silent moments of eating, my face prickles. I realize Wyatt's been staring.

"What?" I ask, suddenly feeling awkward. Do I have ketchup on my face? I start to reach for a napkin.

"It's just... I can't remember the last time one of my dates actually enjoyed her food."

"Maybe you took them to crappy restaurants," I joke.

"Nope. They just nibbled, or ate salad." He takes a big bite of his burger.

I shrug. "That's their thing. I exercise at least three times a week so I can eat what I want. Life's too short to live on lettuce, and it isn't my job to be a size two. That's for models and aspiring trophy wives." I sneer on the last part. "I'm more than a dress size." *Contrary to what my mom insists.*

"I'm more interested in your brain size," he deadpans, while pointedly letting his eyes rest on my chest.

"Rein it in, sparky. Women don't carry their brains in their breasts."

"Hmm. Jury's out on that, too."

I raise an eyebrow, but I also laugh.

"Glad you're feeling better," Wyatt says. "You've been a little preoccupied here."

"It's just... Mom's going to find out we're dating, and she'll probably just show up here one day to 'help things along.'"

"You're close?" he asks, sounding surprised. Everyone in my hometown knows Mom and I have our differences, even if they don't know exactly why. I was too ashamed to advertise my mom's materialistic tendencies.

"No. But she's really going to want to get to know you better and all that."

I stop, wondering just how much I should say. Mom's obsession with marrying rich guys is totally embarrassing. But at the same time, I want Wyatt to know what he's getting into. He's calling himself my boyfriend, and Mom's going to come at both of us, doing her best to manipulate us into marrying each other, not because of love but because of Wyatt's net worth.

Very slowly, I breathe in and out, choosing my words carefully. "Mom wants to live vicariously through me. You know she married, like, five times, right?"

He nods, then offers me one of his fries, which I accept, since it's an act of great caring for a guy to offer a fry.

"She married for money each time, all of them millionaires. Her greatest regret in life is that she never got to marry a billionaire." I bite into my burger to give myself some time to think. "I think she would've had me marry my boss if he were single."

Wyatt's jaw drops. "Your boss…as in Salazar?"

"Yup."

"Isn't he old enough to be your dad?"

Tension creeps into my shoulders, making them rise. "He might almost be old enough to be my mother's dad. But that's not even an issue, as far as she's concerned. The only thing that matters is that he's worth billions."

Wyatt stares, his mouth opening and closing a few times like he feels like he ought to say something but can't think of anything suitable.

I shrug, trying to hide the humiliation churning inside me. Talking with my girlfriends about my mom's endless need to get me to marry the way she wants didn't make me feel bad. But with him, it's different. I wasn't risking the end of a friendship by letting a girlfriend know. Him? Hell, any sane man would run the other way. I would if I were him.

You like him.

That. And I don't want him to think I care about his money because I don't. Except I don't know how to prove that to him. It isn't like you can X-ray the truth in your heart and show it to someone.

Finally, he reaches out and takes my hand in his, gently squeezing. "I'm sorry."

The cold and ugly knot of shame in my belly thaws and loosens at this simple understanding. Suddenly, I'm feeling calmer, more centered and anchored. "Thank you," I say. Sometimes a little sympathy is all I need.

40

KIM

After wishing Wyatt luck with his new assistant candidate, I hurry back to the office. Salazar's coming back from his trip, and I want to be in before he arrives in case he needs something. He *always* needs something after his vacations.

Since I'm a few minutes late, I'm spared the worst of the interrogation from others in the building, even though I have a few messages from my coworkers asking me about "that hottie."

I ignore them for the time being, because Salazar's going to come walking in at any minute. I go over his schedule for the rest of the week one more time so I can be on top of everything when he asks to review his agenda. No stumbling or stuttering allowed in the world of Salazar Pryce.

Ready, I wait. However, Salazar doesn't arrive until almost two.

"The traffic!" he says as he walks in, dashing as ever in a dress shirt with the collar undone and dark slacks. They're new—probably hand-stitched in Paris. "I honestly didn't miss it."

I smile with sympathy. Since I don't want him to dwell on anything annoying, I pick a tack that never fails to make him happy—flattery. "You've got a pretty good tan, there."

As usual, it works like charm. He grins and preens a bit. "I know. Brings out my eyes, doesn't it?"

It actually does. "You look rested and healthy."

He gives a contented sigh. "It's the travel. Nothing like seeing the world with the woman you love."

I refrain from asking why he divorced Ceinlys if he loves her so much. Then I wonder if he's going to propose to her again—and if so, what kind of ring I'll need to buy for the occasion.

"Would you like some coffee?" I ask.

"No, thanks. But here you go." He places a large, glossy shopping bag from Dior on my desk. "A gift from both of us. You outdid yourself for the trip."

Pride over a job well done flows through me. "Thank you." I push the rustling tissue paper aside and see two gorgeous lambskin purses—one in pink and the other in black. Underneath the bags are two large boxes of Swiss chocolates. I pick up the pink bag. Its softness is like some alien technology. "These are...exquisite."

"Glad you like 'em." He starts toward his office. "Ceinlys picked them out."

Making a mental note to send her a thank-you card, I put the presents in my chair and follow him.

He takes a seat behind his massive desk and taps the wooden surface. "Okay, the statue. Where is it?"

Oh shit. François's *Wife*! I totally spaced out and forgot to ask Wyatt about it over the weekend or earlier today. He's probably got it stored in some temperature- and humidity-controlled warehouse, and I'll need to make arrangements to transfer it over to wherever Salazar wants it. "Ah, I don't have it in hand just yet, but we should at least agree on a price by the end of the week."

"Fantastic. Plenty of time. I'm planning to give it to her thirty days from now. Be like a one-month anniversary of our trip together."

Only he would consider a multimillion-dollar statue a suitable for gift for something like this. Actually, only he would think the one-month anniversary of a trip would be worthy of a celebration at all.

"Should I book dinner at a restaurant as well?" I ask.

"Yeah, someplace classy. And flowers. Gotta have flowers."

I nod, making notes to arrange for all of that, plus come up with at least one thing he can try to make Ceinlys happy. He appreciates suggestions. "Got it." Then I add "Start browsing for engagement rings" to the list. At the rate things are going, he's going to re-propose before the year is over, and I need to be prepared. It's my job to anticipate his needs.

That done, I return to my workstation and pull out my phone. Need to get this arranged as soon as possible.

–Me: You remember Dane's housewarming gift? The one you're supposed to let me buy? When can I send somebody to appraise it?

–Wyatt: No need for an appraisal. You can just have it.

I shake my head. He shouldn't give away something that valuable for free, not even to me. Besides, why is he assuming it's for me? There's no place in my apartment that statue would fit, any more than it would fit into his.

–Me: It's for my boss. He can afford to pay for it.

–Wyatt: Still isn't that much money.

Reeeeally? When did he become so cavalier about millions?

I type, *I know you're rich now, but you really need to be more sensible about finances*, then stop and hit delete until all the letters are gone. It's his money. On the other hand, I feel like it's my obligation to tell him, in case he doesn't know how much François's works are worth.

–Me: I insist. It wouldn't be right otherwise.

–Wyatt: Well okay, if you want. Talk about it over dinner tonight? My place.

I find myself smiling at that.

—Me: Sure.

—Wyatt: Great. Oops, gotta go. The interviewee is here.

That's right. His possible new assistant.

—Me: Hope she works out!

I put my phone away and sigh with pleasure. Finally, it feels like my whole life is exactly on the right track. I have a boyfriend I'm crazy about, and I'm about to get my five-hundred-thousand-dollar bonus. Nothing—absolutely nothing—is going to mess things up now.

41

KIM

I leave work early because Salazar insists that I "take a load off." When I'm home, thankfully, Yuna doesn't look like a sci-fi monster. Just her normal self in a dress and watching TV with Champ. He comes over, tail swishing in the air, and sniffs my fingers.

"You're home early," she says.

"Yeah, I have the best boss." I kick off my shoes and roll my shoulders as I go to the kitchen for a glass of water.

"Is there a gym in this building?" she asks.

"No. Why?"

She looks down at herself, a small frown marring her forehead. "I'm getting fat. Like, huge. I need to work off the extra calories."

I tilt my head, wondering where those "extra calories" are. She's gotta be a size zero or pretty close. Still, she looks unhappy about it, so I decide, *Why not?* "My friends and I are going to a barre session tomorrow after work if you want to come." Jo and Hilary won't mind meeting my new roommate.

"Really?" She brightens. "I'd love that. It's like ballet, right?"

"Sort of," I say, hoping she doesn't show up in a pink tutu. I'm learning that you never know with Yuna.

"Awesome. I've done ballet, but not barre. Always wanted to try it."

My phone pings and I check the text. It's Wyatt asking what I want for dinner. I start to type Thai, then stop. Does Yuna want to join us? I feel bad about leaving her alone in the apartment again after the weekend. It doesn't look like she has a lot of friends —at least, I haven't noticed anybody coming over—and she's "hiding" from her mom's evil spies. She must be getting pretty bored and restless.

"Do you want to have dinner with us?" I blurt out before I can catch myself.

"No, thanks," she says. "I'm going to make myself a salad. But maybe tomorrow after working out?"

"Oh. Okay." The girls and I do drinks, and Yuna will enjoy that.

I let Wyatt know I want Thai and take Champ out for his walk, again because I'm feeling bad about the fact that Yuna's been taking care of my dog. She said she would when she moved in, but still, he's my responsibility.

When Champ and I make it back to the apartment—after much snuffling and exploration on Champ's part—I get another message from Wyatt.

–Wyatt: In the elevator. Be there soon.

Happy anticipation fills me. I slide a bowl of food under Champ's nose, then wait for Wyatt in front of his door.

I hear the small ping from the elevator. Wyatt steps out, carrying a brown bag. A smile breaks out over my face, and my heart feels funny. Pounding hard and fast isn't the half of it; more like it's trying out for the U.S. gymnastics Team. I almost put a hand over it, so it doesn't triple-twist out of my chest. Is this what people mean when they say their heart flip-flopped?

Wyatt walks up, puts his free arm around my waist and kisses me. "Evenin'."

"Good evening," I say, a little bit breathless.

"Let's have dinner." He unlocks the door and opens it. I walk inside with him. Princess comes over and rubs herself all around my ankles, her small body vibrating as she purrs. I pick her up and check her crown. *Still white, thank God. Pink would have been—*

"I think she really likes you," Wyatt says.

"Yeah, she does. And I like her too. I just wish she'd stop leaving me presents."

He shakes his head. "I don't know why she does that to you when she doesn't to me or Vi."

I stare the cat in the eyes. "You need to stop, Princess. I don't like dead bugs. Or birds. Or rodents. I like chocolate...but you can't catch that in the wild."

Princess mewls, then twists until she's free from my grasp and lands on her feet.

Wyatt spreads the Thai food on the table and gives me a paper plate from the bag. My mouth waters at green shrimp curry with rice, pad Thai, a sea bass simmered in some spicy broth and green mango salad. All the things I texted him that I loved.

"This is going to be *so* good." I gesture at the salad.

"I've never had it," he says, looking at the food dubiously. "Isn't green mango sort of disgusting?"

"No, it's good. You'll like it."

We split the food. He chews on the salad dutifully, then pushes it slightly more toward my way. I smother a smile, pretending not to notice. Okay, maybe it isn't his thing. It's on the crispy side and spicy.

"So. How did the interview go?" I ask.

"It went fine. Actually, better than fine. Loren's perfect."

I beam, happy that he'll finally be free of Melanie. "Great. So she said yes?"

He frowns. "No. She has two other offers, and another interview tomorrow. So she's going to let me know after she explores all her options."

"You're mad she's being thorough with her choices?" I ask, unsure why he's annoyed by something any sensible candidate would do.

"No. I'm mad that I might've never got a chance to interview her. And also because if I'd interviewed her first—and made the first offer—she might've said yes to me, instead of making me wait."

I pat his shoulder, which is unusually tense. "If she's as good as you say, she knew she would get a lot of offers. But you're a great guy, Wyatt. I'm sure that's going to count when she makes her final decision."

He gives me a small smile. "Thanks." Then he asks, "How'd you decide to work for Salazar instead of somebody else? You had a bunch of offers too, right?"

"Yeah. But I was a bit too new, so they weren't, like, *amazing* offers. I chose Salazar because—despite his reputation—he offered the most generous compensation package, including a significant bonus at the end of my fifth year. Half a million dollars if I never fail in my duties."

"Wow... Never fail in your duties for five years? Is it even possible to earn that money?"

"Sure." I grin widely. "I'm going to get it as soon as I give him the statue."

"A statue? Sounds a little weird, but okay."

Maybe I should've been more specific. "The one Dane gave you. You said you'd give it to me. I mean, I'm going to use Salazar's money to pay you, but..."

Wyatt frowns. "What are you talking about?"

"The statue. That Dane gave to you for housewarming."

The frown deepens. "He gave me this." He goes to the coffee table and picks up a glossy book full of pictures of the architectural wonders of the world. It's a signed first edition, but it's no statue. "That's it."

And a huge ball of ice forms in the pit of my stomach. *"That's* what he gave you?"

"Yeah."

"That's all? Nothing else?"

"Yeah..." Wyatt says, like he knows he's become the bearer of bad news.

No way. Wyatt must be forgetting something. "No key to a warehouse or storage unit somewhere?"

"Uh...no. And he didn't go through Melanie," he adds,

answering the question I was about to ask. "He gave me the book directly."

"Oh shit." I breathe out shakily. "No wonder you kept saying you were going to just give it to me." Propping my elbows on the table, I drop my head in my hands. Five years of hustling and busting my butt down the drain. All because of this one final task! My financial plans are ruined too. Not that I'll be left homeless or anything like that, but this was going to be my nest egg, a source of security so I could claim financial independence and do what I want. I can just imagine my mom's expression now, full of pity and gleeful satisfaction. *What did I tell you? You need a man with money because you can't do it on your own.* She'll start sending me dossiers, like Yuna's mom. The idea is simply too nauseating... In fact, it's infuriating. "Damn it, damn it, *damn it*. I should've known better than to trust him when he said he was giving it to you."

I'm going to murder Dane. He thinks he's so cool and immune, but I'm sure he's not impervious to chlorine. Or I can stir some anthrax into his coffee when he visits Salazar at his office.

"Hey, don't worry. I'll take care of this," Wyatt says.

I lift my head. "How?"

"Easy. I'll just talk with Dane and get it from him."

"It's not going to work," I say. "He's giving it to Sophia."

"How do you know that?"

"Because why else would he buy something called *Wife* and not give it to you like he said he was planning to?" And no matter how close Wyatt is to Dane, he's not going to get the statue out of Dane's sticky grip, not when he's decided it's for his wife, the only person in the world he cares about."

Wyatt curses under his breath. "So if you don't have the statue, Salazar isn't going to give you the five-year bonus?"

"No," I say, feeling like my whole world is ending. I worked so damn hard for that bonus! "It's in the contract. If I didn't know that my boss and Dane don't usually get along, I might've thought they did this on purpose." Then I shake my head at how ridiculous and unfair I'm being. "Actually, I wouldn't think that even then. It isn't like it's a lot of money to him."

"So he might give it to you, especially if it's because of his son that you couldn't get it."

"No, he won't. Salazar sticks to his contracts, no matter what. I've seen him in action." And that's why I still respect the man. Despite all his crazy antics and entitled attitude, he's scrupulous about certain things.

Wyatt drums his fingers on the table for a couple of moments. "What if I give you the money? Technically, I'm partially responsible for the problem. You wouldn't have helped me if you knew I never had the statue. You would've looked for another way, instead of wasting time going off in the wrong direction."

My face twists as though he just offered me a dead mouse on a plate. "I don't want your money," I say, doing my best to ensure my voice is calm even though I'm seriously unhappy that he's even offering. *He's just trying to make things better without realizing how his solution is making me feel.*

"Half a million is half a million, wherever it comes from," he says. "And it's not like I can't afford—"

"But I didn't *earn* it." The money I was supposed to get is Salazar's, paying me for doing my job. This isn't about who's rich enough to give me the money out of pity.

"Yes, you did," he says. "If Dane had given me the statue like he was supposed to, you'd be getting your bonus."

"Yeah, but the fact is he didn't." I don't want to argue about this. I'm afraid I'm going to burst into frustrated tears if we keep talking about it. "I know it's hard to understand because you've never had to live in a situation like I did, but I don't want to just *take* things. That's how my *mom's* life. She never worked to achieve what she wanted on her own. Succeed or fail, I want to do it myself. Does that make sense?"

I hope it does, because I don't have the heart to keep talking about this. I already told him about my mom. He also heard Geneva accusing me of staying with him just for his money. Although I didn't show it, that little jab did find its mark. It's just that I was too upset over Geneva's attack on Vi to really process it.

"Anyway," I add, "don't worry about it. It's my fault for not checking every detail." Because I should've never assumed. That's what makes me good at my job. I don't know why I didn't do my due diligence on this latest task.

"You know why I have broad shoulders?" Wyatt says after a moment.

"Um." I look at him, unsure why he's suddenly talking about his shoulders. "Because you work out...?"

He laughs a little. "Yeah, that, but they're here so I can lend one to a pretty girl who's doing her best not to show how upset she is."

My chin trembles for a moment. He pulls me closer and kisses me on my forehead, offering silent comfort.

WYATT

I HOLD KIM, WATCHING HER SLEEP. SHE FINALLY RELAXED after a few orgasms, then quickly dropped off.

She opened up so much over dinner. Now that she isn't emotionally falling apart in disappointment over the bonus, I'm free to think about everything more clearly.

Her relationship with her mother must be worse than I thought. I knew her mom was a little weird. Hell, everyone in Corn Meadows knew. She was too brash, trying too hard to appear young and fashionable. She even seemed to want to compete against Kim from time to time.

Geneva saying that Kim's only with me for my financial assets probably galled her, too. So if Kim was to take half a million bucks from me to make up for the bonus she lost out on, it really would look like she's with me for money, even though I know the truth. And that'd be unacceptable to her pride. Her mom's already hounding her to marry somebody rich—me, in this case—from what Kim said.

Is my money actually something that *detracts* from our relationship? I've never thought of it that way. To be honest, I'm proud of the fact that I created something so valuable and worthwhile that I was able to sell it for enough to live well, provide for my daughter and still have a lot left over to help other people out.

Kim rejected my help because she thinks I'm just going to wire five hundred thousand into her bank account. That's not the plan, though.

Dane's going to give me the damned statue, and I'll make sure Kim gets it to her boss. She's worked too hard to lose out on my account.

42

KIM

THE NEXT DAY IS HORRIBLE. I TRY TO COME UP WITH A solution to the statue problem, but there doesn't seem to be one. And it makes me feel like a horrible failure. Salazar, of course, has no idea. He's glowing, probably imagining giving the statue to Ceinlys and earning Brownie points. Maybe he's planning on using it as an engagement statue. After all, he's given her a ring already, and he does hate to repeat himself.

If he thinks I'm the reason he can't grandly re-propose to his ex-wife, he might just fire me without reference. He might even put the word out not to hire me because I suck.

Stop. Being. Negative.

Easier said than done. Maybe I should hire a team of Navy SEALs to extract the statue from Dane. Things like that happen all the time in Hollywood movies and it always works out great. And the fact that I'm willing to even entertain such an idea means...I need to stop obsessing about it for the moment, because I'm not going to come up with a real-world solution like this.

After work, I go to barre to exercise with my friends. The plan is to *not* think about François's *Wife*. My brain needs a break, and maybe something amazing will come to me if I just let my subconscious work on the problem for a while.

When Jo and Hilary ask me how my day's been, I tell them it's been fantastic. I'm not going to talk about the big worry or even think about it. *Sticking to the plan.*

Yuna joins us, having arrived just in time for the class. I still don't understand where she's storing her so-called extra calories, because even in skintight workout clothes, she's slim. Amazingly, Jo agrees as we hit the bar afterward.

"You could afford to gain a few pounds." Jo looks Yuna up and down again. "Or maybe not, since I bet you can make anything look good. Love your outfit, by the way."

I shake my head inwardly. Just like Jo to look at people like they're walking hangers, then notice how they're put together. But that's her job—dressing people fabulously. And I have to admit that I haven't yet seen Yuna looking bad, except for the seaweed incident. Even after a strenuous barre session, her makeup is flawless. And she wasn't half-assing it in the studio, either. It's gotta be magic, since my lipstick is more or less gone. My mascara's okay, but only because it's water- and sweat-proof.

"Thank you," Yuna says with a smile, crossing her leotard-clad legs. The pastel pink would make me look pudgy and soft. Not her, though.

"If you look less fashionable, maybe your mom won't ask you to get married," I joke, remembering why she's hiding out in my apartment.

Yuna laughs. "I wish. She'd just hire a makeup artist and outfit coordinator to follow me around and make sure I look perfect enough to suit her."

Wow. Maybe her mother and mine are long-lost sisters. At least when it comes to plans for their daughters.

"Really? Is she very critical?" Hilary asks, her eyes wide.

"No. She just wants what she thinks is best for me." The ironic smile on Yuna's face says she disagrees with what her mom considers "best." Then she turns to me. "By the way, is everything okay? You seemed really distracted this morning."

"Was I that obvious?" I thought I was doing okay outwardly, despite my internal angst about the statue. And thinking about

Dane's grip on the damned hunk of bronze is spiking my stress level.

"Yeah. Because I asked you twice if you wanted me to walk Champ, and you said you didn't want breakfast."

"That's, like, nuclear bomb level," Jo says. "You're never that distracted."

"Everything okay at work?" Hilary asks.

"Or was Wyatt lacking in bedroom technique?" Yuna adds.

That makes my friends sit up straight, and I drop my head in my palm. I haven't had time to talk about my relationship status with Jo and Hilary because I've been busy with Salazar's return and the statue situation and...well, distracted. But right now, they're looking at me like I'm a traitor.

"You slept with Wyatt?" Hilary says slowly, her voice rising a bit. "I thought you hated his guts."

Jo waves an index finger up and down. "Okay, blow-by-blow postmortem. That was the deal."

"Postmortems are morbid," I say, like that's going to be acceptable to either of them.

Our waitress brings our cocktails, interrupting the inquisition. She's getting a fat tip.

My friends grab theirs, and Yuna sips her daiquiri daintily, looking at me through her lashes.

I gulp down half my margarita. "I need to begin with the wedding." And I don't mind starting from there because Yuna hasn't heard the story either.

So in broad strokes, I tell them about the ceremony, how I caught Churchill cheating and Geneva's big revelation.

"Holy shit, that's *makjang*," Yuna says.

"What's that?" I ask.

"Super messed up," she explains. "But it happened over the weekend, so that wasn't why you told me you weren't having breakfast today."

Yuna has to be leading another life as a freelance CIA interrogator. "No." I tell them the rest of the story involving my five-year bonus and the mix-up with the housewarming gift.

Jo smacks the table with a fist. "Oh, that rat bastard."

"Should have checked to make sure." Hilary sounds positively mournful.

I heave a long sigh. "I know. I can't believe I screwed up."

"I'm so sorry." Hilary pats my hand. "Dane's a tricky...um... guy." I'm certain the word she really wanted was "bastard" or "asshole."

I sigh again. *If I'd just asked exactly what Wyatt got from Dane...* On the other hand, it probably wouldn't have changed what I did for Wyatt. I would've still helped out in the end. Not for him, but for Vi. But if I'd known, I would've been working on a way to pry *Wife* out of Dane's cold, tight fist...like bribing his wife, because she can make Dane do anything, up to and including drive a pink car.

Yuna finishes her drink. "If you want, I could hire you instead. I can't do a huge signing bonus, but we can probably work something out."

The offer surprises me. "You?" Yuna's been hiding from her matchmaking mom. Does she need an assistant for that?

Jo and Hilary lean closer toward Yuna. She nods. "Yeah, it's about time I get an assistant who answers to me, not my parents. I have my own money. Grandpa left me a small trust."

To someone like Yuna, "small" is probably like several million bucks. Even tens of millions. "Why haven't you hired one, then?"

"I'm not hiring anybody from Korea because my parents can always buy them off or influence them by dangling jobs for their family and so on. But Americans are complicated. It's hard for me to tell who's, you know...good." Yuna props her elbow on the table and rests her chin in her hand. "But I think you're perfect. I can match or better whatever salary you're getting now. And I can offer a huge lump-sum bonus, too, plus semi-annual ones and so on."

I laugh, certain she's joking. Nobody makes a job offer like this just...out of the blue. She has no idea how much Salazar's been paying me, either, or what my benefits look like. Jo and Hilary both smile as well.

Yuna frowns. "I'm serious. Think about it."

"Would I have to move to Korea?" I say, no longer laughing.

"Well, not necessarily, but you might have to travel with me. I don't let my staff fly economy. Just sayin'."

"Are you going to be upset if I turn you down?" We're sharing an apartment, and I don't want any awkwardness.

"Nope," she says, like a woman discussing a recent meal. "This is America, right? Free country and all that." Now she smiles.

I nod, but instead of the barre and the post-workout drink session clearing my head, now it's more jumbled with this surprise job offer. Not that I'm necessarily willing to leave Salazar for Yuna. To be honest, I don't know what I'm going to do. It's a pretty complicated situation, even if she says no relocation is necessary. She said she might want me to travel with her, and that means I might have to spend time in Korea. What if she marries one of the men her mom chooses?

And even after I get home—Wyatt must still be at work, because he didn't answer when I knocked on his door—I keep mulling it over. Part of me thinks maybe I can leverage it to get a pay raise out of Salazar—maybe even get him to give me the bonus anyway—but the other part shudders at the idea. I didn't earn it, and it almost feels like it would be blackmailing him into giving me the money.

Yeah, but it's just one task out of all the others.

A deal is still a deal, I tell myself, resentful that I'm going to miss the bonus and angry and guilty that I'm even thinking about arguing Salazar into giving it to me.

Maybe half the bonus...?

Champ comes over and licks my fingers. I scratch behind his ear, then hug him as my mind wrestles with all the complicated options.

43

WYATT

The second I stop my Audi in front of Éternité, a valet rushes over. I shake my head. "I'm not eating. I'll be out in a few minutes."

"That's fine, sir, but you can't leave your car here."

I hand him a few bills. "Just a few minutes."

He looks conflicted, but takes the money. "Okay, sir. Twenty minutes, but after that, I have to move it."

I nod, then give him my keys, since it doesn't look like he's going to let me pass otherwise.

The place is packed. I guess L.A. is full of people dying to eat *otoro* and sip wine. And Dane is one of them, since his wife loves it so much.

I tell the hostess I'm here to see Dane Pryce. She looks surprised, but I give her my most confident look, one that says not only do I belong in this fancy-schmancy restaurant, but that Dane is dying to see me. The hostess bites her lower lip.

"I'm supposed to meet his wife, Sophia. It's a surprise." Laying it on a little thick. I'm probably going to piss Dane off, but I don't give a damn. He shouldn't have lied to Kim. And he should've picked up the phone or at least answered my text when I tried to reach him earlier.

Finally, the hostess nods and takes me to a table in the back, by the faux waterfall. I can see why she looked so skeptical earlier. The seating is for two and utterly romantic, with an orange-pink flower centerpiece and a pure white orchid lying by Sophia's side. Dane's wife is stunning as usual, her golden hair twisted up in some fancy style, and pink gems glittering from her ears and fingers. Probably diamonds, if I know Dane. She waves when she notices me.

Dane turns around. The curiosity on his face turns into pure annoyance, which is gratifying. "What are you doing here?"

"Why, hey, Dane. Good to see you." I maintain the friendly smile for Sophia's benefit. She could use a little sunshine. She's married to my ice-cold friend, after all. "You don't think I might be here to eat?"

His expression says I'm not fooling anybody. "No. You don't like anything on the menu."

"Got that right. But look, I need to talk to you for a minute. I tried calling and texting, and you've been ignoring me."

The annoyance sharpens to irritation. "Because I was busy working so I could have a nice night out with my wife." His tone says I'm a pest, and that's putting it kindly. "Did Roxie tell you I was going to be here?"

"I told her it was for Kim." Lying to him to save his assistant would only backfire. Dane hates liars even more than people interrupting his time with his wife.

"She's fired."

Oh, shit. Before I can rise to Roxie's defense, Sophia places a hand on Dane's sleeve.

"Dane, you can't mean that," she says softly. "She's really good at her job. You like her, and so do I."

He lets out a breath, his shoulders no longer extra tight. Just normal tight.

"She's really the sweetest. And she helped me out so much when I first got here. I might not have stayed in Los Angeles without her."

"All right. For that, I'll let her keep her job," Dane says finally, taking her small hand from his sleeve, turning it over and massaging the center of the palm with his thumb.

This tender gesture is so alien for him that I actually feel a creepy sensation. Like a thousand ants marching over my back.

She rewards him with a brilliant smile, then turns to me. "I don't suppose you came here just to crash our dinner. So what can we do for you?"

"It's about a housewarming gift," I say, relieved that Sophia has saved Roxie's job. I turn to Dane. "You told Kim you're going to give me a statue, but I never got it. I promised Kim I'd give it to her if she'd go to my ex-wife's wedding with me."

"I was going to give it to you after you moved into a proper home to serve as a constant reminder of your mistake with Geneva so you don't repeat it," he says, but I think it's more for his wife's benefit than mine. He isn't the type to justify himself to anybody, not even his friends.

Like I'm ever going to forget! "What's wrong with my apartment?"

He shoots me a disgusted "oh please" look, then reaches into his pocket and pulls out a key ring in the shape of the letter D. He searches through it, pulls one key off and hands it me. Then he starts tapping on his phone.

Mine pings in my pocket.

"I just texted you the address and passcode. You'll also need the key to enter the warehouse."

"You've been carrying this all along?" I ask.

"Can't leave it lying around. The statue is one of a kind."

He should've just given it to me earlier, then. But before I can say it, Dane pointedly looks in the direction of the exit. "Now, can I share a nice meal with my wife without persona non grata present?"

"Of course." I shove the key into my pants pocket. "My apologies for the interruption, Sophia. Enjoy your date night."

She waves with a smile, while Dane continues to give me a death glare.

I walk out, doing my best to suppress the urge to pump my fist and dance around. I feel like that dude who just slayed dragons. Come to think of it, Dane is sort of like a dragon.

Excitement swells in my chest. I've fixed things for Kim. Now she can get her bonus.

"Yes!" I say under my breath, then take my keys back from the valet and climb into my car. I can't wait to surprise Kim.

44

KIM

SINCE WYATT'S NOT HOME AND I NEED TO DISTRACT MYSELF, I join Yuna in the living room and watch an Asian historical drama. Champ squirms his way in and lies between us.

"That baby's going to die!" Yuna says, pointing at a cute infant on the screen.

I look at her. "Why do you say that?"

"Because he's the empress's baby. Did you not notice how the concubines have sons, too?"

"Yeah, but..."

"So in order for them to push their sons into power, they have to kill the baby. Mark my words. That baby won't even last a full episode."

"So only girls are safe..." I murmur, feeling sorry for the fictional baby.

"No. If it's a girl, her own mother might kill her."

"The *mom*?"

"Sure. To frame another concubine. Or even the empress. Because who would suspect a mother of murdering her own baby?" Yuna gives me a significant look.

I make a small noise in the back of my throat because I feel like I should...respond in some way. I prefer my entertainment a little bit less gruesome, without any babies in jeopardy.

"*Game of Thrones* could've been better if they'd gone *really* ruthless," Yuna adds.

Okay, I don't know if I want to have a boss who thinks *Game of Thrones* isn't hardcore enough. Who said Asian women were sweet and retiring?

Someone knocks at the door. Eager to escape the darkly morbid drama, I stand up to get it. Champ follows, since he has an overwhelming need to check out every visitor.

Wyatt's standing there, a wide grin splitting his gorgeous face and his eyes sparkling like the ocean. I smile at him, something inside me going all happy and gooey. There's an urge to kiss him, absorb something of his brightness, and an urge to just hug him hard and cuddle and forget about the statue, disappointing Salazar, Yuna's job offer and all the rest of the troublesome, complicated world as well. But before I can decide, Champ noses his way between us and licks Wyatt's fingers. He laughs and scratches Champ's head, making the canine's eyes narrow with bliss.

"Hey. Thought you were working late." I gesture for him to come in.

He does so, waving at Yuna, who gives an anemic hand lift in return, her eyes glued to the TV and a gaggle of elegantly dressed women cooing over the apparently doomed baby.

"Just had to take care of something. And now, I have some very good news." His grin grows wider. "Guess what."

"Your new assistant candidate said yes?" It's the only thing I can think of that could've put a smile this big on him.

He shakes his head.

"Hmm... Geneva fell into a ditch and went bald?"

"Ha! Nope."

Ah, too bad. Karma works very slowly. "I don't know."

He laughs, then looks at me like he's about to tell me I just won a trip to Disneyland. "I got the statue."

"Statue?" I repeat, my mouth suddenly dry. He can't possibly mean what I hope he means. Dane is Satan.

Wyatt nods. "I got Dane's *Wife*. I mean, um, not Sophia. The statue! Had Dane hand it over."

"I can't believe this! You just *asked* him...and he gave it to you?"

Wyatt swells himself up a little. "Dane knows better than to mess with this old boy." But he winks as he says it.

"Oh my God!" I shriek as the words sink in. I jump at him, wrapping my arms around his neck. "Oh my God!"

He hugs me back. "Congratulations, babe!"

I pull back a little so I can see his face. "*Thank* you!"

"Does this mean you won't be working for me?" Yuna asks, as the TV screen stays frozen.

"I guess not," I say. Much as I like Yuna, the idea of working for her is a little scary. "But thank you for the offer anyway." I fan myself, my heart racing with adrenaline. "Okay, um, do you mind if we see the statue?" I ask. It isn't that I doubt Wyatt, but I just have to see François's art for myself. Otherwise it won't really feel real. Even as it is I feel like I'm walking on clouds.

"Not a bit," Wyatt says. "We can go right now."

Swallowing hard, I grab my purse, hands shaking, and say goodbye to Yuna.

I can barely sit still through the drive. The emotional upheaval of the last twenty-four hours is pushing my anticipation to a fever pitch, and my skin is prickling all over.

Wyatt parks the car in front of a very modern-looking building. Probably a temperature- and humidity-controlled warehouse. You don't store art that costs as much as François's works in a U-Haul place. We show our ID to security and walk to the unit Dane must've rented out.

I stand, shifting my weight, as Wyatt turns the key and enters the passcode. With a beep and a flash of green light, the door unlocks. He opens it. "After you."

"Okay." I step inside, my heart pulsing in my throat. I flick on the light switch, then gasp. *What in the name of...?*

The statue is indeed life-sized, but it's hideous. A man is lying on his back, the skin of his chest and belly ripped open. A harpy is hunched over him, his heart in one of her hands and loops of intestine in the other.

My jaw drops, my mind whirring. This can't be what Salazar wants me to get! He's in love with Ceinlys!

"This is...art?" Wyatt asks, his voice barely audible.

I rush to the statue to check. Maybe Dane got the units mixed up. But no. On the man's left foot is François's mark—a stylized *F* and the month and year the statue was completed. This has to be *Wife*.

Oh. My. God. I cover my mouth with both hands.

"Is this really the statue Salazar wants?" Wyatt asks.

"Yeah. But I don't think he knows what it looks like." Or, at least, I hope he doesn't. Because if he thinks Ceinlys will want this, he has another think coming.

"So...does this mean you aren't getting the bonus?" Wyatt asks.

"I doubt he'll ding me for it. He's fair," I say vaguely, more worried about what the statue looks like than my bonus at the moment. I need to save my boss from himself.

"I can't believe Dane thought this would make a good housewarming gift."

I nod, in complete agreement. This is what you keep in your house if you want nightmares.

I snap a quick picture of the statue, then start texting my boss. Suddenly I stop. I need to be cool-headed about this, regain my normal equilibrium. I don't dump problems on Salazar. That's not how I do my job. I always send him solutions or workarounds. I need to research a suitable substitute before delivering this particular bit of bad news.

45

KIM

OUR DRIVE BACK IS QUIET. I THINK WYATT IS STILL STUNNED at the statue, that there are people who would pay money—a lot of money—for something like that. I just can't believe François even made the thing. Doesn't he have better taste?

Eventually, Wyatt tells me how he got the statue from Dane. Maybe he can tell I was curious about it. It isn't easy to get anything out of the Icicle Hog.

When Wyatt's finished, I sit up straight. "You interrupted a date night with his wife?"

"It was the only time I could track him down."

"You were risking your life. Or at least a kneecap."

Wyatt laughs.

But I'm not really kidding. Wyatt went above and beyond to give me what I need. Unlike my mom—and most of my exes—he never once thought it was silly for me to want to be independent or earn my own money. I actually thought he might insist on giving me the money—it would have been easier and safer than confronting Dane.

But he didn't.

Gratitude and something that feels like deep affection bloom in my heart. Everything that's happened since we met again seems like a journey we've taken together. My helping him with Vi and the wedding, his helping me with the statue... We wouldn't have gotten what we needed without each other.

True partnership, my mind says. *You and him against the world.*

It's a new idea. Having a man who's my cheerleader isn't something I ever dreamed of. Maybe it's because of the way my mom harped on men as source of money and material comfort and my refusal to accept it. But I love the idea of being with Wyatt—us leaning on each other and both being stronger for it.

We arrive at our apartment building. I walk with him into his place, pushing the door shut behind us. He places an arm around my shoulder, squeezing gently. I lean into him, loving the physical connection. It cements the team feeling and togetherness in a concrete way.

"Thank you," I say, then turn to him, rising on my toes, and kiss him.

He kisses me back, his lips parting, his tongue probing. I flick his mouth, steal a taste of him that's heady and glorious. I deepen the kiss, my hands on his shoulders, then traveling down his torso until I have them on his chest. His heart pounds against my palms, the beat fast and strong.

Mine races to match his; even in arousal, we're in sync.

I tug at his shirt, untucking it. Then I reach down, undoing his belt and pants, while our mouths are still fused together. His cock is thick and hard in my grasp, hot and eager for me, and an electric pleasure starts to build, making my nipples bead and clit throb.

A deep moan vibrates in his chest, and I smile to myself. He has no clue yet what I have in mind for him. I want him to feel really good. Like, orgasm-blackout good.

I unbutton his shirt and trail kisses down every inch of skin revealed. He smooths my hair as though he can't bear to not touch me. Something warm and sweet that's beyond the searing sexual urge swells inside me, but I try not to think about it too much. I'm on a mission.

Finally, I reach his stomach. His abs are ridged, the skin taut.

The muscles flex as I press my lips, then gently bite the spot below his belly button.

He makes a helpless sound, and heat surges inside me. I tug down his pants and underwear in one motion and his cock springs out, a drop of clear liquid beading at the slit. I trace the veins along the thick shaft with my fingertips, then with my tongue.

Wyatt's breathing grows rougher, filling my ears and turning me on.

"You're delicious," I say, lapping the precum off him.

"You're driving me crazy." His voice is almost unrecognizable, with an edge I haven't heard before.

"Mmm." Gently, I pull him into my mouth. The taste of him fills me—salty and all Wyatt. I move my head, keeping my eyes on his face. His eyes are dark blue slits, and he watches me with the concentrated desperation of a man dying of thirst looking at a tall glass of ice water.

Every little twitch of his muscles, every groan spilling from his mouth, every erratic, uneven breath... They're aphrodisiacs—hotter than anything I've ever experienced. His unbridled pleasure drives me, makes me feel sexy as hell. Right now, it's me giving him this bliss with just my mouth, and it's me who's making him feel so good.

I wrap my lips more tightly around him and move along his cock. The veins in his neck stand out starkly against the tanned skin, and he grits his teeth.

Oh no. You aren't going to try to control yourself.

I run my nails lightly along his balls, while increasing the pressure around him.

"Ah, fuck, Kim!"

He throws his head back and pumps his cock into me, coming in my mouth. His muscles tense, the air in his lungs still. Warm satisfaction courses through me as I watch the orgasm twist through him, wringing him dry.

His chest heaves, and with deliberate care, he pulls away. Then he helps me up and kisses me hard. "Mmm." He wraps his arms around me. "You know I can't let you go like this."

"Like what?" I tease.

"Turned on without any satisfaction." He kisses me again.

"I didn't do it for reciprocation..."

"Not like I have anything else on my plate at the moment," he says with a grin. He pushes me against the wall until I'm resting firmly against it, then pulls my skirt up. "Been wanting to do this for a while."

My breathing grows shallow.

"That skirt is prim as hell, but I know what you're really like when you're aroused. When you're ready to come."

Heat sears my cheeks. His eyes are so brilliant, so blue...and too freakin' hot.

He yanks at my thong, bringing it down to my mid-thigh, then rips it. "I'll buy you a new one."

I start to tell him he doesn't have to. But I don't get the chance, because he sinks to his knees and closes his mouth over me.

I swallow a moan. His mouth is clever, utterly eager. He sweeps his tongue along my clit, then my slick folds. I brace against the wall, locking my knees so I don't collapse like a wet noodle.

Wyatt pulls away for a moment. "Take off your top."

And I do, flinging it on the floor somewhere, feeling hot and sexy at the heat in his gaze.

"Push your bra out of the way. And play with your nipples," he orders.

I hesitate just for a second. I've never...

He gives me another lick, just enough to stoke my need but not enough to ease the sharp desire. "Do it."

Feeling slightly dirty and naughty, I comply. My bra has a front clasp, so I undo it and cup my breasts. The sensation is... novel. It isn't that I've never held myself like this before. But doing it in front of Wyatt makes it a hundred times hotter and more illicit.

He glides a finger through my flesh. "See how wet you are." He licks his finger clean. "Love it."

"Wyatt," I whisper, feeling like I'm going to die if he doesn't do something.

"Don't stop playing with your tits." He closes his mouth over me again as he drives his fingers into my pussy.

I sigh, then whimper as the pleasure builds. He's relentless, sucking and licking, while he pumps his fingers hard and fast, just the way he knows I love. I continue touching my nipples, tweaking them, and the pleasure builds sharply, making my chest rise and fall.

This is unbelievably hot. But more than that, I feel vulnerable —and open. How can sex feel this way when he's the one his knees?

Blinding white bliss swells like a wave and swallows me whole. I cry out, my back arching, my head braced against the wall. My knees buckle, and Wyatt catches me, making sure I don't crash ass-first onto the floor.

He spoons me, his arms around me and my ass snug against his cock, as I fight to catch my breath. When my vision's back to normal, I squirm and stop. "Is that a banana, or...?"

He laughs. "Just happy to see you."

"So soon?"

He kisses me. "Watching you come got me hard again."

I smile, then squirm again teasingly, as I'm turned on by his insatiable need for me. "You *did* say you don't have anything to do... And neither do I."

"Well, then." His eyes twinkle wickedly. "Let's take this to the bedroom."

46

Kim

The next day, I walk into the office with a few solutions to offer Salazar. He can be moody, and part of the job with this boss is to steer him around potential pits of despair.

But to make sure he doesn't reject all my ideas simply out of caffeine-deprived brain malfunction, I take a strong latte to him and wait until he's had half of it.

"So. About François's statue." I keep my voice neutral and calm. He needs to be assured this isn't a big problem. It's a *fixable* problem, and I'm going to do exactly that.

"Ah, right," he says, swiveling in his chair. "How's that going?"

"I have the piece, but...I'm not sure you really want to give it to Ceinlys."

He cocks an eyebrow. "Oh?"

I pull out my phone, get the photo on the screen and hand it over. "See for yourself."

He takes it and stares for a long time, his mouth in a firm, tight line. I continue to keep my expression neutral, waiting for him to absorb the picture.

Finally, he looks up. "What is this?"

"*Wife.*"

"How is that a wife? It looks like a human vulture." He squints at the screen. "Wait. Is the man *alive*?"

"I think so. His eyes are open, so..."

Salazar shudders. "What the hell? Is this what the French consider marriage?"

I shrug. "Can't say. I'm not French." The statue is weird, since François has never been married. His parents apparently weren't married either.

My boss hands me my phone back. "Okay, I can't give this to Ceinlys. She'll think I hate her!"

I nod, trying to project wise agreement, giving him time to let it all out. Otherwise he won't be ready to hear the options I've prepared.

"But then what can I give her? That statue's supposed to represent my feelings. I don't want some run-of-the-mill junk. It has to be unique!"

"I agree. And you don't have much time."

"Precisely!" he says, snapping his fingers.

"So I suggest you try *doing* something for her. That way, it'll be one of a kind."

Salazar looks confused. "Like what?"

"A home-cooked meal? Breakfast in bed would be nice, with a mimosa. You've never done that for her before, have you?"

My boss tilts his head, obviously dubious. "That's Mark's thing," he says. "And you know, I love my son, but he sucks at it. Not even André could help him."

"He's actually gotten better. His pork chops didn't kill my dog." They didn't even cause Champ any indigestion. That's a clear win.

"Maybe, but they're still not good enough for anything above a dog."

Well, yeah, but I'm not going to admit that out loud. "How about a massage, personally performed by you? I can arrange for private lessons beforehand so you can impress her."

"No." He waves a hand impatiently. "That's pathetic. 'Here you go, honey. Have a lousy massage.'"

A lot of women would love that, but okay. Salazar has his own ideas.

"Maybe a yacht or a private jet...? But custom stuff takes forever," Salazar says.

Time to give him the proper nudge. "Ceinlys knows you're rich, so an expensive present won't have a lot of meaning. What made the latest getaway unique isn't that you spent a lot of money on it, but that you spent a lot of time with her."

His gaze loses some focus. "It really was a great trip."

"Exactly. The most valuable thing you have is time, because you can't buy more of it. And she knows that. So if you take time out of your busy schedule and learn a new skill or two just to please her..."

"...it'll mean the world to her." He thinks for a moment, then finally slaps his desk. "You're right! Okay, breakfast and a massage. Make it happen."

"Would you like me to arrange for flowers, too?"

"Yeah, yeah, of course. Roses. Red, but make sure they don't look too common."

Red roses are about as common as you can get, but I keep that to myself. My guess is that Ceinlys admired some roses on the trip, and Salazar decided she should have them.

"Anything else, sir?" I ask, making a mental note to check with André and the masseuse from Ceinlys's favorite spa for private lessons. As for the flowers, I'll have to do some research.

"How much did we pay for the statue?" Salazar asks.

"The market price," I say, hedging a bit. "We haven't actually wired the funds yet, though."

"But we have an oral agreement, right?" He waves his hand again. "Send the money to the owner, but we have to do something about the ugly thing. I'm not keeping it at my place."

I add *Wire money to Wyatt* to my list. "If you'd like, I can have it disposed of properly."

"Yeah, do that. Dump it into some building foundation somewhere. Jimmy Hoffa the damn thi—" He stops, raising an index finger. "No, wait. Give it to—no, *donate* it to Elizabeth. She'll find a way to auction it off for her foundation. And whatever we paid for it, write that off as a tax deduction."

"Got it." François's name alone will net a handsome sum for the charity, and if a harpy eating a man alive can feed some hungry kids, I'm all for it.

"Great. Now I'm having lunch with Churchill today, and I want you to join us."

"Me?" It comes out as a squeak. I've been asked to join business lunches before, but this is awkward. Actually, more than awkward. I don't think I can ever see him again without...*seeing* him.

"Yeah, I'll need someone to take notes. You know how Churchill can get."

Other than sticking his joystick where it doesn't belong right before his own wedding? He's fickle and prone to changing his mind ten times a minute. "I do. I'll be there."

"Thanks." He nods and turns back to his coffee, effectively dismissing me.

I leave the office with a small smile. That went better than I hoped. I text Wyatt to let him know he doesn't have to worry about the statue at all.

–Wyatt: Really? Won't you get into trouble?

–Me: No. He told me to buy it weeks ago, and as long as it's a fair market price, he won't care. He'll just write it off. And trust me, Elizabeth could auction one of François's old socks for a million dollars. The woman's a genius at raising money.

–Wyatt: If you're sure. Hey, want to have lunch? I've got two hours free this afternoon. Also want to celebrate, because I finally have a new assistant!

–Me: Yay! So Loren said yes?

–Wyatt: Yup. She's starting next Monday.

I smile, thrilled for him. Finally, he's going to get the assistant he deserves! But lunch... Damn Churchill...

–Me: Congrats. But I can't do lunch today. I have a business thing. Ugh.

–Wyatt: Why ugh?

–Me: It's with my boss and Churchill.

And it's going to be as fun as caressing a wild tarantula.

–Wyatt: Sorry about that. Sounds nasty.

–Me: And difficult. I don't think I can ever forget what I saw at Geneva's wedding. Hard to put on a professional face after that. But how about dinner?

–Wyatt: Sure. Sounds like a plan.

Woohoo. I can't decide where we should go, though. Some place we'll both like. Maybe the cool Thai place Jo told me about a couple of months ago. I still haven't had a chance to check it out. I start typing the suggestion, but stop when another text arrives from Wyatt.

–Wyatt: Shit. Can't. Just learned the big boss wants to have a face-to-face.

The news both deflates and worries me. I've heard about Alexandra Darling. The woman is hard to please and spares no one. If she flew out here to talk...and if it's going to go long enough that he's expecting it to last through dinner...

–Me: Sounds serious.

–Wyatt: Not that kind of serious. I'll be back by Friday. ;-)

–Me: Friday? How many courses is this dinner going to have?

–Wyatt: No, I have to fly to Virginia to see her. My flight leaves at 3:30. Just found out.

Craptastic Melanie undoubtedly forgot to mention it until now. Wyatt's new assistant can't start fast enough.

–Me: I'm gonna miss you.

–Wyatt: Likewise. But I'll be back soon. And I'll have the warehouse key couriered to your office today so you can get the statue.

–Me: Thanks.

I sigh. I wish it was Wyatt who was bringing the key, even though the chances of that happening are nil. He probably needs to pack and get his stuff together.

Friday's only two days from now, I tell myself. But somehow it feels like a decade.

47

KIM

THE RESTAURANT CHURCHILL PICKED FOR THE MEETING IS Japanese and specializes in sushi. I'm glad of that, because if he'd chosen shabu shabu, I don't know if I'd be able to eat anything. There's limit to my tolerance, and sharing a hot pot with that cheating ass-groper would cross the line. There are some bosses who don't let their assistants eat at lunch meetings, but not mine. Salazar says if I'm working during lunch, the least he can do is feed me.

Churchill looks like he always does—well dressed and smug. I don't understand how he can be okay after the disastrous wedding, but it's likely that shame isn't high on the list of emotions he's capable of. And I bet he forgot I saw his you-know-what.

Salazar and Churchill get some kind of complicated sushi platter. I get a simple otoro and chutoro nigiri set. It's one of the more expensive items on the menu...and Churchill's paying.

When our food arrives, Churchill immediately gobbles up a piece of yellowfin while Salazar studies his fish as though he can't quite decide which to eat first. I take a bite of mine, since I need to eat before the men get down to business.

"It's crazy how Geneva's still upset," Churchill says suddenly. *Is he kidding?* He's lucky she didn't slice that limp stick off.

"Still in touch with her?" Salazar asks, his eyebrows raised.

"My lawyers are. She thinks she should get something in spite of the prenup."

Well, yeah. Because you're the one who cheated. I'm not a fan of Geneva, but my estimation of Churchill has dropped at least another ten notches.

"Brides do tend to get particular if you're caught cheating on the wedding day," Salazar points out, like he's saying that clouds are white.

Churchill scoffs. "It isn't like she's the faithful type. She cheated on her ex-husband with me. That's why she got nothing from that marriage, not even a penny of the billion he made right after the divorce. Stupid. Who the hell gets caught like that when it matters the most?"

Oh my God. I resist the urge to put a hand to my forehead. *Pot. Meet kettle.*

Salazar puts a silver-dollar-sized scallop into his mouth, obviously not wanting to comment.

Churchill turns to me. "You looking for someone to treat you right?"

I resist an urge to recoil. "I'm already in a relationship." *And it'd be nice if you'd start talking about the stupid business thing, so I can get my job done and leave.*

He gives me an insouciant look that I'm sure he imagines is sexy. "And...?"

It takes some serious black magic to make prime otoro and chutoro taste bad, but Churchill's succeeding simply by being in the same room. "And that means I'm unavailable."

Churchill laughs. "That's hilarious."

It'd be really hilarious if I stabbed you in the face with my chopsticks. I keep the thought to myself, though. Salazar really doesn't like blood. It's a difficult stain to deal with.

"Hey, Kim!"

I turn at the familiar voice and see Wyatt waving and coming over. Relief flows through me. He's such a welcome sight compared to the grossness of Churchill. Wyatt's standing with another man I only know from articles—David Darling, an extremely eligible billionaire bachelor from the East Coast.

I wave at Wyatt, a smile breaking over my face. "What are you doing here?"

"Lunch." His gaze is sharp as a scalpel as he looks at Churchill. I'm surprised the old perv doesn't start bleeding. "David's assistant Erin said this is a great place for it."

Ah. He must've had Erin find out where my boss and I were having the business lunch. Good assistants can do the job, but great assistants can find out anything about anyone.

Wyatt places a possessive hand on my shoulder and gently squeezes, communicating that he's here to reinforce me in case Churchill gets gross. I sigh inwardly. My hero.

"And I need to give you this." He hands me the key to Dane's storage. "Figured I'd do it in person."

I smile like a teenager with a crush. I can't help my reaction. I love it that he came here, so I could see him before he leaves for Virginia.

"Are you guys dating?" Salazar asks, entirely too jovial.

"Yes," I say. He's bound to find out sooner or later, if not from me, then from Dane maybe.

My boss beams. "You went above and beyond, Kim. But I approve anyway. I love playing Cupid." He turns to Wyatt. "You can thank me. She's a gem."

Salazar's no Cupid, but I wisely say nothing. It doesn't hurt anyone to let him be smug.

Wyatt smiles. "'Preciate it, Salazar. I couldn't have reconnected with Kim without you."

"I know," Salazar says, apparently having missed "reconnected" in Wyatt's thanks. "I love a good romance. Now, thank me with the best bottle of scotch money can buy. Kim will give you options."

I almost roll my eyes at how shameless he is, but my mind is already making a list of suitable options because nothing less will make Salazar happy.

Wyatt laughs. "Will do."

48

KIM

I love Fridays, but today is extra special. Not only is Wyatt coming back from his business trip to Virginia, I'm getting my bonus payment today!

After I sort out the agenda with Salazar, I check my bank account to see if it's hit yet.

Yes! My heart beats with giddiness. Look at all those precious zeros!

I did it. I'll never have to be like my mom and depend on some man for financial security, worrying endlessly about every little line on my face or extra ounce of weight.

But... As the excitement wears off, I realize the number is wrong. Not that it's too small...it's too...*large?*

Maybe I'm not doing the math right. I grab a calculator, run the numbers... Still too much. Did the payroll people make a mistake and forget to withhold the proper amount? I don't want Uncle Sam coming after me in April. I prefer not to have a refund, but I don't want to owe either.

I open my inbox. There's an email from the payroll department about today's deposit with all the breakdowns. I almost swallow my tongue. A *six-hundred-thousand-dollar bonus*? What the hell?

Ugh. Somebody must've made a typo. I hit reply and let payroll know so they can claw back the overage.

"Why the frowny face?" Salazar says, munching on a danish on his way out to have lunch with his ex-wife. The man loves his carbs and booze.

"Just a minor issue."

"Who? Churchill?" He leans closer. "Is he harassing you?"

It does not bode well for Churchill if he's the first person my boss thinks of when I say "issue." When people start to be on my boss's "issue" list, they don't get to do business with him for long. Not that I feel sorry for the disgusting geezer. "No. It's payroll. They paid me too much."

"Oh, that." Salazar straightens. "Wasn't a mistake."

"But..." I pause for a moment. I'm quite certain my memory is correct. "My employment contract specifically says five hundred thousand dollars, not six."

"Yeah, I know. But Dane and I had a bet."

"Other than the rock paper scissors one?" I ask, totally confused.

"Yeah." Salazar scratches the tip of his nose and lets out a forced cough. "I told him you wouldn't last. He said you would to get my money. And we decided to bet a hundred K."

That explains the extra amount, but... "So why did I get it and not Dane?" I can't imagine him wagering that *I* would get the money.

"He said he doesn't need the money. He said it was your"—Salazar sighs—"'hazard pay.'"

I bite my lip so I don't snort or make an inappropriate response.

"I disagree with the term, but I'm supposed to say it. Condition of the bet."

Never let it be said Dane is a gracious winner. He likes to rub it in, which is one reason I don't bet with him.

"Anyway." Salazar smiles. "Congratulations. I'm very proud of you and happy with your work."

I flush, the skin around my eyes prickling a bit. Geez. I better not cry, even though I'm a little overcome at the moment. I was such a newbie when I started working for him, and I made so many dumb errors, some of which I was able to fix only with Hilary's help.

You've come a long way, Kim.

If my boss notices my reaction, he pretends not to. "Now if you'll excuse me," he says, shooting his cuffs, "I have a lunch to get to."

I clear my throat. "Thank you, Salazar. Enjoy your time with Ceinlys."

My hands shaking, I pick up my phone and text the first person that pops into my head—Wyatt. He doesn't respond, but I check the time and decide he's probably on a plane. He said he was arriving this evening. I can't wait for his reaction to the amazing news, not only about the bonus but the unexpected windfall and praise from my boss.

Then I start a group text. I add Hilary and Jo, then, after a moment of hesitation, Yuna, since she was sweet enough to try to help me out. I let them know what happened.

–Jo: Woohoo! I'm so happy for you, girlfriend! You rock!

–Hilary: You know we gotta celebrate!

–Yuna: Holy cow, my roommate is a superwoman. I'm sad you won't be working for me, but I agree with Hilary. We need to celebrate. Party tonight! All of you and your plus-ones are invited! I'll send you directions to the location.

–Me: Thanks, Yuna, but you don't have to go to the trouble. A last-minute party can't be easy to plan.

–Yuna: It's no trouble. I've organized tons of parties. Every major bonus needs to be celebrated. And I WANT to party. I'm going to invite a bunch of people, but they're all civilized, so it should be fun.

I press my lips together. I'm not sure if civilized and fun go together for a party, not the way she thinks.

Still, I don't want to be ungracious or nitpick. And if Wyatt wants to do something special for just two of us, we can do that this weekend.

–Me: OK. Thanks, Yuna. I'll be there.

–Jo: Me too!

–Hilary: Count me in! Do I need to bring anything?

–Yuna: Nope. Catering's been already taken care of.

–Me: Wow! That was quick!

Yuna doesn't need an assistant. Hell, if she weren't an heiress, I'd try to get her a job *as* an assistant.

–Yuna: Haha, told you I'm good at this! Make sure to show up with a hot date! Or if a hot date can't be found, just come by yourself. Doesn't matter. I love dancing with other women. ;-)

49

WYATT

The plane lands at LAX right on schedule. My meeting with Alexandra went well, and I couldn't be happier with her vision and direction, plus her willingness to listen. No idea was too small, no suggestion too insignificant to consider. No wonder she's one of the most influential tech CEOs in the country.

I turn on my phone to check for messages. A text from Vi pops up on the screen, telling me she's doing well, and she's been hanging out with her old friends in Corn Meadows.

–Vi: But I also miss Krystal.

Who's Krystal again? I think for a moment, then remember that's Vi's new friend. The girl who's really good at "contouring."

I smile. Maybe this is a good thing. She's adjusting to her new school and making friends. And Corn Meadows isn't *that* far. We can always go back and forth if that's what she wants.

–Me: Glad you're having fun. I'm sure Krystal misses you too.

–Vi: I'm going to spend the weekend at Mandee's. Grandma said it was okay.

Mandee and Vi used to be inseparable in Corn Meadows, and the best part is that Mandee's mom isn't impressed or intimidated by Geneva. It'll be good for Vi to reconnect with her and her family.

–Me: Sounds great. Have fun. Say hello to Mandee for me.

–Vi: I hope you have fun too! And say hi to Kim!

–Me: Will do. Love you.

I wait a beat...then another. Finally my phone buzzes again.

–Vi: Love you too, Dad.

Warmth floods through me. The wedding was a total disaster, but going there, plus spending time with people who love her, seems to have mellowed her out some. Maybe when she comes back, things will be less tense and awkward.

The plane stops and the cabin crew open the doors. I grab my carry-on and get to deplane ahead of everyone else. *Gotta love flying first class.*

I fiddle with my phone as I walk through the terminal, checking for other texts and emails I might have missed. Make sure nothing's falling apart—you never know with Melanie holding down the fort—and then I'm going to start the weekend with Kim. We haven't seen each other in two days, but it feels a lot longer.

Before I can get through my inbox, the phone rings. *David.*

"Hey, how was the trip? Alexandra give you much shit?"

"Course not. She loved me."

"Good." His tone says he doesn't really care one way or the other. "Did she have anything for me?"

"If you're asking if she wanted me to give you anything, no."

"Aw, man," David says. "I asked her to pack some of Mom's brownies for me. They're the best!"

For God's sake. "Alexandra might possibly have better things to do than send you a care package, partner. Why don't you just go visit your folks? Have all the brownies you want and be twelve again."

"Can't. Mom's pissed at me for relocating." He sighs sadly. "I had my last decent home-baked cookie today. It's painful, man. Painful."

"How come?" I ask, unsure where he's going with this or where he managed to find home-baked cookies. Normally I'd suggest he simply get himself a girlfriend who likes to bake, but this is David. He doesn't do relationships anymore.

"Today's Melanie's last day. So she brought some goodbye cookies, then made a huge scene before leaving."

Oh shit. "Did she throw stuff?" I didn't think she'd stoop that low. I mean, I never misled her into thinking she'd get a permanent position or anything.

"No. She was just crying a lot. Then she said she did everything she could to stay as long as she could."

"What she did was clip pictures of Ryder Reed and Chris Hemsworth at work. I've seen them. She has stacks—literally *stacks*—on her desk."

David laughs. "Hey, a girl can fantasize."

Easy for him to say. His assistant actually does what she's supposed to at the office.

"'I even brought cookies,'" he adds in a falsetto.

"Too bad bringing cookies wasn't her job."

"Nobody bothered to point that out, though. We all enjoyed her baking." He sounds mournful. "You think Loren...?"

"Hey, you tell Erin to bake you cookies if you want 'em so bad," I say, feeling mildly territorial over my new assistant. "I don't want Loren doing anything except her job."

"No, thanks. I prefer my stomach lining intact. The last time Erin brought me home-baked carrot cake, I thought my mouth would dissolve."

"That good, huh?"

"She used chili sauce."

"*Chili sauce?* In carrot cake?"

"For coloring."

I burst out laughing.

"Fuck you," he says mildly.

"Must've been pretty bad if you can't come up with a better comeback than that."

"Yeah, yeah. Listen, you know if there're going to be a lot of hot single women at the party?" he asks.

"What party?" I'm not going anywhere but home to hang out with Kim. If he's that curious, he should be asking the host, not me.

"You weren't invited?" He sounds shocked.

"I just landed. I haven't had a chance to check my messages yet."

"Yuna Hae asked me to come to her party today," he explains. "I thought she invited you, too. Isn't she rooming with your girlfriend?"

"Yuna? Yeah, she is. How do you know her?" David's talking like he's tight with the woman.

"I've known her brother for a while. We're thinking about using their Internet platform to distribute our app in Korea."

"Their platform?"

"Yeah. She's filthy rich. At least her family is."

Huh. I had no idea. But then, I was never interested enough to look her up.

"Anyway," David says, "I'm gonna sign off here. See you tonight." He hangs up.

He's in for a letdown if he thinks I'm going to show up for this party. I check my texts first to see if there's anything from Kim. Sure enough, I have a few from her that hit my phone a couple hours back.

As I read them, pride and joy for her swell inside me. I knew she could do it, and it's great that she not only got the bonus, but recognition from her boss for a job well done. And that Dane. As assholes go, he's a pretty good one.

Kim also wants to know about Yuna's party. So I guess David wasn't just being groundlessly hopeful when he said, "See you tonight." He's still going to be let down, though.

–Me: I'm proud of you! You deserve every penny and more. As for the party, it sounds good, but how about if we go late or something?

Or maybe not go at all. We should celebrate together. More personal that way.

–Kim: Thanks! I kind of have to be there, though. Yuna said it's to celebrate my bonus, and she invited Jo and Hilary, too. My best friends.

A little disappointing, but okay. It isn't like tonight is the only time we'll have together.

–Me: Then we'll go. See you soon!

–Kim: I can't wait! Missed you.

I can feel the enthusiasm from her text, and God, she's adorable. I wish she were here right now so I could kiss her.

–Me: Me too.

I put the phone in my pocket and drive my Audi out of the airport parking lot. On the way home, I see a florist with bright orange daisies out. They look like they're beaming with happiness. I stop the car and go inside for a huge bouquet. Kim deserves it, and the flowers remind me of her.

Whistling, I return to the car.

50

KIM

I change into a simple black dress that straddles semi-formal and formal, since Yuna didn't say anything about a dress code. But given the location, I think it's best to be just a tad on the formal side rather than going there in jeans.

I brush my hair and let the layers curl around my face and jaw line. Then I freshen up my makeup, and voilà, I'm done.

The clock on my phone says it's been over half an hour since Wyatt texted me. It's going to take a while for him to get here from the airport. The traffic's crappy on Friday evenings.

I sit on the edge of the bed, then let myself fall back onto the soft mattress. I wish he were here right now. Then I could lift the dress up and straddle Wyatt. I was tempted to say we could stay in when he asked about the party, but going is the right thing to do. Yuna's done all the work already, and it'd be rude—like, *really* rude—not to attend.

Champ whines, his nose on my knee.

I use an elbow to lever myself up. "You miss him too, huh?"

Wagging his tail, he gives me a doggy grin.

"Yeah, I know. But he's going to be here soon." I scratch his head. "You're such a *good* boy, Champ. Yes you are!"

We comfort each other for a while, and then...

There are loud knocks on the door, and my heart starts to accelerate. *Wyatt!*

I hop off the bed and dash to answer it. I feel my smile widen when I see Wyatt standing on the other side. He looks so good, his shirt a little rumpled from the travel, and hair slightly tousled as though he's run his fingers through it a few times.

He comes in, Champ's head butting against his hip. I let the door close, biting my lower lip. He kisses me hard, like he misses me more than air itself, and my lungs go tight, my pulse racing. I lick him back, then stroke his tongue with mine, missing the heady scent of him—and the feel of him. How can two days seem this long?

"You look gorgeous," he whispers against my mouth.

I flush. "So do you."

"Here are the flowers for the most beautiful woman in my life." He lifts a bouquet of flowers in his hand.

I take the daisies and inhale their fragrance. "Thank you."

"They reminded me of you."

The simple declaration is sweet and incredibly romantic, and makes my heart thump like Champ's tail before dinner. For a moment, I feel like I have to tell him something, although I'm not sure exactly what. It's as though my mind is unable to sort through the complex pattern of warm emotions swirling inside me.

In the end, I settle for a smile.

"You ready to go?" he asks.

"Yeah. You don't have to rush, though."

"I just need to drop off my bag before the party and change shirts. Mind if I take Princess later?"

"Sure. She seems to get along great with Champ." Champ whines happily, like he agrees. Princess is nowhere to be seen, but she's been playing peekaboo with him over the last couple of days, so I'm not too worried.

Wyatt leaves. I put the flowers in a vase, then place the arrangement on the coffee table. The second I straighten up from the task, he returns. Linking arms, we head out.

"So where's the party?" he asks, once we're in his car.

"Anthony Blackwood's mansion. I have directions. He's apparently Yuna's soul brother-in-law." I still can't hide my dubious feelings about that title.

Wyatt seems to share my sentiment. As he pulls out of the lot, he asks, "What's that?"

"The guy who married her soul sister."

"Was she adopted? I mean the sister, not Yuna."

"No. Anthony's wife is white and definitely not adopted by Yuna's family. It sounds like they're best friends, but I think Yuna decided 'best friend' was too pedestrian to describe their relationship. So, soul sister."

"Ah."

"You don't sound like you get it." Not that I blame him, because I don't get it either, but had to pretend like I did when Yuna explained it to me.

"Because I don't. So other than your friends, who's coming?"

"As far as I know, my former roommate Evie and her husband. Hilary and her husband Mark. Jo, who may or may not come with a date. She didn't say. Edgar and Court Blackwood, who're Anthony's brothers. Court's fiancée. Oh, and Ryder Reed is coming with his wife, too." I try to sound excited about Ryder for Wyatt's benefit, because he probably hasn't seen any of big movie stars yet, having moved to L.A. so recently. But my level of enthusiasm isn't all that high. I've dealt with Ryder plenty of times while working for Salazar.

Wyatt blinks. "Ryder Reed? As in the movie star?"

Is there a weird edge in his tone? "Yup. He's Salazar's nephew. Dane's cousin."

"I didn't realize this was a Hollywood party...or that she knew so many people in the city. Do you know Melanie spent most of her time cutting out photos of Ryder Reed from magazines?"

"She's not the only woman, I'm sure," I say, not at all surprised. "And that's pretty mild, as far as Ryder worship goes. Some of his more fanatical fans tried to kill him so nobody else would have him. Anyway, this isn't a Hollywood party. He's close to Anthony, which is how he got invited. Also, FYI, he's just as incorrigible as Salazar."

The mansion is huge, almost like a palace. The exterior is

very classy—affluence in an elegant modern package. Since Anthony values his privacy more than flaunting his wealth, unlike some billionaires I know, he hasn't let any reporters or magazines feature his home in their puff pieces. And unlike most billionaire homes in L.A., his place doesn't have a pool. Instead, it has a lovely, shallow water garden with water lilies and cute floating lanterns with battery-powered "candles." They make the entire garden look like something out of a fairy tale. Maybe this is the kind of new home I should find for Wyatt. Vi would certainly love it. But then...do I want him to move? I like having him next door.

Wyatt's low whistle breaks my train of thought. "Holy shit. Did he buy this on the market? Because I didn't see anything like this in those brochures you gave me."

"He custom-built it, if I recall correctly. If you want, I can help you find or build something like it. You know, hiring the right architect and things like that."

"No, it's okay. I have a particularly nice neighbor, and prefer not to move." He winks. "Thanks for the offer, though."

I lay a quick kiss on his cheek, happy we're on the same page.

He parks the car, and I put a hand on his shoulder before we get out. Wyatt isn't the type to read high-society gossip rags and tabloids. "By the way, do not, under any circumstances, ask Anthony, Edgar or Court about their parents. Or Ivy's parents."

"How come?"

"It's a long story, but there was a really bad scandal. Best to avoid the subject unless they mention it first. But I very much doubt they will."

Wyatt arches both eyebrows, and his reaction makes me glad I brought it up. I don't think he'll be nosy, but I don't want him to inadvertently step on a conversational landmine, either.

"That bad, huh?" he asks finally.

I nod with a small sigh. The scandal rocked the upper crust for a while. Salazar once said he would've "accidentally" pushed Anthony's mom into an alligator-infested swamp for what she did. "I'll send you an article later if you're curious."

"Don't worry about it. I won't say a word. And I can Google it sometime."

We get out of the car. Wyatt extends his arm, and I link mine with his and we walk to the main entrance. My mood is bubblier than the finest champagne. Even though I was a little reluctant about attending, I'm happy to be here with Wyatt now.

The lights blaze, and loud music is blasting. The interior is just as tastefully posh at the outside—gleaming marble and brilliant crystal. A few pictures hang from the walls, and there's a tall bronze statue in the center that makes you crane your neck to study a woman with a small harp in her arm. She looks like a muse of music.

Wyatt leans over. "So Dane thought I should display that statue in my home? Like this?"

"Most likely, yes. And terrify everyone who comes in." The memory of the harpy devouring the poor man sends shivers down my spine.

He shudders. "Nasty."

Yuna comes twirling in from the hall. She's wearing a white dress and silver stiletto sandals with three thin straps. Her makeup is perfect as usual, and she beams at us. "Hey, so glad you could make it! Everyone's already here!" She turns to a green-eyed man with dark hair, who followed her toward us.

The man doesn't exactly radiate coldness like Dane, but there's an edge to him that says if you mess with him, you'll pay for it with a bucket of blood.

Yuna beams at him. "Tony, meet my roommate Kim and her boyfriend Wyatt."

He smiles, and it transforms him. What a mask, I think. This man is anything but sweet and nice. He didn't build his fortune by being affable after his family kicked him out.

He extends a hand. "Nice to meet you."

Wyatt and I shake hands with him, and he leads us to a hall large enough to hold a concert. A buffet is set up, laden with too-cute-to-eat finger food and fruit cocktails in individual serving cups. There are four fountains of drinks, plush armchairs and couches everywhere. I spot a strawberry blonde with a little pregnancy bump. Evie's speaking with her, a hand over her own belly. Evie's oven has a stealth bun that's going to be showing in a couple of months.

We go over and I introduce her to Wyatt. She tells me Nate is getting her some snack or other.

"I'm *constantly* hungry," she says with a sigh.

"You're eating for two," I point out, pleased that Nate seems to be spoiling her. He'd better.

"Congratulations," Wyatt says. "Is it a boy or a girl?"

Evie puts a protective hand over her belly. "Too early to tell yet."

"Have you made out a list of names?" I ask. Evie is super organized. She must've already created a file on her tablet.

"No. And don't get me started." She scowls hard. "Barron"—her gaze darts in Wyatt's direction—"that's Nate's grand-uncle... Anyway, he wants me to name the baby after him if it's a boy. And if it's a girl, he thinks it ought to be Ethel."

"Ethel?" Wyatt blinks. "That's...um...traditional."

I shake my head. "Let me guess. He wants you to honor his late wife."

Evie nods. "Nate and I have been trying to avoid him for, you know...obvious reasons."

I pat her shoulder. "I'm so sorry."

"Thanks." She gives me a small smile. "Still, it's worth it to be with Nate."

"Love makes everything worth it," I say.

"By the way, I saw Jo earlier if you want to say hi. She was looking for you."

"Thanks. Let me go find her, then. We'll catch up with you later."

Wyatt and I move off toward a big crowd on the other side of the room. "I can't believe somebody else made a fashionably late entrance," says someone from our left.

I turn around and see Ryder lounging there with his wife. His pose is too indolent, and something about it is so full of himself—like he knows he's hot. And why wouldn't he? He's struck more than a few people dumb with his looks. It took me a few meetings before I got used to it.

"Jesus. *That's* Ryder Reed?" Wyatt says.

I pat his hand. Ryder is stunning in movies and photos, but what most people don't realize is that he's actually not particularly photogenic. It's just that he's so damn good looking in real life that it compensates for that particular handicap. "Yup. The rumor is that his mom sold her soul to the devil to have a baby that handsome." And it's probably true. His mom is one of the most soulless witches I've ever known. She hates me, and the feeling is mutual. She resents that she can't just barge into her brother's office because I won't let her. And it absolutely infuriates her that Salazar sides with me instead of his own sister.

I look around some more and see Jo chatting with a dark-haired guy whose face I can't quite see from this angle. Hilary's giggling over something her husband Mark says, then she turns her head and waves.

I wave back. Wyatt and I start moving toward them, but a sudden lowering of the music brings everything to a stop.

Yuna walk to the center of the room and clears her throat. "Thank you all for coming. I wanted to host this party to congratulate my amazing roommate Kim's bonus. Apparently she was perfect at her job for the last five years, so it is well deserved."

Yuna gestures toward me, and suddenly I'm in the spotlight. I smile, although part of me wants to squirm a little bit at the attention. Wyatt links his hand with mine and squeezes, anchoring me. I lean toward him, happy he's here.

Jo pumps her fist in the air. "Yeah!"

Ryder whistles. "Damn, you did it. I didn't think you'd last this long. Salazar's impossible to please."

"So I've heard," Yuna says with a big grin. "And therefore, this must be celebrated! But that's not all."

"What more is there?" Nate calls out, his arm around Evie. "Has your mom finally managed to find a man to marry you off to?"

Yuna shudders, then shoots him a purely evil look. "Perish the thought!" She smooths her expression. "I'm hosting this party because...I just like to party!"

"Hell yeah!" Ryder calls out, lifting his scotch. Marriage might've made him settle down a bit, but you can't scrub the party-loving nature out of him.

Yuna points at Anthony. "I want to thank Tony for letting us have this party in his beautiful home." She waves.

Seated next to his wife Ivy, he waves back.

"The apartment Kim is graciously letting me stay at is lovely, but it's a bit too small to host something like this." Then she turns to a tall, dark man propped against Anthony and Ivy's couch. "Thank you, Edgar, for coming. I didn't think you'd make it, since you spend almost all your time in Louisiana. And do get him to talk, ladies. He has the nicest voice ever."

Edgar waves her away. "Stop. You're embarrassing me."

I raise my eyebrows. Maybe he's a bit embarrassed that she's pointing it out, but she's right. His voice is calm and velvety with a pleasant southern accent. He could be an audiobook narrator, even though that'd be a waste of a nice face. I can see why Mom is salivating over him as a potential son-in-law, even though her motive has more to do with his bank account than anything else.

"Finally," Yuna begins again, dragging our attention back to her. "I had this special treat flown all the way from Tokyo on a chartered plane. When I heard about these things, I *had* to bring them here to share with everyone."

A couple of uniformed waiters push silver carts in. On the trays are white porcelain plates and small, flaky pastries, shaped like mini-strudels, two on each plate. Servers show up with bubbly drinks. I lick my lips, suddenly hungry as I realize I haven't had anything to eat since lunch.

"How did you manage that?" Ivy asks. "I thought your mother froze your account for running away."

The question surprises me. Yuna said she had her own money, but she had these pastries flown in from Japan on a chartered plane. That's one very expensive way to indulge.

Yuna shrugs. "She didn't cut it all off. I can still charge up to five thousand a day, in case of emergency."

"Where can you find a chartered plane that cheap?" Nate jokes.

"You can't. So I had it charged to my brother's expense account." Yuna grins. "He loves me, hahaha. Now come on. Enjoy!" She gestures with a flourish of her arm.

Wyatt and I approach the pastry carts and each take a plate. The other guests do the same. I pick one of the two pastries up. It's still warm to the touch. I take a small bite, curious. If Yuna sent a chartered plane to get them all the way from Tokyo, it must be amazing.

The outside is light and flaky, and the inside is full of thick cream that tastes like cheesecake. But it isn't overly sweet or cloying. Just rich and surprisingly elegant.

"Wow," I say. "This is like cheesecake, but better."

"This one's chocolate," Wyatt says. "But it's like mousse."

I look down at my plate. So the other one is probably chocolate. Awesome. I take small bites to savor the cheesecake flavor as long as I can before moving on to the chocolate.

"Is there more?" Court calls out to Yuna.

"Yes. Do you like them?"

"They're amazing," Court's fiancée Pascal says.

"What are they called?" Ryder says around his bite. "I need to make sure my assistant can get me some."

That's so like him. He probably missed the part where Yuna said she had to charter a plane. Or maybe he doesn't care.

"They're called otona no kuriimu pie."

"Ah, geez," Wyatt says.

"Otona...what?" Ryder asks.

"Otona no kuriimu pie."

I try to memorize the name. It might be something Salazar can have flown in to surprise Ceinlys with. That'll make him happy.

"What does that mean?" Evie asks.

Yuna turns to her with a bright, happy smile. "Adult cream pie."

51

KIM

SOMEBODY LAUGHS AT THE SAME TIME SOMEONE ELSE STARTS choking. More laughter mixes with more choking. A lot of back pounding ensues.

I look down at my plate and stare at the thick, creamy white filling peeking out from the pastry. *Adult cream pie? Really?*

I bite my lip, trying not to laugh, because there's still a small bit of the pie in my mouth and I don't want to join the choking party.

I look at Wyatt. He raises a hand. "Hey. Not my cream."

His response makes me giggle a little, even though part of me is mildly horrified. I mean...there's no way Yuna means what she said, but...

"I can't make it taste like chocolate," Wyatt continues. "If I could, I wouldn't be some lousy billionaire. I'd be worth trillions."

"What's wrong?" Yuna asks, her perfectly shaped and drawn eyebrows pulled together.

Anthony gapes at her. "Did you just say what I think you said?"

She shrugs. "I don't know. What do you think I said?"

I pinch the bridge of my nose. Thank God Evie asked,

because Salazar would've killed me for even thinking he should send something with a name like that to Ceinlys. I mean, she has a sense of humor, but there's a limit...

"Adult cream pie," Anthony says, his face slightly red.

"Yeah. It's a special pie, made to suit adult tastes."

"Ohh," Ivy says. "So it's more like 'a cream pie for adults.'"

"You could say it like that, but the direct translation is—"

"We like Ivy's version better," Edgar says quickly.

Yuna shrugs again. "Okay. But it's really a mouthful to say it that way."

Jo raises an eyebrow. "Oh, adult cream is a mouthful either way." Obviously, one of us girls is going to have to explain things to Yuna.

"We need more music," Ivy says.

Anthony has the music turned up again, and some couples start dancing. Since I'm still a little hungry, and I like the pies despite their name, I gobble mine up. Wyatt looks at his plate dubiously, then offers it to me.

"What's the matter, honey?" I ask. "Adult cream not to your liking?"

"Think I'll try some of the other food," Wyatt says. So I eat his pies as well. I'm not letting a little pornographic translation ruin a meal.

We go over to a cluster of people where Evie, Hilary and Jo are.

"...in Japan once on business with Gavin," Hilary is saying. "And in the 7-Eleven there, they had a product called 'oral cookies.'"

Court comes over in time to catch this and joins the laughter. Then he turns to me. "Hi, I'm Court. I don't think we've met."

"Don't believe we have. I'm Kim Sanford." Unlike his brothers, he has an easy smile and bright, crinkling eyes. But that probably doesn't mean he's a pushover. Nobody from his family would be. Not if they survived the horror of their mother's upbringing.

He introduces me to his fiancée, Pascal Snyder. She's a pretty brunette, sharp as hell. But then she wouldn't be working with Hilary at Omega Wealth Management if she weren't.

"Thanks for taking Yuna in," Court says.

"Oh, no problem. She's great. Have you met Wyatt?" It's a party and supposed to be fun, but it's also an opportunity for Wyatt to meet people in the city. He needs to be friends with people in the upper crust of society other than Dane and David. Opportunities are offered to those who people know first. I've seen that over and over again, and I want to ensure Wyatt doesn't miss out.

"No. I'm Court Blackwood. Nice to meet you."

The men shake hands. I let them chat, giving them a chance to get to know each other. Hilary leans over.

"This is fun," she says. "I like your roommate a lot."

"So do I," Mark says, placing an arm around Hilary's shoulders. The man is still crazy about her. It's surprisingly sweet, given his old playboy rep. People used to call his girlfriends "quarterly girls" because none of them ever lasted more than three months. "And tell me again, Kim, how awesome my pork chop was." He leans closer. "I heard Champ loved it."

That dog loves everything, including cockroaches. But I don't think that's what Mark wants to hear. "Yeah, fantastic." I force a wide smile. "He adored it."

He grins. "I *knew* it! I knew André was just being a dick."

"Probably." *Whatever floats your fantasy boat.* "Where's Edgar, by the way? I've been wanting to meet him." Not because I ever hope to marry him like my mom wants, but because he's going to be the new head of Blackwood Energy. Meeting people who are in my boss's social strata makes my job easier if I ever need to help Salazar do business with them.

"He was here just moments ago." Mark looks around.

"I saw him leave with a woman," Pascal says.

I arch an eyebrow. *Interesting.* He isn't the type to hook up with women at parties, or if he is, he's been *very* discreet. There hasn't been a single scandal with him involved.

"Come on," Ryder says from behind me. "He's the boring, responsible type. Nobody wants to hook up with that."

I shake my head. "You think anybody who's more levelheaded than you is a boring, responsible type."

"Because it's true." He shoots me a spectacular smile. It's

wasted, since I've developed about a five percent immunity to it in the last five years.

"What's true?" Wyatt asks, slipping an arm around my waist as he faces Ryder.

I lean into him. "Nothing important."

Ryder smiles at Wyatt. "She always says that when she knows I'm right. By the way, I'm Ryder."

I watch him extend his hand and can't decide if he honestly thinks he needs to introduce himself—in case somebody hasn't seen movies—or if it's something bred into him by the European boarding schools he was forced to attend.

"Wyatt Westland. Nice to meet you."

They shake hands. Then Ryder asks if Wyatt has seen a picture of his baby. Wyatt barely has time to shake his head before Ryder has whipped out his phone, and I groan. He's just thrilled to find a new victim to inflict the photos of his daughter upon. The man is obsessed.

But Wyatt is nodding, his eyes warm as he looks at the photos. It's adorable. Wyatt, that is, not Ryder. I etch the way he looks right now—the glow, the sweetness—into my memory.

A new song starts. It's one they played at my high school junior prom, and I sigh with nostalgia. Even though I didn't like my hometown, I do have *some* good memories...like junior prom, before everything imploded.

Wyatt looks as though he feels the same way about the song. He excuses himself from Ryder and comes over. "Wanna dance?"

I nod. He takes my hand, his palm hot and firm against my skin, and we go to a wide area near the huge windows. His arms go around me, and I face him, resting my hands on his solid shoulders.

Then something hits me. "Do you realize we've never danced together before?"

His smile grows a little wistful. "Yeah, I was just thinking that, too."

"Can't believe it took this long."

"If you want, we can dance every day."

His sweet offer makes a peculiar emotion swell inside me. I wish

I could pinpoint exactly what it is, but it's too unfamiliar. Sighing, I push the confusion away and let myself relax in his arms. We're at a party, having fun, surrounded by great people. And we're dancing. Why obsess about this strangely warm...lump growing in my heart?

Then I catch a glimpse of the tiny lights glowing over the surface of the water garden as we turn, and I decide this almost feels like...love. I look up at Wyatt's handsome face and wonder if he feels what I'm feeling, or if I'm just getting swept up in the moment.

"You're beautiful," Wyatt murmurs.

My breath catches at the soft gleam reflected in his eyes. Maybe it's just wishful thinking, but I feel...adored.

We turn again, and his head dips. His lips are so close, our breaths mixing and merging. My skin prickles. I can feel my pulse going unsteady and slightly fast, like it's on an intoxicated run. But that isn't such a crazy comparison. I'm drunk on Wyatt's presence. It's scary and exhilarating how quickly and easily he's become important to me.

"Kim..." The soft whisper sounds like a prayer.

I tilt my chin. His mouth closes in and claims mine. His lips are hot and insistent, and my whole body tingles as excitement sparks through me like fireworks, bright and mesmerizing.

The music fades away and there's only Wyatt moving against me. All my senses are focused on a lusty exploration of his mouth, plundering, tasting and stroking—and his hand at the small of my back pulling me closer until I feel the thick, hard length of his erection against my belly.

Oh my...

My knees grow unsteady. Wyatt shoves his fingers through my unbound hair, keeping my head imprisoned so he can kiss me harder. I nip his lower lip to let him know I love what he's doing. It elicits a low, rough growl, the sound vibrating in his chest and throat. Heady lust builds at his reaction, and liquid heat pools between my legs. I wish we were home now so I could strip him naked and do wicked, wicked things.

Cool air brushes my bare arms and legs. I open my eyes and realize we're in a room with a marble floor and very little furniture. It's dark except for the dim, undulating light coming through the windows from the water garden.

"How...?"

"I danced you out of the party," Wyatt whispers against the sensitive spot behind my earlobe, then kisses the skin softly.

"Perfect," I say. This means we can do whatever we want to each other. To pleasure. To adore.

Wyatt pushes my dress up around my waist. "I missed you so much." The pads of his thumbs trace the curve of my hips, making me shiver.

"Me too." I place my palms on my cheeks then pull him down for another kiss.

His mouth fused to mine, he maneuvers me until my butt's resting against the edge of a small built-in shelf. Then he pulls my thong down. I toe my heels off and move my legs so the thong drops on the floor.

He fingers me, the touch sure and hot. "Fuck. You're dripping."

I rock a little, wanting more. "Of course. I'm always hot for you."

He nips my ear. "Did you masturbate, thinking of me?"

My face heats. "No. It wouldn't have been the same. I didn't want a quick orgasm. I wanted you," I say, running the backs of my fingers along his cock and feeling it jerk and grow even bigger and harder.

"Shit." He presses against my hand. "That's the hottest thing I've ever heard."

"I want you right now," I say, spreading my legs and inviting him closer. "I want to feel you moving inside me."

He rests his forehead on mine. "We can't. No condom." His voice is tormented as he drives me crazy by moving his thumb around my pulsing and swollen clit.

"It's okay. I'm on birth control."

His thumb stops, the abrupt cessation sheer torture for my Wyatt-starved body. I can see the muscles in his jaw tense in the dim light.

"You sure? I don't want you to offer because you're too turned on to think clearly. I can make you come with my hand and mouth."

My heart melts. His cock is throbbing against my thigh, and his main concern isn't taking what I'm offering without question, but making sure I'm really okay with it. Laying my palm on his face, I rub my cheek against his softly. "I couldn't be more sure."

My permission snaps the reins holding him back. He unbuckles his belt, his fingers clumsy and impatient, unzips his pants and shoves them—including his underwear—down in one quick yank.

Watching his need for me makes me so hot that I'm shocked I don't burst into flame. I open my legs wider, then cradle his face between my hands. "I want you, want you, want you..."

He surges inside me, making me gasp, cutting off my words. He feels *so good*. The sensation of having his bare cock buried deep inside me is unbearably erotic and intimate.

My breathing is hot and rushed, his thrusts hard and desperate.

Our gazes hold each other in the darkened room. His seems to pierce me all the way to my heart. Unable to bear the sensation, I kiss him, closing my eyes, silently begging him to fuck me until every thought in my head is obliterated.

When he slips his hand between our bodies and touches my clit, I come hard and fast. As I shudder in his arms, I feel wet warmth filling me, his harsh breaths fanning my neck.

We hold each other like that for a long time, just the two of us in the quiet, wavering gloom. And I know he means more to me than I ever thought possible.

52

Wyatt

I'm awake, but I linger in bed, instead of getting up like normal. I don't believe in wasting my mornings.

But it's tough to slip out of bed when Kim's wrapped around me, all naked, warm and soft.

I push a couple dark strands of hair out of her face. Her mouth opens and closes a few times like an innocent baby's. The notion makes me smile. What we did last night—at the party and afterward—was anything but innocent. Thinking about it makes me hard, ready to take her again. Knowing she really needs her sleep is the only thing making me keep my hands to myself.

The party was fun. Kim and I never did get to meet Edgar Blackwood, even though she tried. But she seemed happy enough that I was able to network a little. I let her take the lead, since it's probably good for me to get to know people in L.A.

I stay in bed with for another half-hour or so, then slip out. She's still deep in sleep, and I want to shower and see what's in the fridge for breakfast. And Champ needs to be fed. He spent the night in my living room because Yuna's with Ivy and Anthony at their mansion. I don't know why she didn't just stay at the fortress-like mansion to begin with, but there's probably a reason. Her mom wanting her to marry Anthony's brother or something.

When I step out of the shower, Kim's still curled up in bed. I smile, then pull on a T-shirt and shorts and go to the kitchen.

Champ rushes to me, tail cutting the air back and forth. I scratch his head, then feed him. He isn't going to wait. I also put out food for Princess, who disdainfully scrutinizes Champ like he's some kind of worm, then daintily tucks into her meal.

That done, I open the fridge.

Bacon. English muffins. Eggs. *Hmm. Breakfast sandwich?* Kim seems to love real food.

I lay everything out on the counter, then pick up my phone to see if there's anything urgent. Nothing, but my parents have sent some texts.

–Mom: Do you think I can tell people I was having a stroke when I ran Geneva over?

My heart drops into my stomach. What the hell...? Didn't Geneva leave Corn Meadows immediately after the aborted wedding?

–Dad: Don't worry. Your mom hasn't done it yet. She's thinking about it.

Thank you, Dad, for reading my mind. Relief floods me, then anger fires up. God damn it. Just what is Mom thinking?

–Mom: Planning, honey, planning.

–Dad: Gotta make it airtight.

I shove the heel of my palm against the spot between my eyebrows. I love my parents, but sometimes they make zero sense. Like now.

–Mom: Nobody has to know.

I check the time. They sent those about ten minutes ago.

–Me: Don't do anything. And people will definitely know. You told me!

–Mom: Oh, you're up. Well, you're not people people, if you know what I mean.

–Me: I don't. And you can't kill anybody. I can't perjure myself if asked, and you know cops can read your texts, right?

–Mom: Not if all of us delete them together!

Oh boy.

–Me: No! That's not how it works.

My parents still haven't told me why Mom suddenly felt the urge to murder my ex-wife. Did she parade around with another old billionaire with erectile dysfunction and embarrass Vi?

–Me: What did Geneva do?

–Mom: She came by this morning to take Vi to stay with her! The nerve!

–Dad: Yup. The nerve.

The outrage is palpable even through the small phone screen. But my primary feelings are confusion and concern. Geneva couldn't bother to spend time with our daughter when we were married, so why now, especially after saying all those nasty things at the wedding? If I had even the least bit of charitable opinion about her character, I might think she's feeling guilty, but remorse is a string that isn't on Geneva's guitar. Is she trying to use Vi to make herself feel better somehow? If so, she can go fuck one of my parents' goats! Actually, that would be animal abuse, so she can go fuck herself.

—Me: Did Vi go with her?

If she wants to go with her mother, I can't stop her. At least not without looking like a jerk. But at the same time, Geneva does not deserve our daughter. Not after insulting her in front of everyone at that clusterfuck of wedding!

—Mom: No. Vi's sleeping over at Mandee's.

Oh, right. Relief floods me. Vi told me about that yesterday.

—Dad: You shoulda seen Geneva's face when we told her.

Petty satisfaction courses through me. Geneva can't stand not getting her way.

—Mom: I told her Vi's with her best friend, and Geneva looked so blank. Because she has no clue who her child's friends are.

Then she adds a smug devil emoticon.

Part of me is disgusted, but another part—the decent part of me, no doubt—is sad for Vi. She deserves a better mom than Geneva.

—Mom: Hopefully that witch never comes around again. I don't think I'll be able to control myself next time.

—Dad: I wanted to ask her if she's managed to dig up another walking goldmine...and if it isn't going to stick its you-know-what into another woman.

I'm tempted to laugh. I should be mildly appalled at how juvenile my parents are, but...Geneva asked for it.

My phone rings. Speak of the devil... I'm tempted to pick it up so I can give Geneva a piece of my mind, but I control myself. There's no need to stoop that low, and it'll drive her crazy to be ignored.

So I let it go to voice mail. But my phone rings again...and again...and again.

After fifteen minutes, I finally pick up. "What?" I snap. Rude, I know. Don't care.

"Where did you hide my daughter?" Geneva screeches.

"Oh, so she's *your* daughter now?" Since when did Geneva start referring to our daughter that way or speak of her so...possessively?

"You're damn right! And you can't hide her from me. I'm her mother!"

I roll my eyes. "She's staying with a friend. A sleepover. You've heard of 'em, right?"

"I know what they are! I'm not stupid!"

Just self-absorbed, sociopathic and loud.

"I'm entitled to custody and child support. You understand that, don't you?"

What the fuck? My spine starts to stiffen, and hot rage unfurls in my gut as I realize what she's getting at. "Oh, no. Uh-uh. You're the one who told me you didn't want Vi because your *fiancé* doesn't like kids, and you had no use for her. Your words, not mine."

"But he's not my fiancé anymore, and I changed my mind. It's a woman's prerogative!"

If she were here, I'd throttle her. Changing her mind, my ass. "Not in this case. Vi isn't a purse you can just buy and return because you feel like it!"

"She's not a purse!"

"That's what I just said. And she's not a meal ticket, either!"

"How dare you!"

"Oh I'll dare plenty where *my* daughter is involved!" I say, so pissed off that my vision is going a hazy red.

"I'll take you to court if I have to, and I'll win! Judges love mothers."

I feel my mouth twist into an ugly line. Like she can actually undo our divorce settlement. "Generally. But they make exceptions for harpy bitches like you!"

She gasps. "You'll be sorry you said that!"

"Try me," I snarl into the phone. "I'll fucking destroy you."

And I mean it. I will ruin her if she does anything more to hurt Vi. I will make it my life's mission.

"Fuck you! You can't do that! All you have is money. You're just a pathetic guy who thinks his dick suddenly grew because he got lucky. You know what? You were never any good in bed!"

I change my mind. I'm going to tell Mom exactly how to run Geneva over, then be her alibi. Actually, *I'll* do the running over. Mom can be *my* alibi. "Hard to be good in bed when you're trying to fuck an iceberg. Maybe I should start calling my dick the *Titanic!*"

I hang up, breathing hard. Dammit. That was not what I should've said. Being juvenile and immature is not how to stop my ex-wife, even if she's the one who brought down our exchange to that level.

"Wow," comes Kim's voice from behind me. Her hair's slightly damp from a shower, and she's in a pink robe she brought over earlier this week. "I wasn't planning to eavesdrop, but that was... Who was that?"

I breathe in deep a few times to calm myself. It helps, but only a little. "Sorry. That was Geneva."

"Are you okay?"

"Not really."

She comes over and rubs the tension between my shoulders. I close my eyes at how well she seems to know what I need. *Okay, there's no reason to stay worked up.* Vi is safe with my parents, and Mandee's mom will never just let Geneva take her. And Geneva can't get in touch with Vi directly because I got her a new number after we moved to L.A. As usual, Geneva never bothered to ask for it.

I turn my head a little and see the food on the counter. My appetite's gone, but that's no reason to not feed Kim. And starving won't help me, either.

My jaw tight, I start cooking. As I do, I tell Kim what happened.

She listens quietly, letting me pour everything out, including how much I hate Geneva. "I can't stand her either," Kim says. "But can she do that? Didn't everything get settled in the divorce?"

"Yeah, but I don't know. Maybe she'll try to sue." Geneva will do whatever is in her power to get what she wants, no matter how unreasonable that is. But she doesn't realize I'm going to fight her with everything I've got. I'll call in favors if I have to.

I put two plates on the table, along with some coffee.

"In the process, she'll probably hurt Vi again," Kim says.

"Yeah. She will." And my hatred of her burns even hotter. Then it hits me. Kim isn't worried about my money or a potential lawsuit. They aren't that important to her. What she's most concerned about is Vi's welfare.

We eat. The food tastes like cardboard to me, but I'm going to need calories to fight the upcoming battle. Still, I hand over a strip of bacon to Champ, who's been watching me with pleading eyes. He'll enjoy it more anyway.

"Who did your divorce?" Kim asks suddenly.

"Robert Mann. He's retired, though. I think I was his last case."

"So you need a new lawyer."

"Basically." It hurts my head, trying to think about who to get to crush Geneva. Maybe Dane knows…but then again, maybe not. He's too besotted with his wife to even think about divorce. And David isn't even married.

"I have just the person for you. Samantha Jones."

"Who?"

"She's a family law attorney. You're going to need a nuke, and Samantha is it. She might not kill the roach, but she'll scare it to death. Her hobby is making her opponents cry in public."

How does Kim know this? Is it part of being an assistant to somebody like Salazar Pryce?

"She handled Salazar's divorce. Actually, she worked for Ceinlys, but… Basically amounts to the same thing. Anyway, she's excellent, and she'll find a way to make Geneva go away. Permanently."

"Well, that's the solution I want." If Kim thinks so highly of this lawyer, maybe Samantha is the one to hire. "I'll call her office first thing Monday."

"You don't have to bother." Kim reaches into her bag, which

she left on one of the chairs last night, and takes out her phone. "I have her private number right here."

I fold my arms and watch her tap away on her phone. The sunlight is behind her, making her look like some kind of angel of knowledge and competence. Is there anything she doesn't know how to handle?

I'm a lucky man to have her on my side.

She lifts her head. "Done."

The smile Kim gives me is like a door opening into another, more beautiful and perfect world. My pulse races, and a magnetic pull that has nothing to do with lust floods me.

I love this woman.

If somebody asked me why, I'd say because she's beautiful and smart. But if God were to ask me, I'd answer honestly and say I don't know. It isn't like Kim's the only beautiful woman in L.A., or the only smart one. But everything about her just makes me not only happy but respect her.

"Since she's working today, if we get to her office before noon, she said she'll talk to us for half an hour." Kim's words pull me out of my stunned awareness.

I look at her, my gut tight. It takes me a moment to process what she said. "Uh. Yeah. Sure. Thank you," I say instead of the loud *I love Kim* echoing in my heart, as nervous apprehension holds me back.

53

WYATT

Samantha's law firm is...nice. With lots of warm colors, books on every shelf and some mini-sculptures, the place looks more like a therapist's reception room than a nuclear missile silo. It's jarring. I want the meanest and nastiest lawyer around, not somebody nice.

On the other hand, Kim said Samantha was ruthless, and I trust her judgment.

Kim's with me. I asked her to come. Part of me only wants to appear to her as this perfect guy with nothing bad going on in his life, but another part wants her to be involved in this because she cares about Vi. And also, I just want her support. She's one of very few people in this town who know about my ugly past with Geneva.

A tall guy who seems vaguely familiar comes out from behind a desk. He gives Kim a big smile. "Hello, Kim."

"Hi, Hugo."

Hugo. He's the one she was hugging in the hall that time. I didn't know they were still so...friendly.

"Thanks for your help. I don't know if I would've scored a job here otherwise."

"Ah, you would've gotten it anyway."

"Still. I owe you one."

Kim won't be needing anything from you, buddy. I haven't forgotten the way he hugged her.

She gives him a small nod. "This is Wyatt. He has an appointment with Samantha."

"Of course. This way." He gestures at the door.

We walk into a huge corner office with a sprawling view of the city. A gigantic desk is covered with neat stacks of documents in accordion folders and a slim laptop. A woman who must be Samantha smiles at us and stands up behind the desk.

Dressed in a beige top and black fitted skirt, she doesn't look anything like an evil attorney who likes to make people cry. Her dirty-blond bob lies sleek, and her wide-set brown eyes are warm and trust-inspiring. The friendly expression on her face says you can pour your heart out to her, and she'll hold your hand the entire time.

With any luck, she'll be evil and vicious inside.

She extends her hand. "Samantha Jones. Nice to meet you, Mr. Westland."

"Likewise. Call me Wyatt."

"Please sit down." She gestures at comfortable-looking seats in front of her desk and takes the leather office chair again.

Before settling down, I hand her the divorce documents from my former lawyer.

She smiles. "Thank you. It's nice when potential clients are organized."

Hugo appears with a tray of coffee, then leaves. Samantha gestures at us to help ourselves. "So. Tell me what I can do for you."

I lay it out for her in broad strokes—about the divorce, how the assets were divided and how Geneva didn't want Vi because Churchill didn't want to have small kids around. Samantha listens attentively, her eyes on me the entire time. She nods here and there, then taps her chin when I'm done.

"It seems rather simple. She gave up custody, so there's that. As for the money, it seems like she gave that up too."

"But she's back. And judges do tend to side with mothers," I say, feeling bitter that Geneva might be right about that part.

Samantha looks at me like I'm being overdramatic. "Shouldn't matter. There's a custody settlement, right?"

I frown. Don't remember hearing anything about that. But I was pretty stressed out during the process. "I...guess..."

"You guess? You don't know?"

I shrug. "My lawyer worked on it. That's what I paid him to do."

Samantha leans back in her chair. "But it's your signature."

Damn. She has a way of speaking that makes you feel deeply ashamed that you don't remember what's in the hundredth paragraph of a settlement.

She flips through the thick documents I gave her, then frowns. "Is this all you have?"

Uh-oh. "Yeah."

"I don't see a custody agreement. Your attorney was an idiot for not establishing one. Without one, tenacious, money-grubbing exes can come at you through your children." She shakes her head. "I hope you didn't pay him more than twenty bucks an hour, because that's about all this work is worth."

Ouch. The casually spoken judgment is harsh, but I can't blame her. If what she said is true, my former lawyer screwed up. And it's giving Geneva another shot at hurting Vi. I should've found someone better.

Samantha turns to Kim. "Are you guys dating? Maybe engaged?"

"Dating. Not engaged," I say. I don't like it that Samantha's sharp attention is on Kim. She better not say anything to upset her, even if she thinks it's necessary to hurt Geneva in the end.

Samantha steeples her fingers. "I see. Is there any possibility that you might get married soon? I ask because it would really help your case. Your ex-wife isn't married, and her infidelity was the main cause of the divorce. She gave up all claim to your money, even if it was the result of the work you did while you were married. But I guess now she wants child support."

How did she get all that already from just skimming the documents? I don't think she's guessing. She's way too sure of herself.

She smiles. "Speed reading. It's one of my numerous advantages over opposing counsel."

I'm sure it's a useful skill to have if you're a lawyer. "We're not planning to marry anytime soon."

Samantha opens her mouth, then shuts it. "Well then. I'll do what I can. In the meantime, you should talk to your child. See how she feels about all this."

"She's too young," I say, more out of frustration at having to throw this at Vi than the fact that Samantha wants me to talk about it with her.

Samantha gives me a look. "Your ex-wife's lawyer won't care. They're going to want to know what she'll say when they ask her if she wants to live with her mom or you. And they'll make it sound like if she chooses you, she's saying she doesn't love her mom."

"What the fuck?" My hands clench into fists, and I fight to keep control of my temper. "My daughter's ten! She isn't a pawn to be used like that."

She shrugs, like she's used to this sort of reaction. "I'm just saying. It's what I'd do if I were her lawyer. If she shows even the slightest hint that she might want to be with her mom, it's going to be a factor."

I grit my teeth. Samantha's right, and I'm sure Geneva's lawyer will do that and worse if it will get her the win she wants.

I need to think of this as a war. The prize is my daughter's happiness and wellbeing, so Geneva needs to be fought every step of the way. It's not about money. If paying her once would make her go away permanently, I might just do that. But I'm not letting her take our daughter hostage.

"All right," I say finally, my voice calmer. "Thanks, Samantha."

She nods. "It's no problem."

"I'd like you to represent me."

"Excellent. Hugo will give you the retainer info and letter of engagement."

We stand up and shake hands again, her relaxed and me grim with determination to make the Geneva problem vanish permanently. Kim and Samantha do the same, then we leave her office.

Hugo has the documents ready, yellow arrow stickies on the lines that require my signature.

I scan the information and letter, sign both and write a check for the retainer to get Samantha started. Her hourly rate is high, but I trust Kim's recommendation.

Besides, I can afford it. And if I couldn't, I'd borrow the money. There's absolutely nothing I wouldn't do for Vi.

"Thanks, Kim," I say as we get into the car. "I know this isn't how you wanted to spend the weekend."

She shakes her head. "Not at all. I want to help. For you and Vi." She hesitates for a moment, then adds, "You need to talk to her."

"I know." I don't know how to even broach the topic that her mom only wants her to collect child support. *Fuck.*

"Do you want me to be there?"

It's my turn to hesitate. I kind of want to talk to Vi alone, but the plain fact is she's bonded more with Kim. Her presence might help Vi process it better. I don't want her to think I'm fighting to keep her to avoid giving money to her mom.

"Sure," I say. "That would be great."

54

WYATT

When Kim and I are home, Vi calls me on FaceTime. Apparently, my parents told her I needed to talk to her. I'm not thrilled about the circumstances, since this is the kind of conversation that requires face-to-face interaction, but I know my parents mean well. They probably wanted me to be the one to speak to her and reassure her. At least I can see her expression on screen and gauge her emotions.

Kim sits next to me on the couch, and I angle the camera so Vi can see her as well. Champ comes over, squeezing between us, and Vi waves at the dog, who gives her a smile and pants. Kim asks Vi about her stay in Corn Meadows, and Vi tells her all about Mandee, her tone bright and happy.

I hate to have to shatter her mood. Why can't Geneva just leave Vi alone? She's getting used to life without Geneva and her toxic presence. Didn't Geneva do enough damage at the wedding?

Eventually there's a natural break in the conversation. "Listen, Vi. There's something I need to tell you."

"Okay."

Her slightly guarded expression is like a knife in my gut.

Jesus. Have I been that bad of a father? It's like she's expecting me to deliver some terrible blow.

I choose my words with care and tell her Geneva might want to live with her from time to time. I can't quite bring myself to tell her that her mom's only interested in money. It seems like such a cruel thing to say, and I just don't have the heart.

"So. She wants to be with me?" Vi asks hesitantly like she wouldn't dare believe it. The guarded expression on her face breaks my heart.

What she wants is child support. I kick the thought away, then clear my throat. I can't actually agree with Vi. That'd be a lie. "Do you want to live with your mom sometimes?" I ask, holding my breath. *Say no, say no.*

"Um…" Vi's eyes dart between me and Kim a couple of times, then she looks down. "I don't know. Maybe…?" She shrugs her small, narrow shoulders.

I never realize how cruel and devastating such a little gesture could be until now. It hurts worse than a punch to my solar plexus. This must be what defeat feels like. I knew she wouldn't say, "Hell no," but this sucks. Samantha's warning comes back to me.

If she shows even the slightest hint that she might want to be with her mom, it's going to be a factor.

If I thought Geneva loved Vi, even a little, I might be okay with it. But as far as Geneva's concerned, Vi's a pest she has to put up with until she finds herself a new sugar daddy. I'm certain Geneva won't be happy with whatever child support she can squeeze out of me. She's always been a greedy bitch.

My hands curl into fists. If I'd done a better job of bonding with Vi, maybe she wouldn't still be clinging to Geneva like this.

Kim lays a soothing hand on my back. "Thanks for letting us know, Vi. It's really important."

"Oh. Okay." Vi gives us a forced smile. "Hey, is it okay if I go now? Mandee's mom said she'd take us shopping."

"Sure," I say, forcing a smile of my own. I don't want her to think she's letting me down. She hasn't done anything wrong. She just wants to believe her mom loves her. What kid wouldn't?

"Okay," she says again. "Bye." She hangs up.

I sigh, then lean back, a hand over my eyes. Maybe I should've told her the whole truth, but...

"Hey. Are you all right?"

"Yeah..." I say almost out of habit, then shake my head at how ridiculous I'm being. Kim isn't stupid. "No. This is a disaster. Maybe Samantha can coach Vi." But I wouldn't want Samantha to manipulate Vi into saying something she doesn't want to, not even to stick it to Geneva.

I can sense Kim shifting next to me. "That's not the only way," she says.

"Yeah?" I drop the hand and straighten up. "What else is there?"

"We could always get married."

I stare at Kim and wait for her to laugh and say, "Just kidding"...but she doesn't.

As I keep staring, her cheeks flush. "I mean, it makes sense," she says. "You'll win any custody battle. Samantha said it'd be easier if you were married. And we're friendly and compatible. Besides, Vi and I get along, which is a huge plus. I'm sure that'll count for something with the judge."

Her explanation makes perfect sense. My head is on board, but my gut is saying I shouldn't even consider it because she hasn't mentioned love—or even the possibility of it.

The thing is, I refuse to marry for some other, well-intentioned reason again. Been there, done that, and I've got a messy custody battle coming up as a result. It's going to hurt Vi. And I want what my parents have—growing old together, making jokes, having each other's back no matter what. And they wouldn't have any of that without love.

Kim shifts. "Okay, well...I guess not. Just an idea."

I want to hug her, thank her, tell her she's an amazing person... But I don't. I'm afraid I'm going to say yes because I want her even if all she can offer is a logical rationale, sans love. Feeling sad, I shake my head. "No. That's not going to work."

"Oh..."

And I feel like the biggest tool in the world. "You shouldn't have to marry me just because you want to help Vi," I explain, desperate to ease the sting of the rejection. "I don't want that." I want her to marry for all the right reasons, because...because I love her too much to let her make the same mistake I made. If I said yes, I'd do my best to be a good husband, but she deserves more than that. She should have what my parents have, too.

"I get it. No problem." She gets up. "Listen, I need to wrap up a presentation I'm working on for Salazar."

Her voice is brisk, but I swear I can hear a tiny tremor. "Kim—"

"I really have to go." She doesn't meet my eyes. Instead, she turns to Champ. "Come on, boy. Time to go home."

Then, before I can say more, she takes the dog and leaves, the door clicking closed behind them.

55

KIM

Oh, why did I think it was a great idea to propose to Wyatt?

The urge to slam the door is almost too much, but I resist and close it quietly instead. I don't want Wyatt to hear it and think I'm upset, even if I am. It wasn't his fault he rejected my proposal.

Which is hurtful.

I throw myself on the couch and prop my feet up on the table. Champ hops up next to me, lending me his warmth. Scratching his head, I think about what just happened.

Did I not lay it out right? It's what any of the billionaires I know would do. Ryder, for one, married his wife initially to win a wager with his father. So did his siblings, for that matter. Hilary pretended to date Mark to help him out when Ceinlys was determined to marry him off to some brain-dead heiress.

Maybe he could tell you weren't really being honest.

The thought is embarrassing. Was I that transparent? Because I was remembering how all those relationships, which started out fake, turned into something genuine and real. Every single one of them ended up happy and in love.

But that doesn't mean I expect ours to be that way... Does it?

Yeah, it does. Don't lie to yourself.

I sigh, feeling deflated and defeated. I do want that. There's a connection between us, and I... Well, I love Wyatt. He's fun, sexy, genuine... I adore the way he tries to do the right thing, even if it's unpleasant and he could delegate it to somebody else. Like taking care of Vi. I know so many people who hire "experts" to deal with their kids, especially when they don't have the smoothest relationship. He's big enough to admit when he's wrong and confident enough to ask for help when he needs it.

Maybe he likes to have sex with me and hang out together, but he doesn't care about me enough to get married. Not even temporarily, not even to keep Vi.

God. Now I feel like a cockroach. And about as loved as the ones Princess used to leave on my doorstep. I haven't seen any recently, but it could be that Champ eats them before I notice.

"Argh!" I bury my hot face in Champ's fur. I shouldn't have said anything. Now I've ruined it. I can't possibly face Wyatt now.

My phone rings in my purse, and I pull it out, in case Salazar needs me. I hope he does, even though it's the weekend, so I can keep myself occupied.

But it's Jo.

"Hey, I'm really sorry, but I don't think I can go shopping today," she says, her voice low and raspy.

"Uh...are we supposed to?"

"Aren't we? It's the thirteenth."

"Jo. It's the sixth."

There's a pause. "Really? Shit. Okay, sorry. Brain fart."

Yeah, no kidding. Jo doesn't usually get her dates mixed up like this. Her reputation depends on being organized and punctual. High-end clients hate anything else. "Are you okay? You don't sound so good."

"Um. I'm fine. Just tired. I'm still in bed."

"You are?" Jo isn't the type to laze around in bed all day, even on weekends. "You sure you aren't sick?"

"Just worn out." She clears her throat. "I had a bunch of sex."

I have to laugh. "So that's why I couldn't find you last night at the party. Good for you!" She's been somewhat deprived after dumping her last boyfriend. He was rich and nice, but too clingy, and she said he wasn't good enough to have around long-term. "So. Who was it?" I ask, needing to distract myself. "Somebody from the party? Was he good?"

"Ooh yeah." The way she says it reminds me of a lioness stretching. "That man's like sex crack. I wanna start breaking into people's houses and stealing their TVs to support my habit."

"Wow. You've never said anything like this about a guy. Who was it?"

"Edgar."

"Edgar *Blackwood*?" He's reputed to be so incredibly stiff that I just can't imagine him as the type to go much beyond missionary.

"Yeah. I usually think men sound like lobotomized monkeys when they're doing it, all that huffing and groaning. But not him. The sounds he makes are hot." She laughs. "First time I've had *aural* sex."

Thankfully, she stops there. I don't know if I'm ever going to run into the man, but I don't need to have "aural sex" popping into my head when I do. "So are you going to see him again?"

"Doubt it."

"What? Why not? He sounds like a winner, unless he belches when he comes."

She laughs. "No. It's just... He can't leave Louisiana. His company's there. And I'm not leaving L.A., not even for crack-gasms. All my friends and family are here."

And Jo's really close to her family. I've seen them squabble and fight at times, but when one of them is down, they all come together, no questions asked. The first priority is that everyone in the family is happy and protected. I wish I had that. Maybe I thought I could have it with Wyatt. How pathetic. Maybe, like Jo's ex, I'm being clingy and unworthy.

Jo yawns noisily. "Anyway, I gotta go. I need to sleep."

"It's two in the afternoon."

"Yeah, but he kept me up until the crack of dawn. I need my beauty sleep. Bye!" She hangs up. She must be really exhausted not to have noticed anything wrong with me. That, or I'm a better actress than I thought. Either way, I'm glad she didn't probe, because I don't know what to say.

I toss the phone on the couch with a sigh. At least Jo's happy, no longer dickpressed, as she sometimes says when she's not getting any. And that should make me happy too. She deserves good orgasms—crackgasms. But I still feel flatter than a glass of Coke left out overnight. And that, weirdly, makes me feel like a bad friend.

The door opens, and Yuna walks in. She looks fresh. Her makeup is perfect, and even the Walmart disguise somehow seems crisp and expensive on her.

"Hey, Kim!" she says.

Champ, loyal canine that he is, does not abandon me to check her out.

She notes that with a raised eyebrow and frowns. "You okay?"

"Me?" I inwardly wince at how pitiable I can make that one syllable sound.

"Yes, you. Who else?" She props her butt on the couch's opposite arm. "Okay, tell me. You know you want to."

"No, I don't." It's a lie. Not that I don't want to, but I don't know if I should dump my problems on her. She and I have been bonding more, but still...

She stands. "Ha!"

The sound is vaguely threatening even though she isn't doing anything overtly menacing. She heads to the kitchen and returns with a bottle of very good scotch. A brand Salazar likes.

"How did you get that?" I ask, wondering if she somehow read my notes on the things I need to order for my boss.

"I bought it. With money. Okay, I expensed it to my brother's account." She brings it over with two glasses, then pours. "Here. Drink this and tell me. It's expensive, so make it good."

I laugh a little at that. Like she cares about the cost. But the scotch is tasty, and it dulls the sharp edge of my miserable humiliation. So I tell her as much as I can, withholding anything too specific about Wyatt's divorce settlement.

When I'm done, Yuna takes a long sip of her drink. "You like him, don't you? Maybe even love him a little?"

I say nothing. Acknowledging the situation seems even more pathetic.

"It's okay. You don't have to tell me." She leans closer. "Want me to destroy Geneva? I could do that, you know."

I look at her, wondering if she's joking. She sounds too serious, but maybe it's the alcohol making me think that. "Uh... No. I don't think that's going to help."

"Okay." Yuna considers. "Should I have offered to kill Wyatt?"

The scotch goes down wrong, and I cough as the liquor burns in my throat. "That won't do either," I say, gasping.

"Why not? It'll be satisfying."

"But that doesn't change the fact that he said no and I'm feeling the way I do. Besides, there's Vi to consider. I can't make her an orphan." Geneva wouldn't want her without Wyatt's money. And I don't want him dead. I just... I'm just hurt he doesn't think there could be more between us.

Yuna nods, then sighs hard. "You're right. There's a line. Bastard. I shouldn't have given him any of my adult cream pies last night."

56

Kim

Wyatt and I don't see each other for the rest of the weekend—no calls or texting, either. I'm very careful to avoid him. The wound from the rejection is still raw. If he'd at least acted like he was giving it some serious consideration, maybe it wouldn't hurt as much.

Okay, who am I kidding? I'd still be squirming and wondering. But at least I wouldn't be avoiding him out of humiliation.

I leave for work two hours earlier than normal. As I walk out of my apartment, I look at his door. Maybe I should move. This place is nice, but I don't need a roommate anymore, and it's too big for one person. There are other places that are better suited—probably cheaper, too. The only thing I feel bad about is Yuna, but maybe she can move in with her soul sister Ivy. I'm sure her mom won't be able to pressure Anthony Blackwood to reach her. He doesn't strike me as the type who would just roll over.

The drive to the office is quick and quiet, the traffic much lighter at this early hour. I munch on a granola bar at my desk and work on Salazar's expenses. He left me a note to look into classes so he can do the cooking and massage. He also wants to know if he should sing, and if so, I'll need to hire him a voice instructor.

Normally his unbridled love for his ex-wife makes me shake my head and smile, but right now...

I decide he should sing, although I have no idea how he sounds. Why not? Ceinlys will appreciate the effort no matter what.

His butler Al sends me a text at nine to let me know Salazar's not coming in because he has a brunch date with Ceinlys. A last-minute impulse decision. I check his agenda. Nothing urgent or that I can't handle.

I brood some more. Should I have said yes when Yuna offered to destroy Geneva? That would've at least solved Wyatt and Vi's problem. Maybe he couldn't give my proposal the consideration it deserved because he was too frazzled. I would have been too, if I were in his place.

My desk phone rings. I pick it up. "Salazar Pryce's office."

"Hello? Um... Is Kim there?"

I blink at the familiar young voice. "Vi?"

"Oh, hi!" She sounds much perkier.

This is weird. Didn't Wyatt tell Vi what happened? Maybe not in detail, but that we aren't together anymore? "Hey. What are you doing calling me at the office? You having trouble reaching your dad?"

"No. I wanted to call you over the weekend, but I didn't have your cell phone number. I couldn't ask Dad because I didn't want him to know I was calling you."

You didn't? My wariness slides up a notch. "What do you want to talk about?"

There's a moment of silence. "Is he okay?"

"Fine, I think... Why don't you ask him?" What makes her think she should check with me?

"It's pointless to ask him over the phone. He'll just fake it."

Fake it...?

"He's always pretending. You know."

"Actually, I don't. What do you mean?" What kind of impression has Wyatt been giving his kid? I shouldn't care, but I do. Something like this could mess up his custody battle with Geneva.

"He pretends like he's fine, especially when he thinks I'm

worried about him and Mom. But I can tell. I'm not a baby. And he's terrible at lying, anyway."

"I see." Whew. This isn't as bad as I imagined at first. Or, at least, I don't think so. Should I let Wyatt know anyway?

"Do you think it'll be better if I go live with you instead?" Vi asks suddenly.

"Me?" *Oh, hon. Your dad wouldn't marry me, not even to hand defeat to your mom on a silver platter. I don't think he's going to be okay with you living here.*

"I mean, if I live with you, maybe Mom and Dad won't fight." She's breathing audibly. "I don't really want to live with her. I know she doesn't really like me that much. Not like Mandee's mom likes Mandee."

My heart breaks over the tremor in Vi's voice. She's too young to feel this way. But I can't bring myself to lie and tell her that Geneva loves her.

"I overheard my grandparents talking last night. And…I was so angry. I called Mom and told her I hated her. She said I was an ungrateful little girl." Her voice grows small. "Do you think she's right?"

"Oh, sweetie," I say softly, torn between a desire to wrap my arms around her and wanting to murder Geneva. "You aren't ungrateful. Anyone would feel the way you do. You're a wonderful person, Vi. Don't let anybody, not even your mom, tell you any different. Okay?"

"Okay."

I can almost sense her nod. And I sincerely hope she's not faking it like she claims her dad does.

"So…I guess this means I don't have a mom, huh?"

"Sometimes there's more to being a mom than just giving birth," I say, thinking of my own mother. "Lots of people love you dearly and only want the best for you, Vi. You don't have to let Geneva make you feel inferior or less worthy, okay?"

"Yeah. Okay." She clears her throat. "Kim?"

"Yeah?"

"Thanks. You're a really good friend. I mean, for an old adult."

I laugh, the tension from the weekend lessening. "My pleasure, kiddo. We'll always be friends, no matter how old I get."

57

Wyatt

I feel like shit as I return from taking the trash out in the morning and see the door to Kim's unit. It's firmly shut. I stand there for some time, wondering when Kim's coming out to go to work.

I didn't run into Kim yesterday morning like I'd hoped. Or in the evening either, even though I stood here like an idiot for an hour.

And today's the same. I even got up earlier than normal, even though I'm working from home.

Maybe she's working from home, too.

I shake my head as soon as the thought pops into my head. Salazar Pryce is a generous boss—weirdly so—but he seems to value his own comfort and convenience over everything else. Letting her work from home when he's in the office? Not his style.

Maybe give her a call? But that seems kind of impersonal. She deserves a face-to-face apology.

The knob on Kim's door turns.

Hope stirs, my heart pounding. I said it all wrong on Saturday, but I can fix this. I've put a lot of thought into it. A perfect, flawless script is ready to go in my head. I even rehearsed it a few times in front of a mirror, just to make sure.

But it's Yuna who comes out, dressed in a white T-shirt and denim shorts. She's holding Champ's leash.

The second she notices me, she stops, then peers at me over her huge sunglasses. "You've gotta be kidding."

"Hi," I say with a friendly smile, even though she's continuing to look at me like I just stole her boyfriend.

She pushes the sunglasses back up her nose, then walks Champ right by me without a word. He looks back. I know what he's thinking: *Dude, you're in the doghouse so bad, you might as well be a dog.*

"Hey, is Kim working from home today?" I ask, even though I'm certain the answer is no.

"Why don't you call her and find out?" Yuna says without looking at me, then disappears into the elevator.

Shit. This does not bode well. A woman might not always tell you how she feels, but her friends? They'll say it.

I stare at the door. This attempt to *accidentally* run into Kim is stupid. I should just face her like a man.

I knock hard a few times. Nothing. I press my ear to the door, trying to see if there's any sound on the other side.

Still nothing.

Maybe she already left for work. But when? I've been waiting for—I check my watch—twenty-some minutes out here.

Champ's got it right. I might as well be a dog.

Sighing, I go back to my apartment and try to work, even though the situation with Kim is distracting. How the hell am I going to fix things if I can't see her?

An hour later, loud piano music comes from Kim's place. It's not a recording. It sounds like somebody's actually playing. *When did Kim and Yuna get a piano?*

The performance isn't bad. I'm no critic, but I can tell whoever's at the piano is good. It's just that...it's so damn loud! And it's just really boring scales and drills. Vi had to do those for a while because Geneva wanted her to, until the piano teacher said Vi would never be accepted to Julliard.

I wait for the person—probably Yuna or a guest—to get tired

and quit. Vi could never do the scales and drills for more than half an hour before falling on the floor in an exhausted heap. But this pianist seems to be on steroids or something.

Two hours later, the music is still going at full speed, volume and vigor. It's like an android is at it.

Finally fed up, I knock hard on Kim's door. The music stops, and Yuna sticks her head out.

"What?" she says.

"You mind keeping it down? You or your friend or whoever's playing?"

"My friend?" She arches an eyebrow. "Is that how we refer to pianos these days?"

"Huh?" I frown and try to peer into the apartment through the opening.

"It's me. Why? You don't think I can play?"

"No. It's not like that," I say, suddenly feeling defensive. *Why am I acting like I've done something wrong when I'm making a very reasonable request?* Yuna doesn't own the building. She should be more considerate. "I just need to work, so it'd be nice if you could keep it down, that's all."

"Like you kept it down the night I moved in? Bang, bang, bang!"

I feel my neck grow hot. "Look, I'm sorry about tha—"

"Rejected." She flicks her hair over a shoulder. "I don't accept apologies from assholes."

I stare at her. "Excuse me, what?"

"You don't deserve Kim because you're dumb. I'm going to find her a rich, hot, well-hung dude who's really good in bed. And I have a thick dossier folder full of rich, hot, well-hung dudes who're really good in bed. My mom sent it. She's really good at finding those kinds of guys."

I always knew Yuna is a bit weird, but this... Mom shmom—I'm more focused on what she said about setting Kim up with someone. And not just anyone, but a "rich, hot, well-hung and really good in bed" someone.

An image of Kim laughing and dancing with some rich, hot, well-hung dude plays in my mind like a home movie. Suddenly, I'm no longer feeling bad about putting nails in the wall that night. "Maybe setting people up with strangers is how they do it in Korea, but not here. You need to stay out of this."

"That *is* how we do it, and I'll do it with Kim if I want. She's kind of an honorary Korean anyway."

"What? No, she isn't."

"Her *name* is *Kim*!"

Oh Lord. "You don't know anything."

"I know enough. For one thing, I know you don't love her."

Rage starts to build at her judgmental tone. "Shut up."

She ignores me. "Which is fine, because Kim deserves a man who loves her enough to risk his heart for her."

Her words punch me hard, dousing the rage and leaving me disoriented for a second.

She sticks her tongue out, says something that sounds like "may wrong," which doesn't even make sense, then slams the door in my face.

58

WYATT

Yuna returns to her piano drills, and I go back to my unit and stretch out on the couch with my arms folded behind my head. Exactly twelve seconds later, Princess hops up and decides to sit on my face. I push her away, and she lets out the vilest, most grotesque fart ever.

"Ugh!" I sit up, gagging and trying to wave it away. The army could use this stuff for chemical warfare.

She hisses, then hops off the couch and swishes her tail, stalking away.

I glare at her. I swear that cat is the devil incarnate. She's been impossible since Saturday. It's as though she blames me for making Kim leave—which, okay, is more or less my fault.

Kim deserves a man who loves her enough to risk his heart for her.

It pops into my head, then keeps circling, pushing the cat fart and sound of the piano into the background.

Was I just playing it safe when I rejected her proposal? I had a good reason, and I still think it's a good reason. She shouldn't have to give up the possibility of love to help me with a custody battle. It's just too much of a sacrifice for her.

Don't you think she's thought of that? a voice that sounds a lot like Yuna says in my head. *Don't you think she would be smart enough and capable enough to find a different way to save Vi from Geneva if that's what she wanted?*

Kim hasn't failed her extremely fickle boss in five years and made him happy enough to give her a huge bonus. If she wanted, she could've found some other way. Or at least, she would have tried.

But she went straight to marriage. Which means...

Ugh. I'm an idiot. And Yuna's right. I didn't want to risk my heart, and I excused myself by deciding I'm not marrying for convenience again. But I didn't even try to make Kim fall in love with me. I just said no, telling myself I was being noble by giving her a chance to find love with someone else. But why shouldn't that love be with me?

It isn't like Kim has an issue with Vi. She likes Vi, and vice versa. I've seen them together. They've bonded. Most important, I trust her with Vi.

I screwed up. I let what happened with Geneva take away a chance at happiness with the woman I love. So I need to fix this. Pronto. I owe it to myself, and to Kim and Vi.

I grab my keys and leave for Kim's office. She's at work, I'm sure of it. Ever since high school, she's always thrown herself into work when she's upset.

Besides, nobody could put up with the racket Yuna is making on that piano.

As I drive, anxiety and fear lap at me like waves. Those tight, uncomfortable emotions aren't about the heart I'm about to risk, but the need to make sure I don't hurt Kim anymore...and to see how badly I messed up and how much work I need to do to fix it. I need to put the smile back on her face, feel the warmth of her skin.

On my way in, Salazar waves at me in the lobby. He's looking cheerful, like a man in love, his step light in a crisp outfit that was probably custom-made for him. The urge to go straight to Kim is very strong, but I stop to say hello for form's sake.

"There he is!" he says. "The one behind my lovely assistant's bad mood."

"Jesus, Salazar. Good morning to you, too." Kim's too professional to complain about me to Salazar. For him to have noticed...

"I can always tell. We've been working together a long time." He's staring at me expectantly like he's waiting for me to agree with him.

"Right. Sure." *Stop looking at me like that.*

"And I can just tell it's a relationship problem. Nothing escapes me. I'm Cupid, remember?"

A very old and ugly Cupid. Who is, thankfully, not naked...or carrying a bow and arrow.

It's on the tip of my tongue to say, *If you're so good at romance, how come you're divorced?* But I keep it to myself.

"Lemme give you some advice, son. You need to grovel."

I try not to make a face. I know I have to grovel, and I'm here to do exactly that. Why is he saying it like it's some novel enlightenment only he can think of?

"And as a prelude to groveling, you need the right present. I recommend crème brûlée from Éternité. That's her favorite. One regular and one chocolate. The chocolate one is new, and she Hoovered it up like... Well, I don't want to say. This is a G-rated lobby."

Thank God he didn't go there. But he's right about the present, and I'm realizing I probably should've brought something. It's hard to snarl at a guy who's carrying chocolate crème brûlée.

He adds, "Éternité doesn't do takeout, but if you give them my name, they might. It's kind of like saying, 'Open sesame.'" He leans in slightly. "The name's magic."

"Thanks," I say. "Really." Despite his flamboyance, I know he's trying to help.

"Happy to be of service. But if I were you, I'd rent a yacht and arrange for some fireworks, too."

That extravagant? Not that I don't think Kim deserves it, but the time it would take to arrange...

Salazar checks his fingernails. "Just sayin'."

"Got it. Hey, I have to go."

59

Wyatt

Regular crème brûlée. Check.
Chocolate crème brûlée. Check.
A bouquet of white lilies that smell amazing. Check.
Everything else I can think of... Check, check, check.
I stare at the elegant Éternité box on the dining room table. Kim should be home in about half an hour. But...what if she comes home early? Salazar might've given her some extra time off.
I peer out the peephole. I can't see all the way to the spot in front of her unit, though. Ugh. Annie needs to install a better peephole.
Like what? A peepiscope? A small voice in my head cackles.
Sometimes that part of me isn't very helpful, especially when it gives me *I told you so*s. Princess mewls next to me. Even that sounds like "Moron. You're gonna mess it up more."
Screw it.
I step out into the hall with the box and the flowers, then lean against a spot between her door and mine to wait. She probably won't immediately turn away if she sees my peace offering. Well, more like a bribe to buy some time.

I spent some time thinking while driving to Éternité. It's obvious Kim's avoiding me. And I feel terrible that I ruined the relationship that was growing between us. I even saw the most perfect thing on my way back home—the one item Salazar didn't mention because, despite his claim to Cupid-hood, he doesn't know as much as he thinks.

It's almost nine when Kim finally appears. She looks like she's been sweating, and her hair's a little messy. Somehow, the mild dishevelment makes her more approachable and sexy. My heart picks up a beat, and a slick film of perspiration coats my palms. I surreptitiously wipe them on my pants as I push myself off the wall.

Her expression freezes into shock for a moment.

"Hey, Kim," I say.

She smooths her face. "Hi."

The wariness in her eyes is like a stab in the chest, and remorse floods through me, erasing all the pretty words I've been rehearsing. "Here. For you." I thrust the flowers and the box at her before I can catch myself. *Dammit.* I was supposed to say something—can't remember what at the moment—and make her smile first. "I thought you'd like them. At least the crème brûlées."

She looks at my offering, then sighs softly. "Wyatt, thanks, but...you really don't have to." She doesn't meet my eyes. "It's fine."

"But I'm not fine," I say.

That gets her attention, because her body language changes; she's no longer trying to push past me, but pausing to hear what I have to say.

I grasp at the small opening like a drowning man reaching for a floating oar. "Kim... I have to tell you something. Do you mind if we move this to some place other than the hall?"

Not that a refusal is going to stop me. Nothing's going to stop me right now, not until I erase the unhappiness inside her.

"Okay." She takes a step toward her apartment, then stops. "Actually, let's go to your place. Yuna ordered a cast-iron skillet from Amazon last night."

"Uh, okay. What does that have to do with—"

"She doesn't cook."

I smile a little. It's a good sign that Kim cares about not having my skull cracked open. Or that's what I tell myself, even though a voice that sounds like Yuna says Kim doesn't like to have blood on her floor because blood's impossible to get out and she doesn't want to lose her deposit.

Kim and I walk into my place. There's a really good burgundy breathing on the table, and some bubbly chilling in an ice bucket, which is full of half-melted ice and dripping with condensation.

"What's all this?" she asks.

"I thought you might like something with the crème brûlée. I got it from Éternité."

Instead of sitting at the table, she crosses her arms. "Like I said, you don't have to do this, Wyatt. I didn't say what I said on Saturday to…" She sighs, her eyes going slightly upward, as if she's searching for the right words. "I didn't do that to pressure you into something you don't want."

"I know," I say. "And I thank you for that. But is it okay if I tell you why I'm doing this?"

She nods warily.

I put the box and the flowers on the table and stand in front of her. As I place my hands on her shoulders, she flinches. That hurts, but physical contact is important now. I dip my head, making sure we're making eye contact as well. My heart pounds with anxiety as I see the guardedness in her gaze.

"I didn't—*don't*—want you to marry a guy you don't love just to help him out. Or to help his kid out. I know what that's like, because I did it with Geneva. I never loved her, and what I did was a foolish sacrifice because I was mainly just trying to give Vi some stability. But it didn't even give her that. Just made everyone miserable. I don't want you to be unhappy. I love you too much to let you make that kind of sacrifice."

The guardedness in her gaze softens a bit, and the tension in her muscles eases…maybe ten percent.

"But…I was being a coward. Yes, I love you, but I also didn't want to risk my heart. I wanted to play it safe—told myself I was doing it for you and Vi, but was I? What you offered was a chance. And I should've taken it and made you so happy that you'd fall in love with me, too. That would've been the right thing. And it took me this long to see it."

She lets out a shaky breath. "Well, you're improving. It didn't take ten years."

"I know." I grab the crème brûlée box—the chocolate one—and drop to one knee, opening it. Inside is a platinum solitaire diamond ring that reminded me of her—so elegant and beautiful—when I saw it on my way home from Éternité. The band is set on a long silver pick, which is skewering the brûlée. Kim loves chocolate, and the dark background makes the ring pop more.

She places her hands on her cheeks. Her eyes shine.

"Kim, will you give me a chance?" I say, my voice shaking a little. "Will you marry me? I'll spend the rest of my life making you happy. Making you love me a little bit more every day."

"Yes," she says, her voice trembling too. "And I already love you, you crazy man."

Her declaration goes off in my head like fireworks. I almost jump up, then remember I'm holding her favorite dessert. *Must not ruin the dessert.* I have plans for it. And I want to watch her eat it in bliss.

So I carefully put the box back on the table, pluck the ring off the pick and place it on her finger, where it belongs. Then I kiss her until we're both breathless.

60

KIM

OUR WEDDING TAKES PLACE TWO WEEKS LATER. IF IT HAD just been up to me and Wyatt, we might've gone to a courthouse. But Yuna absolutely refused to let me do that, and Salazar was horrified at the idea as well. On top of that, Vi insisted on attending, and she wanted a pretty dress for the ceremony. She begged Jo to go shopping with her, and they picked out the cutest outfit.

Salazar lends us his immaculate garden. It's so big that we could easily fit five times as many guests, but I only invited my mother and some close friends. Wyatt invited his parents and a few friends as well. We want to keep things small, with only the people who truly wish the best for us.

Yuna watches me get ready, her arms crossed. She's in a pink Dior dress that made Jo squeal a little because apparently not many people can make it look good.

"I knew it," Yuna says with smug conviction. "That Oscar de la Renta dress had your name on it. Written in a red only I could see."

I laugh. The classy, off-shoulder gown is exquisite with intricate lace details. My hairdresser pulled my hair up, but left some tendrils down to frame to my face. I look beautiful in the mirror. Most importantly, I feel loved and content.

"You are absolutely stunning." Hilary beams. "I'm so happy for you."

"Wyatt's going to have a heart attack when he sees you," Jo says.

"He's too young for that," Ceinlys says, walking in. She's probably one of the most gorgeous women I've even seen in my life. Even though she's in her late sixties, she looks better than most women half her age, with her hair still sleek ebony black and her skin smooth and nearly wrinkle-free.

Since it's Salazar's mansion, she's here to oversee the staff set things up, even though I told her I could take care of it. She said brides shouldn't be left to stress about details. I'm so grateful for that, because otherwise Mom would've insisted on taking over the wedding, and turned it into a showy farce only she could appreciate.

Ceinlys smiles at me. "You look radiant, Kim. I'm so happy for you."

"Thank you," I say.

The door to the dressing room crashes open, and my mother appears, along with a cloud of Chanel No. 5. It's a perfume she's never worn before, but she got a whiff of Ceinlys and decided to wear it...as though the scent were the source of Ceinlys's attractiveness. Mom's bleached hair is pristinely twisted into an updo, and she is wearing a dress that's as tight as sausage skin. The colored contact lenses she put on are a strange fakey-blue, and with her natural brown leaching through them, she looks weird.

But she doesn't care as she rushes in to wrap me in her arms. "Honey! So sorry I'm late, but I had to look good."

I cringe inwardly. I love my mom, but there are times I want to pretend she and I aren't related, especially when she does something like this. I don't even want to know what she considers "looking bad" if she honestly thinks this is a good look for her.

She continues, "I knew you could do it! I'm so proud of you!"

"*Mom...*" I hiss, praying nobody overhears what she's about to say.

"Wyatt is *perfect*. What did I tell you? You were always

capable of snagging a billionaire. You just had to put your mind to it."

"That's not the way it is," I say furiously, wishing I could shut her up. I already warned her not to talk about stuff like this, but it's obviously beyond her control.

Vi sticks her head in. She looks like a fairy princess in a flowing pastel pink and lavender dress. "Mr. Pryce says it's time." Her eyes widen. "You look really pretty, Kim."

"Thank you. So do you." Tears bead in my eyes at how settled and happy Vi seems now. I blink them away to avoid ruining my makeup.

"Move aside, I'm here for the bride!" Salazar announces, coming inside in a crisp tux. Since I don't have a dad—at least not one who wants to be involved—he's walking me down the aisle.

I step forward, and he extends an arm. "You look spectacular," he says gallantly. "Ready?"

My heart is fluttering wildly with anticipation. "Yes."

Jo hands me my bouquet—white lilies, just like the ones Wyatt bought me on the day he proposed.

Ceinlys, Yuna, Jo and Hilary take turns hugging me, then Yuna leaves to get ready for her part in the ceremony. Mom just dabs at her eyes, muttering that she *knew* I could do it. She'll never understand that I'm just thrilled to have found a man I love and who loves me in return, and that his money isn't even a consideration.

As Salazar and I walk outside to the garden, Salazar leans over. "Your mother's a little dramatic, isn't she?"

"She really wanted me to...marry well." It's sort of true. It's just that her idea of "marrying well" means marrying a lot of money.

"You're going to have a child your own, right?" Salazar asks.

"I already have a child of my own. Her name is Vi." Geneva's loss is my gain. I'll do everything in my power to let Vi know she's loved.

"You know what I mean. *Your* babies. Biological."

"Maybe..." I say, hedging a bit, unsure where he's going with this.

He smiles like I've already agreed. "If it's a boy, you should name him after me."

I arch an eyebrow. "What if it's a girl?"

"Then name her after Ceinlys. That's the least I deserve."

What about what Wyatt and I want? I keep that to myself, though, and smile instead. "We'll think about it."

"You do that." He pats my hand.

When we're at the garden where the altar's set up, Wyatt's standing in front of it, heartbreakingly handsome in his tux, his eyes bright and full of love and adoration. I feel a big smile tugging at the corners of my mouth. Yuna starts "Here Comes the Bride" on the special piano she arranged for.

I start down the aisle, my eyes on Wyatt—my friend, my lover, my future.

61

EDGAR

THE MEETING IS LONG AND TEDIOUS. AND I CAN'T FOCUS. I keep thinking about the woman from the adult cream pie party. Jo. She said her name was Jo. Then she moaned my name underneath me, her body pliant and hot and wet.

Shit. I shift in my seat. I shouldn't be sporting an erection while the CFO is discussing... What is he talking about? Oh, right. The slide says, "Supply Glut and Its Impact on Our Profit Margin." It's a serious issue for the company, and my meeting wood should soften, except it doesn't, because Jo's sexy "more, harder...please" is echoing in my head over the CFO's decidedly unsexy voice.

Fuck.

When the meeting finally ends, I leave for my office, leather portfolio strategically positioned to hide my condition. My elderly assistant gives me a funny look. Does she notice? But it wouldn't be like her to act like she notices.

"Yes, Susan?"

"You have something from a lawyer in Los Angeles." She hands me a brown envelope.

"Forward it to legal." That's why we employ them.

"It's marked private." She shows me the front of the envelope. Sure enough, it has a big stamp that says PRIVATE.

"Okay." I take it from her, carry it to my office and shut the door. Since I'm annoyed and restless with the fact that I can't *not* think about Jo, I rip the envelope open with more force than necessary, almost tearing the document inside.

My heart almost stops when I read the first paragraph.

Jo wants me to give up the rights to...*our baby*?

62

WYATT

I sneak out of bed early in the morning, leaving Kim sleeping. I tiptoe my way to Vi's room and knock.

"You can come in," she whispers.

I crack the door open and poke my head in. She's sitting up, rubbing her eyes.

"Ready?" I whisper.

"Yeah." She yawns. "Do you think it'll come out okay?"

"It'll come out fabulous. And I promise Kim won't be up until you're done." I made sure she'd be tired last night. That's the least I can do to help Vi.

"Let me wash my face and brush my teeth and meet you in the kitchen." I nod and leave her do her thing.

It's been eleven months since Kim and I got married. Since then, Samantha completely crushed Geneva's legal maneuvering, Yuna gleefully told us my ex-wife is bankrupt—apparently, it's Yuna's motto to follow her enemies' social media accounts, although I'm not sure when Geneva became *Yuna's* enemy—and we moved to a bigger home. Not a mansion like the one Salazar has, but something with more space and a pool. Kim likes to relax by it after work and on weekends, and I like to join her every chance I get. I'm proud and content of the life we're building together.

Vi comes out of her room, pulling her hair back into a ponytail. She's barefoot in a tank top and shorts. She doesn't do all that weird experimenting off YouTube anymore. Kim and she do all that girly stuff together, which is great. Vi's been blossoming with all the love and attention Kim and I have been pouring on her. And based on what she tells us, she has tons of friends now, and she likes her teachers too.

We head down to the kitchen together. Champ whines, and I let him out into the yard. Princess looks on with a feline sneer, then curls back to into a fur ball. Princess quit bringing bugs to Kim. Or maybe Champ's been eating them behind our backs. I caught him a few times, and Princess hissed at him, batting at his head. But she's too small to really hurt him.

Vi takes out two eggs, a couple slices of whole wheat bread and Kim's favorite strawberry jam, bought at a local farmer's market. I show her how to do sunny-side up and toast the bread just the way Kim likes it.

"We have to have coffee, too," Vi says.

"Yup."

She starts the coffeemaker, and I pull out a tray. Vi sets up the rest, then picks the tray up with care.

"You okay there?"

"I'm good. You just have to open the door."

I nod and walk up the stairs with her, and then open the door to the master bedroom.

Kim's still in bed, although from the way she's shifting under the sheet, she's awake. Probably just feeling lazy.

I kiss her on the forehead. "Hey, sweetheart. Look what Vi brought you."

Kim sits up, pushing her hair out of her face. Vi comes over nervously. I know she's remembering the time she did this for Geneva. My ex-wife hated it and said everything was inedible. Not that I think Kim would do that, but I know it was a trauma. I'm actually still a bit surprised Vi decided to do this for Kim on their first Mother's Day together.

Vi lays out the tray on the bed for Kim. A smile splits Kim's face when she sees the breakfast Vi's prepared.

"Oh, *wow*. Thank you, Vi! Everything looks so delicious."

Vi flushes. "Thanks. I mean, you're welcome."

Placing an arm around Vi's shoulders, I kiss her head, relieved and happy for her.

Kim doesn't make a production out of eating—that'd be condescending. But she digs in with gusto. Damn. I couldn't love this woman more if I tried.

"I feel so pampered," Kim says.

"Really?" Vi says, her eyes sparkling

Kim nods. "Yup. You're awesome."

Vi's throat works a little as she swallows. "So are you, Mom."

Kim freezes, and so do I. Vi's never called her *Mom* before.

The light in Vi's eyes dims. "Is that okay?"

Kim moves the tray out of the way and hugs her hard. "Of *course* it's okay! It's more than okay." She kisses Vi's cheek. "I love you so much, baby."

My heart full of love and gratitude, I put my arms around my favorite women and savor the moment, knowing there are more amazing things to come in our lives.

~

THANKS FOR READING *FAKING IT WITH THE FRENEMY*! I HOPE you enjoyed it. If you want to get a peek at how Kim, Wyatt and Vi are doing eight years later, join my VIP List at http://www.nadialee.net/vip to grab a bonus scene. You'll also receive other extras, sneak peeks, new book announcements, sales information and more!

Want to know what happens between Edgar and Jo? Check out their story *Tempting the Bride*!

Did you miss Kim's best friend Hilary's story? Grab *The Billionaire's Counterfeit Girlfriend* today!

If you loved *Faking It with the Frenemy*, could you leave a short review on Amazon? It can help other readers discover and enjoy the book as well! Thank you!

Want to stalk me and see what I'm up to next? Find me at:

Website: nadialee.net
VIP List (newsletter): nadialee.net/vip
VIP Hangout (reader group): facebook.com/groups/nadialee
Facebook: facebook.com/nadialeewrites
Twitter: twitter.com/nadialee
Instagram: instagram.com/nadialeewrites

TITLES BY NADIA LEE

Standalone Titles
Tempting the Bride
Faking It with the Frenemy
Marrying My Billionaire Boss
Stealing the Bride

The Sins Trilogy
Sins
Secrets
Mercy

The Billionaire's Claim Duet
Obsession
Redemption

Sweet Darlings Inc.
That Man Next Door
That Sexy Stranger
That Wild Player

Billionaires' Brides of Convenience
A Hollywood Deal

A Hollywood Bride
An Improper Deal
An Improper Bride
An Improper Ever After
An Unlikely Deal
An Unlikely Bride
A Final Deal

∽

The Pryce Family
The Billionaire's Counterfeit Girlfriend
The Billionaire's Inconvenient Obsession
The Billionaire's Secret Wife
The Billionaire's Forgotten Fiancée
The Billionaire's Forbidden Desire
The Billionaire's Holiday Bride

∽

Seduced by the Billionaire
Taken by Her Unforgiving Billionaire Boss
Pursued by Her Billionaire Hook-Up
Pregnant with Her Billionaire Ex's Baby
Romanced by Her Illicit Millionaire Crush
Wanted by Her Scandalous Billionaire
Loving Her Best Friend's Billionaire Brother

ABOUT NADIA LEE

New York Times and *USA Today* bestselling author Nadia Lee writes sexy contemporary romance. Born with a love for excellent food, travel and adventure, she has lived in four different countries, kissed stingrays, been bitten by a shark, fed an elephant and petted tigers.

Currently, she shares a condo overlooking a small river and sakura trees in Japan with her husband and son. When she's not writing, she can be found reading books by her favorite authors or planning another trip.

To learn more about Nadia and her projects, please visit http://www.nadialee.net. To receive updates about upcoming works, sneak peeks and bonus epilogues featuring some of your favorite couples from Nadia, please visit http://www.nadialee.net/vip to join her VIP List.

Printed in Great Britain
by Amazon